A CERTAIN STEP

MIDNIGHTS AT PEMBERLEY
BOOK 1

GISSANE SOPHIA

Edited by: Kate McGinn

Edited by: Sarah Tompkins

Cover Design and Illustration by Jenna Guidi

For the ones still waiting, hoping, and wanting to be someone's first choice—whether in love or for the dream job—I hope you believe that your time is coming.

I'm rooting for you.

"To be fond of dancing was a certain step towards falling in love."

— JANE AUSTEN

AUTHOR'S NOTE

Dear Reader,

First, thank you for giving *A Certain Step* and the *Midnights at Pemberley* series a chance. I wrote this book as my love letter to the Broadway community and simultaneously because I wanted to tell a quietly sweet romance between two best friends. However, with a space like this comes a bit of world-building that I'll admit made me very, very anxious to dive into. How do you take a whole spectacle that you can so clearly see in your head and put it onto paper for others to envision as well? But here we are. I tried my hardest, and I hope you love these characters and their story as much as I do.

Being the paranoid real-life journalist that I am, I wanted to provide some important disclaimers for the sake of my sanity. All of the characters featured in this story are obviously fictional, as is their success. The shows or movies they are in and the experiences they have are all fictional. Some of them are big names in *this* world, and others are just getting started. Any mention of shows they watch or music they appreciate is drawn from real-life examples, but everything *they're* a part of naturally isn't. Any similarities to something in the real world are purely coincidental.

In telling a story about an industry I know way too much about, I also needed to showcase both sides of fandom. Fans are integral to the success of any film, TV show, Broadway production, or even book series. Without their bustling, beautiful passion, so many people wouldn't be where they are today. However, there's another side to fandom as well, full of entitlement and cruelty. There are gossip magazines that still continue to terrorize artists. With the rise of social media, viciousness has grown tenfold, so it was vital for me to write about that part of it, along with the lovely bits.

At the end of the day, this is a romance novel, and as much as I wish it were, it's not a theatrical production. Still, for references, I'm providing both a cast list and a fictional review of the fictional production to familiarize readers with this wild little world our characters are part of.

Lastly, we don't have nearly enough novels with demisexual representation, so it was crucial to me to have it included in this novel. We all have our unique experiences with intimacy, and I hope I've represented Willa's demisexuality with the grace necessary.

CONTENT NOTES: mentions of grief [past, off-page of grandparents], anxiety [on-page therapy session], one brief conversation surrounding past sexual experiences.

If any of these topics are too sensitive for you, please take care of yourselves.

MIDNIGHTS AT PEMBERLEY
TRACK LIST

1. "Doors Open"

2. "Bennet Sisters Interview"

3. "Hired"

4. "Obstinate, Headstrong Girl"

5. "Smile More"

6. "Lost in the Lights"

7. "Stubborn Bastard"

8. "Midnights at Pemberley"

9. "Marry Me"

10. "Forbidden Corridors"

11. "Elizabeth's Breakdown"

12. "The Letter"

13. "Jane and Bingley Wed"

14. "Shut It Down, Darcy"

15. "All For You"

16. "Midnights at Pemberley Reprise"

MIDNIGHTS AT PEMBERLEY CAST AND CREW LIST

Ethan Everett as Mr. Darcy

Sam Butler as Mr. Bingley

Naomi Driver as Elizabeth Bennet

Sahar Peck as Jane Bennet

Declan McNair as Mr. Wickham

Tanya E. Tate as Lydia Bennet

Mary Ellen Scott as Caroline Bingley

Lea Driver | *Elizabeth standby*

Ensemble

Willa Davidian | *Elizabeth and Jane Understudy*

Christian Galligan | *Darcy Understudy*

Miles Dahl | *Bingley Understudy*

Innila Jani | *Lydia Understudy*

Mena Amin | *Caroline Understudy*

Court Jenkins

Laura Tiu

Breana Miller

Bradley Greene

Director: Jeffrey V. Henderson

Stage Manager: Dina Rollins

Music and Lyrics: Jeffrey V. Henderson and Greta Henderson

Choreographer: Josie Singh

THE BROADWAY TRIBUNE REVIEW

'Midnights at Pemberley' Is Every Austen Fan's Dream Musical Adaptation

By: Louisa Quinn

Midnights at Pemberley is the type of musical adaptation that comes to life once every few decades—boisterous and bustling yet profoundly vulnerable at the same time. From the dynamic duo that brought us *Her Partner's Ex,* Jefferey and Greta Henderson outdo themselves at every turn with the sultriest and most vibrant Austen modification yet.

When the production was first announced, I'll admit that I was *a bit* apprehensive. How are we adapting *Pride and Prejudice* while the entire show will take place strictly inside Pemberley, and how would that change the characterizations and their relationships? Trust the process has never been more true than it is today because everything we get from the performances to the music and the set design, is sure to result in a Tony sweep. To summarize, in this version, Pemberley is a cabaret—open to the public—and the eldest Bennet sisters decide to get jobs to help their family. Little do their parents know...Additionally, while we don't see Mr. and Mrs. Bennet or Kitty and Mary, the narrative still alludes to customary balls and time spent away from the large estate. It modernizes the characters while preserving the traditions of the time to amplify the stakes and ensure that the story is riveting.

The song lyrics are wildly catchy, with the titular track and "Marry Me" likely to become fast favorites that'll play on a loop in many households. (As will the entire album with addicting and thoughtful lyrics that devoted fans will recognize from the acclaimed novel.) However, in more ways than one, it's how tender and strikingly lovely the performances are that sticks out most. The chemistry sizzles between both main couples, bringing two different love stories to the already opulent Hyacinth theatre.

If you're anything like me and are already a fan of Ethan Everett's voice and on-screen—or stage—magnetism, you'll leave the theatre in absolute awe of the man's range. While long-time fans surely know what the artist is capable of, he's on a distinctly new level in *Midnights at Pemberley,* maybe even, and dare I say, born to play Mr. Darcy on stage. How Everett takes the character from the stoic, prideful, and convincingly anxious aristocrat to a man besotted and dazed in love is no small feat. Pair Everett with a stunning performer like Naomi Driver (*Broken Windows*), and we get a tremendous showcase of a hate-to-lovers romance that's brimming with passion.

The production also features Sam Butler (*Down by the River*) as Mr. Bingley and Sahar Peck (*The Case of Loretta Buttercup*) as Jane Bennet in an adorably warm, quiet romance that's as endearing as what readers often assume is *Pride and Prejudice's* main love story. This adaptation takes what's best in the books and amplifies it to underscore the importance of sisterhood right alongside the lifelong bonds of friendship equally with romance. *Midnights at Pemberley* also features *Briar Briar Town's*

Declan McNair as you've never seen him before—vicious, crude, and surprisingly remorseful as Mr. Wickham. Further, with Tanya E. Tate playing the irritating Lydia Bennet, we get something wildly fitting with the two of them.

Maggie Garner's brief role as Lady Catherine de Bourgh leaves its mark, partly because of the three-time Tony Award winner's prowess and because the character is somehow even more terrifying in this adaptation—she's in a single scene, and it's utterly chilling. And, finally, as far as performances go in a Broadway production, the ensemble for *Midnights at Pemberley* deserves every standing ovation possible. Josie Singh's recognizable choreography is often bold and innovative, but goodness, every kick and spin is taken to new heights on this stage. It's mesmerizing to see the stories coming to life with the choreography and how it heightens the words spoken aloud.

I was fortunate to see *Midnights at Pemberley* during the Boston tryouts and have tickets purchased for opening day on Broadway, so it's safe to say the production is a worthy spectacle to travel for. It's not merely for romance fans but for theatre aficionados in general, as it combines the best of the Regency era and modern contemporary influences to create a marriage that feels otherworldly. From beginning to end, it's an undeniably enrapturing sight to behold.

Midnights at Pemberley will officially open at the Hyacinth Theatre on March 14.

1

ETHAN

Ethan Everett felt empty. There was no other way to describe the strange disruption in the air or the sense that a part of him was provisionally torn away.

It sounded melodramatic, even though he wasn't uttering the thoughts aloud. His co-star and best friend, Willa Davidian, had been gone for two days, set to return in five, and five days felt like five hundred right now. Two days without a word from her other than an "I've landed and secured coffee. All is well in the world now" text.

Their close friendship had been instantaneous at the initial table read almost two years ago, allowing them to grow closer during rehearsals and preparations for *Midnights at Pemberley*. But falling this hard for her crept up on him. Sure, he had been in awe of her from the first day; he would never deny that, but slowly and then, all at once, intense feelings descended upon him like a flock of pigeons that'd just been lured with bread-crumbs at Central Park.

He often found himself longing to be around her, constantly wishing to occupy the same space.

It had been a few days after returning from his grandfather's funeral when Ethan first noticed how profound his feelings had gotten. When he realized that she kept his sanity intact while he wished he could disappear from his parents' house. He hadn't even been home a couple of hours before his dad commented that his grandpa would've loved it if Ethan had also been by his side when he passed. *You're the most like him of all his grandkids, and you were the only one who wasn't in that hospital room,* he had said. It wasn't malicious. He wasn't trying to criticize Ethan, but he never quite understood how hurtful those comments could be.

Ethan was already exhaustively aware that he was the lone wolf in his family—the one who chose theatre studies and drama over English literature and anthropology. Everyone in his family had a PhD, or they were working toward it, and Ethan was a two-time Tony Award nominee. He had missed holidays and birthdays not because he chose to but because he had no means of getting away. He'd always make up for his absence, though. He'd try to find the best, most sentimental gifts. He'd FaceTime his sister and nephew constantly. He'd check in on them multiple times a week.

His dad never fully recognized how much he expected out of Ethan as his eldest son, and he didn't mind it usually, but sometimes the words stung.

All he ever really wanted from his family was the assurance that they understood him. He didn't need or want tireless applause. He was proud of the work he did.

The industry was and would always be hot garbage in more ways than one, but when it allowed people to be their most authentic selves, it made the lonely kid watching from the orchestra seats feel a little less scared of the world outside.

People could step into the theatre for two hours and forget the pain they carried on their shoulders. Broadway stages gave people a home away from home—a place to feel safe and loved as they were. And he'd always appreciate being a reason for that.

The entertainers of the world had a place in life's vast storyboard, too.

His grandpa had also been the one to drive him toward the stage—the one who frequently reminded him of how it must've been his grandmother's influence. She was the artist in their family, the one who merged teaching and choir to find a perfect middle. She was the one who taught Ethan how to hold a note. His paternal grandparents were the ones who introduced him to *Lion King*, his first Broadway musical.

So, when the comments hurt and struck deeper than he would've liked on top of the grief suffocating him, Ethan thought of Willa. He reflected upon how she was the only person who never expected anything from him. How he could tell her anything and discern from the look in her eyes that she was never once passing judgment or questioning him. He thought of how, even when she offered him advice, she did so in a way that never belittled or made him feel like he was failing.

He latched on to the fact that being around her felt like home.

At the time, Ethan hadn't even fully processed his grandfather's death until he called Willa, and she ran over to his hotel room. He had suppressed his heartache and tears until he saw her, and she let him cry on her shoulders while holding him tightly without a word. It was everything he had needed. He had later mentioned what his dad had said, and she looked him squarely in the eyes when she declared that his grandpa would've understood. She also reassured Ethan that his dad probably didn't realize how it'd hurt him. She reminded him that his grandfather would've been proud of the show he was putting on every night, and surely his dad was, too. Ethan believed the observations when they came from her. It was easy to.

And then he stopped himself abruptly, bringing his wandering mind back from memories to reality. He focused on the fact that he couldn't and wouldn't jeopardize their friendship because losing Willa would hurt more than anything else he'd been through.

He forced himself to focus on the anguish that would take hold of him if she wasn't beside him.

"Earth to Ethan…" he heard coming from his physical therapist, Jenny Nolan. Right, that's where he was, sitting along the cushioned bench at his second to last appointment for his knee.

"Shit, sorry, Jen. Were you saying something?" he replied apologetically.

"I only asked you to lift your left leg about three times, but who's counting?"

He raised his left leg to oblige. "Sorry."

Jenny gently placed her hand on the back of his stubborn knee. "Where's that head of yours at today?"

Missing Willa.

"Trying to mull over some of the questions I know we'll get during interviews. You know me." Thank goodness he was quick on his feet with a reply.

He could perform in front of sold-out theatres and do whatever was needed of him, never once fumbling, but press obligations always made him far too nervous.

Still, that wasn't the case today.

Today, he was thinking about his best friend, wishing he could have gone to England with Willa as her plus one to her brother's wedding. She joked about it, but he knew a part of her had been serious. Willa was just as nervous about the wedding as she was excited. She was stressed about being the only person in her family who was single, uneasy about people offering to set her up, and asking all sorts of unwanted questions about her love life.

"You'll do fine. You always do. No one would ever know how much you stress about them," Jenny said, shrugging him out of his thoughts.

He sighed, reacting easily when she motioned for him to lift his leg again. "Thanks, Jen."

"I got you. And so does this knee of yours. You're lucky, you know that?"

"Well, you are a miracle worker," he noted, thanking science for in-house aid. He'd taken a minor slip weeks before and slammed his knee against a railing.

"I try," she replied, repeating the pattern three more times before she stopped and sanitized her hands.

Ethan took a moment to look at his phone and check the time in London. He could text Willa. It'd be ten forty at night there—not too late. Hopefully, she was still awake.

He waited until Jenny left the room before shooting the text over.

ETHAN

Didn't realize how attached I am to you. I miss you. Come back.

Subtle, Ethan. Real subtle.

WILLA

Hahahahaha I've been gone for two days. And I'm so damn jetlagged. Please send help.

Excellent, now you've freaked her out, his brain muttered. *You couldn't handle two whole days?*

No, he couldn't. He apparently couldn't nail the art of subtlety either because his fingers betrayed him like they were possessed.

ETHAN

You can call me if you can't sleep.

WILLA

I so would, but I'm at my cousin Emma's house, and the girls wanted to sleep in the guest room with me.

ETHAN

Ah, you're in Bristol already?

WILLA

Yeah! My parents are here, too, but they're staying at a hotel. Alex gets in tomorrow.

ETHAN

Nice. The wedding is in two days, right? There, in Bristol?

WILLA

Yeah. Anna's family is from Trowbridge, but the venue is here in Bristol. Also, I really should've hired someone to fake date. I've already had two aunts from my dad's side hound me about being "too old." You'd think I was 86 and not 33.

ETHAN

I would've been there in a heartbeat if I didn't have in person press to do.

WILLA

I know.

ETHAN

If you need me to play pretend from a distance, tell everyone I'm yours. I'll vouch for us.

WILLA

Hahaha noted. I should try to sleep. Miss you too, by the way.

He stood up, swung his backpack over his shoulder, and trekked out of the theatre's rehabilitation room. He was thankful Declan had invited him and Sam to have dinner tonight because he needed to shut off his mind. He needed it to be tomorrow and for interviews to start so that he could distract himself from all things Willa.

"Ethan, you're too quiet. It's weird. What's going on?" Sam asked, taking a swig from the beer bottle in his hand. The three of them were sitting out on Declan's balcony, the weather slightly warmer than it had been the past week.

Had he been too quiet? Ethan tried to unfreeze his gaze. "Nothing. I'm just beat."

"He's sulking over Willa," Declan chimed.

Well, shit. Had he been *that* obvious? "Why would I be sulking over Willa?"

"Oh, mate. Come on. How long are you going to deny this?" Sam asked.

Ethan arched his eyebrows. "You're both off."

Declan laughed. "Bro, you've been a sad sack of shit for two days. I know why. You know why. Everyone knows why."

There was no way they could read him that closely. There was no way that everyone knew. Did this mean Willa could figure it out, too?

"Everyone knows what?"

Declan downed a final gulp and knocked the bottle against Ethan's shoulder. "Everyone knows that you're into Willa."

He responded too rapidly. "I'm not into Willa. She's my best friend."

"I'm also your best friend, but you don't look at me like I put stars in the sky. Why don't you look at me like I put stars in the sky, Ethan?" Sam remarked, doing some abysmal kissing face.

Ethan grimaced. Yes, he thought the world of Willa, but he also thought he was successfully cloaking his more romantic feelings. "I don't look at Willa like she put the stars in the sky. Stop going method into Bingley. You're growing soft."

Sam chuckled. "And you're brooding, so who's method acting now?"

"Fuck off," Ethan bit back.

Declan turned to whisper to Sam. "Oh, he's down bad. The lines between his eyebrows are getting deeper."

Ethan rolled his eyes, kicking the foot of Declan's chair while he'd been tipping back in it.

"You're lucky we love it when you're broody and annoying," Declan said.

"You're annoying," Ethan replied. Jesus, they sounded like twelve-year-olds.

"You're annoying," Sam and Declan mimicked in unison.

Declan's wife Carmen conveniently popped her head out, returning from where she'd gone, putting Ethan out of the heckling misery. She kissed Declan's head. "How was dinner?" she asked.

"Great, love. I left you a plate to heat up." Declan was the best cook in their entire circle, often joking that if he weren't an actor, he would've dabbled in the culinary world. He'd made them beef gyros and the best damn homemade tzatziki sauce Ethan had ever had. As irritating as Declan was being, Ethan would swallow it up with gratitude.

"Sounds amazing. Anything new and exciting here before I go eat and watch my shows?"

Declan looked at Ethan with a wink. "Oh, yeah, our boy is in love," he noted.

Ethan let out an exasperated sigh.

Sam chortled.

Cocking an eyebrow, Carmen gave Ethan a knowing smile.

"Not you, too, Carmen," Ethan nearly whined.

"Silently. I'll think it in my head, but I won't say a word," Carmen remarked.

Declan grinned. "You two showed up at Naomi's Halloween party dressed like Gonzo and Rizzo from *The Muppet Christmas Carol.* Carm was the first person to have noticed that there was something more going on there."

Ethan shook his head. "It's not my fault none of you get the reference, which isn't romantic, by the way."

"Eh, everything can be romantic nowadays. People ship my Wickham and your Darcy."

Ethan held back a laugh.

"I'm going now. Stop hounding him. He'll tell us when he's ready to own up to his feelings," Carmen declared.

Ethan released an exhale. *Was he really this obvious? Did the entire cast know? Could everyone just tell that he was missing her like a limb was torn from his body and left 3,461.34 miles away in England?*

This was not how he imagined the night would go. He hoped it'd be a welcome distraction from Willa, not a whole discussion dedicated to her. The air thickened around him, and the sounds of sirens wailing at a distance drew his attention away. He needed to change the subject because these two weren't going to. They'd keep probing and pushing.

His eyes darted indoors, remembering the game of *Super Smash Bros.* from last Thursday that had nearly started a war between them. They'd promised each other a more fair rematch. "If you two are done getting on my nerves, we're due a rematch from last week," Ethan noted.

"Shit, that's right," Declan agreed, rising from his seat with Ethan and Sam following.

2

WILLA

Willa was used to darker makeup, a sharp and thick cat-eye, false lashes, smokey shadows, and blush in its most overt form to be seen by all members of the audience. The softer colors she got to explore for her brother's wedding were a pleasant change. She blended oranges and burgundies with a sparkly peach that brought out the hazel in her eyes. And as much as she adored red lipstick, the subtle mauve felt nice after wearing "Midnight Dance" daily at work.

She placed a napkin between her lips to blot the excess. While she got to do her own makeup, she needed someone else to do her hair, which resulted in a sleek, straight ponytail, a hairstyle that always seemed easy but was impossible to get right for someone more used to fashionable wigs for every act.

"Willa, darling, are you almost done?" she heard her mother call out.

"Be down in a minute, Mum. I just need my shoes."

Willa slid her feet into the nude pumps and stepped back for one last look in the long mirror. The caramel-colored A-line dress, decked out in glowing sequins, thankfully complemented both her body type and olive complexion.

She took her phone from the dresser and snapped a quick photo.

Willa opened the messages app on her phone and clicked on Sahar's name in her pinned contacts.

WILLA

As promised, here's the full look.

The three dots appeared immediately.

SAHAR

HOTTIE OF THE DECADE AWARD GOES TO…

WILLA

lmao I love you. I'll send more photos of the
bride and groom later.

SAHAR

Have so much fun, babe!

A part of her wanted to send the same photo to Ethan, but she couldn't figure out if that would be weird or not. She could send him random things, sure. An old photo of her with her childhood dog where she's grinning from ear to ear. Another one yesterday with her hair and makeup done dramatically by her nieces, Catherine and Lily.

Maybe she could post it on social media. Why did she even want Ethan to see it? Being away from him was odd. It was making her feel strange.

You hate social media. Why are you even questioning this?

She did it anyway. Willa opened the app and added the photo to her stories, captioning it with "time to get my big bro hitched." Then, she posted it to the Close Friends circle she'd curated away from the public eye.

Walking down the stairs, Willa heard her immediate family's chatter grow louder. While they weren't having a traditional

Armenian wedding, Anna thought the detail of the groom's family going to the bride's house could be a lot of fun, so they were keeping that element sans zurna and drums blasting upon their entrance.

Willa looked around the room, and every single person—excluding her and the kids—was paired up. Emma was adjusting the flowers in Catherine's hair, and Lily was having a very animated conversation about candy in her dad's arms. Her parents were talking to her paternal aunt and uncle. Her youngest girl cousin, Maria, was giggling with her boyfriend, Andy.

Violet, her cousin Ben's wife, was fixing his tie while quietly laughing about something he was saying. It was sweet seeing him like this, the quietest person she'd ever known, openly smiling and wholly in love with a woman who was just as in awe of him. He was a traitor, though. They'd joke often about being stuck together in the single's zone, but then he had to go and reunite with the long-lost love of his life. She'd be selfishly furious with him if their story weren't so adorable. Violet had also given birth to twins when she was forty-two, a boy and a girl. In truth, that detail gave Willa a bit of hope because despite people annoyingly telling her that her biological clock was ticking, she did, in fact, have plenty of time. At least, she hoped she would be as fortunate as they were.

She sighed. These were the moments when loneliness hit her the most, the fragments of time when she wished with everything in her that she could find someone, too.

Therapy next week was going to be a doozy.

Her phone vibrated at the exact moment her brother spoke. "Can we please not be stereotypical Armenians and get there late? Let's go!" The Armenians rolled their eyes affectionately. The non-Armenians chuckled.

ETHAN

I just saw the photo you posted. You look so beautiful, Wills. Give your brother my love.

WILLA

Thank you 😊 and I will! He's cranky and eager to get to his girl.

ETHAN

I'll bet. How are you feeling? Is anyone harassing you yet about making you their son's next bride?

WILLA

Hahahaha we're safe for now. Ask me in a few hours when we get to the venue.

ETHAN

Duly noted. I take my fake boyfriend from across the pond duties very seriously.

WILLA

Enormously grateful for you!

She placed her phone back into her cream clutch and averted her attention back to the chatter. Everyone was thankfully getting ready to leave the house, even though there'd likely be at least one more conversation in front of the door.

ON THE RIDE over to Anna's family home, Willa spotted a treehouse and squealed openly in the car. Her dad laughed, knowing her obsession. So did her mum. Since she was a little girl, Willa had adored the idea of treehouses despite never even stepping foot in one. Their houses growing up weren't big enough, and she'd never known anyone who had one either.

She didn't often dream of a big house, but she always wished for a space that could hold a small treehouse, at least something she could maybe give future children and live vicariously through them.

Willa picked up her phone to text Ethan.

WILLA

Spotted a treehouse on our way over. I almost jumped out of the car.

ETHAN

LOL but did you cry?

WILLA

I was so close.

ETHAN

Her fascination couldn't be explained. There was something about them that made her feel like things were going to be okay. It might've been silly, but merely looking at one felt like a long, needed hug, an all-time favorite song coming on shuffle right when you need it most, the first sip of coffee—a combination of all her favorite things secured in this small space surrounded by leaves.

❧

WILLA WAS OPENLY CRYING. No, she was sobbing. Alex looked at Anna like every answer in the world was written in her eyes, stored somewhere only he could see. Their vows were one thing, but the language they spoke in silence was another—tender and intimate.

This was what she wanted. This was why she kept longing for that deeper connection, where the inability to grasp a life without that person was a thought too devastating to entertain.

Willa had never felt that before.

She'd begun to think that it was never in the cards for her. But this moment, watching her brother and new sister-in-law slow-dance to Dean Martin's "Welcome to My World," was proof of its existence.

Love was indeed a very real thing.

And she wanted it for herself. She didn't want it from the guy eyeing her from across the room since they got to the venue. She most definitely didn't want it from Alden Price, her ex-boyfriend, who was convinced demisexuality was a made-up construct, and she'd get over it if she just had good sex.

As if she didn't wish it could be easy for her to go out there and have a mindless romp.

She heard the host invite all the other couples to join the bride and groom on the dance floor and caught the guy on the other end of the room rising from her peripheral vision. Willa sprinted up and beelined out to the loo.

Hard, definite, no.

Closing the restroom door behind her, Willa leaned against the nearest wall.

There were so many things she appreciated about being half-Armenian, but she loathed so much about how people approached relationships. Armenians in foreign lands often bonded quickly, an inherent effect of the displacement their ancestors faced during the Armenian Genocide, embedding a deep fear in them that someday their entire race would cease to exist. So, even though her family wasn't close to some of the people who'd been invited, it was done out of respect. She'd deal with the nosey comments for one day and try her hardest not to internalize them. Inevitably, she'd fail at that last part.

At the very least, she'd thus far managed to avoid the one

lady who'd been actively trying to set Willa up with her son since they were nineteen. Respectfully, no.

Her phone buzzed again. Yet another unfamiliar spark flared inside of her upon seeing Ethan's name.

ETHAN

What time do you get in on Wednesday?

WILLA

3:17ish

ETHAN

I'm off the whole day. I can come pick you up.

WILLA

You don't have to do that. We'll get stuck in traffic.

ETHAN

I don't mind.

She smiled to herself. What on earth were these feelings creeping up? Good God. She couldn't think this way. Ethan was her best friend. That was it—nothing more. They were just experiencing a weird, maybe natural, spell of separation anxiety. It'd happen between any two people who saw each other every day and who genuinely liked spending time together. That was it. Nothing more. It couldn't be.

So, why was her heart fluttering?

WILLA

Who am I to say no then? You're a godsend.

ETHAN

After a solid five minutes, Willa returned to the hall, which was now buzzing with livelier music, crowds circling the bride and groom, and flashing lights with faux smoke. Now, this was the party she was used to. The slower moves only felt safe on the stage, with a partner she could trust. She didn't need it here in any capacity, however casual it might be. She maneuvered her way toward her people, ready to disregard all unwanted thoughts to bask in the joy of love with the people *she* loved most.

Later in the night, she'd also learned that the chap eyeing her was Anna's relatively nice co-worker but not at all Willa's type. He had approached Anna, asking about Willa, to which she instinctively replied that she was taken, so he'd back off. But also, with very minimal effort, she caught the bouquet because it quite literally landed on her head. *Yay*? If she believed in that sort of stuff, maybe she'd take it as a sign, but nope.

Seven days with her family was both too much and too little at the same time. She was ready to return home to New York, even when she wanted to stay a little bit longer. But she'd be back soon, and her parents were set to visit in a few months. Willa moved through the security line rather swiftly, desperate to sit down with one last airport coffee from Costa and scones freshly baked by her mum.

She entered the nearest shop to buy a bottle of water before walking over to her gate. Willa sat down and opened her phone, doom-scrolling social media until she noticed a saved Instagram live on Sam's account.

Ethan looked like his skin was crawling, and he needed the camera off him. He had a few smiles—most of which she appreciated, but not this. This was the uncomfortable smile. The one he'd force when a fan was out of line or if he was feeling uneasy in a room. She picked up her phone to shoot him a message.

WILLA

I saw a bit of Sam's live. You had your uncomfortable smile on. Did something happen?

ETHAN

How on earth did you notice that?

A fan spotted me going into the theatre and ran over to grab my ass. It was the weirdest thing.

WILLA

What the hell!? I'm so sorry, Ethan.

ETHAN

And they had their friend film it, too. So who the hell knows where that'll turn up.

WILLA

That's horrid. Jesus. Why'd you get on camera after that? Did you say anything to them?

ETHAN

I turned around and said what the fuck, but they ran off. I'd promised Sam I'd do it with him, so I didn't want to back out.

WILLA

He would've understood if you'd told him.

ETHAN

I know, but I was already in such a shit mood that I didn't want to sulk about it. Are you at the airport already?

WILLA

Fair. I'm here to talk if you want. And yeah! Boarding soon, hopefully.

ETHAN

Can't wait to see you. Have a safe flight!

WILLA

Saaaaame.

ETHAN

Thanks for checking in.

WILLA

Always.

She wanted to be by his side. If she had been nearby, Ethan would've found her, put his head on her shoulder, and told her that he was annoyed. That was the familiarity crystalized in their relationship.

Small touches here and there, like second nature.

Eight hours and some change. She'd be there soon, and then she'd have them back again.

3

WILLA

There were people in the world, blessed in a way she could never fathom, who came out of airplanes miraculously still looking like gods and goddesses. But Willa always felt like a deliriously disgruntled raccoon who'd just raided every rubbish bin in the neighborhood. She hadn't even moved. Why did she look and feel like she tried and failed to run a marathon?

She regretted telling Ethan he could pick her up. No human should see her like this. After securing her luggage, Willa ran to the loo, freshened up by brushing her teeth, and sprayed a bit of perfume.

When she walked out of the airport and saw him through the window of his car, the familiarity of his smile sent every other thought running.

He stepped out, popped the boot, and took her luggage from her.

She set her backpack down next to it, and then he enveloped her in a firm but brief embrace. God, he smelled divine, the recognizable cologne he wore hitting her like a striking gust of wind.

He let her go, and she released a breathy laugh. "I feel so gross coming off that plane; you'd think I haven't showered in seventy-two years. And now you have to destroy your clothes, too. Sorry."

"You look great, and your perfume hasn't worn off either," he said, glancing at her with a regard that felt like home. *Well, good. I touched it up.*

At the very least, Ethan would never lie. If she had smelled as gross as she felt, then he would've kept quiet.

"Well, I'm glad the interior raccoon feelings aren't translating to the exterior."

Ethan laughed, wondrously deep and warm, then opened the passenger door for her. "Let's get you home, little raccoon."

"Are you coming over?" Willa asked.

"Do you want me to?"

"No, I asked because I wanted to hear you say yes, only to respond that no one invited you, and you're not welcome," she deadpanned.

His lips curved upward. "Aggressive."

"You're coming, and we're continuing our *Peaky Blinders* watch after I shower. You didn't watch any new episodes without me, did you?"

"Would I ever betray you like that, little raccoon?" Ethan answered.

"I'm not into this nickname. It's not doing any favors to my self-esteem."

"How about a cute little raccoon?" he specified, and her heart did an alien gallop.

"My raccoon state will end soon. What then? I have to live with this pesky reminder?"

He shrugged. "We'll think of something else."

"What we should think of is what we're drinking."

Ethan looked toward her. "Now you're talking. Is Sahar going to be home?"

"No, she's gone to the Hamptons with the prick's prissy friends. She'll be back tomorrow."

"You really don't like that guy."

Willa rolled her eyes. "I don't like blue cheese. I loathe that guy. He's the bloody worst. I have no idea what she sees in him or why she puts up with all his bullshit when she could have literally any man falling at her feet."

"He's a kiss ass. The only thing he has going for him is a decent voice and a face to match. He shows everyone what they want to see."

Huffing, Willa replied. "Yeah, except the woman he supposedly loves—the one who's too good for him. Anyway, enough about him. Are you feeling a bit relieved now that interviews are done?"

"Excluding the red carpet for the premiere, you have no idea. Though, I think it went okay this time. The group interviews and behind-the-scenes content went especially well. I wish you'd been a part of them," Ethan answered.

Willa smiled at him. "Sahar told me! It makes me so happy to hear that. I'm sorry they make you so nervous, though."

"Yeah, well, some journalists haven't made it easy in the past."

She arched her eyebrows. "Journalists, fans, even some fellow actors; it's the curse of not having any boundaries in our industry."

"I hate that this is also why social media freaks you out so much," he added.

She didn't want to think about that right now. She didn't want to think about the fact that their lives would always be brimming with chaotic highs and lows without the added privilege of privacy.

"Yup," she replied.

"I can't say I blame you. At all."

She shrugged. "Oh, any updates on your guest room? Forgot to ask about that."

He let out a sarcastic laugh. "Fucking hell, Wills, I thought I told you. A damn pipe burst in the guest bathroom, flooded into the damn room. I swear it's just gonna be storage space until I actually get some actual time off to deal with it."

"Christ. That's some shit luck, mate."

"Tell me about it," he said.

They stayed quiet for a beat, letting the music stretch out and fill the comfortable silence between them. Willa glanced over at him. Why did everything feel so...different suddenly?

The two of them had been nearly joined at the hip from the moment Willa quoted *The Muppet Christmas Carol*—specifically the line about jellybeans—and Ethan was the only one who got the reference. Come to find out, they were both obsessed with the film and watched it multiple times every year during the holidays.

From then on, it'd been movie nights almost every other day and regularly starting TV shows together. The nights turned into breakfast the next morning and easy conversations about anything and everything.

She had been the first person he told when he found out his grandfather passed, smack dab in the middle of their Boston run. He got the phone call right as he'd gotten to his hotel room. She ran up to his floor. He threw himself into her arms. She stayed with him until he fell asleep. He was only able to get away for one day, and then he'd called her after the funeral, too. Willa met him at the airport upon his return, wanting to be beside him in case he needed anything.

She held him when he cried silently on the couch. She watched him pour his heart out into an emotionally taxing performance the next day, then sat with him as he crumbled in her arms in his dressing room.

They'd become each other's safe space.

And then came her birthday, two weeks after his grandpa's passing. He had called her at midnight, his voice a little muted and husky. *"I set an alarm for you,"* he had admitted. *"I wanted to be the first to say happy birthday."* She thanked him, laid back against her pillow, phone resting along her ear. *"I wish I had eloquent words, Wills, but they're escaping me right now. You're my best friend, and the world is better with you in it. I hope this year is extra kind to you, and I hope you get everything you've always wished for,"* he declared, the vulnerability in his voice staying with her during the loneliest nights. The sincerity, the warmth.

She thought she had imagined it when she woke up in the morning, checking her phone's caller ID to confirm that it had indeed been true.

There was a moment that night when she questioned whether she could feel something more for him, but she buried the feelings as quickly as they materialized. This was merely a friendship—a lasting, life-altering, perfect friendship.

Plus, she had rules against dating actors and an even more rigid belief that best friends should never venture toward the uncharted territory of becoming lovers.

And the entire cast was close, too. How they'd quickly become like a family after the first few gatherings made the Boston tryouts that much more comforting. Coffee runs, ridiculous social media-led lives always conducted by their Bingley, Sam Butler, many nights playing "Werewolf," and breaking into bonkers arguments as a result of the tension.

Willa faced Ethan in the driver's seat. Things were shifting. She wasn't quite sure why, but her reactions to him felt different.

He had a face carved exclusively for the spotlight. It was made even more beautiful because of all the ways she knew him.

She knew of Ethan Everett long before she worked with him, but what she learned was that despite the roles he'd take on, despite what a heartthrob he was, he could be quiet, a little shy even. He had the biggest heart of any man she knew.

His presence suddenly overwhelmed her, like the sun making a quick appearance on a day that assured only rainfall. Kaleidoscopic hues waltzed through her mind, begging her to marvel at him—to stare for a little while longer.

Bloody hell. What was happening to her? Missing him had done something she wasn't prepared for.

WILLA APPLIED hyaluronic acid and topped it off with a generous amount of moisturizer to combat the dryness of her skin after the plane ride. She then detangled her hair with a wet brush and ambled over to Ethan, who was standing in her kitchen, mixing cocktails. They had picked up a pie from Leo's Pizza on their way over, and she quickly scarfed down a slice before jumping into the shower. Ethan had taken the pepperoni off his and left them on a plate for her. She popped two of them into her mouth at once and gave him a gratified grin.

She eyed the drinks then. "What are we having?" she asked. He looked obscenely hot handling the silver shaker. If she hadn't known he'd bartended back in the day while still making his way into the industry, she would've assumed he was a natural at it.

"Sour cherry negroni," he replied.

"The telepathic part of my brain that signaled to yours I wanted something sour deserves an award."

Ethan winked, a delicious smirk rising alongside it. "I got you."

Willa took the rest of the pepperoni slices and beelined over to the TV stand; grabbing the remote, she plopped herself on the sofa. They should watch something. It'd help her shake whatever emotions were nagging at her.

Or, there was that puzzle she wanted to start—the one of Paris bathed in moonlight. Would Ethan want to make it with her?

She stole another glance at him. Something about Ethan looked different today, and it wasn't the light scruff dusting his face after two days of no press or show duties. It wasn't his tired posture or the natural waves of his hair falling forward after a long day. No, it was something else entirely—something she couldn't quite figure out.

Nope, nope, nope.

They were friends.

Best friends.

That was it.

She not so subtly looked at her phone once she saw him walking toward her. The nerves bubbled into a volcanic explosion directly in the middle of her throat.

He placed the two glasses down and sat beside her, the weight of him making the sofa feel smaller and simultaneously cozier.

There was no way she could handle serious television right now, not with all her feelings muddied like this. "I know you've been waiting to watch new episodes, but my headspace is a bit...convoluted right now, and I don't want to watch something heavy. Would you want to do a puzzle with me?"

Concern chased away the ease in his expression. "Sure. Is there anything you want to talk about?"

"Nope. It's just the usual dose of anxiety doing its due diligence and making its presence known because what else would it do?"

"Okay," he acknowledged tenderly, without judgment. "You know you can always talk to me, right?"

Willa reached forward to grab the glass in front of her. "Aren't you tired of me always having something frustrating to say?"

His expression turned serious, wholly sincere, and promising. "Never." The conviction in his voice was palpable, easy to believe.

"You're my favorite," she replied, the words slipping effortlessly off her tongue.

"Good, because you're mine."

Willa scrunched her nose in a closed-mouth smile and took a sip of her drink before rising from the sofa to retrieve the puzzle. She crouched down and pulled it out from underneath her bed, then she punctured the sharp end of her nail into the spot where the two boxes joined and ripped the plastic. Removing it fully, she tossed it in the bathroom's rubbish bin before going back out to the living room.

She glanced between the coffee table and the kitchen table, trying to decipher which would be a better location. Ethan seemed to intuit her choice quicker than she did because he got off the couch and picked up their drinks. He set them down on the kitchen table and went back for the wooden coasters. Willa opened the box, tore the bag inside, and spilled the cardboard pieces onto the white oak surface.

"Do you have the sheets to glue them together?" Ethan asked.

"No," she answered.

He gaped. "So, what are you going to do when we're done?"

Willa beckoned her hands upward. "Undo it, then throw it back in the box?"

He looked horrified. "What? All that work and you're just

going to toss it back in a box? What is wrong with you? Is this the British way of doing puzzles?"

"Don't bring my people into this. It's a puzzle. It's not that deep."

He shook his head, a small laugh escaping through his astonishment. "We're not doing that. I'll order the tape, so don't you dare touch this until I bring it over."

"But I feel like doing it now. What would we even do with it afterward?"

"Frame it? I don't know, Willa, what do people do with a piece of artwork?"

Willa took a long sip of her drink. "Oof, I didn't know you were so passionate about puzzles."

"And I didn't realize you were such a chaos demon. It's a good thing you're not into gaming. We'd murder each other."

She concurred with a nod. "Sahar's rage is enough for me to know I wouldn't survive playing with any of you. I'll stick to Tetris on my phone."

Ethan shuddered dramatically and turned to the pieces scattered across the table. "Please tell me you at least start with the edges; otherwise, I'm leaving."

She laughed. Ethan was so ridiculously precious when he got heated about something. It reminded her of when she once sat with him and Sam while they played some sort of football game. Was it *FIFA*? Sahar would know better; she'd sometimes play with them, too. Anyway, Ethan had been convinced that Sam was cheating, so they went at it with every insult known to man, immediately sounding like five-year-olds who'd learned how to swear for the first time. At one point, Ethan smacked his plastic water bottle over Sam's head, and then Sam smeared guacamole onto Ethan's face. They bickered for maybe five minutes before begrudgingly agreeing to a rematch. She was used to the yelling since living with Sahar, but seeing her typically easy-going best friend get so riled up was hilarious.

"Yes, Jesus Christ, I'm not a monster. I just apparently like to work hard and then demolish everything," she remarked, sticking her tongue out at him.

He swiped from left to right and signaled with his hand. "Okay, good. You take that edge, and I'll take this."

"Wait, we can't start yet. I need to put something on the TV for noise. Any suggestions?"

"*Moulin Rouge*," he answered off the bat.

She smiled. "I see how you got there, and I applaud your brain's desire to remain on a theme, but unless you want me to start sobbing halfway through, we need another option."

"*Ratatouille*," he countered.

She clicked her tongue in agreement.

Willa pressed the microphone on the remote and spoke into it. "Play Pixar's *Ratatouille*," she commanded. The apps on the TV heeded her request and brought the animated film onto the screen. When the volume was at her preferred level, she spun back to the table.

"And go," she said.

Ethan's eyes widened. "Wait, are we competing?"

She laughed. "No, weirdo. We're doing a puzzle, not fighting zombies or whatever it is you lot battle in those games."

A moment of truth? Willa secretly adored how competitive he could get. The way the tips of his ears flared when everything got heated and tensions built. He would be on her side at any given moment except when it came to any sort of game. So, while she was partly glad she wasn't into playing much, Willa wished she could be. But she could barely handle her nerves when a TV show got too intense; she wasn't strong enough for the gaming world.

Their hands moved and brushed against each other along

the plane as they worked through finding the edge pieces for their respective sides, swapping and testing selections to find their exact match. This was the perfect distraction, the TV doing the talking for them, the occasional sound of gulping down their drinks.

They completed the edge pieces and bits of the middle before Ethan left for the night, reminding her not to touch anything until he was back tomorrow.

4

ETHAN

Ethan appreciated many things about Willa, and he especially appreciated the way she moved her body. As a dance captain—or co-captain, rather, as she shared the title with Miles Dahl—she was transformative in her coaching.

"Let's take it from the top with 'Marry Me'. Naomi, your form is excellent, but Ethan, I need you to make the grip on her arm more believable. Darcy's proposal has to come off too strong—too brash. The edge is there in your voice, but your movements are a bit on the graceful side today," Willa called out.

Ethan nodded, positioning himself to face Naomi again.

He placed his hand underneath her chin, waiting for the orchestra to begin the charged opening notes of the number. *Wait, stop—there's something I need to say,* he sang.

What is it you want from me? Naomi belted out, Elizabeth's frustration pushing through.

They moved and meandered in their blocked space, voices blending together. Then Ethan gripped onto her forearm, using his physicality and facial cues to make it appear tighter.

"Yes! Perfect! Just like that," Willa shouted through the melody.

It was a good thing that "Marry Me" fell right before intermission because the intensity of the number drained Ethan in a way nothing in his career ever had. From the use of the gruffest parts of his vocal cords to the movements in the choreography, his body could have given out if he hadn't trained so vigorously for it. It was both depleting and rewarding to experience something like it as an artist. He knew as much, and he was grateful for it.

When they came to a stop and parted after the kiss, he briefly angled his head toward Willa's gaze. A smile rose on her lips.

His eyes mapped out Willa's curves, which were accentuated by her fitted taupe workout set. Ethan wanted to drag his hands along the hard planes of her abs. His lips and teeth, too.

He thought about what it would be like if she ever went on as Elizabeth, knowing how rare it would be because Lea Driver, Naomi's sister, was the role's standby. He imagined trailing his lips along Willa's neck, up toward her mouth. He shouldn't think any of these things about her, and yet...

The past few days since Willa's return from England made him feel foolish: two whole nights spent doing a puzzle together, takeout meals, and one too many instances of catching himself staring. He was so raptly tuned into everything she did, so incontestably besotted that he didn't know what to do with himself.

He couldn't stop himself from wanting her, determinedly attempting to push aside those thoughts, knowing she wasn't interested in him like that.

Despite his efforts to ignore Sam and Declan's pestering, they were right. Ethan was a goner. He liked Willa far more than he ever thought possible. Being around her day and night fueled him, both on and off the stage.

She made him a better person and a better performer, too.

"Incredible, team," stage manager Dina Rollins noted. "Take five."

Ethan sauntered over to the edge of the stage and sat down. Willa jumped down and strolled to Sahar, Tanya, and Innila, who sat in the orchestra's first row.

He wanted her to look at him again. He wanted to ask her to come over tonight, eat takeout Chinese food, and continue *Peaky Blinders.*

Declan crept beside him, resting his head on Ethan's shoulder. "You're in a daze, lover boy," he said, low enough so no one else would hear.

Ethan shrugged him away. "Fuck off. No, I'm not."

"Yeah, you are, boo," Declan remarked, then snorted loudly. It made Willa look, a smile dancing across her face. She turned and walked back to them.

Thankfully, Declan would never say anything near her. He had too much respect for Willa—too much respect for both of them unless it came to hounding Ethan in private.

She stood in front of them. "You're smashing the new bits of the choreography Josie implemented. I'm so damn proud of you."

"I'm also proud of you," Declan added.

His face heated a bit. "Thanks, Wills. You too, Dec."

Declan smacked Ethan's back flippantly and stood up. "I'm going to call *my wife*," he emphasized.

Ethan suppressed an eye roll, sure of the fact that the overt use of the words "my wife" was on purpose.

He stretched out his hands to lock his fingers with Willa's. *Were other friends like this? Did they touch each other this freely?*

She was like gravity sometimes. No matter how hard he tried

to fight, he couldn't prevent the steps his body took to be near her.

"Come over tonight after rehearsals for Chinese and *Peaky Blinders?*" he suggested.

"Can we do tomorrow instead? Prissy little prick is being extra shitty to Sahar. We're going out with the girls tonight."

He nodded. "Yeah, of course. Is she okay?"

"We'll make sure she is," Willa answered, determination present in her voice.

Ethan pulled her closer to him with his hands entangled in hers, rocking her back and forth. "You really mean what you said about the choreography?"

Willa squeezed his hands, leaning forward into the space between them. "Would I ever lie to you?"

"No, but you could be sparing my feelings, settling for mediocre."

"I wouldn't. I'd offer to work with you if I thought you needed more training, but you're doing great. You're in your head about it. Get out."

"Yes, ma'am."

She smiled and released her fingers from his, pushing herself up on the stage with a swift and easy hop. Ethan turned to face her, swinging his legs back onto the stage. Willa placed her hands in front of his, and he took them again, all sorts of emotions coursing through his veins.

She tugged him up, released her grip, and bumped her hip against his.

Ethan enfolded his arms around her waist and spun her, prompting a low, startled giggle to rush out of her. Deftly, he swung her over his shoulder and carried her to the position she'd have to be in for the next number.

Moving like this was never seamless for Ethan. He had rhythm and could learn a dance routine with enough practice, but someone as talented as Willa made it easier for him to try more impromptu steps. Months of practicing and standing in with her while she made up dances for fun improved his form spectacularly. Or, maybe her body was meant to be in motion with his.

It almost felt instinctual in a way he only ever mastered with his voice and acting. Spinning someone else felt awkward if he had not rehearsed it.

She bowed dramatically. "Thanks for the lift. The effort it would have taken to walk this distance felt monumental."

Ethan shook his head and laughed, stepping into the wings where he'd have the complete view of her during "Forbidden Corridors"—the most erotic part of the show. He shouldn't watch. The last few rehearsals proved he was too enraptured to make it through the entire thing without growing hard.

He should turn away. But God help him, watching Willa lunge against a ladder, move, and twist through the space occupying the very reason for the show's title was one of the hottest things he'd ever seen. It wasn't until he understood the depth of his feelings that everything that happened in this number ripped him to shreds from the inside.

Ethan would give his whole being to be on the receiving end of each move. He would treasure her facial expressions while standing in front of her, instead of watching from behind. He berated himself for it. He shouldn't be thinking these thoughts about his best friend.

He turned away as she lay on the ground, hands splayed across her breasts. He knew what would come next. She'd thrust her hips and move her hands lower and lower to where his gaze shouldn't follow. In a few beats, Miles would join as her partner in the number. He had to look away.

Thank heavens, Darcy was nowhere to be found in this scene, so Ethan could avoid this number altogether during live performances. He mostly did during the tryouts, but even seeing Willa quickly run by him in the leather cut-out leotard was enough to make him lose his mind.

He took deep, steady breaths, forcing his mind to trail elsewhere. He thought of the boiled chicken he had to feed his cat two nights ago for her stomach, trying to recall the foul smell he couldn't stand. He focused his attention on the larger-than-normal rat that nearly had a staring contest with him this morning at the subway station. Mushy vegetables, soggy fries, feathers of any kind, sounds at the dentist, the smell of apple cider vinegar, people who chewed loudly, slow walkers...

The worst things were far better than thinking about Willa in leather. Willa and her pretty eyes and her wildly brilliant laugh and all the ways he could love her.

Focus. What is wrong with you?

Declan made his way into the wings with him, leaning back against the opposite side of the wall. Part of "Forbidden Corridors" meant that Elizabeth would catch Wickham with two women here, learning that he wasn't who he said he was. He'd run out of the scene when it happened, reappearing only after the off-stage marriage with Lydia.

"I don't know how the hell the ensemble pulls through this entire number. They're such legends. I feel like I'm dying every time," he joked breathlessly.

Ethan snorted a laugh. "What blows my mind is how flexible they are."

What blows my mind is how flexible she is. He kept that thought to himself.

Declan agreed, still heaving.

"Bro, you're lucky you don't have to do anything else for three more songs," Ethan said.

Declan bobbed his head. "Don't I know it? Oh, listen, you still down to come with me to my buddy's show on Sunday?"

"Yeah, is Sam coming, too? Or is it just us?"

"Us and Miles."

"Cool, cool. I'm psyched."

Declan grinned ghoulishly. "My hero," he declared.

"Am I not always your hero?"

"Naw, only when you do things for me."

Ethan shook his head back and forth. "You're an idiot."

"I'm tired, so I'll let you have that," he said, sliding down onto the ground.

Ethan chuckled, then quickly averted his eyes to the stage, noticing the number's approaching ending. Since the number sped up and the ensemble moved around the entire stage instead of staying in the marks where they began, at this point, Ethan couldn't spot Willa as easily. Good, because he needed to calm himself down still.

REHEARSALS TOOK an hour longer than usual, and by the time it ended, he was exhausted and thrilled, nevertheless. Though so much was heightened by *Midnights at Pemberley's* scale, the juxtaposition of being tired and fulfilled would always be one of his favorite things about being in a Broadway musical.

It's why the couch in his dressing room, where he would unwind with Willa, had become such a comforting fortress. The secluded little space they often occupied together stretched out to develop into something bigger, better. She was standing a few feet ahead of him at the stage door, hands animated in a conversation with Christian and Miles. She stepped forward when she spotted Ethan, hugged them both jointly, and then hurried over to him.

She smiled when she got closer. "Okay, so girl's night turned into everyone is coming. Sam and Priya are meeting us there, and so are Miles and Christian now. Would you come, too?"

"Sure, what time?" he asked.

"Seven. We don't plan on staying long since we're all tired, but it's something to do," she specified.

He angled his wrist up and glanced at his watch. Three hours from now. That was doable. "Yeah, sounds good." The dimples in her cheeks surfaced as her smile grew into an excited expression. It was bolstering for him to know that, if nothing else, she cared for his presence as much as he did hers.

It was comforting to understand that even if she never felt the way he did, she still appreciated spending time with him.

She wanted to include him in her plans.

She wanted him around.

That would have to be enough.

5
____

WILLA

Typically, Ethan and Christian would be heading in the same direction as them, but Ethan needed to pick up cat food on his way home, and Christian was in physical therapy.

"My hips hurt. Do your hips hurt?" Willa asked Sahar.

Sahar grinned cheekily. "You know, I'm partly jealous you have the intensity of 'Forbidden Corridors' as one of your numbers but also not."

Willa maneuvered awkwardly down the stairs. "It feels like a truck ran into me. I don't even know how that's possible. It's not that rigorous."

"It's not that rigorous, she says when Josie called it one of the most grueling pieces she's ever choreographed," Sahar noted.

Willa groaned, stretching quickly as they got to the bottom of the subway stairs. "I call dibs on a shower first, please."

"Take your time, boo. I'm going straight for a nap."

"Did the prick text you?" Willa inquired.

Sahar shook her head, sadness creeping its way onto her expression. "Nope."

"You tell me when, and I'll kill him."

"No need for murder, but I'll take all the distractions," she said, moving aside to place her phone against the turnstile.

Willa stepped in after her. Two seats were luckily available, so they sat side by side. Sahar laid her head against Willa's shoulder. "Why am I such shit at picking men? I swear it. I'm never dating another actor again."

"Okay, you know where I stand with my rule, but it's not the actors that are the problem. It's dumbasses who can't see your worth."

Sahar sighed quietly. Willa knew this wasn't over yet. He'd likely come groveling, she'd take him back, then he'd piss her off again, and the cycle would repeat. She could never understand why Sahar would put up with it, but then again, Willa admired the risks Sahar took, wishing she could be like that when it came to love.

WILLA'S PHONE vibrated on her bed while she was drawing on eyeliner. Like his company, Ethan's name on her lock screen would perpetually elicit a joy she couldn't put into words. Something familiar and warm.

ETHAN

Would you hate me if I bailed tonight?

A sense of gloom eclipsed her excitement with dark clouds and spattered onto her like heavy droplets of rain. She could never hate him, but now that it was no longer just the girls, his absence would be palpable. She'd feel it in the same way she did at her brother's wedding during quiet moments in the night when she'd looked around the venue in longing.

WILLA

Of course not. You alright?

ETHAN

Yeah, just a bad tension headache crept up and
painkillers aren't doing jack.

WILLA

Is there anything I can do?

ETHAN

Have fun and make it home safe.

WILLA

I meant for you.

ETHAN

Your joy is my joy.

WILLA

And your well-being is mine.

Three dots came and went for a solid minute. It was
maddening.

ETHAN

The feeling is mutual.

Ugh. What did she expect? Willa needed to pull herself
together. These emotions were starting to get weird as hell.

She needed a drink, or three, maybe four. She needed to stop
thinking of him as anything more than her best friend. She had
to stick to her beliefs and remember that he was an actor at the
end of the day. And she'd sworn to herself that she'd never date
one because she wanted a partner whose life would be a bit
more stable than hers. Someone who would balance her chaotic
career.

. . .

THE BAR WAS NOISIER than usual and more packed, too, which was odd with no game on an arbitrary Tuesday. And, in an unsurprising turn of events, her feelings wouldn't let her be.

Coming here was a bad idea. Three gin and tonics were a bad idea, while the fourth sitting in front of her, which was now tempting her with its invisible crystal claws, was shaping up to be another.

Willa was indebted to her dad's genes and the ability to hold her liquor but not so grateful for her mother's sensitive nature.

She averted her eyes toward the wooden pole where Miles stood, hitting it off with the guy who'd been gazing at him all night before Willa and Christian made him walk over to start a conversation. She felt herself growing a bit envious over the possibility that they'd probably go home together, spend a delightfully solid night rolling around in sheets, and then maybe tomorrow they'd get coffee together. Maybe coffee would turn into dinner when they were free, and dinner would turn into late nights curled up on the sofa.

Another happily ever after unfolding in front of her while she pined like an utter buffoon over her best friend. She felt icky and selfish and sad. Miles deserved every bit of happiness in the world. She was thrilled for him, wholeheartedly wanting this to work out even if her emotions were all over the place.

The night turned sour so quickly, too, as she sat in a swarming bar where they were supposed to be comforting Sahar instead of watching the prince of pricks intrude and beg for her forgiveness.

She should've just left when Sam and Priya did. There was no need for her to be here anymore. *Ugh*, but she also didn't want to abandon Sahar until she was certain she would be going home with the prick.

Christian poked her hand resting on the table. "Penny for your thoughts."

Willa sighed, speaking before her brain could counter against sharing some of her more personal thoughts. "Why is everyone paired up? Have you noticed it? I'm quite literally the only single person in the cast."

He pouted apologetically. "You and Ethan, actually. But also, does it make you feel any better that my fiancé is in LA and won't be back for another ten months because of his schedule?"

She placed the glass in front of her mouth and sipped. She hated feeling this way. "No, because you still get to talk to him every night. Gah, I'm sorry for sounding like such a whiny little shit. I'm just sad. I shouldn't have drunk this much."

She pushed the glass away from her. She and alcohol should only mingle when her headspace was kinder.

"You're good, Wills. I've been there, too. Before Dan, I was the only single person in every friend group for three years. It made me so damn cranky, and I was thoroughly convinced I was cursed to be alone forever."

Christian's empathy was genuine. At the very least, it was apparent that he didn't think she was a horrible person for her feelings.

"Dan's an absolute peach. You two are perfect together." She pointed toward Miles. "And those two are too hot for words, so we've got to make sure it works out."

Christian smiled with understanding.

Willa sighed. "I need to get home. I'm going to see if Sahar will come. If not, would you wait outside with me while I get a lift?"

"I'll head out with you," he answered.

Willa stood up and veered through a crowd of rowdy college students to get to the corner where Sahar stood with the prick. She stepped right in between them, not caring a lick about his feelings, and placed her hands on Sahar's shoulders. "Are you going to stay with him? I don't think I can hang anymore. Plus, we have an early morning tomorrow," she whispered.

Sahar concurred. "No, I'll come with you. Give me two minutes."

"I'll be waiting outside with Christian."

She turned away and moved toward Miles, debating whether to cut in on their conversation to say bye. Instead, he caught her nearness and pulled her in for a side hug.

"Heading out?" he asked.

She bobbed her head and smiled amiably at the man whose name she still didn't know. "I'll see you tomorrow," she declared. "Goodnight, you two."

"Get home safe, Wills," Miles added.

She stepped outside to where Christian stood, his hands tucked in his pockets. "Is our girl coming?"

Willa nodded and shivered slightly. The late winter night pierced with a subtle blow. "Said she'd be out in two minutes."

They stood there for a beat, neither saying a thing before Sahar finally met them—two minutes on the dot. "Sorry...about all of it," she said.

"All good. What'd the prick want?" Willa inquired.

Sahar sighed. "He apologized. Blamed it on stress and shit. I told him it wasn't an excuse and I needed to think about what I want. He claims he understands, so we'll see," she finished with a shrug.

Willa put her arm around Sahar's shoulder. "I'm glad you're thinking about it."

"Yeah, so am I."

Christian looked up from his phone. "Ride is approaching."

"Thank God, I'm so knackered," Sahar added.

Willa groaned and tugged her falling bra strap up from inside her jumper. "I'm going to hate myself if I'm hungover tomorrow."

Sahar turned her head, shock dawning in her eyes. "How much did you drink?"

"Enough to make my future self hate me. I was sad. And the bartender must've noticed because he gave me the extra one on the house when I went up to get water instead."

Sahar chuckled slightly. "Oh, babe. We'll get you some ibuprofen, and I'm not letting you sleep until you've emptied two entire cups of water. Want to tell us why you're sad?"

"No, because it's embarrassing." And because she was already feeling bad for basically disclosing half of it to Christian, minus the part about her feelings for Ethan.

Sahar pursed her lips.

Christian patted Sahar's shoulder, gesturing for them to follow him into the silver Kia SUV that had approached.

Willa bit her tongue as she entered, forcing herself not to swear aloud.

Of all the songs in the world, this driver had to be playing Keane's "Somewhere Only We Know." She was going to lose it. Her eyes welled so hard it would be downright humiliating if she started crying.

Fuck alcohol. Screw emotions.

She wanted to call Ethan.

She wanted to beg this driver with great taste in music to please change the damn song. It hit her in all the places she had zero stamina to combat against.

It was touching the familiarity and tender emotions that only Ethan's presence could evoke.

It was too much.

Her discomfort must've been evident because Christian placed his hand on her bouncing knee. "You okay?"

She shut her eyes for a second and then drew closer to his ear. "The song isn't helping the mood."

The driver must've overheard her attempt at a whisper. "Would you like me to change it?"

Yes, she wanted to say. "Oh, no, that's okay," left her betraying lips.

"At least we're close to home," Sahar added.

The car came to a halt five minutes later, no traffic being a much-needed blessing. They stepped out of the vehicle and gave each other quick hugs before Christian walked to his building next to theirs.

She wanted to check in on Ethan and see how he was doing, but it suddenly felt intrusive. A thing she would've done without an ounce of hesitation now sparked a storm of doubts and uncertainties. It's not like Ethan would think she liked him because of a simple text.

The man was focused intently on opening day, married to his work, as she should've been. He wasn't pushing boundaries in his mind as tirelessly as she was.

It's just a text, woman. Send it. Check in.

Sahar pressed the fifth-floor button in the elevator, and Willa leaned her head against the cool metal. She opened her messages, clicked on his name, and stared. She stared until a ding alerted her of their arrival.

"Where'd you go?" Sahar asked.

She sighed quietly, looking down at her white trainers against the floor. "Has this floor always had such an ugly tile pattern?"

"Oof, it's that bad in your head that you're deflecting with another question? Noted. And yes—how are you just noticing this?"

"It's squishy."

Sahar held back a laugh. "Something is going on in that head of yours, and I'm gonna pretend I'm not offended that you're keeping it from me."

"The only thing going on in my head is how I can't stop thinking about Ethan, and I'm not at all chuffed about feeling these things."

Sahar stopped, flat key mid-turn. "Ethan, as in Ethan Everett?"

"Do we know more than one?"

"No...but are you saying what I think you're saying?"

"I was going to text him to see how his head is, but I started spiraling."

"Because?" she asked, fingers still tightly wound against the silver.

Willa sighed, reaching forward; she spun the key in Sahar's fingers and pushed open the door. "Because my brain is going down the kind of path it should stay far away from, and I don't want to talk about it."

"OH MY GOD." Sahar didn't move, standing still in the doorway.

Willa turned back. "What?"

"How are you just casually sharing this with me like it's some random thing you bought at the shops?"

"Well, I'm glad it's not obvious because today's been *a lot,* and I started worrying about how I must be wearing every little emotion all over my face."

Sahar scoffed. "No, it's obvious because I know you, but I didn't think you'd figured it out yet. And I assumed that once you did, your arse would share it with me."

Willa took off her shoes beside their rack near the door and strode to the kitchen. She filled a glass with water, popped open a bottle of painkillers, took one, and then turned to look at her friend. "To be fair, I haven't processed shit."

"When did this start?"

"It's come and gone a few times, but it's never been this...I don't know, loud? Things have been different since I got back. I missed him so much when I was away. He said he missed me, too. I think we're just a bit too attached."

Sahar laughed. "Wow! I'm going to assume you probably can't admit this or maybe even see it, but you know he feels the same way, right? You two are conjoined at the hip."

Willa placed the glass under the filtered dispenser and filled it to the brim once more. "And this is where I head to bed now because you're just talking nonsense."

"I'm not, and you know it."

Willa shook her head, frustration mounting in her chest. "You know where I stand with dating actors, Sahar. My brain is just disheveled in all sorts of ways right now," she flipped her hair to the other side and sighed. "None of this means anything. It's pre-opening jitters, coming back together after time apart, and a whole bloody mess of confusing emotions that'll go away eventually."

Sahar shrugged and leaned against the fridge. "Just checking to make sure you know that's a rule you set yourself, right? It can be broken."

Willa pinched the bridge of her nose. "I set it for a reason. The field alone is complicated; look at the divorce rates and the amount of time people spend apart. It'd be a recipe for a disaster."

Sahar was about to speak, but Willa cut her off. "*And* on top of that, I don't want to deal with death threats from his fans or hear about how I've only gotten this far because I dated him. You know how it's been for us, Sahar. We've worked our asses off for years in smaller roles, and this is our big break. We got here on our own. We got here because someone somewhere finally looked beyond my last name and your first name. We got here because of our hard work. They saw what we were capable of. It'd all go straight to hell if I got with Ethan."

Sahar grimaced. "Do you hear yourself? First, yes, we got

here on our own, and we should be damn proud of that. But people will talk and make assumptions *regardless.* Someday, you might also have a few toxic fans who'd give your normal accountant boyfriend hell just because they think you can do better. That cannot be a reason you stop yourself from being with the one person you might fully connect with," Sahar countered.

"The distance could be hard on us. Things are easier now that we're in the same production. Things are too unpredictable in our field."

Sahar gaped at her. "Willa, listen, I know you believe this with everything in you, and I know I'm not the best example with my track record, but you have to know that not every actor's relationship is the same. Like how every Middle Eastern person isn't the same even though ignorant people love boxing us in, every demisexual isn't the same, every dancer isn't the same, etc. You know this."

Willa exhaled heavily and took another large gulp of water. "Yeah, okay, I hear you. I get that. But, Sahar, all of that aside, there's also the fact that I'd never jeopardize my friendship with him. I know it's only been two-ish years, but it feels like he's been the missing puzzle piece in my life, and I can't imagine getting together, breaking up, and losing that friendship. I'm not risking that."

"And what if you don't break up? What if it lasts? What if he's the one? Jesus, Willa, look at the love stories in your family alone. How am *I* the hopeless romantic who gives every dick a chance even when they keep screwing me over? Meanwhile, you have concrete proof of all the ways that love lasts and endures. My sister just divorced her childhood best friend, for crying out loud, and I still think love is a very real thing that can last."

Willa threw her hands up in the air. "Exactly! Amina is proof of why you don't get with your best friend, let alone your childhood best friend."

"The problem here isn't that Amina and Keith were friends; it's that Keith has always been a womanizer. Amina thought she could change him, and he wanted to change but realized sticking his dick into one woman for the rest of his life was too challenging. They aren't a bloody rule here. Plus, Amina is, quite frankly, doing all right with the chap from her office. There might be something there that lasts."

Willa closed her eyes and took a deep breath. "Still, she and Keith are no longer as close, and they used to be inseparable."

"That's just life, babe. You can't live in fear of what'll happen."

"I'm not living in fear. I'm being cautious."

"Cautious could be stopping you from experiencing something extraordinary."

"Cautious is what you have to be when you're thirty-three, and you'd eventually like a family someday."

Sahar released an empathetic sigh. "I get it. I do, but sometimes, all of that—kids, a family, happy endings, require taking a risk. Ethan isn't Jesse, he isn't Robert, and he sure as hell isn't Alden."

"How did we go from my headspace feeling fuzzy and these emotions will eventually go away to an entire deconstruction of my love life? I'm too drunk for this."

"You would be reacting the same way even if you were sober because these feelings aren't going to go away overnight, and you're doing a lot of work to deny yourself a chance at happiness," Sahar noted, reaching up to the cupboard, she took out a bag of sour belts and ripped the seal open.

She inched the bag close to Willa, who shook her head in a wordless, *I'm good* gesture. Sahar pulled out a green one and stuck it in her mouth. "I'm guessing we're going to forget this conversation happened in the morning until you're ready to admit that your feelings aren't just a batch of nerves?" she asked.

Willa nodded and reached over to take the bag of white cheddar Cheez-its sitting on the counter. "Yup. Good talk."

She beelined toward her room, fully aware that Sahar would be shaking her head. She wanted—no, needed—a quick body shower, but God, the effort—*the effort*. She picked up her phone again and stared at Ethan's last message. A simple text would be harmless.

Contrary to everything Sahar believed, none of these emotions would last. They'd go away. They had to.

WILLA

How's your head?

ETHAN

Still hurts but no longer has me in a death grip.
How was tonight?

WILLA

Good to hear. It was fine. Nothing special.

ETHAN

Did you get home safe?

WILLA

Yup, about to crash.

ETHAN

Okay, good. Sleep well.

WILLA

Goodnight!

She released a tortured groan, ate the remaining Cheez-Its, and forced herself to shower before bed.

6

WILLA

Jay Callahan's resting expression switched into a natural smile when Willa and Sahar walked into Amanda's Coffee the next morning. Almost every cast member had been coming here for months now, which meant most of the staff recognized them.

"Sahar, Willa, morning," he said.

"It'd be a better morning if we weren't so knackered. How's it been today?" Sahar asked.

His communication softened even more. "Eh, fine so far. Nothing too irritating yet. The usual?"

"Yes, please," Sahar confirmed.

Willa looked up from the pastries she'd been eyeing.

She watched Jay's countenance as Sahar paid for her drink and everything bagel. There was something distinct about it she couldn't place, and as she thought on it further, it was fascinating how he always said Sahar's name before Willa's. It was also riveting to suddenly recall that he didn't smile as much on the rare occasions when Sahar wasn't with her.

Perhaps it was because Willa would never start conversations with him the way Sahar did. Maybe it was the similarities they had. Regardless, taking note of it today was an intriguing distraction from her own anxieties.

She approached the register next. "Add a guava cheese strudel and a plain iced Americano to my order, please."

"You're getting Ethan's coffee, too?" Sahar asked.

Willa consented with a nod. She had texted him this morning saying she would, wanting to go back to their routine of sorts—break the metaphorical ice she'd piled up herself.

"You got it," Jay confirmed.

Willa tapped her phone against the pin pad, tuning herself out of the conversation Sahar and Jay resumed over some new game.

Dahlia, the other barista on shift, handed Willa Ethan's drink first. Then, she called out for her iced Americano with Irish cream syrup and a splash of oat milk, along with the pastry in a brown paper bag. "Thank you, thank you," Willa acknowledged, stepping aside while they waited for Sahar's drink, which Jay was making himself while they talked.

She placed the pastry carefully inside her backpack, freeing her hands to carry the two liquid lifelines.

A slew of six people came into the shop at once, the sounds of their chattering bringing Sahar and Jay's conversation to a stop. They seemed to take a beat as they stood back to look at the menu. Dahlia moved to the register and another barista came out from the back.

Jay handed Sahar her drink and some type of note on a purple Post-it before heading to the register.

It was a good thing for them that Amanda's Coffee wasn't as crowded as the Starbucks down the block. Or even Tom's Bagels across the street. It made it easier for them during busy days.

"What's that?" Willa asked curiously.

Sahar folded the Post-it note in half and placed it in the back pocket of her jeans.

"It's a new game code. His mate was part of the developing team, so he had a few extras to give out."

"Nice!" Willa remarked.

After signing in, Willa beelined straight toward Ethan's dressing room, noticing the door slightly ajar. She knocked lightly.

"Come in."

She pushed it open, finding him seated on the sofa, looking up from his Switch. She strode inside and handed him his order. "Your coffee, sir. How's your head?"

Ethan smiled, popping out the straw by tapping it against his thigh muscle. Willa's eyes trailed toward his forearm, marveling at how it flexed with the motion. "Better. Thanks again for the drink. How are you?"

"Only slightly hungover but fully functioning, thankfully."

"Did you guys drink a lot?" he questioned.

"I sort of did."

He cocked an eyebrow. "Sort of? Bummed I missed it. Sounds like a good time."

"Ha! It wasn't...trust me."

She wasn't about to explain that the drinking occurred because she was sad about wanting him. *Nope.* Ethan didn't say another word, studying her for a beat too long, which brought those peculiar feelings back to the surface.

She turned to walk away, but his fingers circled her wrist, signaling her to halt. She looked back at him, eyes flicking to where he held her.

"Are you okay?" he asked.

No. No, she wasn't.

"Yeah. Just a little stressed and anxious. Nothing out of the ordinary."

He tipped his head to the side with a knowing gaze. "You sure?"

She crossed her heart with the hand that held her coffee cup, hoping the gesture would suffice for the words she couldn't say aloud. She was indeed stressed and anxious—none of that was new. She didn't need to disclose the parts about his contribution.

His understanding smile.

His comforting hugs.

His careful attention to everything she did.

The probability of something more lurking beneath his kindness and thoughtful gestures was not something she should have been reading into.

It had been easier to share her anxieties when her feelings for him hadn't been the reason. It was easier to share secrets when she wasn't hoping that one day she could see the vault he stored his in.

Something in his eyes said he wasn't buying her wordless promise, but he'd have to. With a courteous look, he released his fingers and moved aside for her to sit.

"Full-on dress rehearsal, remember? I need to get prepped with hair and makeup."

His lips curved into a straight, almost sad line. "Right, yeah. See you out there then."

She needed to get her shit together because whether Ethan felt it or not, she was sure she was making things awkward. She could feel the cold intensifying. She wasn't melting the glaciers, she was creating icebergs along their path.

She sauntered toward the dressing room she shared with Sahar, finding Miles there as well. "Good, you're here. I need to catch you two up."

Willa placed her coffee on the vanity and squealed. "Go on then."

"We went back to his place and talked until three in the morning before things escalated, and we're meeting tonight after rehearsals for dinner if I'm not too tired. I'm pretty sure he's the one, and I don't even care if it's too early to tell. I've legit never experienced something like this with a man before. I told him things last night that people who've known me my whole life don't know, and he opened up a bunch, too."

Sahar and Willa glanced at each other in unison before looking back at Miles, luminous expressions flashing in their eyes. Sahar bounced out of her seat and pulled him into a bear hug. "Mate, this is everything you deserve and more. I need this to work out more than I need my own relationship to," she proclaimed.

"Listen, this whole concept of two people disappearing into each other in a room full of people has always sounded a bit far-fetched, but I watched you two all night, and *I* was entranced. Pretty sure I've planned out your whole future," Willa added.

Miles grinned from ear to ear, radiating in a way that appeared to be ethereal. This must've been what her brother felt when he met Anna, claiming he knew from their first date that he would be marrying her.

It was harder for Willa to picture what that was like, but it was a lovely detail to cling to, an idea that two people could be so entwined with invisible strings that they'd know they belonged together from their initial meeting. She hoped with everything in her that it would be true for Miles.

She also hoped, *needed*, to get her mind off all this—love, companionship, Ethan—all of it. When Miles left, Willa opened her phone to the dance playlist she had curated for getting ready. The first song, "I Don't Want to Talk (I Just Want to Dance)" by the Glass Animals, did the job pristinely.

She started pinning her hair back to put it in the first wig, a snappy high bun with braids and a fringe. It was one of the more exciting ones, as it was the only time she could pull off the style without getting tired of it when her hair grew out.

She bopped her head and mouthed the lyrics.

Sahar dragged her feet behind her, dancing to the song instead of getting ready. "You're trying to distract yourself, right? That's what we're doing here?" she asked.

"Distract myself? From what?" Willa smirked.

Sahar arched an eyebrow. "It's working that well, is it?"

Willa rolled her shoulders rhythmically. "As the song title says, 'I don't wanna talk.'"

"Noted. But can we talk about how this is the first time we're going to dance in the new costumes? I feel so giddy I could run a marathon."

"I *know!*" Willa emphasized, flicking her eyes to the new bejeweled leotards in their wardrobe. The base was a gorgeous hue of burgundy, but the crystals were different shades of bright reds, big and small, glistening in the light. It featured a plunging neckline and two cuts near the ribcage. Most of their costumes, Willa's ensemble getups especially, were on the sultrier side. Still, this was the most stunning, right next to Elizabeth's final outfit: a shimmering gold dress that stood out like it had been stitched by goddesses in the skies of Mount Olympus.

Despite being the understudy, Willa would likely not go on as Elizabeth during their run. She'd love to, though, if only to have a chance to dance in that dress. And, all feelings aside, sharing the stage with Ethan wouldn't be a chore either.

Willa turned back to the mirror, itching to get up and start already. It was astounding how the prospect of performing could vanquish everything else in this world.

When she was on the stage, no anxious thought had its clasp on her—no distraction, only an unsurpassed form of escapism she was immeasurably thankful for. This was one of their last few dress rehearsal before previews started, and she couldn't wait to do this eight times a week.

.   .   .

THE LIGHTS BEGAN TO DIM, and the pre-show music started its slow ascent to a thumping cadence—the sound matching a slow, eager heartbeat. Naomi and Sahar made their way onto the stage, walking through a feigned misty morning.

"No one can see us here, Lizzie. Father and mother would disapprove if they knew where we were," Jane said.

A large blast struck from the orchestra, and the curtains moved from left to right, signaling the doors of Pemberley as *opened.*

"Welcome, ladies and gentlemen," Sam as Bingley began. *"Here, the gentile society is of no concern to us—here, the rules of society are meant to bend."* He moved aside, and the ensemble made its way onto the stage, Josie Singh's sensational choreography pushing them through an introduction that Broadway critics raved about during tryouts.

Willa and Innila stepped forward to greet the two women, helping them out of their country ensemble and into the bejeweled leotards. *"Let yourself be free, ladies. You'll find that life is more pleasant with a little less fabric and a lot more skin,"* Willa declared.

For this number, though all the women wore the same costume, different pieces like a garter or a hat and hairstyles would differentiate them from one another. A begrudging Darcy was then pulled out from the wings by Bingley to introduce his hideaway of iniquity: a place for no skin trade unless, of course, it was consensual—in the forbidden corridors only.

Willa kicked her foot up before lowering to a split, her dance partner in the number, Miles, coming up behind her to drag her swiftly through the floor, back up, then in between his legs. How Josie combined classic waltz movements and contemporary steps was a brilliance Willa still couldn't fathom, and she'd been dancing her entire life.

It was quiet, then loud, and artificial smoke started to rise, signaling the transition from "Doors Open" to "Bennet Sisters' Interviews."

DRESS REHEARSALS WENT ALMOST SEAMLESSLY, a miracle they hadn't achieved yet, which put everyone in the cast in a great mood. They even finished in time for Miles to get dinner with the bar-boy-maybe-the-one Clyde. Willa walked out of her dressing room to Ethan, who'd been waiting nearby, leaning against the wall.

She stopped in front of him, a little too close for comfort but not as hot and bothered, the adrenaline from the rehearsals still coursing through her. "Are we still on for *Peaky Blinders* and Chinese?"

"Fuck yeah," he confirmed.

7

ETHAN

"I'm so sick of characters dying! God, why? Why did we do this to ourselves? I looked up spoilers. I *knew* what was coming. I told myself I'd be fine. But I take it all back. I'm not fine. I'm mad. Good characters don't deserve to die on-screen. Isn't it bad enough that we have to watch real people die? Now we have to watch characters we love have the same fate, and for what? Good television? Fuck that. I'm over it. Never again."

Ethan wanted to weigh in, but he knew she wasn't done venting yet.

Willa got up off the couch and started pacing around the room. "And after everything they had been through." She sighed heavily. "This sucks. This sucks so bad," she said, wiping a few tears from her eyes.

She moved toward where Tulip sat, and as though sensing her agitation, his cat rose and leaped behind the couch. "See, even Tulip is sad. She's gone off to hide. Or she thinks I'm a mad woman; either way, we're not having a good time anymore," she remarked.

He stifled a laugh. He had rescued Tulip from a shelter in

Boston, a tiny little nugget who'd been abandoned at six weeks old. Willa had insisted that he keep the name the shelter had given her, so Tulip stuck.

Willa walked back toward the coffee table, took her can of Dr. Pepper, and chugged what had been remaining.

"Do you need something stronger?" he asked.

She stopped her pacing. "I need my memories wiped. I have massive regrets now."

Ethan curled his lips inward to suppress a smile.

She pointed a finger at him. "Don't you dare laugh at me."

He tried with all his might to hold it in.

"You're telling me that after three seasons of investing in this love story, you're not the least bit upset at this outcome? The same man who cries every time they show what Tiny Tim's future would be if Scrooge doesn't change in *The Muppet Christmas Carol?*"

And then he laughed. He was upset, but Willa's adorable face was a bright spot in the moment. He couldn't help himself. "We knew this was coming. We'd been preparing for it."

"It still doesn't make it any better," she said. "And it's a shitty reflection of the real world I'm trying very hard to escape from."

"It doesn't, no, and I'm not laughing *at* you. I was laughing at the *way* you got up. And at Tulip's reaction," he replied honestly.

She scoffed affectionately, her belief in his response falling somewhere in between "nice try" and "whatever, it'll do."

In an instant, Willa squared her shoulders, and the sudden spark of an idea flashed in her expression. An entire story danced in her eyes in a way he recognized from all the times she'd done this before.

"Get up, please," she said, confirming his detection.

He did as she asked, pushing his coffee table against the couch to free up space on his living room floor.

Willa opened her phone and played what he recognized as

Billie Eilish's "No Time to Die." She stood before him, bopping her head first, moving her fingers afterward, lost in thought. This was how a choreography with Willa always started.

"This song always felt too sad to ever choreograph anything to, but it's perfectly appropriate right now," she noted.

He nodded in agreement. It wasn't one he'd ever think about, but he understood exactly how she got here from where they'd been. He understood the mood she was trying to convey—the emotions she wanted to release.

"We're going to start with the gradual waltz that Jane and Bingley have during the wedding song. The first one that is a little slower, where it's basically the two of them sort of losing themselves in each other," she waited for him to verify that he knew which one she meant.

Ethan lifted his left hand for her to take and placed his right hand against her back. She put her hand in his, gliding the other to the slope of his shoulder.

They moved as she'd suggested for what felt like less than ten seconds. "Follow my lead for when it gets a little quicker, yeah? We're going to focus more on the bridge," she detailed.

He let her guide the motions, reveling in the fleeting sight of her in his arms.

They waltzed in the way she'd suggested then she nearly ripped herself away from him, spun in a clip turn, then fell back toward him where he caught her in his arms. She looked up at him, her eyes gleaming. "Excellent catch. I figured you'd get exactly how I wanted that one."

She pulled away from him, listening to the music, moving in-place in small ways he gathered she was trying to piece together. "Ugh, we need a bigger space for what I'm picturing. And I'm going to need Miles' input. No offense," she added apologetically.

He chuckled. "None taken. I could train for years, and my body would still never move the way his could."

"Still, you got me started on something, and I'm now thoroughly excited that I could channel my sadness into a dance, so thank you," she said with a bow.

"Anytime," he replied.

He looked at her for a beat, head tilted toward the ground, listening intently to the music once more.

He remembered when they'd first danced together. During a day off in Boston, Miles was out sick with the flu.

She'd been fixating over Duncan Laurence's "Arcade," so she had called Ethan to see if he'd be willing to step in with her. He had plans with Sam and Declan, but he canceled on them, selfishly happy to spend more time with Willa—to move with her, see what it was like when she worked through an entire choreography from scratch.

It wasn't the kind of number that required too much from him, more acting in a sense, less dancing. It didn't have them touching as much as he would've liked, either. But it was also the first time he learned how to lift her, consumed immediately by the sensation of her in his arms like that. His hands splayed against her waist, her body sliding slowly down his form.

She was perfect for him. He considered it then; he was positive about it now.

The repeated motions were intoxicating.

He recalled coming home in a daze that night, tossing and turning with his fingers still buzzing from all the ways they'd touched her. His mind racing with all the little smiles she'd given him, the way she lost herself in the music—the movements.

There had been a point during the whole process where she made him crawl to her, making him realize at that second that he would do anything for her. Crawl, jump, run in circles—whatever she asked of him. He'd do it without hesitation.

He'd always try a little harder for Willa. Stay firmly anchored if she needed someone's arms to fall into. He'd lift her higher if she wanted to leap toward the skies.

The memories pushed him over the edge every time.

She had been so patient with him, so at ease and open in how she taught him every routine. He remembered the way she glowed when they finally nailed the entire thing in one go.

On the nights when he craved her touch, he thought of that day.

He remembered the teal legging set she'd worn. The cut-off pattern in the back of her sports bra, her bare skin between the fabric; the grueling humidity that was made a thousand times more bearable because of how the two of them moved.

Ethan had memorized all the ways she looked at him that day. He cherished the healing narrative that unfolded through the choreography she created. He savored the way she giggled every time they messed up and how she trusted him fully. The way she lay across the floor where he joined her side by side, their exhales hard and heavy until they stabilized into something more measured.

She was back with other dance partners after that, Miles mostly. Sometimes Christian. And Ethan understood that entirely. The two of them only shared small numbers here and there, moments of her helping him with his form for *Midnights at Pemberley* that ended too quickly.

Nothing had been like that day. Slow. Rewarding. Emotional.

No amount of time spent with her felt like it was enough.

He'd never felt that way performing before. No matter how engrossed he'd been in a role, no matter how closely he knew his character or his scene partner, he could leave it all behind once the ghost light turned on or when the director called cut.

The emotions never followed him home. But with Willa, every move was different—every gaze from her felt like discovering constellations for the first time.

God, how he wished again that she could go on as Elizabeth. One time only. A single show, though he knew that would inevitably make him greedier, drive him to want more of her.

What if he told her? Right here at this moment while she stood in front of him with her mind worlds away, creating something magnetic?

What would happen if he blurted that he'd metaphorically been transported back to the past, where memories of them dancing left him breathless and wanting?

What if he told her he went back to that place often?

What if he told her that he thought about her constantly, on and off the stage?

Willa felt like coming home after a long day of pretending, falling onto the couch, and knowing he didn't have to try as hard. He didn't have to force a smile if he was too tired to. He could just be Ethan, content and happy. He could be hers and no one else's.

She stopped the music and looked up at him, forcing him out of the memories and immersing him back into the present. "I should head out. I can't believe previews start tomorrow."

He wanted to ask her to stay, but he knew that'd be a step too far. Still, he wished for it desperately, with everything in him.

"I'll take the subway back with you, so you're not alone. My car chose the worst time to require servicing," he said.

She shook her head. "No, it's late. You need to rest. We both do. I'll just order a ride."

He and Willa stood outside his apartment, waiting for her Lyft to pull over. When she looked at her phone and noticed that the driver was fast approaching, she turned and wrapped her arms around him. "If I have nightmares about this fictional death, I'm waking you up and forcing you to suffer with me."

He laughed into her velvety hair and faintly pressed his lips against her temple. *Could she tell? If she did, she didn't say anything.* "And I'll answer the phone with only a few complaints."

Willa peered up at him, her arms still circled around his waist. "There better be zero complaints. You're the one who suggested it. Now you pay the price."

"Okay, no complaints. Call me whenever." He secretly ached for that, too. He'd maybe grumble for a millisecond, but his tired mind would link itself with his heart and realize that it was Willa—every part of him could stay awake for her and do anything she wanted.

Releasing his arms from her, Ethan opened the car door and ensured the driver saw him. "I know I have your location, but text me the second you get home," he said.

He didn't actually know her location, but it was something he figured he should say to guarantee her safety.

"You got it," she replied.

That sentiment wasn't a lie, though. He wouldn't be able to sleep peacefully if he didn't know she got home safe from leaving his house, so he'd wait for her text. He walked back up to his apartment and plopped himself onto the couch. Tulip jumped forward from behind the couch and straight into his lap. "Thanks for giving us the privacy, Tulip. You're a real champ for that."

She gave him a death glare.

"Are you mad that Willa left or that we made you hide?" he asked as though she'd answer.

Tulip lifted her little head and stared at the wall next to him.

He scratched underneath her chin. "I'm going to pretend

you're mad at me because I was too much of a coward to tell Willa how I feel."

She did not react. Still, he took it as validation. He sat there until Willa's text vibrated on his phone.

WILLA

I'm home, alive, and found fix-it fan fiction to read in the car.

He chuckled.

ETHAN

Send it over if it's good.

WILLA

8

WILLA

Sahar and Willa sat side by side in their dressing room when Naomi walked in, phone in hand, giddy smile on full display for the *Midnights at Pemberley's* social media account takeover.

She looked toward the screen and pressed record. "And these two rockstars are absolute icons in our production," Naomi chirped. She had already done her hair and makeup, so she only needed to change into her first costume before starting the show.

Sahar leaned back in her chair, extending her arm out to pull Naomi closer. Naomi wedged herself between the two women and then turned the camera sideways to catch all three of them in the frame. Willa and Sahar looked at each other and kissed either side of Naomi's cheek.

Naomi squealed jubilantly. "Honestly, if you aren't welcomed into work like this, you need to quit, friends. It's not worth it otherwise," she said to the camera.

"Cheers to that," Sahar concurred.

Naomi perked up and stopped recording. "I still can't believe they wanted me to do this takeover on the first night of previews, but it's surprisingly helping with the jitters."

"You're gonna kill it, love," Willa pointed out.

Naomi's eyes expanded with warmth. "Thank you. It's just so unbelievable to finally have this moment after all these years on Broadway. There are so many of us on this show who've been fighting tooth and nail. Gah! I'm emotional. I love you both so damn much. I'm going to go bug some of the boys now."

"And we'll be refreshing to watch everything you post," Sahar said.

Willa turned back to the mirror to apply false lashes. "Do you ever think about how lucky we are with this show? Like every single person is a genuinely good egg, no one is fake, and we all get on so well that it's basically unheard of."

Sahar agreed. "No, you're right. A cast like this is once in a lifetime. There's always someone who messes something up or causes drama, but we hit the jackpot here. We should be a package deal in all other productions. Hire one, hire all."

Willa chuckled in agreement and inched closer to the mirror, holding a set of lashes in her hand. She stuck one on and used her hand as a fan to dry the glue. After she placed the second and picked up her lipstick, they heard a loud screech that sounded like a gaggle of people bursting into a fit of laughter.

Charging out of their dressing room, they found Sam on the floor, cackling his head off, holding his stomach, and pointing toward Declan's dressing room.

"What on earth is going on?" Sahar asked.

Naomi shook with mirth, her phone camera aimed right at Sam.

"He...he..." Sam tried to explain but lost his words to another snort-laugh. Naomi stopped recording again.

Declan stepped out of his dressing room, revealing a gigantic split in the middle of his leather pants.

She could hear Ethan's delicious laugh behind her and twisted back to see him standing over her shoulder.

Willa tried to hold hers in. "Oh, mate, what happened?" she asked Declan.

Sam's laugh was so wildly infectious that even Declan stopped pouting to have a hoot over the incident. He pointed down to the black leather pants on his person, then to Sam. "This idiot bet that I couldn't squat in these, and I did…"

"I caught the whole thing on camera, too. Thank heavens we weren't live," Naomi added.

Sam was still clutching his stomach and roaring. "I can't breathe. The damn confidence he had."

"But you have an extra pair, don't you?" Ethan inquired.

"Bro, these aren't for the show. They're mine," Declan answered.

The sea of laughter spread throughout the hallway. "Sam is going to lose his voice before the show even starts," Christian noted from the doorway of his dressing room.

"Why would you buy leather pants?" Sam questioned, still snorting so hard that his whole face looked like it was doused with blush. "I didn't even notice he was wearing them until he stood up to show them off for Naomi's video. He was so proud."

"Because they looked epic. Don't be jealous," Declan replied.

"Jealous? I pity my future self who'll probably never experience something funnier in his life. Goddamn, please don't ever change, mate."

Thirty minutes to showtime was called from the speakers.

They all dispersed, laughter simmering to quiet giggles.

Willa turned back to Ethan, who was already in his first costume and ready to go—high-waisted trousers, jet-black tailcoat, a muslin shirt unbuttoned, chest hair peering through. On

Midnights at Pemberley, Darcy only wore a cravat once in the entire production, during Jane and Bingley's wedding. In the gaudy, glistering corners of the fictional estate, his clothing was almost as loose as everyone else's.

She smoothed her fingers against his lapels, taking note of the velvety texture that was absent from the Boston shows. "I'm obsessed with this new tailcoat. It's so much nicer than the first one. The audience is going to lose their minds."

He smiled shyly. God, it was adorable. Ethan was a perfectionist through and through, so she knew how much he appreciated statements like this.

"Thanks, Wills. You're good for my ego."

She huffed. "Please, if you ever get an ego, I'd celebrate it. Your humility is more intimidating."

He chuckled. "Go get ready. I'm going to hound Declan about those pants some more."

She smiled and then bounced away to her dressing room. Willa sat down and drew closer to the mirror to finish the last step in her routine, adding the lipstick all the women wore. It was a brilliantly universal shade of red, which miraculously did something stunning for each of their different skin tones. And its name, "Midnight Dance," was a coincidentally delightful bonus.

Willa then started with the base of her costume, three pairs of skin-colored pantyhose to make her legs appear nude, and then the first bodysuit: an enchanting scarlet piece adorned with crystals. Afterward, she put on a massive jeweled necklace, her most prominent accessory in the show, for the slower, more tamed dance movements.

Sahar had begun vocal warmups, as had a few other cast members, their different voices spreading through the corridors. She stood for a few beats, stretching her legs before putting on her shoes.

Willa was gearing up to head out, waiting for the ten-minute mark to get called.

Sahar turned to her. "Break a leg, sister."

"You too, beauty," she returned.

Willa, Innila, and Laura Tiu were meant to go on before the rest of the cast. The production's pre-show would keep audience members engaged while everyone took their seats, with Christian and Bradley standing by the doors as though to guard the entrance.

She strode past Ethan's dressing room, then a few others, and up the stairs toward the stage's right side, where she would enter from.

It was an underrated part of the show Willa especially appreciated because she could easily catch people watching and pointing, waiting to see how their favorite Austen story would come to life with the twist Jeffrey and Greta Henderson created.

It made the entire experience that much more immersive.

She stepped out when the time was called, a slow sauntering walk with a champagne glass in her hand.

She spun once, twice, stopped, and took a sip. She walked toward the doors and eyed Christian and Bradley. Willa, Laura, and Innila then spun around each other, clinked their glasses together, and turned again, ending up on opposite sides from where they had entered.

They quickly disappeared into the wings, handed over the glasses to the props crew, and moved back out just as swiftly.

The stylistically slow music started to rise in rhythm, the percussion of low drums ascending higher, and then she stopped center stage where all three women pretended to converse. A woman's voice in the track subtly sang the word *enter*, but no one other than the cast and crew had yet distinguished those lyrics as part of the remixed melody.

Willa then arched backward, twisted, and moved around the

stage. The music came to a crescendo before its fall brought Naomi and Sahar onto the stage as Elizabeth and Jane. Slow claps from the audience came first at the sight of the women, then for the curtains opening to reveal the vast staircase, signaling their formal entrances into Pemberley.

The "Doors Open" number introduced the entire ensemble, with Bingley coming to greet the women.

AND WITH THAT, their first official preview on Broadway had begun, resulting in the kind of exceptional performance only possible in a state of dreaming. It had been deliriously wondrous. Enthralling. Willa couldn't believe she'd get to do this daily. Eight times a week.

The dressing rooms buzzed with chattering sounds and glasses clinking together as everyone came together to salute a successful new beginning backstage.

After they'd finished, they got word of an overly packed stage door taking up the entire block.

Her eyes darted toward Ethan. He stood in front of her, right next to Declan and Naomi. He cared about meeting fans and was so good about understanding their perspective, but more often than not, stage door meetings made him anxious.

He had told Willa that during his third Broadway musical, he learned about a group of fans who stalked him daily without attending the show, making the process even more frustrating. At the same time, they also discovered things about his personal life that felt deeply invasive.

Still, he never wanted to disappoint people, especially those who'd traveled to see him. If he didn't show up, they'd call him stuck up.

Some days, it was a breeze for him to go out and meet people; other times, she knew it required laborious willpower.

Willa clocked the change in Ethan's posture easily—shoulders stiffened, fingers digging into his palm. Heaviness now replaced the effortless magic she'd watched come to life on stage.

"Wait for me?" Willa asked him.

He concurred with a nod and then went into his dressing room to change.

Willa removed the glittering emerald costume and switched into distressed denim jeans and a white T-shirt, completing the outfit with her camel-colored coat. She took off the lashes and tossed them in the rubbish bin, leaving the rest of her makeup to wash off at home.

She waited for Sahar to finish before walking with her to meet Ethan by his door. The three of them strolled out together, finding a few cast members already signing playbills. The crowd erupted like a volcanic explosion at the sight of Ethan.

An avalanche of pride poured out of Willa as she turned to look at him.

She understood it. She'd be in their shoes if she wasn't an actress and merely watched him perform as a fan. Ethan Everett was magnetic in every way—and his voice, *good lord, his voice should come with a warning*. Side effects include the risk of heart palpitations and ovarian explosions.

The fact that she knew him beyond his talents made the praise far more worthy. They were right to root for him. He was one of the good ones, on and off the stage, the type of man Hollywood unquestionably needed more of in its horrendous ranks.

They started signing, kind words being thrown to them all, like long-stemmed red roses onto the stage.

"Oh my God, how does your body move like that? Also, can I please get a photo?" a fan asked her, gushing with a huge smile.

She couldn't believe the kindness. She adored compliments

about the way she danced. Who didn't want to hear that they were good at the thing they loved doing the most?

"Aw, that's so sweet! Thank you, and, of course," Willa responded, signing the playbill and posing in front of the fan's phone.

"Thank you," she said again before walking to the next, making their way through the riotously long queue.

They made their way down to the end of the crowd, signing for almost everyone who showed up. When they rounded the corner of the block, Willa lunged herself onto Ethan's back. His hands drew back to hold onto her. "I'm so freaking proud of you," she screeched before jumping down. "And *you two*," she added emphatically to Sahar and Christian.

Ethan exhaled a monstrous sigh of relief. "That might've been the smoothest preview of any show I've done. I'm so damn glad it went well."

Willa was equally thrilled with his mood; the temporary tension in his shoulders had shifted, and the look in his eyes found their natural glow again.

He put so much weight on his shoulders that she knew he'd blame himself if anything were slightly off. If even a single person were out of line at the stage door, that would have messed with his headspace.

"Everyone was so good. Like, so freaking good. Holy shit. I don't know how I'm going to sleep," Sahar commented.

Willa agreed. "Same."

"Not to burst anyone's joyous adrenaline bubble, but in two months, we're going to leave that stage and be sweating in the gross heat," Christian dropped out of the blue.

"Good. I'm tired of being cold. You heathens have had your time. Now it's my turn to thrive," Sahar countered, looking specifically at Willa.

Willa looked dumbfounded. "Give it a week, and you'll start grumbling about it."

"Not with the last winter we've had. I'm tired. Let me be happy."

"If I hear you complain, so help me God," Willa added.

"You won't," Sahar affirmed.

Willa turned to Ethan. "Weigh in, Everett."

"You know I'm with her on this. I don't like being cold. But fuck the heat. Give me whatever we've got going on right now, and I'm solid."

"Ha!" Sahar bit back affectionately.

"He didn't side with you, mate."

Sahar stuck out her tongue. "Yes, but he didn't side with you either."

Willa turned to Ethan, then to Christian, and shook her head. "Look at the rift you've caused. We're a house divided now."

"And here I was making a random observation about the weather," Christian remarked.

Ethan chuckled heartily, extending his arm out to set it around Willa's shoulder. He brought her closer to him. "Could be worse. My sister's husband is always cold, so their thermostat is perpetually set to seventy-seven degrees."

Willa gasped dramatically. "Yeah, no, I'm pretty sure I'd die."

They strode in companionable silence for a beat. Christian and Sahar went head-to-head on the weather some more. Willa looked up at Ethan, and he pulled her in tighter. It was tough not to want more of him during moments like this—too hard not to bask in the glow of how happy he looked.

Stop staring, Willa. Jesus. What's wrong with you?

Ethan looked at her, not saying a word. He detected her staring and held onto her gaze. Somehow, she understood it—

whatever he was trying to say. Any other person and she would've sunk into the ground from humiliation.

Maybe all of this *was* awkward. It should be.

The putrid smell of the subway station pulled her away from her thoughts. His spicy leather cologne left her senses far too soon. When had they reached the top of the stairs?

He turned to face her and tucked a strand of hair behind her ear. *Don't fixate on the moment, Willa. He's just being polite.*

Ethan and Christian fist-bumped, and then he moved aside to hug Sahar quickly.

Ethan looked back at Willa again, a transitory glance but powerful in its hold. "Get home safe, you three," he said.

See, he didn't single you out. He was just being nice. With more and more crowds showing up when the show officially opened, she knew that Ethan would need to have a ride waiting for him instead of joining them at the station. He lived close to the theatre, so it was convenient, but public transportation after a while wouldn't work.

Well, that thought upset her.

Willa shook away the feelings. She focused on her steps down the stairs. She threw herself into Christian and Sahar's conversation, standing firm on her beliefs about hot weather.

Tomorrow would bring another exhilarating performance, another one after that, and another one after that. Willa had her best friends by her side despite very obviously crushing on one of them, but nothing would have to change.

It shouldn't.

9

WILLA

Willa had just finished redoing her makeup and was prepping to curl her hair when she heard Sahar yell from the opposite side of their flat. "Willa, come help me decide what to wear, please!"

She walked into Sahar's room, where she stood over a green dress shirt paired with a denim jacket and a green knitted dress. Miles' sole request of the night was that if they could, they should wear something green. The man hated the fact that he was born seven minutes before St. Patrick's Day, so he always took up the opportunity to celebrate his birthday on it. And since it fell on a Sunday this year, it was also convenient for their schedules.

Weighing Sahar's two options, Willa bit down on her bottom lip. "What bottoms are you thinking?"

"If I go with the shirt, then black jeans. If the knitted dress, then pantyhose."

"Go with the dress. I love the concept of the top, but the denim jacket would ruin it. And knowing you, you'd get cold, so you need it. Are these the only green things you have?"

"Yeah," Sahar confirmed.

"You're welcome to my wardrobe, but that dress is lovely."

Sahar approved. "Knitted dress it is, then. Are you wearing heels?"

"The black, heeled ankle boots," Willa specified.

Sahar pointed to the black Dr. Martens next to her bed. "I think I'm going to stick to my Docs. Would that look weird?"

Willa shook her head. "Not at all. Pair it with some jewelry, and you're set."

"Aces. Thanks, boo. You still wearing the skirt?"

Willa nodded. "Yeah, I haven't worn it a while, and I'm in a tartan mood," she answered, referring to a green and blue mini skirt she was going to pair with a simple black long-sleeve.

"Sometimes I'm envious that you run so warm, but other times, I know I'm the one who's better off," Sahar replied.

Willa chuckled at the statement. It was true. She'd so much rather run cold than hot.

She sauntered back to her bedroom, stopping at the record player in their living room to switch the A-side vinyl that had come to a halt. Tonight's album was David Bowie's *Legacy,* and Willa was in particularly good spirits.

The last month had been a dream, with every preview show going better than the one before, and one week ago, *Midnights at Pemberley* had its official premiere and opening.

With busy schedules keeping them occupied and too tired to function at times, Willa managed to leave her thoughts and feelings about Ethan mostly at bay. Except during Sunday nights when they tried to sneak beyond the wall she'd built, badgering her when they'd catch up on shows together, sitting a little too close for comfort on his sofa. Ethan in his tortoise shell-colored glasses that somehow and unsurprisingly made him far too attractive for his own good.

It was, however, easier these days than those initial moments after her return from London. She could push the emotions toward a barricade and divert herself with other mind-numbing thoughts until her brain decided it was tired of fighting with her.

Tonight was the first night they'd skip their Sunday night routine for Miles' party, which would make for another excellent distraction. A *necessary* distraction.

Willa stood over the clothes splayed across her bed and changed into them one by one. She was still trying to decide whether to wear her leather jacket. It'd complement the skirt and top with her boots, but the thought of wearing it indoors was already making her sweat. She put it on, checked the mirror, then took it off and settled on draping it across her shoulders. At least this way, she wouldn't suffocate, and the outfit would still feel finished. She completed the final look with a chained necklace set that she couldn't wear during the production and switched out of her standard lobe studs for hoop earrings.

Willa ambled toward the door and waited there. "Are you done?" she called out to Sahar.

"Coming!"

"Is the prick meeting us there?" she asked when Sahar came closer.

"Miles invited him to be polite, but who knows if he'll actually show up."

Willa tried desperately not to make a face, nodding with as much nonchalance as she could. She'd stopped talking to Sahar about her awful boyfriend since she decided to give him another chance. It was no longer Willa's place to fight for someone else's relationship. Plus, Sahar knew where she stood on the matter.

Miles had reserved spots for the majority of the cast who had RSVPd at an underground speakeasy decorated with red and gold trappings, quite similar to some of the set designs of

Midnights at Pemberley. It felt like being back at work, even when they weren't, but she wouldn't want to escape it by any means.

Ethan walked to where she sat, placing two cocktails in teacups before her. The aesthetics of this place reminded her of home a bit, like the posh corridors of London marrying with the rugged edges of what their version of Austen presented. It was effortless to appreciate, making her feel a little lighter, a bit more free.

He sat beside her and leaned forward, inching closer to Willa. "Miles just introduced me to Clyde. He's the guy from the bar, right?" he asked, his eyes fixed on the pair.

She nodded excitedly. "Yes, aren't they adorable together?"

"Yeah," he agreed, taking a sip of his drink. "They look alike. You know how people start to look alike when they've spent a lot of time together? They already have that."

"You're right," Willa exclaimed.

Did they look alike? People had said that about her and Sahar sometimes. But she wondered about her and Ethan now.

She mentally swatted away the thought, returning her attention to their friends. "They also have such a sweet opposites attract situation. Miles was telling me how Clyde is a massive introvert and an accountant. But they share so many similar morals."

Ethan smiled and leaned against the settee's cushion. Willa wanted to recline, but instead, she looked forward for a beat.

She thought she spotted... no. *Wait.* She shut her eyes briefly, then opened them again, but much to her regret, the last man she thought she would ever run into again was also here tonight.

Please be a nightmare.

Alden Price. Shit shit shit. What the hell was he doing here? Had he seen her? God, she hoped not.

Willa took a deep, painful breath, trying to contain her

dismay. She turned toward Ethan, but he was saying something to Christian.

She swung her wavy hair fully to the side of her face and tilted her head at an angle that would keep her hidden from people on her right side.

As though he caught her head in his direction, Ethan faced her, his eyes widening immediately. He drew closer to her, his arm lowering from the top of the cushion to her back. "Wills? You look like you've seen a ghost. What's up?"

She bit back a curse, trying not to rile herself up. Alden Price, with his starchy tailored suits and slicked-back hair, didn't deserve a fraction of her attention anymore. What on God's green earth had she ever seen in him?

She brought her hand to her temple, hiding her face as naturally as possible while leaning closer to Ethan. "Alden is here."

"Where is he?" Ethan asked, a hint of rage in his voice—something dark and unlike him.

"He's at the bar with two other people. I don't think he's seen me yet."

"And which one is he?"

She forgot that Ethan had never met Alden. They'd been so close that she sometimes failed to remember there were parts of her life and people who'd never crossed his path. "The one with black hair," she answered.

Ethan looked forward subtly.

Willa tried to exhale, but something sharp pierced her gut. The music was suddenly too loud, the bass too sufficient in its thumping. It was all inside of her. Panic rose in her chest; tinnitus made its way through her ears.

She couldn't, *wouldn't* let this happen. He wouldn't get to her like this. She'd spoken to her therapist, Marie, about this after everything Alden did; she had healed from it. Or, at least, she thought she had.

The anxiety boiling inside of her said otherwise.

Ethan's voice torpedoed through the rising quakes. Safe and serene, he had moved closer, his knee brushing against hers, his hand hovering over her arm. "What can I do? Talk to me."

She closed her eyes for a beat, willing herself to focus. "I need air."

He speedily stood in front of her, blocking her body, and then extended his hand out to pull her up. She took it, warm and comforting under her now clammy fingers.

He turned to Innila and Christian, who were sitting beside them. "We'll be back," he said. The two of them bopped their heads to the music while simultaneously acknowledging they'd heard him.

Ethan methodically shielded her body from where Alden and his friends stood, placing his hand against the small of her back as they walked out. Willa was 5'8, and even in block heels, Ethan could still hover over her with his 6'1 frame.

They stepped outside to the dingy corners of the hidden speakeasy. Willa braced herself against a wall, and Ethan stood in front of her, covering her body from anyone who'd come out the door. "Of all the bloody places in this enormous city, he had to show up here tonight. I haven't seen him since things ended," she noted.

She tried to calm herself, breathing in and out.

"Are you ever going to tell me what he did to you?" Ethan asked, his voice low and gentle.

Willa shook her head, fear shooting up her spine.

He looked empathetic, his eyes cascading a warmth straight into her. "Does anyone know? Sahar, at least? Your family? Or your therapist?"

"Yeah, Sahar and Marie know."

"Okay, good," he answered. "Want me to get Sahar?"

"I'm fine. I just need to mentally prepare myself in case he notices me. I'm the one who broke up with him, but it wasn't pleasant. He's not dangerous or anything like that, just a dick. And in all honesty, I'm disgusted by him."

Ethan's eyes darted back toward the opening door. Sahar walked out to them. "Oh my God. Willa?"

Ethan moved a little. Willa looked at Sahar. "Did you see?"

"Yup, I tried to find you, but when I noticed you and Ethan were gone, I figured you'd be out here. I'm going ram my fist into his throat. See how he—" She stopped mid-sentence, likely and thankfully remembering that Ethan didn't know about what led to their breakup.

"Maybe let's not ruin Miles' night with you getting arrested?"

Sahar's fury was palpable, heat nearly sizzling from her eyes in a cartoonish way. "I will say something if he even dares to look in your direction," she countered.

"You will say nothing; we're going to play it cool and hope that he's too stubborn to even come near me."

"And what if he does?" Sahar asked.

Willa shrugged her shoulders. "I'll be fine. I just need to get over the shock of seeing him."

Sahar sighed and nodded with understanding. "I'm so sorry. I wish you hadn't."

"Yet, here we are," Willa declared.

Sahar took her hand and squeezed it. "Okay, I'm going to go inside, and I promise to behave myself. Come back whenever you're ready. Or if you need to leave, I'm sure Miles will get it."

Willa looked back at Ethan when Sahar left, his gaze so intensely fixed on her that it was concerning. "You don't have to tell me what he did, Willa, but..." he swallowed. "Sahar's response...that isn't the kind of reaction a friend has just because someone was an asshole. Did he hurt you?"

A giant lump formed in her lungs, extending up toward her throat. "You know Sahar. She gets like that even while gaming."

"I know she's passionate, but that was something else." She could recognize all of Ethan's smiles, every one of his tired expressions, his frustrations, his excitement, but the look on his face right now was new. She hated it. She hated being the reason for it.

She also didn't know how to answer him. She didn't want to make the situation worse, but as close as she and Ethan were, she couldn't tell him about her one, horribly failed attempt at doing something with a man that went beyond kissing. Their friendship had few barriers, and this was one of them.

"He didn't hurt me. At least not in the way you're probably thinking. He just..." she questioned how she could tell him a portion of the truth without disclosing all the details. She'd have to share this again someday, likely with a future partner if she ever found someone she wanted to be intimate with.

How she wished for a moment that it could be Ethan.

"Let's just say he was under the impression that demisexuality was a made-up construct and thought I had to 'grow up' for the way I reacted to him," she said.

And yet, somehow, she did, in fact, say too much.

Ethan's eyes darkened, fire bouncing from the streetlights above them into his sapphire hues. He remained silent for a moment, unpacking what she had said like an equation in front of his face.

"Hey," she called out.

Ethan looked at her, his face softening slightly from the anger that had undoubtedly pooled through him.

She brushed her hand along his bicep. "I'm good, I promise. It's just ghastly to see him after all this time."

Willa hadn't seen Alden since their second to last rehearsal before starting the show in Boston, which was almost two years ago now. They didn't run in the same circles; they'd met at a bar, which was a seemingly cute occurrence where he spilled his drink all over her and then asked to make it up to her with dinner. He had been an absolute sweetheart until his true colors appeared when he grew tired of waiting until she was ready to fuck him.

"You sure? We could leave if you want. Sahar is right; Miles wouldn't mind if he knew."

"No. I'm not letting him ruin a perfectly good night with my favorite people," she answered firmly.

Ethan nodded, the glow in his eyes making a slow return.

"Thank you for being you," she said. No other words came to her, but she needed him to know. She was grateful for him, fully in every way.

He pulled her tightly into his arms, holding her for a quick second. "I got you, Wills. Through everything. You know that."

She smiled up at him when they parted. "And I've got you. You got lucky with decent exes. I don't have to fight any of them for your honor."

Ethan gave her a closed-mouth smile. *Wait...was she wrong? Had any of his exes hurt him in any way?* He had told her that distance had broken him and Michelle up, but a hint of sadness quickly emerged in his eyes and then vanished. Was she reading into it too much?

"Ready to go back in?" he asked.

"Lead the way."

He held the door open, walking close behind her the entire time. She felt his hand settle along the small of her back again, signaling a comfortable warmth to spread through her.

So much for her feelings for Ethan taking a night off.

But seeing Alden again was proof that Sahar was right. Despite her rules—the ones she felt she had to stick to—Ethan Everett wasn't like other men, let alone other actors.

He most certainly wasn't like any of the men she'd dated. But no matter what else was bubbling inside her, he was still her best friend, and she wanted that to remain unmarred.

They ambled back in, standing with their friends at the corner of the room. Naomi and her wife, Jeanie, were telling a story about a club in Nice where a bunch of people from the States met each other. "No, but I'd *never* seen a crowd like that. I'm pretty sure we're all bonded for life. The whole club went to get breakfast together the next morning," she finished.

"We need to get that crowd to a show," Sahar added.

Naomi gaped at her. "Oh my God, I so wish." She turned to Jeanie. "Babe, don't like three of them live here? We should text them. Give them an invite," she said with a laugh.

"Oh, I'm so game; let's do it," Jeanie replied.

Christian chimed in with a drink in hand, pinky out dramatically. "Are we talking about the club in Nice again? How many times have I said we're not allowed to discuss this near me because the FOMO levels have become uncontrollable? I'm but a mere mortal, you heathens."

Naomi swung her arm around his neck. "We're going to make a couples trip out of it next year when Dan comes back. You'll experience the whole thing with us—and you three as well. All of us. We'll make it a celebratory *Midnights* thing."

"Okay, fine, proceed with the conversation," he gestured artistically, his hand rolling thrice.

Willa chuckled, wanting to add a comment about already prepping outfits, but right as she was about to speak, someone touched her shoulder. She swung her head back to Alden standing behind her. "Willa! Hey, you."

She conjured an ersatz smile, pretending she hadn't just mentally prepared for this horrendous outcome. "Alden, hey," she said, keeping her tone casual to contrast his overly cocky approach.

He leaned in for a hug, and she met him halfway courteously. She could feel Ethan's body tense next to her, could feel Sahar's eyes burning a hole through her back. "How've you been?"

"Good, yeah, you?" she responded.

Willa was thankful that Naomi, Christian, and Jeanie were still talking about the club. She didn't need all eyes on them.

"Oh, you know, same old. Working a ton." She wanted to laugh. The bloke worked at his dad's company and could take days off whenever he wanted to. He always made it seem like he was saving lives when he'd discuss his job.

"Aren't we all?" she replied, pausing to muster another grin while attempting to cut the conversation short. "It was good seeing you," she commented.

He poked Willa's hand with a finger. It grossed her out. "Can I buy you a drink? Let's catch up."

She tried to sound as sincere as possible. "Thank you, but I'm good, though." The thing about men like Alden was that they were so stupid, so far up their own asses, that they'd never realize the effect their actions had.

He clicked his tongue. "Well, all right. Take care; it was a friendly gesture anyway. No need to take it so seriously."

Asshole, she wanted to say, "Take care" was what thankfully came out of her mouth.

She turned back right in time to catch Sahar's eye roll. "Was he always that stupid?"

"Honestly? I have no freaking clue, and I don't know what that says about me," Willa questioned.

Sahar shrugged. "That you're human?"

"Yeah, I suppose so."

Willa turned back to Ethan, the crease between his eyebrows far more pronounced than she'd seen before. He was tense and rigid. Had Alden's presence riled him this much? Fury had made its way back into his eyes with full force, making her feel guilty.

She wrapped her fingers along his forearm, drawing his eyes from throwing daggers at her ex to where she touched him. He blinked once, twice, refocusing to meet her at eye level.

She didn't say anything. He remained silent.

The conversations around them distorted to muffles, the bass growing louder. "Are you okay?" Willa asked.

Ethan nodded. "Promise me that *you* are," he emphasized.

"I am. I really am."

She released her hand. He drew closer to her ear, whispering, "Be right back."

She watched him stride away toward where she assumed were the toilets. God, Alden was the world's biggest buzzkill.

She shuddered out of her unpleasant thoughts, returning her attention to the banter occurring beside her. She needed to refocus. She had therapy tomorrow and could discuss all of this with Marie if she still needed to.

10
____

ETHAN

The bathroom was too small, and the growing anger ballooning inside him made it worse. It was suffocating. He wanted to go back outside, into the fresh air, away from the loud music, but he knew that if he stepped out, Willa would follow, guilt sauntering right behind her. This way, he could pretend like he was fine. Nature called.

Nothing more serious.

Except it was.

Ethan could tell that Willa was hiding portions of the truth from him—details that he knew she didn't owe him but ones he couldn't help but care about. It also riled him up to witness her dumbass ex's audacity, his inability to take a hint and understand the difference between diplomacy and interest. He momentarily contemplated punching the obnoxiously veneered teeth out of Alden's mouth.

He knew she could take care of herself; she didn't need him, yet he couldn't help but worry. He wanted to wrap his arms around Willa's waist and steal kisses from her all night. He wanted to show her off and let men like her ex know that she was off limits.

Except the only person she was off limits to was to him.

The closer he and Willa got, the harder it became to deny the reality of his feelings. Ethan had never felt this way about anyone before, never wanted someone as much as he wanted her. He never needed someone so desperately in a crowded room. Their connection was deeper than anything he thought existed, despite having family and friends who'd been happily and irrevocably in love before. The intensity of his emotions was unfathomable and staggering.

He wasn't sure she'd ever feel the same way, and he loathed the thought that he could potentially push her away because he wanted something more than a friendship.

Far more times than he would've liked, he'd heard her say that she wasn't interested in dating actors, noting that all her exes had indeed been men in entirely different fields—a lawyer, a teacher, a big-city architect. Despite what letdowns they'd been, Willa had shown no desire to reconsider her rule.

Ethan took a deep, painful breath and released a forceful exhale. Everything was too overwhelming. Thank goodness no one had entered the bathroom after him. The heaviness in his chest wouldn't subside. It took everything in him not to profess his true feelings every time they were alone together. Pulling his mind away from how her body felt underneath his touch required herculean effort every time he thought about her for a bit longer than he should.

Willa overpowered him, day and night, in the most wholly encompassing way.

He needed the space to collect his thoughts—thoughts he shouldn't have in the first place, thoughts that shouldn't have crossed his mind as her best friend, and nothing more.

Fuck.

He never wanted to let go when she hugged him. He wanted nights like today to end with her coming home with him. He wanted to press his lips to the three little moles on her collarbone, rake his tongue up her neck, and kiss her pretty mouth all night. He wanted to kiss her in places no one else ever had, hear the sounds she'd make, and love her so reverently she would know, without a shadow of a doubt, that she could trust him.

She was safe with him. She'd always be.

He shook his head, almost violently, as though that'd somehow drive his desires away.

Another heavy exhale.

Ethan turned on the faucet and splashed water on his face, willing himself to stop stewing and get back out there. He took a brown paper towel from the dispenser and dabbed away the droplets on his face.

He needed to go back out there and be her friend.

He swung the door open and walked out, spotting the cast in the same place, all of them together now as opposed to dispersed.

When he approached, they were hovering around Miles, Clyde's arm around his waist while he tried to down what appeared to be six shots of blue liquor. Two of them were already emptied.

Ethan turned to Declan. "What'd I miss?"

"The owner just told him if he could take all of those and keep it in for an hour, the rest of the night will be on the house," Declan answered.

Ethan folded his arms, tilting his head. "And do we think he can?"

"Oh, hell yeah, have you forgotten July of last year? No one can hold his liquor the way Miles can."

That's right. July twenty-four. It came rushing back to him at once, all of them shit-faced beyond comprehension, swearing off alcohol for the foreseeable future after the worst hangover. And then Miles walked in, completely fine, laughing at all of them for complaining.

He took the shots one by one without flinching, and the whole group erupted into a roar with each one. Ethan looked over to Willa then, her brown eyes glistening with a sweeping, stunning smile on full display.

This woman. The best friend he'd ever known. She was an all-consuming force to be reckoned with. She was everything to him.

A knot formed in his stomach suddenly, a roiling disgust at yet another intrusive thought—one far worse than all of his desires combined. He looked around the room, catching Alden and his friends somewhere in the distance, his eyes hooked on Willa.

Neither he nor Willa had dated in the two years they'd been friends. His mind pressured him to confront the idea now—the thought of her in someone else's arms, introducing him to the cast and crew and bringing him out on nights like this.

Ethan didn't think he had a jealous bone in his body until bile climbed up his throat. He'd lose his damn mind if he had to share Willa with someone, watch her arms wrap around another man's body, knowing that he'd know how she kissed. Christ, the thought alone filled him with such horrendous dread that he was sure he could never face the reality of it.

Miles took the second to last shot. Another outbreak of hollers filled the room.

Here he was, in a place full of people who were having a blast, and his tortuous mind was having an outburst over something he had no business thinking about. Ethan shut his eyes for a split second. At no point in his life had he wanted a woman this deeply. He sincerely believed that he loved his recent ex, Michelle, but her infidelity aside, it was clear now that she had never impacted him with the vehemence that Willa had. She never consumed any part of him or became the one person he was positive his life would have no meaning without.

And maybe that was something else entirely. Maybe it was the mere detail that Willa was his best friend, different from all his other friends growing up who were still a big part of his life, or even how he connected to Declan and Sam in the cast.

Their gazes met each other across the room. She was other-worldly, rare and distinctive in a sky full of stars.

Declan angled his head back toward him, forcing Ethan's thoughts to pause. "You coming over tomorrow for D&D?"

Ethan shook his head. "I have plans with Willa," he replied.

He was thankful they had postponed their usual Sunday night arrangement to Monday. He appreciated having time alone with her because, if nothing else, sitting with Willa on the same couch, talking to her, and reaching for the same bowl of popcorn would keep his aching desires contained. Or would it? Would he simply continue falling farther and farther?

Declan dipped his chin with a smirk. "Right, yeah, you two have Sunday nights locked. Should've assumed you'd be making up for it tomorrow."

Ethan didn't say anything; no refuting remark came to him. He had no energy left to fight against his feelings. Let Declan and Sam mock him. They were right about all of it anyway.

ETHAN CAUGHT up with Willa as they all proceeded to walk out of the speakeasy. He had given her space while she was around the rest of the cast, locked in conversations and laughter. "Are we still on for tomorrow?"

Her lips curved upward. "We better be."

"Okay, good. I wanted to be sure." He paused for a beat, tempted to ask if she was okay after seeing Alden again but skeptical if he should. Still, checking in on each other was *their* thing. He'd feel terrible if he didn't, and worse, what if she thought he didn't care? "Are you sure you're okay after what happened tonight?" he asked finally.

She nodded with a conviction stabilized in her eyes. "I am, and I mean it. Plus, I have a session with Marie tomorrow, so I'll get to work through the situation."

Ethan accepted the answer. She was, after all, a lot stronger than she let on, especially when it came to owning up to her emotions. He admired that about her. He admired many things. And dear God, he couldn't wait until tomorrow.

They had a small distance to walk, so Ethan draped his arm around Willa's shoulder. He had to; he was sure the balloon swelling inside of him wouldn't let up if he didn't touch her, even for a short period. She might not have needed him, but he ached for her. Thankfully, this had always been normal for them.

Willa looked up and smiled, sliding her arm around his waist in response. A familiar spark of light hurtled through him, and for the briefest moment, he was content with sending the worries in his chest packing.

One of these days, he was going to lose it.

She would give him that beautiful smile, and he'd be too far gone not to confess every one of his feelings aloud. He was terrified of when that day would come and how he'd put their friendship on the line in the process, but he was hanging on by the flimsiest thread in existence.

11

____

WILLA

Willa took her morning tea and a piece of dark chocolate with almonds, then sat at the small desk in her bedroom. Sahar went to the gym earlier on days when Willa had therapy, giving her the space to sit wherever she wanted in the flat.

The night ended in better circumstances than it had begun, but it was a whirlwind still. Willa was extra glad that her biweekly session fell on this Monday instead of the next because she really needed it.

Her run-in with Alden unleashed a fury of demons she hadn't thought of extensively in a while, and she wanted to shove them back into the cesspool they rose from. She felt small again, far from okay. Initially, when they got home, she thought she'd be fine. She'd been so knackered during the car ride back that she figured she'd fall asleep immediately after she showered.

Instead, she tossed and turned until three a.m. while her mind chased the comfort of Ethan's arm around her shoulders. How concerned he'd been, the irritation she'd noticed in his eyes.

She couldn't believe that any of those emotions had stirred inside of him because of her. There was no way. There had to have been something else bothering him when he walked away for a solid five, maybe ten minutes.

And so, with sleep continuing to escape her, she had called her mother, wanting to check in, knowing she'd be awake with the time difference. Willa mostly caught her up on work, limiting the details of her personal life, but when Beatrix Davidian asked at the end of the phone call if she was sure there was nothing else she wanted to talk about, Willa felt the crushing weight of the words she couldn't say aloud.

It was a simple, generic question any good mother would ask, yet somehow, the tornados in her mind swirled every logical approach away from reach, leaving the worst possible thoughts holding their ground.

She'd told her that she was fine, that everything was good. She didn't dare mention the possible feelings growing for Ethan, and definitely not how she was questioning everything—her past, her present, her future.

She flipped open her laptop camera, which was covered by a small adhesive sticker, and waited. Marie entered the video call a minute after she did.

The woman on the other end of the screen smiled. "Good morning, Willa. How are you?"

Willa sighed and waved. "Hi, Marie, I'm okay...I think."

Marie tilted her head slightly. "Just, okay? Has something happened?"

Willa exhaled audibly, convincing herself to spill it all—she couldn't go over more minor issues today. She needed to let all of this out without holding anything back, and she needed to address the majority of these pent-up emotions.

"I saw my ex-boyfriend yesterday. The one who gave me the

most shit about demisexuality and the one I felt pressured to have sex with."

"Were you expecting to see him, or did it just happen?"

Willa swallowed a lump in her throat. "It was purely coincidental. We were out for Miles' birthday, and Alden was there with his friends," she paused before starting again. "The initial realization that he was there made me freak out a bit, but the conversation itself wasn't too bad. He had the gall to offer to buy me a drink, but I politely declined, and he let it go."

Marie nodded empathetically. "This is the first time you've seen him since the breakup, correct?"

"Yeah, I never thought we'd run into each other. New York City is massive, and the odds of it are slim to none, especially when we don't run in the same circles."

"I see. How do you feel about it at this moment, now that it's already happened?"

Willa bit the fingernail on her thumb, mentally talking herself out of ripping the Gel-X on it. "I don't think I care so much about seeing him, but it sort of stirred all these feelings inside me that are becoming too suffocating to contain."

"What kind of feelings?" Marie asked.

Willa entwined her fingers together, cracking her knuckles and moving them around out of habit. "Of why I even dated a man like him in the first place, why I let myself think that maybe he was right for me. I know we've been over this. I know it's not my fault, but maybe I had all these convoluted feelings about sex because I hadn't had it before. The desperation I felt when I was with him because I was in my thirties. It all comes down to this loneliness I've often felt in the pit of my stomach that's never gone away. And it's a feeling I've always felt so guilty of."

"We're going to take this one issue at a time. With everything we've covered prior, you know that it wasn't your fault, correct? That your feelings, no matter how convoluted they might seem, aren't up for debate by another person, especially if you aren't actively harming them."

Willa nodded. "I know, and I think I sort of brought myself back to that understanding after last night, and everything was fine, but then I came home and couldn't sleep all night, so I called my mum, and when she asked me if something was bothering me, I sort of just spiraled."

Marie bobbed her head, nudging Willa to go on.

"She had every right to ask. I'm sure she could sense I was off, but that's just it...I became more aware of my loneliness when I was back home for my brother's wedding. I couldn't help but feel like everyone was secretly concerned for me. Poor little Willa, quite literally the only single person in her entire family. That's also not a hyperbole, Marie. Even the youngest person in my family has a significant other. And then there's me."

Willa fought back tears. "These feelings I have... it's just," she hesitated, unsure how to continue and bring the most painful part of her reality into words. The part she always felt was too petty and silly to experience this much agony over.

"It's just what?" Marie commenced.

"It's just foolish to feel so lonely because you aren't someone's number one choice romantically. It brings all these other emotions to the surface because I've never been someone's first choice. I've never been the first phone call. All my friends have their people. I've always been so fortunate to have many close friends, but I am never the first person on the list, coming only after various other people. And again, I *get it*. This is life. It feels childish to care. It feels selfish. I should be content in my singleness and my freedom. I just...I—that's why I give men like Alden a chance, hoping that I might be their first choice in everything. Their person. Their partner."

Marie looked at Willa with the very warmth that always comforted her during these sessions.

"This is the first time you've expressed this without bouncing around the words, Willa. I'm proud of you. It's a big step to admit and see what's so clearly bothering you. There's nothing wrong with wanting a romantic relationship. It's a perfectly natural desire."

Tears prickled Willa's eyes and fell as quickly as they made their presence known. "But it hurts, and I want it to stop. And the worst part is that I...I think caring could be more harmful than helpful."

"Well, if you didn't care, then you wouldn't be you. It's not uncommon to be aware of this type of loneliness, especially when you're surrounded by people who are coupled. It's also not wrong, but it's something that we can work around. What's making you think that caring causes more damage than good?"

Willa sighed, pushing the pain down and willing herself to open up. "Because I might've found the person who's most important to me, and I'm scared I'll ruin everything because I'm developing feelings for him."

"Ethan?"

Willa confirmed wordlessly.

"When did this start?"

Willa placed her elbows on the desk and drew her fingers back to her face. "Very recently. I realized a while back that I felt close to him in a way that's so sizably different than with anyone else. I feel safe with him, entirely comfortable in every way, and I know he cares about me in the same way. But what if I only feel that way because I'm lonely and because I desperately want someone or something who's all mine? What if I'm projecting my desires and seeing something that isn't actually there?"

"Anytime you've spoken about Ethan to me, you've made him sound like an absolute gentleman, even in the early days when you weren't as close. Do you think he feels the same way?"

Willa shook her head. "I don't know. We do a lot of things

together. We check in on each other constantly, but even if he had the same romantic feelings, I...I wouldn't want to date him. I wouldn't want to risk it."

"Why is that?" Marie asked.

Willa huffed a sharp inhale. Every single one of her worst-case scenarios, playing on a loop like a song stuck on replay. "Because I'm terrified beyond comprehension to lose him. I can't—I can't imagine my life without him. And the thought of losing him in any capacity shatters my heart into pieces. I can't even think about the day when we complete our run of the show and what will happen then. But the idea of dating him when we're as close as we are and then something ruining it would hurt far more than anything else. I just know it."

Small tears weren't merely falling; Willa was openly crying, everything inside of her tight and heavy. "Ethan is...Well, he's Ethan. He's my best friend. He's my choice in everything. If he weren't the one beside me yesterday when everything happened, he would've been the one I'd have wanted to run to. He's the one I'm looking for in a crowded room, the one I'm sitting next to and gravitating toward. I know now that it will devastate me when he finds someone—when I have to watch him fall in love with someone who isn't me. But I'd rather have him as my friend than lose him fully because we screwed up something perfect. I don't know if I'm his choice, but it scares me in every way because he's mine."

"But what if it lasts? What if he feels the same way, and you two make it? You're good at taking risks, Willa. It got you where you are today."

Willa looked down for a beat, her eyes stinging, her heart in shambles. "I know, but it's Ethan," she managed to mumble.

"Do you believe that you have to choose yourself every day? That this is something we've worked on for a while now together?"

Willa nodded.

"Have you been keeping up with it?"

She thought about it for a beat. She hadn't, not intentionally, at least.

"I think I've gotten better at it, but I haven't been deliberate about it."

Marie smiled at the response. "I believe you have your answer there. You do a lot of things with careful intentions; you've expressed as much to me time and again, but you don't choose yourself. And sometimes, choosing yourself means taking those chances that terrify the daylights out of you."

"I just don't want to be in the same situation again, reeling from another breakup that didn't work out and losing my best friend in the process."

"None of us ever want to lose those we love. But if it happens, we have coping mechanisms for a reason. You've gone through many hurdles and heartbreaks in your life. You'd get through that, too," she took a beat. "You cannot control his feelings if they aren't there, but if they are, it could also work out."

Willa took in her words, trying to fuse them into the loud corridors in her mind that were bustling with hard-to-ignore screams.

Their session was coming to an end with five minutes left on the clock. Willa couldn't say anything; she didn't know how to respond, what to add—she needed to think.

"I wish I had the answer to whether it'd work out or not," she said aloud, more so to the air than to Marie.

"Unfortunately, in that regard, only one other person can give you the answer you're looking for."

Willa concurred.

"How has the show been going?"

She gleamed at the question. Talking about *Midnights at Pemberley* always brought elation to the forefront. "Every night has been magical so far, grueling and so very exhausting, but it's worth every minute. I wouldn't change any of it."

Marie smiled proudly. "I'm so happy to hear that, Willa. I'm hoping I can see it one of these days. My husband and I are both fans of musicals."

"I love hearing that. The critical reception has been great, so I'm sure you'd enjoy it."

"Is there anything else you'd like to address before we end our session today?"

Willa considered for a moment but shook her head. "I think I'm okay for now. It does feel a bit liberating to say those words out loud to someone else."

"That is why I'm here," Marie affirmed. "I'll see you in two weeks?"

Willa waved her right hand. "Yup. Thank you for everything, Marie. Really."

When the video call ended, Willa leaned back against the chair and took a deep breath. She reached for her tea, but it'd gone cold. She took a small sip, letting another lone tear fall at the aches and consolations clashing in her chest.

She was going to see Ethan in a few hours and be with him for a little while, just the two of them. And no matter her feelings, with Ethan, even when the time they spent together was short, it was always comfortable.

Being around him was easy—calming, even when she gazed into his deep blue eyes and thought of kissing him.

12

ETHAN

Willa was wearing an oversized, dark-heather Muppets T-shirt that covered her like a mini-dress and a pair of black cycling shorts. It was the exact outfit she'd worn during their first rehearsal.

Ethan couldn't keep his eyes off her then. He failed even more miserably today.

Something about it was hotter now—more intimate and familiar. He watched as she grazed her pearly-white painted fingernails against the marble counter, waiting for the kernels to finish popping in the popcorn machine. He prized these quiet moments with her.

He didn't care how dramatic he'd sound when admitting that the thought of not having time alone with her made him feel like he couldn't properly recharge.

Unwinding with Willa was Ethan's favorite place to be outside of the stage.

He knew he was staring at her, thankful she was leaning against the counter, eyes fixed on their impending snack, her mind evidently elsewhere.

Part of him knew he should stop, but he couldn't.

Ethan could gape like this for hours, take her in like she was a novel discovery every time. The physical and the emotional. The way she had smiled when he walked in. The gorgeous curve of her ass, the exposed part of her neck showing because of the high, messy bun holding her long hair together. He wanted to wrap his arms around her, hold her tight, and scatter kisses all over her pretty face.

He wanted to tell her how beautiful she looked and confess what that outfit did to him.

He'd never do anything Willa didn't want him to, but he couldn't suppress his imagination from running wild.

The machine came to a halt. She dumped the finished product into a large Ziplock bag, sprinkled Old Bay seasoning and a little pepper on top, then shook the entire thing. She tossed everything in an orange bowl and finally looked over at him.

"What do you want to drink?" she asked.

"Whatever you're having," he answered.

She sighed softly. "But I'm not drinking alcohol; my uterus is on a mission to murder me. So, I took meds."

"I'm sorry. Is there anything I can do?" He asked without a second thought.

"Think you can somehow go back to the dawn of time and magically make it so periods don't exist?"

He chuckled. "That one might be out of my hands. But I'm serious; if there's something I can do, I'll do it."

Her smile was so soft that his heart galloped in his chest. "You're an angel. Anyway, what do you want because I know you're not going to want tea?"

He made a face that he was sure was unattractive. "Water then," he replied.

"Mate, drink for the both of us, please."

He shook his head. "I'm good with water."

She poured him a glass, and he took it from her.

Ethan ambled over to the couch and sat down, then Willa handed him the bowl before plopping herself cross-legged beside him.

"Look, I'm not ready for *Peaky Blinders* to end, but after this, we're doing something light. Rewatching *Schitt's Creek,* or I don't know, *Brooklyn Nine-Nine.* No dramas for at least a month," she commented.

God, she was adorable.

"Except when we have news of *The Bear's* return," he rebutted.

"I appreciate that you're finally acknowledging it's not a comedy."

He chuckled. "You made valid arguments."

She winced slightly, and if he hadn't been so in-tuned to her every move, he might not have noticed. He hated that she was in pain. No wonder she'd been quieter today. He had discerned it when he first came over, but he didn't think anything of it, assuming it might've been from yesterday, which he shouldn't continue prying on. They were initially supposed to meet at his place, but she'd called, said Sahar was going out, and asked if he'd come over instead.

He chanced another glance at her. He supposed it was a good sign that she seemed invested in the first few minutes. However, she grew silent when the episode opened and apart from the initial reactions, her responses were minimal, unlike Willa, at all. There were no audible gasps or comments here and there.

After a few short minutes, her head fell against the cushion, angled to his shoulder. He leaned closer, letting her head rest there for as long as she needed. He debated pausing the show, but that would require reaching toward the other side of her and potentially waking her up.

If she fell asleep, then she must've needed it.

He looked toward her, pretty pink lips slightly open, her soft breathing, creating a melody he could drown in. Musicians wrote songs about moments like this; poets etched such memories into the sacred parts of their beings. They held them there forever, immortalizing the emotions through words.

Ethan had no words, but he felt like he could rupture.

A few minutes passed—fifteen, maybe, judging by the scene changes on the TV screen—and her head moved, her eyes popping open with a sudden jolt.

"Crap, did I fall asleep?"

He smiled down at her. "You did, yeah. I didn't want to wake you, figured you needed it."

She placed her hand in front of her mouth, covering a yawn. "I'm so sorry."

"Why are you apologizing?"

She didn't say anything; she merely gazed at him, her eyes searching his for something he wasn't sure he could give but wanted to.

Fuck it all. He wanted to hold her. He would've stayed there all night if she hadn't woken up. Okay, no, he would've gently nudged her to at least go to her bed so she'd be more comfortable, but still.

He wanted to pull her to his chest.

"I don't know." She settled herself back against the cushion, eyes reverting to the TV. She rewound to where she last remembered, looking up at him one last time before pressing play.

Minutes later, Willa laughed heartily at a scene, repositioning herself at the same time and curling her legs behind her.

"How are you feeling?" he asked.

The mirth lessened, a smile lingering in its place. "My uterus is still choosing violence, but I'm okay."

They stayed unmoving for the next thirty-five minutes or so.

Her eyes darted toward him after she pressed stop on the remote. Goddamn, her eyes—the hypnotizing flecks of gold shimmering from underneath the perfect shade of russet— enamored him. They were so different indoors, darker but comforting nonetheless.

What if he said something? What if he just laid it all on the table, here and now, at this very moment? What if he confessed to feeling something more? Would she run? Would she tell him he's mad and that she only sees him as a friend?

He knew her rules—he wasn't an exception to them.

"That was so good," she said, undoubtedly referring to the episode.

His attention returned to the fictional world. "Yeah, it was," he managed to say.

She smiled, moving slightly from what he noticed was a vibration near her side of the couch.

She picked up her phone, opened it, and excitedly typed something out, then set it back down. "Alex and Anna got the house they'd been looking at! They can finally move out of his crappy flat," she mentioned.

"They did? That's great," he added.

She reached toward the bowl of popcorn, still relatively full because he refused to touch it while she was asleep, and they hadn't finished when they resumed. She took a handful, popping them into her mouth.

He needed to get his mind off all the ways he wanted to get closer to her. He didn't want much. Not at this moment, at least, but he would've given anything to simply have her in his arms.

"Is your family going to visit anytime soon?" he asked, pushing every other thought away.

She nodded with a big grin. "Yes, Mum and Dad are coming during the week of my birthday. Alex and Anna in either November or December."

"Nice. Are you excited for them to see the show?"

She grimaced. "Oh, Dad won't be coming anywhere near it. My father is very much an Armenian man in that regard and doesn't need to see me grind against a ladder. Mum will be coming, though."

He arched an eyebrow and laughed. "Fair point. Anyone else from your family?" He'd only met her cousin Ben and his wife, Violet, very briefly when they'd attended a show in Boston.

She popped three more pieces into her mouth, chewed, then spoke. "Possibly. Emma really wants to, but it's so hard for her to take proper time off. We'll see. I'm not sure about anyone from my dad's side. They aren't big theatre folks."

He nodded along. Willa had met most of Ethan's family, except his sister, who hadn't been to a performance yet because of her schedule. He wanted to know so much more about her, see the streets where she grew up, the places where she hung out. He'd been to London before, but he wanted to experience it through her eyes. He wanted to be there with her.

"Ethan?" she called out.

He broke himself from the gaze he must've held. "Hmm."

"You zoned out. Tired?"

No, just thinking about you, he thought. "A little. Is Sahar not coming home tonight?"

"She'll come. Probably later. She doesn't stay over at the prick's anymore."

If he didn't get off this couch and go home, he was sure he'd lose it. He stood up to leave, holding his hands out for her. She rose to her feet, meeting him at eye level. "Let me grab us lunch tomorrow. Tell me what you're craving."

She tilted her head. "You're the best, but you don't have to do that.

"Either you tell me, or I'll get us one of everything from all our favorite spots, and then you'll wish you made a choice."

She jokingly shook her head. "Why are you like this?"

"My mother raised me well," he answered.

She smiled proudly. "Damn right she did! Patty is a queen."

"She sure is. Now tell me what you want."

She bit her lip in thought, eyes narrowing. "Fine, Jacob's Deli. The usual but extra pickles."

"You can have my pickles, weirdo."

She rolled her eyes. "No, Ethan, you're the weirdo. Something isn't right with your taste buds."

He made an unappealing gagging sound, prompting her to punch his shoulder playfully.

"I don't know why you're complaining. You get extra pickles because of me every time."

She shrugged her shoulders. "Fair, but when you insult them, it's personal. It's war, Everett. We are no longer best friends; we're sworn enemies."

"It's bedtime for you. The theatrics are coming out. Save it for tomorrow's show."

She laughed heartily. "Will do. Now, get out of my flat."

"We're in New York, it's an apartment."

"It's a *flat.*"

He smiled wide, leaning in to take her into his arms. "I won't insult pickles in your presence again."

She held on just as tightly. He didn't want to let go.

"Yeah, you will, but thanks for being a gem about changing plans," she added.

They parted from each other. "Of course," he replied.

He walked out, the scent of her perfume still lingering in his nose. The feel of her in his arms reverberated through his entire being.

On his walk over to the station, he opened his phone multiple times to text her. *God, I want you more than anything.* Delete. *My chest hurts every time we separate.* Delete. *I can't believe you fell asleep on me like that. I hope you do it again, but not because you're in pain.* Delete. *I think I love you.* Delete. *I know I love you.* Delete.

He almost wished someone would bump into him and force him to accidentally hit send. That way, he wouldn't be such a coward. He would own up to his feelings.

I want to turn back around and kiss you. Delete. *You're the most beautiful woman I've ever known. I'd give anything for you to want me like I want you.* Delete. *I miss you already.* Delete. *I could still smell your perfume, it's like a damn perfect garden.* Delete. *I love that T-shirt you wear. It reminds me of the first day we met.* Delete. *What would it take for you to want me like I do? I'd do anything.* Delete.

Delete. Delete. Delete.

He could erase it all in writing, deny it like his life depended on it, but the feelings would grow tenfold still.

Ethan Everett loved his best friend, with every bone in his body.

13

WILLA

Ethan forked out all the pickles in his sandwich onto Willa's plate, spiritedly rolling his eyes in the process.

"You're my hero today," she claimed.

He took a bite of his pickle-free sandwich and chewed fully before speaking. "What about tomorrow?"

"That depends on whether you have pickles for me or not."

He chuckled, taking another mouthful.

She took a bite of her pickle-heavy sandwich. They were seated on the grey sofa in Ethan's dressing room, his Bluetooth speaker humming with a customized Bon Iver mix. Close and comfortable, as they'd always been.

For once, she was thankful for her period. Grateful for the fact that she crashed immediately after Ethan went home last night instead of letting her mind fixate on the way he hugged her before he left. Then, this morning, she woke up and distracted herself with laundry and cleaning around the house, blasting upbeat dance music to keep her mind singing along instead of marinating in unnecessary thoughts.

But now that she was beside him again, his cologne deliciously prickled her nose with the maddening temptation to breathe him in. He wore the kind of annoyingly tight white T-shirt that made his bulging biceps stand out in an even more tormenting fashion and light blue jeans with his hair tousled, sans any styling products before the show.

These moments with Ethan were among her favorites. She knew that if this were any other day and she laid her head on his shoulder now, he'd allow it without a word. He wouldn't question it. But because she was thinking about it—because she wanted it, she wouldn't let herself have it.

She wanted to be more intentional about choosing herself, but she wasn't sure what that looked like when it came to Ethan. He glanced at her for a split second and smiled, taking another bite of his sandwich.

She loved the quiet conviction in his eyes with everything in her—the low baritone he kept to preserve his voice. This was another part of the reason she respected him so much. His work ethic was unquestionably admirable. His drive to bring the best of his abilities to every performance and every interview, even while the vast majority of the attention made him uncomfortable.

And no one really knew that about him, either. People often assumed that anyone in the spotlight always wanted the attention, signed and vetoed their freedom away like a sheltered princess desperate for an escape and bargaining with a sea witch. But that wasn't part of the deal any of them ever made, even when they acquiesced to endure the fatiguing heartaches the industry entailed and demanded.

And Ethan Everett sacrificed so much of his own comfort to please others that she wished he'd stop. He did it for her, too. She could tell as much. He was doing it now, choosing to eat whatever she wanted, instead of doing something for himself.

He'd gotten better at moving at his own pace, not giving into every stage door demand when his body necessitated that he should leave straight after a show. At the expense of his mental health at times, she'd even watched him wrestle against his demons, trying to convince himself that he should do something just because he could—because it was expected of him, even though it'd take too much out of him.

Maybe he also needed to be intentional about choosing himself guiltlessly.

She adored the fact that she got to sit with him during these quiet moments before a show. She remembered the first time they did this, and how he'd stopped her when she got up to leave, asking her to stay, to be with him for a little while longer. She'd obliged, appreciating the silence that filled the space between them, bringing them closer in a way that eased her just as much.

Only then, Willa hadn't developed feelings for him. She hadn't wanted anything more. She didn't think about what it'd feel like to kiss him, to move with him in a way that was intentional and not for show. She didn't think about what it would be like to hold him when he was tired and kiss away that look that told her something was eating him up inside.

She'd thought about what would happen if she ever went on as Elizabeth, but the idea seemed so impossible—plus, in that case, they wouldn't be Ethan and Willa—they'd be Darcy and Elizabeth. It wouldn't mean anything. He couldn't possibly want the same things she did, which must've been why he felt so comfortable with her. She was his best friend. Nothing more.

She put the last piece of her sandwich in her mouth and folded the wrapping paper into the larger plastic bag sitting beside them on the floor. She took her Dr. Pepper in her hands and leaned back against the couch.

Catching the movement, Ethan's face angled toward her, his eyes gentle and warm. "Are you feeling better today?" he asked.

She nodded. "Much. The first day is always the worst for me, but I'm lucky; some women are in pain for days."

"I'm still in awe you perform like that."

She gave him a lopsided grin. "Oh, mate. You have no idea how much we're capable of. There'd be bloody national holidays if men ever got periods."

He bobbed his head to the side. "I wouldn't doubt it."

She was about to respond when they heard a rap on the door.

"Yeah," Ethan called out.

"I'm live on Instagram. You decent? Can I come in?" Sam called out from the other side.

Ethan let out a low chuckle. "Yeah, come." Sam ambled in, prompting another laugh out of Ethan before he continued. "Decent? Dec's the one who sits in his dressing room without a shirt all day."

"Willa!" Sam bellowed, turning the camera to face them both. "It's a bonus round, folks. One of our queens is here, too," he started, pausing to add, "Also, do you all hear this asshole's tone? I'm out here considering his comfort, and he has the gall to be rude to me."

Willa moved closer to Ethan on the couch, giving Sam room to crash with them. Sam plopped down, holding the camera in such a way that all three of them would be in the frame.

Sam immediately pointed to an incoming comment that read, *Ethan's hair looks especially good today* with a bunch of fire emojis. Willa turned her head to face him. "It does, ZROB2019; it does," she said.

Sam reached over from beside her to grab onto it gently. "It's soft, too. He knows how to use conditioner."

Ethan forcefully shook off Sam's hand, but Willa knew it didn't actually bother him. He bobbed his head with a small bow. "Thank you. Thank you, and you," he added, pointing to Sam, "Paws off my locks."

Faking a dramatic frown, Sam laid his head on Willa's shoulder. "How do you put up with this bully, Wills?"

She patted the side of his temple. "There, there. He's getting into character, remember?"

A second later, Ethan crumpled up a piece of napkin and threw it on Sam's head. Willa looked at the camera and shook her head jokingly. "Do you two need me to give you some space?"

Ethan's hand swung down to her knee and squeezed. "Don't you dare leave me alone with him," he quipped. He kept his hand there briefly.

The three of them broke into a shared chuckle.

Ethan then pointed to a question that read, "Is Declan really always shirtless?"

Still chuckling, Sam answered first. "Yes. We're not exaggerating. He's shirtless like ninety-five percent of the time. It's obnoxious. It'll be negative nineteen degrees out, and he's still walking around with his chest out."

"Can confirm, but push that percentage up to ninety-eight," Ethan added.

Another two or three comments flew by them, with some variation of, "Show us!"

"I will. We'll go there next. Any interesting questions for these two while they're in an obliging mood?" Sam said.

"Who said we're in an obliging mood? You just barged in here," Ethan deadpanned.

Sam rolled his eyes lovingly. "I did. You wouldn't disappoint the fans like that."

"No, but I'm happy to disappoint you."

Willa looked between them in the extremely tight spot, then burst out laughing. It prompted them to follow.

They looked to the camera then, reading, waiting for something interesting and appropriate to answer.

"This person wants to know if we were Austen fans before signing on to the production. I'm so sorry, I didn't catch the username quick enough," Willa read.

Ethan looked to Willa first, initiating for her to start the conversation. "I was! I grew up going to Bath frequently, so it was a big deal for me to get to do this. But, okay, no one kill me. *Pride and Prejudice* is my third favorite. I'm a hardcore Henry Tilney girl first, Mr. Knightley second, then Darcy."

Ethan and Sam let out audibly fake gasps. "Leave, you can't sit here anymore. Security! Get her off this damn production," Sam exclaimed.

Willa rolled her eyes, laughing. "Oh, is that so, Mr. I Watched 2005 *Pride and Prejudice* First Then Read the Book?"

Sam put up his free hand in surrender. "Fair, but hold. *Pride and Prejudice* wasn't part of my curriculum. I didn't do well in school. Leave me alone. I did read it extensively, though, to study, so jokes on you."

Ethan chimed in next. "I read it in school but didn't think much of it at the time. I really liked the Colin Firth mini-series," he added, turning to Willa. "Which year was that again?"

"1995, BBC," she answered.

"Yeah, I really dug that one. Ooh, and the zombies one they did a while back was hella cool. But I do know it like the back of my hand now. I don't know if it's this performance or my age, but I appreciate it way more than when I was in high school."

Willa nodded with understanding. "You just made yourself sound ancient," she started with a laugh. "I get that, though. It's hard to appreciate most of the books we're forced to study, but then when you read it when *you* want to, it's an entirely different experience. That was also a great question."

Sam brought his face closer to the camera to hold the screen and read. "Oh, this one's good; what number makes you the most nervous? ETHANEVERETTDAILY asked."

"Oh, I know that account," Ethan said. Willa smiled, knowing it'd make their day. "What number makes you the most nervous, Everett?" Willa repeated.

He took a breath, thinking the answer through. "I don't think any of it makes me nervous anymore, but Maggie Garner is such a legend that I always feel like a little kid during, 'Shut It Down, Darcy.'"

Willa and Sam nodded in unison. "God, she's so good. I still can't believe we get to work with her in this show. It doesn't help that she basically yells at you throughout the whole thing," Willa said.

"The first time we rehearsed it, I almost forgot my lines, and that rarely happens to me," Ethan said.

Willa gave him a sweet look.

Ethan's gaze averted toward them, waiting for either one to answer next. Sam went first. "Honestly, nothing? My scenes aren't as intense, maybe 'Doors Open?' Just because I sort of kick things off, but it doesn't actively make me nervous anymore."

"Mr. Perfect over here," Willa said, gesturing toward the camera.

Sam scoffed. "To be fair, if I had Ethan's role, I'd be shitting bricks constantly. There's a reason I'm the soft boy," he noted, placing his hand under his chin in a motion to showcase said softness.

"Okay, but you are also most like your character, so that makes sense in a lot of ways," Willa added.

"What about you?" Sam asked.

"I used to get really nervous with 'Forbidden Corridors.' The ladders lock in place, but I would picture the worst possible outcomes with them solely because of the angle we move in. It took a while for my eyes to adjust, if that makes sense, but not so much now," she answered.

Sam's eyes grew wide. "Oh, shit yeah. Those ladders do look like they move, especially from the wings."

Willa nodded along. "They do technically. The mechanics are wild, but there's only so far they go from the bookshelves."

"It's wild to me that the show's sexiest moments are in some hidden passageway through a library," Sam remarked.

They laughed.

"Right?" Willa concurred. "It's one of my favorite details, though, because I'm such a massive fan of murder mysteries that this lets me live out those fantasies."

Sam continued to look through incoming messages. "Oh, I really like this one," he noted, pointing to a username. "TAYJENNNJONES wants to know what we listen to when we get ready."

Ethan curled his lip between his teeth, thinking.

"I go through phases. Right now, I'm back on an early 2000s emo kick," Sam answered, doing a dramatized rendition of Fall Out Boy's 'Dance, Dance.'"

Willa and Ethan chuckled collectively, with Willa joining Sam in the singing. "You know what I love? Everyone said the emo stage wasn't forever, but when you're in deep, it's engraved in you. I have some of those songs memorized way better than I do more recent obsessions."

"It was integral to our development, so it probably did something to our brain chemistry," Sam said.

"No, but it's true. People have been using that statement a lot recently, and I genuinely do think it's applicable here. I can recognize the notes in so many of those songs quickly, but I'm not good at that generally."

Ethan tilted his head. "You're pretty good at it, I'd say."

"No, that's you. How many times do I have to figure out

what's about to play when we're watching something, and you already know," she countered.

Ethan clicked his tongue. "She's being modest."

Willa made a face to the camera to dispute the statement.

Sam read the next question, or rather, statement, aloud. "This whole cast is so hot, it's borderline offensive."

They all laughed loudly at the sentiment.

"That was part of the auditions. We're trying to compete with the Firths and the MacFadyens, people," Sam said.

Willa put up a forefinger. "And don't you dare forget Matthew Rhys."

"Right, right," Sam acknowledged, eyes searching again for another question. "Oh, what's something you want to see on Broadway and be a part of?" he read.

Willa's eyes darted toward Ethan. She knew his answer better than her own.

Sam caught the look. "Am I supposed to know his answer? Do you?"

"I do," Willa declared proudly.

"What is it?" Sam asked.

Ethan started whistling to the tune of "Lovin' You Lots and Lots" by The Norm Wooster Singers.

Sam's eyes lit up in understanding. "Oh! *That Thing You Do!*"

Ethan bobbed his head up and down. "Yeah. It's one of my favorite movies. It'd be so fun to perform those songs."

Willa smiled, remembering how he'd been the one who introduced her to the film.

"Okay, but only if we're cast in it together," Sam remarked.

Ethan winked. "There's no other way we're taking it on."

He and Sam started singing part of the film's main track. Willa giggled in the middle of them and leaned back against the couch to let them serenade each other, but Ethan turned to her, and Sam followed. It made her blush. *Hard.*

"See, people, sometimes they *do* get along."

Ethan and Sam both laughed. God, *Ethan's laugh*.

Sam pointed to a question about who breaks character most. "You know what this reminded me of. I don't think anyone knows this story?" Sam said.

Ethan gestured for him to go on.

"Remember the last dress rehearsal before opening day at Boston?"

Willa laughed at the memory. "You have to tell them now. They deserve to know."

"Okay, okay, okay," Sam tried to say while laughing. "You guys, Ethan doesn't break character. Like, it's annoying how good he is. And I'm horrible. If anyone's breaking, it's either me or Dec. So we're in full-on dress rehearsals, running the show, everything's going great..."

Ethan interrupted. "Wait, no, hold on. Give them the disclaimer. During the last half of 'All For You,' we don't actually have a set choreography. So most of what you see we improv. Like sometimes, Elizabeth kisses Darcy. Other times, I'll do it. It's free rein. We just roll with it, so keep that in mind."

Willa tried to suppress her laugh.

Sam kept going. "So, during this second half, Sahar and I come in, and we sort of have this cute little couple's celebration. We're doing our thing. They're doing theirs. Sahar and Naomi sort of look at each other and hug, and it's such a quick moment that Ethan and I are supposed to hug, too. I fucking trip and stop myself by accidentally grabbing his ass." Sam breaks into a laugh. "Does he flinch? Not even for a second. And I'm trying so hard not to lose it because we were doing *so well,* so we keep going."

Ethan had his hand over his mouth while he laughed silently.

Sam continued. "We get back with our wives and we're carrying on the song, and Sahar loses it."

Willa laughed hard. So did Ethan. They leaned into each other instinctually.

"I feel bad telling this without her. Where is she?" Sam asked.

"She's in PT. Don't worry. Go," Willa answered.

Sam shook his head with another laugh. "So they're singing, we're dancing. And Sahar's trying to question it, thinking it's something we improvised, but I have no clue what she's wordlessly saying to me, so all of a sudden, she grabs my ass, and I think I yelped or something. All I hear is Ethan's laugh, and Naomi's on the floor; Sahar goes down with her. Dina looks like she wants to fire all of us. For a good five minutes, I couldn't explain that it was an accident," he paused. "What was the point of this story?" he returned.

"You were trying to answer that you break character the most," Willa said.

Sam concurred. "Basically, yes, and this guy makes us all look bad on stage because he's too damn perfect."

Willa turned and smiled at Ethan.

"You're perfect, too, Sam," Ethan commented.

Sam blew him a dramatic air kiss, then got up suddenly. "Okay everyone let's go, it's time to harass Declan in his man cave."

Ethan rolled his eyes but rose to his feet, beckoning for Willa to step ahead of him. They walked into the next room, finding Naomi and Innila standing in front of Declan's door.

"Oh, shit, it's a party," Sam declared. Naomi and Innila turned around.

"We've been expecting you," Naomi said with a laugh.

Much to their unfortunate surprise, Declan put on a shirt solely to spite Sam.

"You bastard," Sam started. "How dare you disappoint the fans like this?"

He looked straight into the camera. "If you're at the show tonight, don't talk to this asshole at stage door. He won't give the people what they want."

Ethan poked his head through the door. "How could you?" he added, using his Darcy voice and the British accent he'd surprisingly gotten very good at since training thoroughly with a dialect coach. "This is why you're Wickham," he taunted, pretending to storm off from the frame.

Everyone burst into laughter. Declan lost his shit simultaneously at the remark. "I was going to dramatically strip out of it, but you know what? You get nothing now," he hollered, hands above his head, supposed fury in his eyes.

Goodness, she adored this cast with everything in her.

Sahar came up the stairs from PT. "I see we've all collectively lost it."

"Declan won't give the people what they want."

Sahar whistled on the dot; Willa was envious she couldn't. "Show us what you've got, Dec. It's what the people deserve," she shouted.

A roar ruptured throughout the hallway, and the whole ensemble made their way out in no time. It was during moments like this that Willa stood back for a beat and counted her blessings. She had been part of a few West End productions in her lifetime, nothing like *Midnights at Pemberley*, but work she was proud of nevertheless.

They weren't just co-workers; they were a family, people she'd love and cherish for the rest of her life, even if there would come a time when they wouldn't see each other every day. None of this was for show; it wasn't for the Instagram lives or the behind-the-scenes footage.

It was real and wild, and it made New York City feel like a forever home.

Their distinct personalities blended in a way that only happened once, maybe twice, if you're one of the lucky ones. Declan took off his shirt, threw it on the floor with jokingly deliberate force, and ran to the toilets.

He provided an exaggerated bow. "Duty calls, my friends."

The laughter engulfing the room was infectious, glorious, and warm. Goodness, her period was making her a little sappy. She'd let it anyway.

14

WILLA

Time often passed strangely when you did the same thing every single day, one gloriously rewarding sold-out show after another. But some days, they'd all be so exhausted that Willa wasn't even sure how she was functioning. Somewhere between it all, she and Sahar managed to schedule their interviews for dual citizenship (on different days, but still).

It'd also been over a month since her run-in with Alden, and now, more than ever, nothing was clearer to Willa than the fact that she was actually falling hard and fast for Ethan. So much so that at one point last night, when she watched him leave in the car designated for him, a sudden ache pierced her chest because it wasn't Sunday, and they wouldn't be hanging out.

Instead, the following morning, Willa woke up to her phone buzzing. A moment of panic swelled through her when she saw Dina on the caller ID. *Fuck.*

Had she slept through a critical, crack-of-dawn live performance? *No.* There wasn't anything on their calendar for that.

"Hello?" she croaked, catching herself and uttering the greeting again.

Dina sounded like she had been running a marathon.

"Willa, hey, I'm sorry to call so early, but Naomi has had a family emergency. Naturally, that means Lea can't go on either. They're both on a flight to San Diego right now, so you have to go on for Elizabeth. A swing has already been called in to fill your role in the ensemble."

Willa couldn't process, couldn't think. Quite frankly, she *never* in a million years thought she'd actually go on as Elizabeth. The few times Naomi had to take time off, Lea Driver, her sister, and standby went on for her.

The odds of this happening were exceptionally rare. "Jesus, I hope everything is okay," she said first. Should she text Naomi? Should she reach out to Jeanie? Maybe they had to keep it private for a reason, and she wouldn't want to overstep.

"I do too. Right now, they aren't sure whether they'll be out all week," Dina replied.

Willa's heart dropped to the pit of her stomach. Did something happen to one of their parents? Their sister? She imagined it must've been bad if they had to get on a plane immediately, with no time to disclose specifics. "Good lord," she managed to reply.

She thanked every molecule in her brain that no matter how bad her memory was, she was great at retaining lines and dance numbers. She knew this production like the back of her hand. Just because she never thought she'd go on, Willa never stopped herself from prepping at random intervals.

"I'd love to rehearse it at least once with Ethan before we go on, though. It's different being on the coaching side."

"Yeah, that's why I called so early. I was going to call Ethan right after I spoke with you. How soon can you get to the theatre?" she asked.

"About an hour, hour-and-a-half max," Willa replied.

"Excellent. I'll see you soon," Dina noted before the line went dead.

"Bloody fucking hell!" she nearly screamed. *Ethan.*

For a split second, her mind had been so focused on Naomi's family that she hadn't even thought about the fact that she'd be performing closely with Ethan.

Willa would be *kissing* Ethan? As Darcy, no less. It was fun, albeit torturous, to imagine what it'd be like—to think of it back when she was fully convinced it wouldn't actually happen, but now, it was going to.

Tonight.

In a few hours.

Oh, God.

She had to wake up Sahar. Christ. She'd never been *this* panicked about a performance before. She went on as Jane easily in Boston for two days when Sahar was sick. But the story behind Jane and Bingley wasn't nearly as sexy as Elizabeth and Darcy's. And even if it had been, she wouldn't have given a damn because it wasn't Ethan she was sharing the majority of her scenes with.

Willa could scream. She wanted to. She had to be a professional, but she hadn't had feelings for a coworker before. And this was the big, huge reason *why.*

He probably had no idea what was going on inside of her, and he certainly wasn't a bundle of nerves because, on stage, Ethan Everett was one of the most skilled actors she'd ever known. It was a gift to work with him. Willa knew as much, and now, she'd have the chance to be his partner. As he always did, she had to give one hundred and ten percent. She couldn't screw this up. She couldn't be a schoolgirl with a crush. She had to pull herself together and bring the best of her abilities onto the stage.

Willa took a deep breath and nearly bolted to Sahar's room. "Sahar, wake up; I need your help."

Sahar grumbled. "What time is it?"

"Too early, c'mon."

Sahar's eyes flung open. "What?" she whined.

"Naomi and Lea had a family emergency. I'm going on as Elizabeth," Willa blurted.

Sahar propped herself up so quickly that Willa was concerned her head would spin. "Oh fuuuuuuuuuuuuuk," she elongated.

Willa sat on the bed. "Sahar. I can't breathe. I'm so. I'm— *Ethan,*" she emphasized.

Sahar released a giant exhale. "Mate, I'm so sorry. Jesus Christ, it's one thing to know in advance, but like this? When you feel...all of that?" she gestured a clunky circle with her hands.

"And you know I don't have a problem with last-minute performances. Frankly, I think I killed it as you. But Sam isn't Ethan."

"Oh, I know you did," Sahar agreed, blinking rapidly. "Okay, let's go. We gotta get you to the theatre."

"I have to shower," she contested.

Sahar nodded. "Have you spoken to Ethan?"

"No, I ran here. Crap, my phone..." Willa didn't even finish her sentence before she sprinted back to her room. She would have to apologize to their downstairs neighbors for the early morning disturbance her feet were causing.

She picked her phone up from her bed and saw a missed call from Ethan.

Fuck fuck fuck! she stressed to no one in particular.

"Willa Catherine Davidian, get your shit together," she whispered aloud.

She called him back, the ringing making her heart rate blow speedily.

"Hey, Wills," he drawled, his voice low and hoarse.

She took a soundless breath. "Hey, I'm guessing Dina called you already."

"Yeah, she did. I'm skipping the gym today. When are you heading to the theatre?"

"I'll be there in about an hour."

"Cool. I'll see you there."

Willa hung up the phone and sat on the bed for a moment. She could do this. She was a grown adult, for crying out loud.

It didn't matter if these were technically uncharted waters. She'd danced with Ethan before. Hell, she'd rehearsed the "Midnights at Pemberley" number with him multiple times when he'd been nervous. She'd used him as a partner when she had a choreography in her mind that she wanted to nail down. Yet, as hot as those moments might have been, none ended with a kiss. None had the heat and fire that "Marry Me" contained.

Sahar ambled into her bedroom. "You've got this, babe. Pretend he's the most hideous person on the planet."

Tilting her head to the side, Willa narrowed her eyes. *Like that was possible with Ethan.* Chestnut-brown wavy hair falling in his face, the most alluring smile she'd ever seen, eyes so uniquely blue...It was unreasonable to pretend with that man. And knowing what a gentle, brilliant person he was on the inside, too? She was shit out of luck.

"Okay, right, yeah, that's not the best advice. But you've danced with him before."

She sighed. "Not 'Marry Me'—the intensity of that choreography isn't one I've actively rehearsed *with* him. And, hi, yes, I haven't kissed him. He's never had his damn perfect lips on my neck? I realize we're changing during that number, but you've got to remember what it entails. Plus, how many bloody times do he and Naomi have to kiss during 'All For You'?"

Sahar's face fell, her teeth baring. "Oh shit. Yeah..."

"Yup," Willa said, popping the p.

Sahar shook her head. "I don't have any good advice I can give you. Frankly, even with all my initial crushes, I haven't been in your shoes. But the most important thing I can say is that it's Ethan. Everything aside, it'll be a great show day because you two are both excellent performers. Everything else? His mouth? Yours? Leave it to the end of the show. Right now, just force your mind to focus on the dances, the music, everything but the kiss. I know it's easier said than done, but you've got to try."

She nodded in agreement. Sahar was right. Willa had no other choice right now.

"Okay, I'm showering. I'll try to talk myself out of a full-fledged breakdown in there."

"Do you need me to come early, too?"

Willa paused for a beat, thinking it over. "Our numbers are easier, but I'd love for you to be there. Just so I have someone with me who knows how I feel? But if you're too tired, I absolutely get you wanting to stay behind until your call time."

Sahar nodded. "I'll come. I'll nap during breaks."

"You're the best," Willa emphasized.

Sahar smiled. "You'd do the same for me."

15

ETHAN

He was going to kiss Willa, place his lips on her neck, skate his hand up her thigh, and draw his fingers along her breastbone. Well, Darcy would do those things to Elizabeth, but today—maybe for the rest of the week—Elizabeth wouldn't be Naomi. She'd be Willa. His best friend. The woman he wanted more than anything—the woman he was sure he loved more than anyone else.

Ethan wasn't prepared for any of it. What made matters worse was his certainty that she couldn't possibly feel the same way. She'd be nervous, sure, but not for the reasons he was.

He couldn't think of this as anything other than a performance. He couldn't risk slipping up. It wasn't them. It was an act. He'd touched Willa's body and swayed with her many times, but despite how those instances had left him wanting, he couldn't give in to the desires coursing through him. He wouldn't risk jeopardizing his friendship with her.

This could be like the other times.

It had to.

He was already sweating, and the spring humidity was coming in with full force. Ethan stripped off his clothes and stepped into the shower, setting the lever to the coldest temperature possible. He needed to forget. Snap out of it urgently.

The piercing water worked on his body, but his betraying mind still wandered. Willa's long, gorgeous legs, her beguiling lips, those beautiful brown eyes, her sweet, dimpled smile. And good lord, her laugh—her breathtaking, perfect laugh. He desperately wanted to play it on a loop like his favorite song. Listen to it over and over and over again.

He scrubbed his skin like his life depended on it, as though the earthy-scented body wash would somehow whisk away his thoughts of her.

Nothing would help. He was a lost cause.

Ethan got out, reached for a towel to dry off, and braced himself for the most excruciating bout of self-control he'd ever have to exercise. He secured the towel around his waist, planning to style his hair here instead of at the theatre, when a small creature wobbled into the bathroom with a loud meow. "Shit, Tulip. I'm so sorry, girl. It's been a hell of a morning," he declared.

He forgot to feed his cat. Tulip meowed at him again, her little attitude more pronounced. "I'm coming. I'm coming. Let's get you food," he said.

He hurried over to his cabinet, opened a new can of wet food, and added it to the bottom of her automatic feeder bowl. He was going to have a long day, and she might as well have some extra sustenance so at least one of them could experience a modicum of comfort. He took her bag of dry food, filled the inside of the feeder, and added more water to the mini fountain before nuzzling her fluffy orange coat.

He bent down to place a kiss on the top of her tiny head before migrating back into his room to change and leave.

~

WILLA WAS ALREADY on stage when he stepped in from the wings, taking the show from the top with Sahar for "Doors Open." God, even the simple way she moved was transcendent. She wasn't doing anything other than walking, head in the clouds for the act, and it was already too much for him to deal with.

She wore forest green leggings with a matching sports bra and her hair in a high ponytail. Ethan hadn't switched out of his glasses yet, and a part of him didn't want to now. He thought of sitting in the stands and watching her. Good lord, he almost sought to tell Christian to go on for him, fake an illness or something. Except, he wouldn't do that to Willa. He had to be the strong one for her debut—the anchor for any of her possible needs. If she even needed him at all.

Get your shit together, he nagged at his brain.

She spotted him after concluding the number, and her eyes flicked in his direction, a sweet smile rising on her lips.

He shuffled closer, taking her quickly into his arms. "You're going to be amazing," he whispered, loud enough so only she'd hear.

"Glad one of us has that faith in me. I'm extremely nervous," she admitted.

He tucked his fingers underneath her chin, nudging her to look up at him. *It doesn't mean what you think it does, Ethan. She's just nervous about the performance. These are common debut jitters.* "Don't be. I've got you. You can do all of this in your sleep."

She nodded, the apprehension in her eyes mollifying a tiny bit. Ethan removed his fingers from her chin and slid his hands to her shoulder, holding her in place. He wanted to say something and toss a few more compliments in the ring, but he couldn't speak.

He moved aside, letting her resume from the top, waiting until it was his turn to enter the scene. With all their movements and singing occurring while seated, "Bennet Sisters' Interview" didn't require much physical labor from the women. Ethan couldn't do his part without Sam yet, so he stood by until it was his turn for "Obstinate, Headstrong Girl."

It was riveting to move beside her like an equal—to mark Darcy's cold gaze upon her stunning frame. It was even more rousing to experience a new side of their rehearsals, a shift utterly different from their dynamic as friends.

The meat of "Smile More" and "Lost in the Lights" were heavier for the ensemble, leading to "Stubborn Bastard," which required Declan, then to the "Midnights at Pemberley" title theme and one step closer to "Marry Me."

One step closer.

They got into position for their small solo in "Midnights at Pemberley."

He rubbed his palms up and down her bare shoulders.

She squared herself to start.

"You two are doing so great I can't handle it," Miles called out at one point. "We won't be giving Dina an ulcer today," he continued with a laugh.

Willa had turned to face him through a spin. "Keep throwing compliments at me, Miles, it's helping," she joked.

Miles obliged with a huge smile. "You're a beautiful stage mermaid, Wills! At least I didn't wake you up at four a.m. screaming because I had a dream about a video we should make this time around."

Her dimpled smile morphed into a hearty laugh, and Ethan could swear her eyes shimmered. He was grateful for Miles' charm at a time like this. Pleased that he knew Willa so well as a dancer.

Yes, Ethan and Willa had danced before, but watching her act like this was a breathtaking experience he wouldn't ever take for granted. Watching her transform into someone else and evoke all sorts of emotions while simultaneously in *his* arms was a gift he'd hold onto for the rest of his life.

Smooth sailing was almost inevitable with Willa, as if their bodies were made to dance together. He wondered if she felt it, too—if it was as seamless for her as it was for him when they were together.

While many of these numbers required intimate moments—Darcy's notable hand flex included to excite the audience—the ensemble's presence made the movements far less daunting.

It was "Marry Me" he was shitting bricks about.

Ethan wasn't a particularly religious man, but when it was time for "Marry Me," he sent a prayer to the ethers. He implored for the strength to pull off the moves without keeling over in front of her, begging on hands and knees for her to be more than his friend.

Miles got closer to them, his hands animated, eyes twinkling with excitement and a bit of concern simultaneously. "You two are dazzling together, but here's where you need to be more mindful of your movements, E. Willa is taller than Naomi and Lea, so you don't have to bend as much. But when you reach for her as you sing, *"Wait,"* I want you to still carry some of that nervousness Darcy does. Curl your shoulders slightly, and then you'll straighten your posture again when you pull her up."

Ethan nodded, taking in Miles' every word, trying to focus on nothing but the performance.

Miles clasped his hands together. "The most important thing to remember about this number is that the aggression is passionate. Darcy's feelings are raw, and he's deeply conflicted, so I almost want you to go even harder with all the movements. Because Willa trusts you, and I trust you with her, I want your off-stage friendship to push through here because it'll make the momentum more palpable."

Miles nudged Willa to face Ethan and instructed him to grab onto her forearm. He did so and with as much force to create an impact without hurting her. Miles turned to Willa then, gesturing the next movement himself for both of them to see. "And you, my wondrous stage mermaid. You're the most flexible dancer, so what if you bend back as much as possible when he grips your hand during the climax, then suspend it right as you touch the ground? Lea can dip somewhat as low, but Naomi can't. I know you can, so I want us to use that. Then you rise slowly and thrust forward but pause, a little too close for comfort before the kiss happens. In other words, I want you to give Ethan's leg the ladder treatment."

Willa let out a boisterous laugh. Ethan's breath caught in his throat, and he tried to smile.

"Oof," she noted, half joking, half something he couldn't quite decipher. "Thoughts, Dina?" Willa asked.

Dina beamed. "I'm obsessed, and Team Miles on this one. He's right."

Miles grinned gleefully. "You have no idea how psyched I am to see this. Josie is going to flip out, too. I know she'd be so excited that you're finally dancing in these numbers. Now, from the top, just the choreography, no singing yet. I want us to grasp the movements before we add the lyrics."

Ethan and Willa positioned themselves, then she turned as if to walk away like Elizabeth was meant to. Ethan's hand flew to hers, and he indicated for her to face him by tipping her chin with his other hand. They performed the start of the number rather successfully.

Miles continued to throw compliments left and right until they stopped right before the first kiss. Ethan's glasses slid slightly down his nose, breaking the tension a bit.

"And perfect. We can hold the kiss since E's in his glasses. Unless you want to take them off and try? But I think you should be good to work it into the moment since it's you two. Now, let's finally take it back from the top with music."

They resumed positions. Naomi was a tremendous singer, and she could hold a note in a way Ethan hadn't seen in all the years he'd been doing this. She was one of the best scene partners he'd ever have vocally, but *Jesus*—Willa's voice sounded the way happiness felt. Soft and euphonious, filling his entire being with a melody he was sure he could feel in all two hundred and six of his bones. He could drown in it, listen to it for hours, just like her laugh. He had heard her sing before, but this was something else. This was magic.

Dina clapped heartily when they finished, stopping again right before the kiss. "I didn't doubt either of you, I swear, but this last minute? I'm pretty sure my blood pressure skyrocketed at one point."

Willa smiled, and Ethan did a small curtsy. "Would we ever let you down?" he said.

Dina shook her head. "Not ever. You've nailed the hardest bit once again, so take a beat, go get food, rest, whatever you guys need, and we'll take on the remaining numbers when everyone shows up."

Ethan faced Willa. "I'll go out and get us food. What do you want?"

"Coffee," she said.

"And?" he clarified, knowing something else was on her mind from the expression on her face.

She shut her eyes briefly. "Just coffee."

"Wills, come on. You need food, so I want you to tell me before I get one of everything. Haven't we been over this before?"

She wrinkled her nose. "I don't have an appetite, but you're right. I probably should eat something. Blueberry bagel, please."

"That's my girl. What's Sahar's order?" he asked.

She thought about it for a beat. "Take her with you. She and Jay get on well. I'm sure he'd like to see her."

Ethan narrowed his eyes, questioning the small but riveting fact. Did Jay have a thing for Sahar? If so, he was certainly a better option than the clown she was currently dating, and though Ethan didn't know much about Jay, he also seemed better than the assholes she'd previously dated. He obliged Willa's idea, turning to Sahar, who was half asleep in the audience seats. The woman's ability to fall asleep on any surface, comfortable or not, floored him. No pun intended.

"Sahar," he called out.

She perked up and blinked, once, twice. "What, what'd I miss?"

"You and I are going to Amanda's," he stated.

She groaned sluggishly and pointed somewhere toward Willa's vicinity. "Take her. I'm tired." She seemed to be thinking something through, almost like it clicked in her brain that Willa was taking on the principal role tonight. "Alright, yeah, fine."

16

WILLA

Willa stepped into her dressing room, took her water bottle, and gulped down the entire thing in one go. She couldn't believe that this wasn't some sort of a fever dream. She couldn't grasp the fact that she'd just rehearsed the show's most emotionally and physically charged numbers with Ethan and that it'd felt completely different from any other time she'd danced with him.

It took all her might not to crumble from the ways Ethan had touched her. How would she get back on the stage and function after he kissed her?

Setting the bottle down, she steadied herself against the vanity's edge. Willa thought of how he looked at her when he first entered the stage, eyes gentle and warm with belief shooting through the lenses of his tortoise-shell frames. She also hated him a little for wearing those bloody glasses because it made her weaker in the knees, but how was he supposed to know that? Maybe she could teasingly let him know.

Heavens, it was hot in here. She obsessively fanned herself with her hand, then reached for a notepad, which she hoped would add more wind.

She felt like she was an having out-of-body experience. She was miraculously fine on the surface, but inside, her heart, mind, and body wrestled in a chaotic match set to destroy each other. *He's the love of my life,* her heart clamored. *Shut up,* her mind argued. *I need him,* her body cried. They were throwing calculated volleys at each other constantly, and she couldn't stop any of them.

We've discussed this.

Don't go there.

Don't ruin this one good thing.

He. Is. An. Actor.

I trust him.

I love him.

It's against every rule you've set up to succeed in this industry.

It's too risky.

He. Is. Your. Best. Friend.

Her mind was getting louder, logic attempting to bolt the other two back into the cage where they belonged.

She should call her mum and tell her she was about to go on as Elizabeth. *Yes, that'd be a good distraction.* She picked up the phone to ring her, but the line on the other end went to voicemail. The woman would pick up any phone call ever, but the one time Willa needed to talk to her.

The universe was determined to draw out her torturous emotions and make her anxiety much worse until she finally got off that stage, day one in Elizabeth Bennet's shoes behind her.

Her phone vibrated as she was about to set it down. She looked at it, realizing she was being a bit overdramatic because her mother called her right back.

"Hi, Mum," she answered.

Her mother sounded tired. *Had she been asleep?* "Hi, love. I was having a nap; I caught something a few days ago," she added.

Willa's face fell. "Oh, no. Are you feeling okay?"

"I'm all right, yeah, don't worry. Just a little cold. How are you?"

Willa sat down on her chair and started spinning in it. "I'm good, but I'm going on as Elizabeth today, and I'm quite nervous. I really didn't think it'd happen, but the Driver sisters had a family emergency, so they're both out right now."

Her mother squealed on the other end of the line, every bit of her energy seemingly returning. "Oh, Willa! I'm so thrilled for you. I hope the girls are okay, but this made my whole month. Maybe my whole year. My girl is going on in a lead Broadway role!"

"Thanks, Mum!"

"But go on, love, why are you nervous?"

Willa took a deep breath, got out of the chair, looked around to ensure the hallway was empty, and then closed the door for extra measure. "Because it means I'll be kissing Ethan, and I've got feelings for him that go beyond our friendship."

"Ha!" she declared a little too loudly.

Willa perked up. "What's that supposed to mean?"

"I knew you had feelings for that boy from the moment you started talking about him, Willa. I raised you, remember?"

"And what on earth did I say to make you think that?"

She let out a small laugh. "Mother's intuition. It's not what you say, but it's how you say it. You light up every time you talk about him, and as much as your dad and I raised you to be a loving person, you don't talk about anyone else the way you do about Ethan. It's different."

Willa pursed her lips. "And you didn't think of voicing your opinions to me?"

"No, because you're a grown adult, and despite what my generation might believe about meddling, it's up to you to come to these realizations on your own. When have I ever interfered in your love life? Or your brother's?"

Willa nodded. "Yeah, true. Fine, anyway, that's what I'm currently dealing with."

"Do you reckon he feels the same way?" Mum asked.

Willa closed her eyes for a beat. "Marie asked me the same question. I don't know. I can't think about that right now, even though it's exactly what I'm thinking about. Ugh, nothing makes sense, Mum."

She could feel her mother smiling through the phone. "Well, it's a good thing you've always been someone who could escape into a role. You'll smash it, I'm sure."

The compliment filled her with a bit of ease. "Thank you. I'm going to go prep some more. Is Dad sick, too? Do I need to check in on him?"

"He was. He's the one who brought it home to me, but he's fine now. I'll give him the news, and we'll phone you together tomorrow."

Willa smiled. "Okay. Love you, Mum."

"Love you, too, my darling. Break a leg!"

Sahar and Ethan both sauntered into the dressing room, talking excitedly about something she couldn't quite decipher from the first few words. Ethan brought over her drink and the bagel.

"We told Jay you're making your Elizabeth debut tonight, and he was extra meticulous with your drink," Sahar noted.

Willa's lips quirked upward. "Thanks a million. You two are the best," she said. Pushing the straw in, she took a sip, the smooth, cold liquid hitting in all the right ways. No one made her coffee the way the baristas at Amanda's did, but something about the taste today was indeed different. It wasn't like he had changed the flavor, but maybe it was the thought of it—the care and attention. She could swear things like that made all the difference in the world.

Ethan turned to leave, but she stopped him. "Where are you going?"

"My dressing room?" he replied, making it sound like a question.

She pouted slightly. "Stay for a bit?"

What is wrong with you? Let him go.

He gave her a familiar smile, a little crooked, light in his eyes, and contentment written all over it. It was a smile she loved profoundly, coming in right after her favorite one—teeth bared and eyes gleaming as though the sun shined straight through them.

Ethan turned back, walked over to where she sat, and leaned against the vanity. "Are you still nervous?" he asked Willa.

She bobbed her head in a slow see-saw motion. "Eh? Yes and no."

Sahar bumped her shoulder with her fist. "That's way better than a full-on yes."

"I suppose so," Willa started to say. "I think what's also bothering me is knowing how many people are going to be disappointed that they won't be seeing Naomi or Lea. I hope their family is okay."

Sahar nodded. "Yeah, I wonder what happened and if there's anything we can do?"

"I imagine one of them will tell us when they can. And then we could maybe talk to Jeanie and see what would be most helpful," Willa answered.

Ethan sighed. "Yeah. I don't think Dina can say anything. And knowing Naomi, if it's really bad, she won't say a word to any of us until we're done with tonight's show." He took a sip of his coffee and then turned to Willa. "And you're not going to disappoint the audience, Wills. It'll be the opposite. You're going to stun them."

She looked at him like he was speaking another language. "That's a generous statement."

"It's the truth," he rebutted.

"He's right," Sahar agreed.

They were both wrong, and it was wild how they couldn't see it. Naomi was a force to be reckoned with—the type of performer who made her scene partner better and stronger. And that, despite her feelings for Ethan, was another reason she feared the audience would question whether they got their money's worth. But she wouldn't show them how hard she was fighting against her demons or the inability to comprehend that maybe she also belonged on that stage.

She pushed the bagel up from underneath the paper bag, holding on carefully so she wouldn't have to use her hands. She took a bite and chewed thoroughly before speaking. "If I fumble this, I expect you both to buy my coffee for a year. The price for false belief."

"And what do we get when you're met with a standing ovation?" Ethan propositioned.

"Whatever you want," she replied.

Sahar winked. "You read two books I recommend to you each month."

Willa looked at Ethan.

"I have to give mine more thought," he teased.

Oddly, somehow, this helped ease some of her nerves.

AFTER ANOTHER ROUND of rehearsals and more cast members joining in, they dispersed for the afternoon. Wanting to be alone for a while, Willa ate her lunch at home, took an emotional support shower, and left for the theatre two hours earlier than normal.

"Five minutes, people."

Sahar turned to Willa and looped her hand into Willa's folded arm. "Let's do this," she said, a massive grin forming along her matching nude-colored lips. This was another interesting adjustment. Willa was used to maroon red lips, but Elizabeth wouldn't don that color until after she was hired to work in Pemberley's gorgeously gaudy corners.

The show started smoothly, the crowd reacting to them with the grace and applause she hoped for. Having to share the first three numbers closely with Sahar made easing into the production more seamless. For a beat, it was hard to think of the Ethan of it all. Her mother was right. Willa could always disappear into a role once the audience started reacting and her co-stars filled the space.

It was also enthralling to closely witness her best friend's acting chops—how he exuded Darcy's initial unkindness and prideful stubbornness; it made the banter and tongue-lashing more fun. It made catching the minute changes in his character more riveting as an actor. She caught him staring at her, as the role required, during "Smile More" and "Lost in the Lights," but his true reactions would come in "Midnights at Pemberley." It was then Darcy realized that Elizabeth fit in better at the Pemberley grounds than he thought possible—where he began to see how the others appreciated her.

Willa had gone off stage quickly after sharing the stage with Declan as Wickham for "Stubborn Bastard" and quickly stripped out of the hostess getup to a maroon sequined costume before "Midnights at Pemberley." This was the show's biggest ensemble number before "Marry Me."

Oddly enough, she was ready for it. Her mind was focused so intently on the performances that the rest of her emotions blurred behind the music and lyrics. The verbal sparring inside her had temporarily muted.

Plus, the titular theme was always one of her favorite performances as an ensemble member, but it was intoxicating to experience it from another side. She had two big jumps in the ensemble, while Elizabeth had four smaller ones, plus a long drag from all the male performers, which was just as fun during rehearsals as it was during the show.

When the dancers dispersed backstage, Elizabeth talked to Jane about taking a walk outdoors. She needed to clear her mind, and funnily, so did Willa, but the upcoming performance would do the opposite of that. Sahar winked at her. She wasn't sure if that was in character or not. Willa appreciated it, regardless.

She began walking toward center stage, and the bright gold lights dimmed into cooler blues. The back curtains fell, and a gazebo came out to the forefront. Shortly, Ethan, as Darcy, was in front of her again. *This was it,* she thought. *You can do this, Willa. Be Elizabeth. Stay here, in character. Don't go anywhere else.*

They began arguing again. She shook her head, turning to walk off— *"Wait..."* Darcy called out. She turned to him, eyes narrowed, brows raised, anger brewing inside of her.

They began the choreography as rehearsed, Ethan's hold on her tighter, his emotions on full display. She arched back, touching the ground with her hand, before he lifted her, prompting her to ride up his leg in a slow, drawn-out thrusting motion.

Darcy held her knee in place and grazed his fingers up her thigh with a reverence that would've likely made Willa say yes to this horrendous proposal if she were Elizabeth. She faced him, foreheads touching, their breaths mingling intimately in the space between them. He skated one hand delicately down her breastbone. Willa's body scorched in the wake of his touch. *"Marry me,"* he sang, voice low and gruff to match the now slowed-down melody.

She shook her head, looking down and away from him. *"You don't want me,"* she blared out, a little more anger in her tone.

He curled his fingers underneath her chin and turned her gaze back to him. His eyes were bright spots in the low-lit room. *"Yes, I do,"* he sang.

She moved away from him again; Ethan methodically dragged her back, flipped her sideways with his hands around her frame, and then slid her underneath his legs. She came up with a turn. *"Against your better judgment,"* she spat out. He gripped her hand and spun her thrice before bringing her close to him once more.

His lips fell to her neck, and she gasped, thanking the heavens this was part of the script, too. *"I want you,"* he declared, voice breaking with Darcy's uneasiness. The aggression and passion simmered into a shuddering vulnerability.

She leaned her head back, giving him more room, allowing him further access in a moment where Elizabeth briefly lost herself to the temptations building inside of her. His lips were warm, soft, and staggeringly enticing. *"Against your better judgment,"* she repeated, her voice marrying rage and intrigue. She could feel him shake his head against her neck, his breath sending tremors down to her toes.

He brushed his lips delicately up her neck, hand rising to hold her cheek with a hunger in his eyes that eclipsed his frustrations. *"It came out wrong,"* he uttered, a near whisper in Darcy's voice. And then his mouth crashed into hers, magnetic, commanding.

Willa opened hers slightly, and he tugged on her bottom lip with a tenderness that made her knees buckle. She willed herself back into character, ignoring her fragile state of mind that was begging to give in to her desires.

Fuck, kissing someone had never felt this right before.

No no no.

Then, as the script demanded, she pushed him off.

"*Never,*" she bellowed. "*Not when you've belittled me and declared that all of this is against your better judgment,*" Elizabeth screamed. She shook her head, then spoke again, her voice lower now, more vulnerable and heartbroken. "*Never,*" she whispered and then ran off the stage as the intermission curtains fell.

None of this was real.

None of this was Ethan and Willa.

It couldn't be...

Her whole body trembled with nerves and a bustle of emotions over which she had zero control. She almost wanted to stop and let Ethan catch up with her, but the tension was too high. She rushed to the bathroom to catch her breath.

When she came out, hoping maybe five whole minutes had passed at least, it'd only been two. There were thirteen minutes left to... *What?* Ponder her overbearing feelings? She didn't even have to change out of this outfit because it was the costume Elizabeth would still be wearing when she stumbled into the forbidden corridors. God, she missed her ladder. It was far less intimidating than Ethan's eyes pleading with hers.

She walked back out, hoping Ethan was occupied.

Somewhere, *anywhere,* far away from her.

She went into her dressing room, where Sahar sprang out of her seat and wrapped her arms tightly around Willa's neck. "Holy shit, Willa!" she screeched.

Willa could feel Sahar's excitement pulse through her, the

giddiness in her voice, the way she rocked her back and forth. "Was everything okay?" she asked.

Sahar pulled away and glared at her. "Okay? *Okay?* Willa, I watched bits of you two rehearsing, but I've *never* seen anything like that. I swear you could see the flames rising from in between you two. I would've paid big money to have seen that from the audience's point of view."

Willa swallowed a rigid lump in her throat, moved toward the vanity, and chugged from her water bottle. Her voice quivered slightly. "Okay, good. That's good. That means we did our jobs."

"Babe, you didn't just do your job. You went above and beyond. How do you feel?" Sahar asked.

Willa shook her head. "I can't go into that. Do I need to touch up anything?"

"Lipstick and a little blush," Sahar answered honestly.

Willa sat for a beat and tried to steady the tremors in her leg. She leaned forward, opened the red lipstick, reapplied it, and then blotted. She then added more blush, focusing on the spot where Ethan's hand had lingered.

She took deep breaths, cleared her throat, and drank more water. She was glad not to have scenes with Ethan for two numbers, until the end of "The Letter," at least. And though they'd be more of a couple during "All For You," it would be easier to know the end was near.

Willa looked at Sahar through the mirror. "He told me earlier that we could keep things a little more tamed during 'All For You'. I know you all improv some of those moments."

Sahar concurred. "That's understandable. He and Naomi are used to playing off one another with it. I think it'll also help that Sam and I will be there with you two."

"Yeah, definitely. Apart from that last confession. I can't wait until both of you are with us. The spotlight is so rewarding as an actress, but the Ethan of it all...well."

Sahar gave her an understanding look.

Perhaps it was the ferocity of the emotions in "Marry Me" that were driving her into such a frenzied state. Outside of her own feelings, the tension and vulnerability demanded a lot from the actors. Maybe it was knowing how much audience members loved that scene that also added far more pressure. It could've also been the aftermath of kissing him that made her reactions more electric, but fuck, it was...*everything.*

THE SHOW SPED through in the second half with a different point of view on "Forbidden Corridors," putting her in the necessary state of despair and frustration to push through the rest of the numbers. Thankfully and surprisingly, "Elizabeth's Breakdown" was a cathartic release of the emotions roaring inside of her. Willa had only ever had one solo before, and she'd completely forgotten how gratifying it could be. The cheers were loud and lovely, and for a moment, she was convinced that fully embodying the character would put her desires aside.

But that turned out to be near impossible because Ethan's appearance upon delivering the letter to Elizabeth was something else entirely. Defeat and determination brought forth an expression that nearly astonished her. He wore such a bewitching gaze that if she had any control in awarding accolades, she'd give him every single one solely for this moment alone. She hadn't fully seen him while he performed during this number because she was changing, and rehearsals seldom did the real thing justice.

And even if she had seen it, up close like this was an indescribable sight to behold.

Did his eyes always look this misty?

Their hands brushed as he exited, and when she looked back, she couldn't say if she did it as Willa or Elizabeth. She opened the paper, read, covered her mouth with her hand, and slowly sauntered out.

The ensemble prepped for Jane and Bingley's wedding, moving around the four of them to bring to life the quaint celebration that'd take place at Pemberley's grounds. Sam and Sahar were always adorable during this number, but Elizabeth's eyes remained glued on Darcy's.

Conversations in silence moved them to new grounds and a more profound understanding.

She went off stage as "Shut It Down, Darcy" brought the legendary Maggie Garner into the spotlight. She could've stayed to watch—she wanted to since she rarely got to witness this number and didn't have to change this time around. But she went out into the wings and grabbed Elizabeth's valise instead.

Willa, as Elizabeth, prepared to leave Pemberley, but as she reached the doors that had once welcomed the Bennet sisters inside, a hand stopped her. Gentle and warm. ~~Ethan's.~~ Darcy's.

"*Wait,*" he sang, the same as before but different in its cadence. She turned to face him. Darcy's words didn't hit Willa as hard as Ethan's performance or the vulnerability in his voice. The character was so different from her best friend, but it still struck deep, signifying that no matter the parts they played or where they went in the world, his eyes would always be home to her.

He sang his confession to her, his voice sweeter than in "Marry Me."

When it was her turn to sing, she cupped his cheek, thankful that Elizabeth did this because Willa might've done it instinctually.

"*I thought only of you,*" Darcy spoke.

Elizabeth smiled. *"You're quite the wordsmith when you want to be."*

"It was all for you," he reiterated, drawing closer to her. He traced his fingers along her arms and then tipped her. Elizabeth was meant to laugh, but where she began, and Willa ended, Willa couldn't say, not at this moment. And when his lips met hers with a more tender touch than before, she willed herself to focus solely on the characters.

They could giggle together. He could carry her in his arms and spin her because none of that was new to them. It was familiar and comfortable enough to play off their friendship and give the characters a happy ending. She shouldn't have feared this number, thankful that he didn't try to kiss her again, keeping his promise to tame some of the fire he and Naomi kept up.

When Sam and Sahar joined in as Bingley and Jane, the warmth in the air grew tenfold. The laughter doubled before the track continued.

Darcy wrapped his arms around Elizabeth from behind and kissed her cheek gently. Willa couldn't process the softness—the delicacy of his mouth along her face. She leaned further back as she sang. He spun her once, twice, then pulled her back into him for a tight hug. After parting, she smiled in his arms, peered up at him, and drew his hands up to her lips.

As they neared the bows after the "Midnights at Pemberley Reprise," reality started to set. Backstage, hearing the music and audience cheers blend, every other noise reduced to a murmur. The standing ovation was a sign that they'd done their jobs right.

She turned to Ethan, his smile bold and bright as he extended his hand out for her to take. They presented each other, took their final bows, and walked off the stage together. They stopped at the end of the passageway. The entire cast also took a moment to clap and cheer loudly. Conversations and laughter muffled together and spun into a spectacular array of light she couldn't fully process.

He pulled her in for a hug, and she held on like her life hinged on it. For a split second, the world around them faded away. She felt his head angle toward her temple, a barely there whisper uttering, "Wait for me in your dressing room?"

She parted from him and nodded, watching him disappear down the hallway.

17

ETHAN

His lips had trailed along Willa's neck, and his hands had grazed her thigh, albeit covered in three layers of pantyhose, but still. *The kisses*—each one, in their distinct way, had wrecked him to a state of no return. During intermission, he had bolted to his dressing room, catapulted himself against the small couch, and tried to catch his breath.

She had to feel the same way. He couldn't be the only one whose entire being felt like it'd been shoved into an inferno.

Ethan had kissed countless co-stars before, but it never did anything for him. None had converted every cell in his body into blazing embers.

It couldn't have been Elizabeth responding to Darcy's fiercely misplaced kiss. It surely wasn't the heat of the number. It also wasn't Elizabeth finally accepting Darcy's offer and realizing how deeply he loved her.

It couldn't have been.

It was Willa opening her lips for Ethan. It had to be. He desperately hoped that he was right.

He couldn't hold back anymore and continue fighting against the relentless emotions keeping him up every night. He couldn't come into work the next few days and put on a show while hiding the fact that he was longing for her. Ethan couldn't be selfless here—he was too fragile for that, a shell of himself brought down by the force of feelings demanding all his attention. He was too far gone.

He had to try.

He had to be honest with her.

He had to beg *her* to try.

He had to know how she felt.

She did owe him for the standing ovations he was sure she'd get. Maybe this could be it. A chance. An honest conversation, if nothing else.

Ethan's feelings were clearer than the sky after a dreadful storm. He'd never been more sure of anything in his life than the way he felt about Willa.

While changing out of Darcy's clothes into jeans and a grey T-shirt, he debated switching out his contact lenses but decided against it to save time. He'd do that at home.

He wasn't even sure how he'd say it. What could he possibly do to get her to talk to him?

He closed his dressing room door and walked toward Willa and Sahar's, knocking quietly.

"Come in," he heard Sahar say.

When he stepped in, Willa was applying some kind of balm on her lips. God, she was beautiful—so indescribably radiant. His breath hitched. She perked up when she saw him and stood to face his direction. Her stance was more rigid than he would've preferred, but he understood it fully.

Sahar looked from Willa to Ethan, got up, grabbed her tote bag, and grinned. "I'll wait outside for you two," she stated before leaving them alone.

Ethan drew closer to Willa. Her eyes gleamed despite the apprehension stuck in her gaze.

"Hey," he said.

"Hi," she replied.

"You were sensational tonight," he asserted confidently, the words slipping from his tongue more effortlessly than he uttered any line written for him.

Her cheeks flushed prettily. He wanted to press his lips there.

"Thank you. You're an A+ scene partner."

God. A compliment from Willa, no matter how simple, had a way of getting to him. His heart hadn't thumped this rapidly since his very first curtain call. He wanted to profess it all right at this second, but he knew that would overwhelm her. He had to wait. A few more minutes, until after they left the theatre grounds at least—until their workday was well and truly over.

They stood there for a beat, holding each other's gaze, a promising stillness stretching between them.

For a few more minutes, he had to be her best friend first. He had to give her a safe space to release the anxieties he knew she'd be harboring. "How are you feeling?"

Willa then shut her eyes and swallowed. "Overwhelmed," she whispered. "I don't know if I can go out there and face everyone's reactions. But I also don't want to sprint out of here and be rude. I haven't processed half of what went on tonight, and I don't think I can do it with a whole herd of people who came here hoping to see Naomi."

Ethan's eyes narrowed, disbelief slamming down on his face. "Did you not hear the part when I called you sensational? Willa, you were perfect. You were transcendent. You're the best damn scene partner I've ever had. Did you not hear the standing ovation?"

She leaned forward, laying her head against his shoulder. God, he was so appreciative they'd always been like this, close and familiar in the small but monumental ways they'd touch each other. "They get louder with every show, but I'm also about ninety percent sure I must've been on another astral plane during the entirety of the second act."

He cradled her head. "You know I'd never lie to you, Wills, just like you wouldn't lie to me. If you don't feel comfortable going out there, we can leave together, but I'm positive there are people who'd be excited to meet you. Whatever choice you make, I'm with you on it."

He felt her exhale against his neck, making his heart drum faster. She propped herself up, then turned and reached for her denim jacket. She put it on over her white crop top and black jeans, then squared her shoulders.

"Okay. Maybe for a little while. I keep trying to be in the moment and actually take in what's happening, but I feel like I'm somewhere else."

He pulled her in for another quick hug. "You'll get used to it. You deserve the spotlight and so much more," he stated.

Chuckling, she said, "Be mean for once."

"Never," he disputed.

She shook her head playfully and walked toward the door.

He followed behind her, wishing he could take her hand in his and show the world how much he loved her off-stage, too. It wasn't just their characters.

He might've been reciting lines from a script, but Ethan was very much talking to his best friend.

18

SAHAR

Sahar sat at the top of the backstage stairs, waiting for Ethan and Willa to finish talking. Knowing the two of them, Ethan was probably checking in on her. Willa was probably fighting an internal battle.

But something *had* to change after this performance.

Sahar would lock them in a bloody room herself and force them into a confrontation if they didn't act on their feelings themselves.

She looked toward their dressing room and then back at her phone.

Earlier, she had snapped a photograph of Willa while they waited in the wings before the "Midnights at Pemberley Reprise." The gold slit dress accentuated her physique, with the shadows of the stage lights painting her with a stunning glow. Sahar scrolled through various filters, eventually chose a classic black and white, and then added the Polaroid background she always used.

It made the shot look and feel more timeless.

Because that's exactly what this moment in their lives was— a timeless memory bound to stay with them. And what a gift for

Sahar to witness it, standing beside Willa, playing her sister of all characters.

The majority of Sahar's Instagram account was photos she took of other people. It's why she kept the app anyway. She valued centering those she cared for.

She captioned it: *"This beauty had her Elizabeth Bennet debut today, and I'm in AWE—obsessed beyond words, stunned, screaming, crying, etcetera. So wildly proud of you, @*WILLADAVIDIAN*!"*

Most of them were pretty active on social media, but Sahar and Sam were the ones who spent more time online. She couldn't help it. And frankly, most of the time, the reactions to shows were great. Between Ethan and Declan's popularity as actors known in TV and film along with theatre, their fandom was a riveting, albeit wild place.

Sahar also knew Willa would likely be in her head about the performance for a while, so she wanted to find positive reinforcements to send her.

She opened the show's Subreddit first. *Jesus Christ, the internet is something,* she thought.

One user wrote: *"OMMMMGGG! Willa Davidian had her debut as Elizabeth today, and I'm pretty sure I've ascended!"*

Sahar let out an audible laugh at the following comment: *"Okay, I hate real-life shipping, but you can't be friends with chemistry like that. I've never seen anything like that? I know they are super close, but does anyone think there's something more?"*

This person wasn't exactly wrong. You *couldn't* have chemistry like that and simply remain friends. Ethan and Willa were electric together. Ethereal, in more ways than one, and everyone could see it, extraterrestrials included, she was sure.

Most of the comments were thrillingly positive, and not a single person was being vile or unkind about Willa's performance. Good, because Sahar would've had to fight them otherwise.

"THE WAY HE GRAZED HER THIGH. I THOUGHT I WAS GONNA PASS OUT," someone wrote in all caps. Sahar laughed out loud.

"I lost it when she sang, "It wasn't supposed to be this way—" *The whimper in her voice was so raw. I'm obsessed. Need to see them again immediately!"* Sahar also lost her shit. Willa had such natural talent, and the world needed to hear her sing more.

User ETHANEVERETTOBSESSED02 wrote: *"OMG! I was bummed to see that Naomi Driver was going to be absent from this show, but Willa Davidian?! Hello?! I'm ready to pledge my loyalty!!! Marry me? like I can't believe what my eyes witnessed! I came here to scream during intermission because my friend and I were just dying!! And we were so close, too! Third row orchestra right at the center. Best purchase of my life."*

Her favorite comment came from user MAPONBROADWAY23: *"Can Ethan Everett fight? Because if he doesn't marry Willa, I will."*

Sahar could definitely send some of these to Willa in due time, particularly the few about her performance. She continued reading until Willa and Ethan stood over her.

"Ready to go?" Willa asked.

Sahar nodded. "Are you guys signing?"

"A bit," Willa responded. Ethan concurred with a nod.

"Let's do this then," she said, standing up and gesturing her hands forward to nudge them to go before her.

Zayn, one of the primary security guards, opened the door. Sahar watched Ethan and Willa walk out together, bodies effortlessly leaning toward one another. As though itching to touch, their hands swung closely beside one another in a synchronized dance. They were more reserved today; typically, she'd be *much* closer to his frame, and he'd maybe have his hand hovering over the small of her back. Funnily, they probably didn't realize all the ways they gravitated toward one another, but she spent enough time with both of them to see how different they were around each other.

They were cautious tonight, undoubtedly unsure of how to move forward, which made sense considering what they'd all witnessed today was so much more than a mere performance.

The roar of merriment overlapped every other sound nearby. Sahar's eyes darted toward Ethan, his eyes fixed on the crowd as though he were scoping out the perimeter. There were three guards nearby, but Ethan was still so cautious of Willa, so keenly aware of her moves.

Sahar kept watch on them covertly while she signed, thrilled to hear so many people compliment Willa's performance. She deserved to hear all the praiseworthy feedback.

But it was Ethan's smile at every sincere word that stood out when Sahar caught it.

Sahar knew Ethan loved Willa; he was far more obvious about it than her flatmate was—far more aware of his feelings, but it was still refreshing to see his visible pride when she took the spotlight. Ethan wasn't in this industry for tireless praise; he was in it because he loved acting. He also had no issues with a woman's success, which ultimately made Sahar realize that her boyfriend, Martin, would have had the opposite reaction if they were in Ethan and Willa's shoes. He wouldn't be as proud of her. He wouldn't be an equal partner the way Ethan was Willa's.

She tried to bypass that realization as she kept smiling and signing for the fans. "You're so great as Jane—can I please get a photo?" the person in front of her asked.

"Of course," Sahar answered, drawing closer to the phone, which was turned toward them. She smiled for the camera. "Thank you so much for coming!" Sahar added.

Apart from the few questionable fans that Ethan had a few years ago while he was on *Detective Vice*, most of the people they met at the stage door were delightful. It made their nights brighter when they shared the joy with people who appreciated theatre as much as they did.

Sahar continued making her way down the queue, signing for one fan after another and taking as many pictures as possible. She overheard someone say, "I've seen the show twice now, but this was the first time I cried during 'All For You'! You guys were so amazing during the show. I'm speechless!" to both Ethan and Willa.

Sahar couldn't stop smiling.

When they reached the end, realizing they'd gotten through the crowd, she turned back toward Ethan and Willa.

She could tell Willa was overwhelmed by the reactions because she kept looking at Ethan, easing in her stance when he smiled back at her. It was lovely to catch and understand that they were two people acknowledging one another as life vests in a sea of unruly waves. It had been a constant with them: picking up coffee for each other, movie nights, sitting together at most events, eyes locking together in crowded rooms—parallel lines at every turn.

Ethan and Willa gravitated toward one another in a way that looked as wholesome as it sounded.

Sahar had never felt that way. She wanted to, desperately. But every time she tried with Martin and her exes, she scarcely felt at ease. And good lord, she hoped that her friends would do the right thing and give their feelings a proper chance to grow.

"Thank you so much," Willa replied to the last fan, her voice shaking slightly. They beelined quickly back into the theatre.

The air had shifted. The late spring night was suddenly a little warmer.

19

ETHAN

Ethan couldn't process half the words spoken by the fans outside because all he could think about was Willa. And heavens, he was thankful to hear about all the ways they loved her performance. He did, too, in more ways than he could say.

Their emotions had subdued, a few glances here and there. Willa, especially, he could tell, was uneasy. She kept fidgeting with her nails.

He didn't want to make it worse. He didn't want to add to her agitation, but his damn heart wouldn't stop thrashing inside of him. If they were in a quieter place, they would've all turned and asked him if he was okay.

Ethan wasn't okay. Far from it. He was a man on the precipice of declaring his love for his best friend smack dab in the middle of the theatre's hallway.

He'd have to ask her to wait for him, to get word from the guards that the crowds had dispersed, so he could safely step into the ride back home and hopefully have Willa come with him.

She turned to face him before stepping into her dressing

room to grab her bag, likely to say goodbye for the night as they'd be going in opposite directions.

His heart thrashed faster.

He inched closer, grazing his fingers along her hand. Her eyes flicked down to where he touched her. "Wills, can I...uh, have a second," he asked, pointing to his dressing room instead.

Willa nodded, sauntering over.

He took a deep breath and tried to speak, but the words locked in his throat. He regarded her for a second, willing himself to pluck up the courage to confront the emotions swimming around them, taking up the space he desperately wanted to close with his body.

She looked up at him, her face so lovely that it gave him the strength to continue. "Would you, uh, come over tonight? I... uhm, there's something I want to talk to you about. Privately."

Willa took a breath, an unreadable expression mounting itself in her eyes. "Okay."

Grabbing his backpack from the hook behind his door, they walked out together.

Sahar came out of their shared dressing room, holding Willa's bag as well. Taking it from her, Willa swung her arms around Sahar's shoulder in a tight hug.

He was sure Willa whispered something to her because he could catch Sahar nodding.

Willa pulled away. "Text me the second you get home, Sahar. I mean it."

Sahar crossed her heart. "I won't forget. But also, you have my location."

"Text. Me." Willa emphasized.

Sahar rolled her eyes. "Okay, mum." She walked toward Christian's dressing room before the two of them headed out together.

· · ·

APART FROM A FEW WORDS, Ethan and Willa were silent during the car ride over to his place. When he opened his front door, and they stepped inside, Tulip looked up from her favorite corner at the top of his sectional and silently uttered all her grievances with eyebrows squared and annoyance in her grumpy eyes.

He'd been gone all day today, and with the way she was looking at him, one would think he'd abandoned her with no food or water the entire time. *Cats.*

Willa's gorgeous eyes lit up at the sight of her, and she released an audible little squeal.

She shuffled closer to Tulip, who'd already jumped onto the cushion and rolled over for comfort. Willa nuzzled her head, moving toward the place under her chin where she loved scratches most. "Hi, cutie," she added. "It's been two weeks too long since our last reunion."

Well, he'd have to have Willa come by more, but he also understood why she preferred her place in Queens to his in Manhattan. She wouldn't have to worry about going home late, and they could easily pick up a pie from Leo's Pizza.

She picked up Tulip, who calmly steadied herself in her arms, and they moved toward Ethan. "Treat me," Willa declared, holding out her free hand for treats. Tulip meowed, understanding the exact word.

He reached for the cabinet and pulled out the foul-smelling chicken sticks.

Opening the snack, he handed one to Willa, and she repositioned herself to feed Tulip while she was still in her arms. Tulip chomped down eagerly, tiny sounds of overexcitement coming out of her. When she finished, she jumped out of Willa's arms and strolled toward her water fountain.

Willa went over to his kitchen sink and washed her hands.

Afterward, she turned and leaned against the counter, eyes fixed on him.

"You hungry?" he asked.

She shook her head. "No, my appetite is still wonky."

"Tea? I have the rose-flavored one you like."

She cocked an eyebrow. "The one from Whittard's?"

He confirmed with a nod, trying to read the expression on her face.

"Did you order it online?"

"Obviously not. I hired bootleggers, and they illegally smuggled some for me in exchange for my best cattle," he deadpanned.

She laughed, then tilted her head, still trying to understand. "I—just. When did you buy it?"

"About a month ago. When we were hanging out, you opened a new pack, and I saw the brand, so I ordered it when I got home."

"But you hate tea."

"Which is exactly why I didn't ask you to tell me what it was because you'd know it wasn't for me."

"So, you bought it for *me*?"

His smile grew tenfold. "No, I bought it for Tulip. It's her latest fixation. I also have Dr. Pepper in the fridge. She's really into them both and alternates between them every other day."

Willa sighed, opened her mouth, and then closed it, hiding a smile. "I'll have the tea for your extraordinary efforts, please."

He bobbed his head, washed his hands in the sink, filled the kettle, then turned it on. Ethan opened his fridge and took a Dr. Pepper out. He initially bought them for Willa but eventually got accustomed to the taste and started drinking them, too. He looked back at her, both leaning against his kitchen island now.

Neither said a thing for a beat, their silence blending with the sounds of simmering water coming from the kettle.

Ethan took a deep, painful breath and turned to face her.

It was now or never. Between the kettle and his hammering heartbeats, he was losing his mind.

"Willa...tell me you didn't feel something more out there. Tell me it wasn't all for the show," he nearly begged, not caring how he sounded, wanting only her reassurance, her honest answer.

Willa swallowed. She shut her eyes, then peered up at him, uncertainties clouding the sparkle that had been there moments ago.

"It wasn't all for the show," she confirmed. Willa held his gaze, big brown eyes peering into his soul. "But...but it has to be."

Ethan's insides felt punctured—like a dagger rammed into his chest and twisted all his organs around.

"Why? Why does it have to be that way?" he asked, surely sounding small. Defeated.

She stepped closer, took his dangling hand and squeezed like she was trying to tell him something he wasn't picking up on. He caught her slow breathing. She was trying and attempting to combat something standing in front of her. He knew that look well enough by now.

"There's just... It's too much of a risk. There's a lot to talk about. It's not...simple," she said, her eyes a little heavy.

Ethan lifted his hand and caressed her cheek, delicate and reverential, with meticulous touches. She slid her fingers up and curled them around his wrist. "Then let's talk about it. Please, Wills. It sounds dramatic, but I feel like I'm drowning. I can't keep all of this inside anymore."

She leaned into his touch. Hope made its way back into him, a little less pronounced but resuscitating still.

Willa was about to say something, but she stopped to look down at her vibrating phone that rested against the black marble.

"Oh, shit. It's Naomi in the group chat," she announced.

The cast had a group chat they'd started from their first official rehearsals, mostly memes, occasionally check-ins on plans, and affectionately named "Pemberley's OG-Hoes," courtesy of Sahar. No one bothered to change it. Ethan drew forward to read from her phone as well.

NAOMI

> Hi, my loves. I'm sorry if Lea and I worried you by leaving without a word. Our little sister Siena was in a horrible car accident last night, and the doctors told our parents they weren't sure if she was going to make it. But praise be, they're hopeful that she'll make a full recovery. She's out of surgery now, and we'll be back by Sunday at the earliest. If you believe in prayers, please keep our family in your thoughts. If not, we could use all the good vibes. Love you all! And congrats on your debut, Wills!! We're positive you were perfect on all fronts!!

"Fuck—" Ethan uttered, looking toward Willa, her shock on full display.

"God, I can't even imagine what they must be going through. And the fears they dealt with in the last twenty-four hours," she said.

She started typing out a response. Her phone buzzed again with a text from Christian, another from Innila, followed by one from Sahar. Ethan took his phone out of his back pocket, and Willa's message appeared as he prepped to respond.

WILLA

> I'm so sorry you're all going through this. Thank goodness she'll be okay. Your family will be in all my prayers <3 big, big love, my darling girls! Please keep us updated.

ETHAN

> Please let us know if there's anything we can do! Sending your family all my love and prayers!

They both set their phones down and looked at each other. Ethan felt guilty for having had such a great day when his scene partner was struggling in a way he couldn't comprehend. He thought of his siblings for a beat, making a mental note to give them both a call tomorrow.

It was strange what happened to a person when they heard bad news of any degree—how rapidly and effortlessly precious life could become in the blink of an eye. A rush of gratitude flooded through Ethan, growing into a bravery that made him certain he didn't want to waste a single second pretending like his heart wasn't beating out of his chest.

The electric kettle's handle made a popping sound, indicating the water had finished boiling. Willa looked toward him and then reached up to open the cabinet where he kept his mugs. She placed one down, and he handed her a tea bag.

"Milk?" he asked.

"I'm good for right now. Thank you, though."

He sauntered over to his fridge, took out a can of Dr. Pepper, snapped it open, and then walked toward the sectional with her.

Ethan picked out two plain black coasters for them; Willa placed her cup down on one and then sat farther than she usually did.

He gave her a puzzled glance. Physically, maybe two other people could fit in between them.

"What?" she asked.

He tilted his head. "Why are you sitting so far away?"

"I'm not," she disputed.

How was she so calm about this? Was every part of her not torching with rambunctious flames? Was she doing this because she was nervous? He didn't want to push her, but she was Willa. He was Ethan. She'd jump on his back for shits and giggles every chance she got. They were farther now than when they'd sit in his dressing room, for crying out loud.

"It feels like you're on another continent. Can you come a little closer?" he pleaded.

Shaking her head affably, she moved a little. Her hand was close enough for him to reach for, but he stopped himself from doing so.

Her expression was indecipherable. He looked attentively at her for a second, trying to understand whether she was uncomfortable, shy, or something else.

His heart lodged in his throat. Willa was everything to him. He could finally divulge it all, every little thing he kept veiled out in the open.

Ethan broke the silence. "You mean the world to me, Willa, you know that, right?"

She seemed dejected at first, like he'd said the wrong thing. She swallowed, the sound of her slow breathing filling the space between them.

"You mean the same to me, Ethan. You're my best friend. I'm pretty sure you're my person. But that's exactly what scares me."

He closed his eyes, processing. Willa was among the smartest people he knew, but good grief, none of this made sense to him. "Why? How? That doesn't add up. If there's something more between us, why do we have to deny it?"

"Because..." she answered quietly, turning her head in the opposite direction.

Drawing a bit closer to her on the couch, he placed his fingers underneath her chin and gently tipped her head toward him. "Because why?"

She bit her lip, releasing a shaky exhale. "*Midnights at Pemberley* isn't forever. Our contracts will end. We'll move on to the next show, and even though you're stuck with me as a friend, we can't guarantee that the distance and changes won't drive us apart. We don't get full-time steadiness. It's all temporary. And if any part of our new jobs affects us, everything could crumble. You and Michelle didn't survive it."

His head was spinning.

She made sense, sure. But distance didn't work out for people when they weren't willing to make equal effort. She had to have known that wouldn't be the case for them. "I hear you, but it's not the same. Michelle and I had different issues. Plus, I was with her for almost two years, and I didn't experience a fraction of what I feel with you. That alone says something."

Her eyes were a little sad.

"It's too big of a risk on so many levels. What if I want to move back to London? What if...what if I decide I want a more consistent lifestyle? I've always wanted a family and a quiet life away from all the spotlight and chaos of our jobs. Your life is here. It's always been here."

His choice was inevitable—he'd choose Willa every day and follow her to the ends of the earth if that's what she needed from him. But he had no idea how to convince her of that. He had no inkling of how to explain that he was convinced his heart would only ever beat for her without blurting that he was head over heels in love with her.

"I want a family, too. I want all of that. And as long as you don't force me to start drinking afternoon tea, I'd go wherever you want me."

She tilted her head, looking at him like she couldn't believe the words out of his mouth.

"You say that now, and I believe you mean it, but when the time comes, it might not be what you want. Not to mention the fact that I would never force you to. I'd feel guilty about it. You're too magnetic and brilliant to ever leave the industry behind. The loss would be tremendous."

It took everything in him not to reach forward and kiss her like the world was ending. His words clearly weren't enough—they weren't selling his feelings like he wanted them to. Maybe he'd have to show her. But he didn't want to scare her away, either. Intimacy was acceptable as long as she was playing a part, but he couldn't guess where Willa stood on that matter outside of acting. He didn't want to push past the walls she'd built for herself. Not without her permission. Her certainty.

But God, he wanted to somehow take what was inside of him and weave it into the very fabric of her being, so she'd know. So, she'd believe that he'd never been this serious about anything before.

She was *it* for him. She'd always be. She wouldn't be forcing him to go anywhere when he was certain he only ever wanted to be beside her. It'd be impossible to be apart. For crying out loud, he couldn't even last a week.

His adoration wasn't fleeting. It was infinite.

Ethan reached for her and intertwined their fingers. "Can I ask you something? Yes or no. Just answer the question."

She bobbed her head.

"Put aside everything else for a second. If you had things your way. If you knew, with utmost certainty, that we would last, even with distance, would you be with me?"

"It's more complicated than that."

He swallowed a lump in his throat, the finality in her tone made his chest grow heavy. "Willa, *please,* yes or no."

"Yes."

His eyes stung. Warmth blasted into his heart. "Then tell me what I can do to convince you that this could be good for us—that we could be good *together,* that it could last. I'll do anything,

Willa. I appreciate the faith you have in me and how you see my abilities, but you're more important."

Sliding closer to him on the couch, she lifted her other hand to Ethan's cheek and traced his skin tenderly with her thumb. "That's the problem. I think deep down, I know that you'd take big leaps to convince me. I know how much you give to other people. But I'm scared—terrified, Ethan because I know that if something happened and we went our separate ways, it'd break me that you were no longer in my life. My therapist said I could survive anything, but she was wrong. I could lose so many people, and I'd be fine. I'd move on eventually, but you—you've carved a space for yourself that's so crucial in my life that if anything happened to us, I'd be walking around with a perpetual hole in my chest."

He didn't know what to say. He moved their entangled hands to his lips and pressed a delicate kiss to her wrist. "You've done the same for me, Wills. It's how I know that we'd fight like hell to keep what we have. Distance, hectic schedules, calm, quiet nights, I know we'd make it work. Please take a risk on us. We could take things slow, give it a try, see what unravels, and how we feel. And if we see that it's not working, or if it changes us too much, then we'll stop, and nothing will shift between us. We could still be friends. I promise."

"What does giving it a try look like?"

"However you want it to."

"You could get impatient with me."

He shook his head hard. "I'll be as patient as you need."

She sighed somberly, the sound so small, it broke him a little. "Everyone I've been with has said that."

"Well, they're all morons, and I'm selfishly grateful. I didn't know I had jealousy in me until the thought of you being with someone else crossed my mind. I couldn't share you with another man. I couldn't stand the thought of someone else being your person."

The sentiment made her smile, the honeyed awe-struck wonder in her eyes making its gradual return. He wanted to ask about Alden and what he'd done specifically, knowing he was the worst of them and that whatever it was, it had messed with her the most.

He swallowed. "Will you tell me what Alden did? So, I know never to make that same mistake."

She huffed. "You'd never."

Ethan stayed silent for a beat, unsure of what to say, wondering if she'd continue. She sighed heavily and put her face in her hand like she was stabilizing herself. He waited patiently.

She arched back, taking the cup in her hand and drinking from her tea. She set it down and looked at him. "Both Jesse and Robert got tired of waiting, so they dumped me early on," she started.

Well, fuck both Jesse and Robert, he thought.

"But it'd been five-ish months with Alden, and he would frequently say things like 'I believe demisexuality is real, but maybe you should just try to, 'break the dam and all.'" Those must have been his exact words because she emphasized them with air quotes.

"He said it so much that I started feeling like there was something seriously wrong with me. I was thirty-one at the time, and in my head about everything. I talked about it with my therapist often, and I kept feeling like his words just wouldn't leave me alone—that maybe he was right. He also kept saying how it made no sense that I felt so comfortable using my body the way I did while performing but couldn't do the same with men I was dating. As if it was the same thing."

She shook her head, willing something out, he assumed.

"No one knows this but my therapist and Sahar."

Ethan guided his hand to her cheek. "You're safe with me, Willa. Whatever you say, I'm taking it to my grave. And if you can't tell me right now, that's okay, too. I want to know so I can understand how I can be good to you. But if it's too much for you to say it out loud, then I get it. I'll follow your lead and all your cues."

"Thank you," she said first. "I might as well just say it. Plus, I know you, and I know that even after I reassured you at Miles' party, you probably played it over in your mind."

He agreed. He had done that.

She continued. "I think, to some degree, I just wanted to have something so badly that I sort of convinced myself he could be the one because he'd stuck out longer than the rest. So, I started persuading myself that I owed it to him to see if he was right. And maybe even to myself—to just get it over with because it kept gnawing at me."

Willa paused, taking another deep breath. "So, one day when we were hanging out, I let him touch me...And I hated every minute of it, tried my hardest not to cry, not because it hurt or anything but because I felt so disturbed by him touching me like that. I should've known before, really, because even kissing him wasn't enjoyable. After a few seconds, I asked him to stop, and he was an asshole about it..."

She worried at her lower lip before continuing. "He pulled away, thankfully, but then he basically mocked me. His exact words were, 'You need a good fuck, Willa. You need to grow up because you're not gonna get over this shit if you don't.' And then he left. I broke up with him after that."

Fuck. A lump housed itself sharply against his pipes. He tried to speak, but her name came out in a croak.

He tried again. "Willa, I'm so sorry." He pulled her into his chest and held her there. He didn't know what else to do. "I'm so sorry," he repeated.

Willa straightened herself but stayed right beside him, mere millimeters away. "That's just it, Ethan. It's human to get tired of waiting and…"

He shook his head a bit too aggressively, but the thought alone ripped him from the inside. "Willa, stop, *please.* Yeah, men fucking suck sometimes. I'm not above it, and I'm not going to make myself sound like a saint when lord knows what's crossed my mind when I've watched you dance. The things I've thought about and the ways I've wanted you. But beyond anything else—in spite of all my feelings and urges—you're my best friend *first.* I wouldn't forgive myself if I did something to push you away. And I know that might not be easy for you to believe, but I'll prove it. I'll be as patient as you need. I'll do whatever you want me to, but I can't keep pretending I only see you as a friend."

She nodded. "There's something else."

"What is it?"

"Your fans."

"My fans?" he questioned. "What about them?"

"The public in general, really. I'm pretty private when it comes to my personal life on social media, you know that. I post here and there, but I'm not as active when it comes to my private life, nor am I as known as you are, thankfully. I like it that way. But you've been around much longer. And I know how you're going to counter all this because I know you, but I don't think I have the willpower to be called a gold-digger or a leech. I know you understand my hesitations and fears to a degree, but I can't stand claims that I'm using you and God knows what else. I'm too damn anxious and insecure. I realize I chose the wrong career, but alas…"

His eyes went wide. None of this would've ever crossed his mind, but he could see where Willa was coming from. He hated it but understood it, nonetheless. His fans could be hostile at times, and he wasn't sure how to handle that either, advised by his publicist to ignore it as often as possible.

"The ones who'd talk would talk no matter who you were. A bunch of people would love it, and a select few would loathe it. There's no rhyme or reason. I am sorry about that, and I wish I could control it. But please don't let that be a reason we stop ourselves from trying. *Please.* We can keep it as private as you want. We hang out often anyway. It wouldn't look any differently to those who don't know us, no matter how closely they pay attention. All of this—we'll...we'll figure it out."

She took a breath, a sadness he couldn't place making its way into her eyes again. "I know. I do. I'm just scared. Please don't break my heart," she begged, and at those very words, the pain in her voice, the fear in her eyes, his heart sank. He knew exactly what she meant by it, too.

He lifted his hand and pressed it to her cheek. "I'd demolish my own if I ever hurt you. You're safe with me, Willa. I promise."

"Can we keep it between us for now?" she asked.

"Yeah, but you're going to tell Sahar, aren't you? Isn't that a girl code thing?"

The question made her chuckle. "Yeah, that's true, not a girl code, but I'm also sure she already knows what's happening. Now that I think of it, Christian probably does, too, but I guess, just...not everyone? Not yet, at least?"

"If that's what you want," he replied, thinking through the next question he wanted to ask, hoping and praying that it wouldn't come off wrong. "What are you comfortable with?"

"What do you mean?"

"In terms of intimacy. I'm not talking about sex but other things. I know performing is different, but can I kiss you when we're alone?"

Her dimpled smile was so perfect that it shattered him.

"You better kiss me," Willa declared, inching closer.

He could feel the canyon carved by her doubts slowly shrinking. Lips to lips, thighs to thighs, whatever came from her willingness to fill the space between them, Ethan Everett knew that he was about to become the happiest man in the world.

20

WILLA

Willa's heart raced. Ethan cupped her face, his eyes illuminating with a gleam she hadn't seen before. The heavy tethers holding her together snapped one by one—restraint, hesitation, doubt, and uncertainty. For a moment, nothing mattered the way Ethan did. Or, rather, that was always the case, and she was brave enough to admit to it now.

There was plenty of time to play back the poetic promises he made—to perhaps question and sit with the dread of how it could all fall to pieces. That was the kind of self-deprecation her brain held a master's degree in. But right now, inches apart, all she wanted to do was press her lips to his. To kiss him, not as Elizabeth, but as Willa. His touch against her cheek burned through her. She blinked, once, twice, drew forward, and rested her forehead against his.

"We're really doing this?" she asked.

The brilliance in his smile could ignite the entirety of New York City.

"Yeah, beautiful, we are," he confirmed, his voice unbearably tender and affirmative.

And then his lips were on hers, languid and gentle, parting and pulling with a softness she could blanket herself in.

His kisses were tormentingly dazzling in the frenzied fury of their earlier performance, delicious even, now that she was being truthful with herself. But this—this dance was theirs and theirs alone. He was utterly in tune with her body, so methodic in his attention that it enraptured her.

Keeping her body upright would've required enormous effort if they hadn't been sitting. She would've melted. She was already halfway there, stunned by the fact that kissing someone could feel like this.

He wordlessly asked for permission, undoubtedly wanting more but leaving the decision in her hands. Willa boldly darted her tongue in response, swapping tender tugs for more hunger and heat. A low groan reverberated from somewhere deep inside his throat, pleasing her to no end with the knowledge that she had been the one to elicit it.

She bit his lower lip, pulling another satisfied sound out from him. Willa draped her legs over his, and he wrapped his arms tightly around her waist, squeezing her closer to him. She could feel what she was doing to him, the substantial proof of his desires, dizzying and gloriously intoxicating.

Ethan's mouth moved against her with more fire, and he quickened his pace while still maintaining respectable boundaries—too many if he asked her. She didn't need him sticking to just her lips. She wanted, *needed* him elsewhere. Her own feverish longings were now addicting. His fingers trailed to her hair, down to her shoulder, back up toward her neck and jaw.

She'd never had a first kiss like this before. Scratch that, she'd never had *any* kiss like this before.

She'd never felt this safe and revered in every way.

They parted for a beat, breathless and flushed, foreheads pressed against one another. He stole another quick kiss, prompting Willa to giggle. His eyes held her, impossibly over-whelming and gorgeously warm.

"You're... you're something else, Willa. You're everything," he rasped.

The hunger in his eyes burned a hole through her chest. "Is that so?"

He tipped her chin and kissed her again, once, twice. Slow and sweet. He didn't need words to answer. His lips were meticulously drafting an entire novel. "Was all of this okay?" he questioned.

She couldn't help but smile at that—the amenity in his genuine and selfless care. "It was more than okay. I don't want you to tiptoe around me, Ethan. I might not be ready for certain things right now, but you don't have to be such a gentleman. I feel safer with you than I have with anyone else, plus *I've* been wanting to kiss you for quite some time now. You don't have to ask."

His eyes crinkled at the edges, and one of her favorite smiles made its way onto his face. "So, if I want to pull you inside my dressing room after a show and make out with you until your lips are swollen, I don't have to ask?"

She shook her head with a laugh. No, he definitely didn't have to ask. And God, now she wanted that—badly. "You don't have to ask. You don't have to stick solely to my lips either," she added.

He swallowed abruptly, his eyes blown wide. "Are you telling me the three little moles against your collarbone aren't off-limits?"

Her lips parted. "Oh, we're *that* observant," she noted.

"Willa, I wouldn't even know where to begin with what I've observed."

Her breath hitched. She wouldn't know where to begin either. His neck, his hundred-watt smile, those damn biceps and forearms. "No, they aren't off-limits. Not to you," she assured.

She was selfish with her declaration, too. She'd happily give Ethan what she wanted to take, the places she wanted to plant her lips—to lick and bite and kiss without restraint.

He lowered his head suddenly, carefully moved her shirt aside, and planted his lips against the moles on her collarbone. Lingering there, he kissed her softly, then skated his lips toward her throat. A low whimper threatened to emanate out of her, but she repressed it. His fingers moved to her jaw. His mouth was all over, avidly taking from wherever she'd permit.

He met her lips again, dazed and warm. They stayed like that for a few moments again, kissing like their lives depended on it.

He nipped at her bottom lip. "Stay, please. I'll take the couch," he asked breathlessly.

"I want to, but I need to shower before I can sleep."

He peppered kisses along her face as he spoke. "You know I have a shower, right? And, also, an extra, unused loofah. You can have it."

"You have an extra loofah because?" she questioned, planting a kiss against his nose.

"I buy things in twos, just in case I need a new one."

She laughed, moving away for a second to look him in the eyes. "We live in one of the biggest cities in the world. Are you scared Target is going to run out of loofahs?" she mocked sweetly. Frankly, it was adorable, but she loved riling him up.

"No, it was all a part of my devious plan to get you to stay here."

"That's less concerning than you're secretly worried there will be shortages of basic human necessities."

"Is that a yes, then?"

She smiled. "I'm going to have to borrow your largest T-shirt. None of the fitted stuff that puts your biceps on blast."

He hummed, moving his hands up and down her arms. "What does that mean?" he teased.

"You know damn well what it means."

He smirked, smoldering almost. "I didn't think you'd be checking me out, but I'm happy to hear those bench presses aren't for nothing."

She kicked her legs off him and stood up, holding her hand out to him.

"Only your arms," she lied. If she could wink, she would have. "Now get me that shirt."

Ethan laced their fingers together and led her to his bedroom.

"Also, you're not sleeping on the sofa. We can both fit on your giant bed."

"You sure? I honestly don't mind. I'd prefer you were comfortable."

"I'll be more comfortable knowing I'm not stealing your bed. I am, however, slightly concerned about your other girl," she pointed to Tulip, sprawled along the middle, sound asleep without a care in the world.

He shrugged off her concern, released her hand, and headed toward his wardrobe. "Tulip loves you. You're fine."

"Yes, but she's never had to share you with me. Am I going to wake up with claw marks on my face?"

He chuckled, pulling out an oversized grey T-shirt and handing it to her with a kiss on her forehead. "You're not going to wake up with claw marks on your face."

Willa ambled back to his living room for her tote bag, then reached for a pair of new knickers, thanking her past self for always being prepared with show essentials. She should start carrying pajamas, too.

He came out of his bathroom, offered her the new loofah,

and opened a cabinet inside the wall to hand her a clean, beige towel.

"I also have brand new toothbrushes," he mentioned.

"I have my toothbrush," she replied.

He tipped her chin up, gazing into her eyes with fond excitement. "I want you to have one here."

A laugh escaped her. "One day, and we're already talking toothbrushes."

"I'm telling you. It's all part of my master plan," he said, inching forward for another kiss.

"Sea salt and cedar is an impressive choice for body wash. It's fainter than your spicy leather cologne," she asserted, stepping back into his room with nothing but his T-shirt.

Ethan was sitting on the bench at the foot of his bed, looking down at his phone. He set it aside and extended his arms out for her. She stepped in between his legs and wrapped her arms around his neck.

"My spicy leather cologne?" he repeated.

The words sounded so silly coming from his lips, his voice a little gruff, slightly tired.

"I don't know how else to describe it. Your cologne—the one you usually wear. It smells like leather and a spice of some sort. Therefore, spicy leather."

His hands tracked along her arms. "And are we a fan of said spicy leather?"

She bobbed her head up and down. "Big fan—the body wash, too."

He pulled her tightly against him and held her. "It smells even better on you."

"Does it now?"

He looked up at her, eyes wide and sparkling. "Yeah, a close second to the floral notes in your perfume."

"Jasmine, rose, and gillyflower, according to the bottle's description," she specified.

"What on earth is a gillyflower?" he asked.

She shrugged. "I have no idea. I'm not even sure why I have the specific ingredients memorized."

"It's doing its job. I'm surprised it's not lilac-scented."

She tilted her head, wordlessly asking him for clarification.

"It's your favorite flower, isn't it?" he questioned.

Had she told him that? When would that have come up in any of their conversations? It was, yes, courtesy of her mum's obsession since she was little—both the color and the scent, really.

"I told you that?"

He shook his head. "No, I just assumed since you usually have the soap in your bathroom and the candles burning when I'm over."

Huh. Christ, he had been observant, and it sent a prickle of elation down her spine.

"Your assumption is correct. You can thank Beatrix Davidian for that—we have lilac trees in our backyard, and she stops to smell them every time we pass one. She also keeps candles around for when they aren't in bloom."

His lips curved into a sweet, satisfied smile. "I'll jot that down for when I eventually meet her." He rose from her seat, and she swapped with him, turning to pet Tulip as he left to shower.

She browsed through the comments Sahar had curated, then finally braced herself to open social media and focus *only* on the messages and tags from people she knew and followed.

Clicking through their stories one by one, she saw that all their cast members had shared the photograph Sahar had posted on her feed. She sent each of them a small reply and commented underneath the actual photo with, "I love you to the bloody moon, you bewitching creature." She refreshed the app, noticing Ethan's icon (an unfairly *hot* promotional still of him as Darcy) pop up with a new story.

He had also shared Sahar's post ten minutes ago while she'd been in the shower. *Proud and grateful to share the stage with an absolute powerhouse of a performer and my best friend.* She turned to Tulip, who was now on her back, paws in mid-air, belly up. "He's something, isn't he, girl? How do I not fall madly in love with a man like that?" she added, rubbing the spot underneath Tulip's chin.

She replied to Ethan's story with a sobbing emoji and a purple heart, set her phone down, and released a purposeful exhale. Right now, isolated and alone in his bedroom, everything felt right. She could stay like this, in the shadows where the outside world had no say in their relationship. But aggravating thoughts tried to crash through her barricaded happiness anyway.

People are nice right now but just wait. The horrible comments are out there. Sahar is shielding you from them. You don't deserve to be up on that stage. You haven't earned it. You don't deserve Ethan's love. You're a nobody; he's one of Broadway's biggest stars. He'll get tired of you—your face, your body, your personality. Whatever opportunity you get after this show, it'll be because of Ethan, not you.

Willa shut her eyes, taking in another deep inhale and releasing a forceful exhale. Inhale, exhale, repeat. None of that tonight—*please.* The noises inside her head were too loud, too demanding. Ethan's neighborhood was quieter, but there should've been some noise still. Where was a fire engine or loud group chattering when you needed them most?

She willed herself to focus on what she could control—the present, the truth behind Ethan's eyes, his kindness, *his friendship* above all things. How he cared for her. His innate goodness.

Then she unlocked her phone and put The National on shuffle. The first few notes of "You Were a Kindness" bustled through the speakers. Appropriate and perfectly on cue, universe.

Who helped regulate an emotional downward spiral better than the Sad Dads? No one.

She looked around his room from the spot she sat in, taking note of how organized he was. His house was always neat, but this was her first time seeing the inside of his bedroom. The dark green walls were a pleasant touch, and most of his mahogany furniture had a homey feel. He had more things in his living room than in the bedroom, but a scenic painting of Italy hung above his bed.

Ethan ambled back in just as the song ended and switched to "Light Years." He wore his glasses again, stimulating a somersault in her chest and a massive grin over which she had zero control. At least she didn't have to hide it now.

He arched an eyebrow. "What?"

"Did I ever tell you I have a thing for men in glasses?"

The most enchanting chuckle escaped his throat, a wildly picturesque smile on full display. "What else do you have a thing for?"

She rose from the footboard bench. "Forearms."

He took in her words, eyes darting up and down her frame. "You already told me that one. What else?"

She smiled. "That's all you're getting now."

"I'll take it. Which side of the bed do you want?"

"Whichever one you don't usually sleep on?"

"The right."

"Works for me. If murderers come in, they're taking you first."

He laughed, drawing the covers and handing her a new pillowcase that'd been sitting atop them.

"Are you a blanket hog?" he asked.

"Not that I know of. Do you snore?"

He shook his head. "I've never been told I do, so I'm going to say no."

"We'll see," she drew her shoulders inward a bit, "I...I, uh, might kick you."

His eyes widened adorably. "Aha, ladies and gentlemen, we've uncovered a flaw. And you were worried about Tulip causing problems."

She tried not to smirk. "*Sometimes,* I talk..."

"Now that I can't wait for," he emphasized with a sly smile.

He kicked off his socks and got underneath the covers; Tulip made her way to a spot next to his feet.

"Does she not go up higher?" Willa asked.

"Only in the morning if I snooze my alarm. Sometimes, she'll go to the living room in the middle of the night. Depends on her mood."

Willa joined him in bed, sat upright, and stared at him. The whirlwind of tonight's revelations dawned on her once more, flirty banter taking a backseat to trepidation.

He must've noticed the change in her expression because he straightened in his reclined position immediately. "Willa?"

She was fine. She would be fine. This was Ethan. She was safe with him. She'd always be safe with him. "Right, sorry. I'm okay. I just...it keeps hitting me that we're doing this, and I start freaking out."

He took her hand in his, sweeping his thumb against her knuckles. "What are you freaking out about? How can I help?"

She blinked rapidly, trying to steady her heartbeat. "I'm okay. I promise. It's just—it's you and me and this. I'm not used to it, but I want it. My brain is going to illogical places."

"I can still go to the couch. I promise I don't mind. I've fallen asleep there countless times. It's comfortable."

She shook her head. "No, I want you with me. Welcome to

my brain. One minute, it's fine, and the next, it's conjured up a zillion scenarios that make no sense."

He drew his lips to her palm and kissed her there. Another at her wrist. "You can talk to me about those scenarios, too."

"Yeah, I'd rather we not go there," she admitted.

He drew his lips higher, kissing along her forearm, up toward her bicep.

She smiled easily, allowing herself to focus on the man sitting before her. Ethan kissed her like she was the most precious thing in the world, and she felt it every time his mouth touched her somewhere.

"I'm not going to wake up with both you and your cat spooning me in the middle of the night, am I?" she asked.

He laughed, placing kisses along her neck now. "I don't move at night unless I need to actually get up. So, no, but if you want me to, come closer."

She raised an eyebrow. "How do you not move?"

"Some of us don't do acrobatics in our sleep."

Valid. "Do you dream?"

"Occasionally," he answered.

Willa bobbed her head up and down repeatedly, taking it all in. "This arrangement could work for me personally, not sure about you."

He smiled and tipped his head higher, pressing his lips softly to her temple. "Kick me all you want, Wills, just stay."

"What time are you going to the gym tomorrow? I'm assuming you're not missing another day," she added.

"Seven. Want to come with?"

"Nope, but I'll head out with you and go home."

He made the silliest pouting face, an expression she didn't know he was capable of. "I won't be long. We can go get breakfast afterward."

"Let's do lunch instead? I should do laundry, and I'll probably try to get some extra runs of the numbers just in case."

"Sure. Did you want something specific?"

"Yes, I thought about the jalapeño poppers at Blazing Salmon earlier today, so now I need them."

He nodded, his face so serene and welcoming, so effortless to look at and want. "Sushi it is then. Twelve-thirty?"

She slid under the covers and positioned herself comfortably on the pillow. "Works for me."

Ethan removed his glasses, set them on his bedside table, and did the same. Willa looked at him for a beat, lingering for a few moments longer than she should've. She wanted to say more and fight against the exhaustion that was taking over her. She wanted to say that maybe she'd be okay with him holding her. But she settled with, "Goodnight, Ethan."

"Goodnight, beautiful."

She could get used to this, comfortably shutting her eyes next to her best friend after a wildly sweet endearment left his lips.

21

ETHAN

The early morning with Willa flew by too soon for his liking, but it dragged afterward.

He was glad the lobby in his apartment was empty because he could steal a quick kiss from her before they went their separate ways. They'd gotten ready together, fed Tulip, and left the house.

It had been perfect.

Annoyingly, training at the gym passed slower than usual, and so did the remaining hours at home, where he had no idea what to do with himself after his post-workout shower.

He'd gone to the highest-rated florist shop nearby and ordered a lilac-mix bouquet, thankful the flowers were now in bloom and scheduled delivery to the theatre two hours before their call time. It'd be there when Willa arrived, and even though they were meant to keep things clandestine at work, this was a small, subtle way for him to congratulate her debut.

He would've done it sooner if yesterday hadn't been so hectic.

Now that he was set to see Willa again, Ethan was buzzing with serotonin. He stood outside the Blazing Salmon, leaning against red brick walls with one foot kicked up. He spotted her at a distance, skin glowing with the sunlight and her long hair flowing down in its natural wavy form.

He reminded himself not to kiss her, to lean in only for a quick hug, and not to linger no matter how badly he wanted to.

Ethan didn't always get recognized on the street. The perks of an intensely bustling city meant that people were either glued to their phones, absorbed in their own conversations, or focused solely on where they needed to go. If anything, recognition often occurred near the theatre, mostly on quieter afternoons. Sometimes at Amanda's Coffee, more than anywhere else. Still, he shouldn't take the risk.

His breath harnessed in his throat as she got closer, and he caught her beaming smile in full effect. She had on a pair of light-wash ripped jeans, white sneakers, and a black, short-sleeve crop top with her bag slung across her chest.

Willa could wear a burlap potato sack, and he'd probably still fawn over her.

He outstretched his arm, somewhat grateful for the bag's intrusion in their embrace. She wrapped her arms around his frame briefly before letting go and giving him a massive, toothy grin. "Guess who did her laundry *and* folded everything back into its place. Honestly, real proud of myself there."

He swung the restaurant door toward them and stepped aside to let her in first. "That's way more than what I accomplished. I fell asleep on the couch for two hours."

"Mate—how?" *Mate.* Sometimes, he forgot how British Willa could be. He loved it.

He bounced his shoulders. "Because naps rule?"

"Yeah, like twenty minutes maybe, but two bloody hours? That's mad."

The restaurant's front desk host showed up to her podium and broke their conversation. "Hello. Table for two?" she asked.

They both confirmed.

"Booth or bar?"

Ethan and Willa looked at each other, generally preferring a bar in such cases to not wait as long, but a booth could be more private, better for the conversations they'd want to have.

"Booth," he answered for them.

The host took two menus from the stack in front of her and motioned for them to follow. "The server will be with you soon," she noted, leaving them the menus.

They took their seats, somewhat secluded but near four teenagers who might've been ditching school and an older couple on the other side of them. They generally stuck to the same things on the menu, so neither of them looked at it.

"I need to get it on record that this isn't an official first date," he started in a whisper, trying to judge her reaction.

"I didn't assume it was," she responded casually.

He kicked her foot gently at the bottom of the table. "Right, but I want you to know that I'm thinking about it. There's a place near my parents' cabin where I grew up, and I want to take you there for the official first one."

She smiled a little wickedly. "Is that where you take all your paramours, Ethan Everett?"

He rolled his eyes, taking note of the way she said paramours, mocking his use of it in the show. "I've never taken anyone there, which is why I want to take you."

"You had to go and make it sweet? Dammit, go on then—tell me the story," she declared.

He clicked his tongue. "Not yet."

She narrowed her eyes. "Well, you're no fun. Now I'm going to picture all sorts of weird things."

He laughed louder than he intended to. "Patience is a virtue."

"No, patience is life's most enraging plot device."

Their waiter came in just in time, took their drink orders as well as food, and left them in comfortable silence. God, he wanted to reach over and hold her hand, but he stopped himself. Someday, he'd be able to do that, and he made a mental vow to himself that he'd never let go.

"It's taking everything in me not to hold your hand right now," he whispered.

She smiled amiably at him. "I know, I want you to, but not right now," she paused for a beat. "There is something I want to ask you, though."

"What is it?"

The waiter returned with their drinks, Dr. Pepper and water for both. She took a quick sip before speaking. "I gave you some hefty details about my exes, but all you've ever told me about Michelle is that you were long-distance for a couple of years. Why did you two break up?"

He swallowed a lump in his throat, gulped down some water, then squared himself. He looked around the restaurant, taking in the noise of their surroundings, determining what he could say aloud. Surely, these people didn't even know him. There was no need for him to be paranoid, but he wanted to respect her wishes, just in case. He lowered his voice.

"I was at a rough spot when I met her. *Detective Vice* had been canceled, and my agent didn't have any leads. I'd also been super drained. It was a brief period where everything in my career felt grim. So, while we were dating, she was there for me and understood me because we were both in similar boats. Conveniently, a month later, we both booked separate gigs. That's when I did the run at West End. While I was there, she was filming a show in Vancouver. We'd been together for almost a year at that point, and long-distance was going fine. She visited once. I went to see her after my run ended. But then she cheated on me with her co-star."

Willa's jaw dropped.

He continued. "She told me about it, so I sort of took her honesty as genuine regret. That's when I was cast in *Fired Up*, and I went to film on location in Vancouver, so we got to physically be together for a while. She seemed remorseful, so we kept things going. But as my project wrapped, she cheated again with another co-star, and that time, when she told me, she ended things because she wanted to be with him."

"Are you kidding me?"

"Nope," he said, leaning back in his seat and taking the Dr. Pepper in his hand.

Fury filled her eyes. "Ethan, tell me you're joking right now."

"Want me to lie to you?"

Her cheeks went fiery red, the blush and natural anger blending to a raging hue. He hated it. "She cheated on you again after you took her back? With another co-star? On the same show?"

"She was in a bad place, too. I—"

Willa cut him off. "Don't you dare defend her. Once, fine, *maybe* you could've used that reasoning, but twice? She made a choice, and it was a really shitty one. And on you, of all people? God, I hope I never work with her."

The waiter came by with their food and extra spicy mayo for Willa. She stared at it. "I'm so furious I don't know how to eat."

Great, now look what you've done. You've made her angry with your sob story. "Wills, look at me."

She looked up at him, chopsticks propped up in her hand like some sort of weapon.

"I'm not hung up on it. Did it make me more skeptical and distrustful? Yes. But frankly, that's exactly why I had no interest in anyone else until you. And in that regard, I trust you fully. Now, please take the first bite so I don't feel like I've ruined our day."

She shook her head, shut her eyes for a beat, then reached for the grilled appetizer. "I'm still mad," she stated, popping it into her mouth aggressively and then covering it with her hand to chew.

"Welcome to the club. If I ever see your ex anywhere near me, I'm punching his veneered teeth out of his mouth."

Her eyes widened. She swallowed the piece she'd been chewing and shrugged. "Go for it. Just don't get caught. We don't need you getting arrested then going from Broadway's darling to Broadway's bad boy..." Her thoughts trailed to a place that brought on a mischievous smile. "Although, you know what, I'd still dig Broadway's bad boy, too. Go forth. You have permission to defend my honor."

He made a bowing gesture with his hands. "Your wish is my command."

She reached for another specialty roll and stopped before putting it inside her mouth. "But in all seriousness. I really am angry. And I'm sorry. You didn't deserve that."

"Thanks," he said, unsure how else to respond. They ate the rest of their food during a brief silence before changing the conversation to ranking the spicy mayo at all their favorite Japanese restaurants.

HIS DRESSING room had been fully open when Willa strode inside and closed the door behind her. Her eyes flickered even from afar. A reaction, he hoped, was from the flowers. Ethan stood up from the couch, dropping his Switch on the small table.

She flung herself into his arms, full force, holding him tightly with her arms encircled around his neck. He inhaled the delicious notes of her perfume, savoring the feel of her so close to him. "What's this for?" he mused in a low whisper.

Willa faced him then, her one hand traveling through his hair while another came to rest against his chest. He burned white hot where she touched him. "You had to know how much those flowers would mean to me. What the hell am I going to do with you, Ethan? When did you even have the time?"

He held her hand against his lips and placed a kiss on her wrist. Another on the tip of her nose. One more on her forehead. He returned his mouth to hers, tracing her soft, sweet lips with languid brushes. "Sometime in between my nap and meeting you in the afternoon," he answered. "I'll get you flowers every day if it means you'll charge into my dressing room like this."

"Christ, have you always been this romantic, or did playing Darcy somehow alter your brain chemistry?"

He released a closed-mouth laugh. "That's all you, beautiful. You're the one who's bringing all this out of me." If she hadn't decided to keep their relationship a secret, he'd have confessed every one of his feelings. He wasn't testing the waters, even though they'd decided to *try,* he knew where he stood.

He loved Willa more than anything in the world, but he understood that she wasn't ready for that confession yet.

She sighed with deep contentment, then sprung herself into his chest again. He squeezed her close, trailing his fingers along her back. They stayed that way for a minute or two, rocking back and forth against each other in a languid, slow reprieve.

"I don't know what to say." She glided her fingers against his cheekbones. "But...my heart feels like it could erupt, and I'm trying really hard not to cry right now because thank you simply doesn't suffice. I know they're just flowers, but it means everything to know you heard me—that you've always heard me."

"And I always will," he promised.

She reached down to the silver watch on his wrist and

checked the time. "I have ten minutes before I need to start hair and makeup."

He beelined to the door, locked it, and hurried toward her lips.

Ethan kissed her deeply, drinking in the giggle that cascaded out of her. Willa swung her arm against his neck, her hands knotting in his hair. She met his lips with equal fervor, identical desperation, tugging and pulling so exquisitely he could swear he was dreaming.

22

WILLA

Sahar looked up from her phone when Willa sauntered back in, eyes widening like a mother who knew what her kid was up to. "For two people trying to keep things a secret, you're both shit at it."

Willa turned to the mirror on their table. She'd fixed her hair when she left his dressing room. "You live with me. You notice the smallest changes."

"Sweet baby child, every one of our friends would be able to tell if you suddenly walked out of Ethan's locked door with heart eyes on full display."

Willa leaned closer to her reflection. "What on earth are heart eyes? They look normal."

Sahar pressed on, raising her eyebrows in a silent scold.

Willa tried to suppress a grin.

"Naomi is going to know the second she takes one look at the two of you when she's back. She and Innila have a bet going."

Willa gaped her. "You're all terrible people, gambling on our relationship."

"It's because we love you."

Willa sat down on her chair and reached for her face primer.

Sahar let out a laugh and turned over to face the mirror. She took her phone and asked Siri to play from a curated playlist titled "Something About Silly Love Songs."

Elton John's "Tiny Dancer" suitably came on first.

Willa gave her a knowing look. "You're the worst," she joked.

"I'm the best," Sahar countered.

They had almost finished getting ready when Greta Henderson came in. "Knock, knock."

The women lit up and then jumped out of their seats to hug her. "Gretaaaaaa," they both called out excitedly.

"Hi, my loves," she said in their clasp.

One of the things Willa appreciated most about this company was that Jeff and Greta were involved long after they had to be. They both attended multiple shows and visited frequently, making the cast and crew feel like a family. "Dina had such amazing things to say about you, I had to come and see for myself. My sister is around here somewhere," she said to Willa.

"Gah! Thank you. You've been so missed."

Greta smiled. "Also, Dina is wondering if you'd like to take over the show's account tomorrow. It could bring some exciting buzz since it's a two-show day. It was supposed to be Tanya, but we could hand it over to you and highlight what it's like when an understudy goes on for the principal role."

"Ooh, Wills, you should. People are genuinely lovely during the takeovers. I had a blast when I did it," Sahar noted.

Willa thought it over for a beat. *Would it be too stressful on top of two performances?* It could keep her distracted. It might even be fun. She hated social media, but she could control parts of it this way. She probably should get it over with, too, and maybe it'd help later on. She nodded in agreement. "Is Tanya okay with it?"

"Oh, yeah," Greta noted. "I spoke to her earlier."

"Sure, yeah. I'll do it then."

Sahar faced Willa when Greta left the room. "This is also the best time to do it, babe. People are apparently obsessed with the way Ethan grazes your thigh."

Willa gave her a pronounced look. That detail hadn't been part of the comments Sahar had sent her. "And how is it any different from the way he touches Naomi?"

Sahar brought her hands forward in a nonchalance gesture. "No idea, but I overheard it when I went out to sign last night and then saw a few comments in the show's Subreddit."

Willa laughed. "I don't even know what to say to that."

"You have nice thighs, boo. Let the man appreciate them."

"So does Naomi."

"True, but Ethan's not in love with her."

Willa gave her a sidelong glance.

Sahar arched her eyebrow. "You know I'm right."

Willa shook her head, leaving the conversation at that.

ETHAN WAS LIGHTER during this performance. He moved with her far more comfortably, like on the days when she'd force him to run a choreography with her, alone in one of their living rooms or the middle of the stage during rehearsals. Now that most of their feelings had been worked through, the nerves had converted into an effortless contentment that she was confident brought out better performances from both of them.

When it came to the kiss in "Marry Me" again, she could swear Darcy was somehow even more feverish, crushing her lips with the force of a man who was agonizingly besotted. It was a spellbinding, gorgeously heated moment with what she was sure was Ethan's longing piercing through.

He was even beaming during their bows, his smile so big that there was no mistaking the pride and joy in his demeanor.

How she wished for a single moment that their cast members knew because restricting herself from leaping into his embrace was becoming a herculean task.

Yet, while she was thinking of it, the next minute, Ethan swept her in his arms, spinning her around like they were the only two people backstage. The sounds beside them muddled, and then clear laughter dissolved into howls and whistles. "You two are unreal together," she heard Declan call out.

"Respectfully, fuck you for taking away my dance partner, Everett. I'll get you back for this," Miles remarked lovingly.

Ethan set Willa down, and she swung her arm around his torso without a second thought. "Two more days, and I'll be back with you," she replied to Miles.

Christian gestured as though tears were falling from his eyes. "Seriously, man, your voice was wild today. Whatever that gravely note was during "Marry Me" should've been in the original cast recording."

Ethan choked on a swallow. "Thanks, brother."

Willa looked at him with bursting pride; Christian was right. It wasn't just Ethan's body she could feel the ease in; his voice had been on another level, too, and she loved the idea that she maybe had something to do with it.

Ethan had always been the type of actor to challenge himself, bringing one hundred and ten percent to every performance even if he felt off, yet throughout the two years, she hadn't seen something like this in him. It amazed her to no end.

Maggie Garner strode over to Willa and held her face in between her hands. "You, darling girl, are going places. You were incredible tonight."

That did it. Willa's eyes welled up, and her soul ascended. It wouldn't matter where she went from here, *the* Maggie Garner, three-time Tony Award winner and two-time Academy Award winner, Maggie Garner told her she was incredible. Could her words be projected on Willa's tombstone?

"Oh my heavens, you cannot be serious. Thank you!"

Maggie wiped the single tear falling from Willa's eye. "I don't give out empty compliments." She pointed to Ethan. "He would know, he gets an earful from me every time his pitch is even a little off."

"It happened twice, and once, my form was off, so I got a neat lecture afterward. I'm better for it," he added with a wink.

Willa looked at him with a surprisingly shy smile.

The fact that people were taking notice of their performance together was inspiring. What her body did while dancing, she'd never thought of in terms of her love life. It was storytelling; it was art in a way where she detached from herself and her thoughts to break into something otherworldly for a little while. It's what acting was, too, playing around in someone else's head, embodying their own unique space.

Yet, a part of Willa moved with pieces of Ethan. It wasn't just Elizabeth and Darcy. It was Ethan's fingers grazing down her breastbone, his hand gripping tightly against her waist as she arched back, then swayed back against his form with a sensual thrust. It was his fingers clutching her wrist, hoisting her up to him while his other hand slithered up her thigh.

It was his lips brushing against her ear as she sang tearfully about the condition their characters were in. She recognized that they were bringing two stories to the stage, escaping and finding themselves somewhere in the middle where their relationship ignited into a spectacle for people to witness.

23

———

ETHAN

When Ethan came home from the gym the following day, he kept refreshing *Midnights at Pemberley's* Instagram account to see when Willa would start her takeover. She'd been nervous about it, opting out of hanging out the night before in order to mentally prepare herself for an entire day of bringing people on a virtual journey of her day.

He fully understood it as someone who appreciated talking about his work but loathed the anticipation of an interview. Some actors were better at it than others, and despite how long he'd been doing this, there was only a handful of times when he didn't get nervous.

On two-show days, he made sure to have a heavier breakfast to prepare for a lighter lunch. He also went much easier at the gym. He made himself two avocado and spinach omelets with feta cheese, topped with Trader Joe's "Everyday Seasoning," a handful of blueberries and raspberries, and a cup of coffee.

Her first video came through when he'd made his way through one of the omelets. Christ, she looked adorable. She had some sort of a lilac tank top on, and her hair was tied up at the top of her head in a messy bun with a few wisps dangling from the sides. It looked like she was wearing the barest bit of makeup.

"Hi, everyone! I'm Willa Davidian, and somehow, people thought it was a good idea to have me hijack the account on a Saturday matinee."

She giggled slightly, and his heart galloped.

"For those who don't know me, I'm in the ensemble as well as an understudy for some of the glorious stars in our production. I'm also one of the co-dance captains. Today's a bit wild because I'm still on as Elizabeth, but normally, and this is a fun fact that isn't mentioned in the show: my character's name is supposed to be Abigail. So, follow along and be nice to me so I don't have to cry before the show."

He appreciated how Willa could address something that triggered her anxiety by making a joke about it. Maybe he could learn from her.

Another video popped up while he'd finished that one.

"For starters, one of my favorite parts about this show is that I get to do it with one of my best girls."

She put her arm around Sahar, who stepped into the frame and took a bow.

"Most people know we've been friends since we were in a West End production of Macbeth, and this is the first time we booked a show together since moving to the States for other gigs. We both moved to New York about six-ish years ago and we've been roommates since."

"We have attachment issues," Sahar added. *"Especially now, after working together every single day. We even share a dressing room."*

"It's true," Willa chimed back in. *"Anyway, first things first on our agenda, we're going to get coffee, run a few quick errands, then head to the theatre."*

He knew it'd be a while before she returned with another post, so he sent her a text.

ETHAN

You're gorgeous 😍

Three dots appeared almost instantly.

WILLA

I'm a nervous wreck is what I am loll

ETHAN

you're extraordinary. I could watch you read off a grocery list.

WILLA

Hahaha unfortunately for you, I never make one.

ETHAN

It's a good thing I do. Tulip and I missed you last night. Mostly me.

WILLA

Convenient because I missed you both, too.
(You a little more.)

He smiled to himself, wondering how in the world they finally got to this place where they wouldn't have to tuck away their feelings.

ETHAN

see you soon, beautiful.

WILLA

He knew they'd be going to Amanda's Coffee, so he called the store to make an arrangement. The line rang five times before someone answered. "Amanda's Coffee, this is Jay."

"Jay, hey, buddy, it's Ethan Everett."

His voice grew less robotic. "Hey, Ethan. What's up?"

"Listen, the girls are going to come in today for their drinks. Can you opt out of charging them, and I'll give you the amount when I'm there instead?"

Ethan heard chatter grow louder on the other end of the line. Jay didn't speak. "Sorry, it was noisy. Yeah, sure. I'll put them on my tab, and we can square away later," he noted.

"Appreciate it, man. Thank you."

"Of course, see you soon," he added before the line went dead.

WILLA TEXTED him an hour later while he was standing in the subway.

WILLA

Did you do something? Why did Jay at Amanda's say that our orders were taken care of?

He held back a chuckle.

ETHAN

Maybe I did. Maybe I didn't. Maybe Jay is just being nice. Who knows?

WILLA

You're a lousy but hot liar.

ETHAN

Come to my dressing room when you get to the theatre. I miss those pretty lips.

WILLA

So demanding.

ETHAN

pleaaaaaaase?

WILLA

Maybe I will. Maybe I won't. Who knows?

ETHAN

I'm not above begging if that's what you want.

WILLA

;)

He shook his head at her, drawing his attention back to the music coming from his earphones. He refreshed his feed, seeing that a new story had finally appeared. This time, it was a portrait photo of her coffee, held up against the shop's wall of vinyl records. She captioned it: *coffee secured, now ready to be a human and answer your questions.* He jokingly added his own little note to the query box. "Who's your favorite person, and why is it Ethan?"

He entered the theatre, signed in, and went straight for his room, where she was already on his couch, legs crossed and waiting. "Now, what was that about you begging?" she said amorously.

He shut his door, hung his bag against the hook, and rushed to her. Ethan kneeled, eyes beaming up at her beguiling gaze. She batted her lashes in a state of shock. Christ, how had men let her go because they weren't willing to be patient with her? How had they not realized what they could've had with her beside them?

He would stay on his knees forever if that's what she wanted.

He would refrain from innuendos if she asked for that.

He would even opt out of kissing her if she no longer felt that was something she desired.

He would do anything. No questions asked.

Willa brought her fingers to the bottom of his chin and tipped his gaze higher. She brushed her fingers against his lips, then she bent lower and clasped her mouth to his.

Her lips moved rhythmically, nudging him to part and take her tongue in. Her wish was his command. She tasted like the notes of Irish Cream syrup in her drink, simultaneously sweet and smokey. Her soft lips danced methodically against his, picking up pace when his hand rose to tangle itself in her hair.

A low, barely-there groan of need broadcasted itself, meeting the discreet chuckle from her. She pulled away from him, her eyes flashing with heat and desire equally. "Okay, okay, I have to go give the people what they want. I'll come back to those lips later."

Ethan held her gaze. "You'll come home with me tonight?"

Willa dipped her chin up and down to answer.

He took her face in his hands for another quick kiss before letting her go.

Whoever was on his side up above, he'd send a thousand thanks in their direction. He felt like a kid at Christmas, giddy and teeming with excitement.

Ethan changed into Darcy's clothes and sat back against the couch. He opened his phone to see if there'd been another video from Willa, surprised to find about four waiting for him. The question someone had asked was, "Who is the other dance captain? Is it Miles?" She recorded the video with her arm around Miles's shoulder in his dressing room.

"Yes! This brilliant beast of a dancer is indeed my delightful co-dance captain and scene partner in most of the numbers." Miles concurred with a nod. *"We joke about it a lot, but we basically share a singular brain cell when it comes to dancing."*

Miles spoke next. *"It's true. Just last week, we were at rehearsals, and I wanted to work through something in my head, so I called Wills down, and I kid you not, she knew the movements step by step how I envisioned it in my head."*

"Or you know, you call me at four in the morning, saying you had a dream about a dance, and we need to make it happen immediately."

They both laughed.

"And what was the result of this visionary dream? The most viewed choreography video we've ever made thus far."

Willa continued. *"No, he's right. It's always just a ton of fun because any time there's a new song that I want to choreograph something to, Miles is the first person I'll text or vice versa, and the other person's response is 'I was just thinking the same thing,'"* they say in perfect unison.

The next story played. The question was, "Would you ever teach a dance class?" She answered with a picture of her, Christian, Miles, and Sahar during rehearsals. She captioned it: *"I would love to! I've talked about this a few times with Sahar and Miles, actually. It'd be a load of fun. I taught a bit back home in London!"*

He'd take a class taught by her any day.

The next was a video; she was back in her dressing room again, and someone had asked, "What's your favorite number to perform as Elizabeth?" Willa came alive when she began to answer.

"We all talk about this a lot, but 'Marry Me' is probably one of the most gorgeously produced numbers. When our brilliant goddess choreographer Josie Singh first showed it to us, we were in awe. It's one of the performances that always mesmerizes me when I'm watching Ethan and Naomi or Ethan and Lea execute it in rehearsals. I don't get to see most of it because I'm usually changing costumes and wigs for 'Forbidden Corridors,' so getting to be a part of it is a real gift." Her eyes glistened then, a small change and one he was sure only he'd catch. *"And, plus, sharing the stage with Ethan, who's my best*

friend, makes the experience even more magical. So, I'm going to have to say 'Marry Me,' followed by the encore, which is my second favorite overall."

Another follow-up question was about which costume she loved the most.

Willa had walked over to the wardrobe in her dressing room.

"Look, it's a crime to pick a favorite when our amazing designer, Marla Jennings, has created so many gems. I mean, just look at the details," she said, gesturing toward the adorned, emerald corset. God, he loved that one on Willa.

"Tell them about the leather outfits!" He heard Sahar yell from the back. *"Sahar wants me to show you all the leather costumes we have for 'Forbidden Corridors' because she tragically doesn't get to be part of this number and has no leather in her wardrobe."*

Sahar came into the frame. *"Do you guys understand how jealous I am? I begged for them to put Jane and Bingley in this number. Begged, I tell you. Solely so I can wear these."*

"You get a whole wedding dress, babe," Willa replied.

Sahar shrugged. *"Should've been leather. We're just going to have to switch out one day. Put me in the ensemble, and you go on as Jane."*

They both laughed.

"The leather is also surprisingly comfortable, too. I was initially worried that it wouldn't be, but the inside is soft for us, so it works with the grueling choreography. It is one of my favorite costumes, but if I have to pick one, the emerald wins."

That was the end of her videos; she likely went to get ready.

"I NEED A NAP SO BAD," Sahar announced after their bows.

Willa reached for her hand. "Go, go take one. Do you need painkillers, too?"

Sahar shook her head. "I have Midol."

Willa turned to Ethan. "What are you doing?"

He quirked his lips to note that he had no real plans. "I was going to see what you were doing. You can come and hang out in my dressing room. We can get food delivered."

"Sure," she replied.

Willa had changed out of costume and returned to his room shortly after.

"I got us sandwiches from Jacob's Deli. Extra pickles for you," he announced from the couch.

A huge smile made its way onto her face as she sauntered over to him. "Good because this takeover is giving me an ulcer. How do people talk to their phones so often? What's the secret I'm missing here, and how do I channel it?"

"I'd tell you if I knew." Ethan was far worse than her in this regard, which was probably why he wasn't ever asked to participate in the account takeovers. He could only get on camera if someone else was holding it and conducting the flow of where the video was going, which is why Sam's Instagram lives weren't a drag for him.

Willa giggled, then brought her phone to his face so he could read. "There are a ton of these," she declared, scrolling through various messages saying, *where's Ethan? Show us Ethan, please!*

She held up the phone to her face, hit record, and said, "*Show number one done. I'm beat, but here's the man of the hour, folks, Ethan's location has been secured. I won't let him out of my sight in case you have any burning questions for him.*"

He said *hi* to the camera, unable to stifle a chuckle from Willa's tone.

She looked at him and smiled, scrolling through the feed of questions. "Oh, this person's asking if we could go anywhere in the world right now, where would we go? Want to answer it with me? I'm sure they'd care more about your answer than mine."

"The question came to you. Of course they care. But sure, if you want me to," he replied.

"Should we say anything about why we're hanging out?"

"We're allowed to hang out. That wouldn't be suspicious to anyone."

She grimaced with an expression that said *yes, but...* "True, but this is the internet. Gah, sorry, I'm in my head about how our feelings must now be stamped on our foreheads or something."

She had a point. He was sure his love for her had always been on full display. He drew his hand to her knee and squeezed lightly, releasing before she propped her phone into recording position.

Willa began talking first. "*Inside of a cozy treehouse with biscuits and a blanket,*" she answered.

Willa pointed the camera in his direction.

Inside the same treehouse with you, he wanted to say.

Ethan pondered for a second. "*The Cliffs of Moher,*" he said quickly, a small smile quirking on his lips as he remembered the family vacation he'd been on nearly a decade ago.

"*Oh, you actually went somewhere far. My brain had a different perspective.*"

He smiled. "*If we're thinking more attainable at this moment, then on my couch with my cat.*"

Willa turned to him, the camera still aimed at them both. "*You know what you need to do now, right? You've got to give us a picture of Tulip when you get home. I demand it. It's what the people deserve.*"

She was careful not to use the word *we* in speaking, implying that they'd be going their separate ways. But sure, he'd oblige and post a photograph of Tulip.

His eyes darted toward her hand when she turned off her phone and placed it on the coffee table. His own hand flexed instinctually like it needed hers. But they couldn't do any of that right now; he'd respect her wishes, and he'd control his impulses, however small they seemed. It'd be too obvious if he closed his door again, with Willa inside until the next show. They had to keep this casual.

There were countless ways that evidenced how he and Willa were cut from the same cloth. Two sides of the same coin, similar but different. But what he admired most was her work ethic, the willingness to do whatever it took in an industry that often had its cards stacked against her. He understood his privilege in more ways than one from the moment he had his foot in the door.

He was a white man, conventionally attractive, and somewhat good at his job. Good ol' imposter syndrome would never let him admit to that last one. The reality was that there would always be a role for him, even if it wasn't the one he wanted. There was a space for him in the industry, even if he disappeared from social media for days and weeks without a word. He could come back, and people would still care for him. But women like Willa had to keep fighting to be seen, and he loathed the idea that anyone would think her ties to him diminished the work she put in.

His desperation to be with her gnawed at him consistently, but he'd do anything to shut it down, to satisfy himself with whatever she gave, even when he understood the sheer immensity of what being with her would entail. She wouldn't be the lucky one—it'd be him. To walk beside a woman who loved so deeply, so fiercely. She brought out a fire in him he didn't know existed—an urge to push beyond his capabilities and try new things, not because she asked him to but because her passions made him curious, eager, and excited.

"Where'd you go?" she asked suddenly, drawing him away from his stupor.

He dragged himself away from the thoughts in his head and

the sounds of their co-workers muffling to indistinct chatter. "I was thinking about everything you said, why you want to keep this quiet. I get it. I hate it, but I get it."

She smiled with understanding. "Why do you hate it?"

"Because I want to close that door and kiss you. I want to hold your hand without anyone wondering what's going on with us."

She tilted her head, sadness making an appearance on her face. "If it helps, I want to do all of those things, too. It's only for a little while. I think we can tell our friends once we're more settled. I just want it to be us for a while."

He nodded and rested his head against her shoulder. This wouldn't be weird, not to anyone passing at least, holding her hand however would be another story.

She turned her head and snuck a kiss on the side of his temple. "I'll make it up to you tonight," she added.

WILLA WAS in Declan's room, recording a video with him before their evening show, answering a question about whether he had his shirt on.

"Unfortunately, Dec has his Wickham costume on right now. But Sam is best at catching him without one."

Declan choked on a laugh. *"Nosy, nosy people,"* he remarked. *"I'm going to have to start wearing a shirt and change all my ways. What's a man got to do to get some privacy in his own dressing room?"*

Willa laughed loudly, and his screen lit up with her smile. She had Elizabeth's first wig on and makeup fully done, but she was still in her own clothes.

She walked out of the room, still holding the camera to her face.

"Let's see who else we can go bug."

Sam made an appearance behind her, trying to scare her but failing. Tanya came into the frame, placed a kiss on her cheek, and then strolled away. The video cut off, but another one came in where she answered about the show's biggest prankster. She'd found Sam again.

"This guy. This one. He is the worst of them all, and by worst, I mean the absolute best. He tries to startle everyone, but he's never gotten to me because I don't spook easily. Poor Sahar, on the other hand..."

"Listen, I'm going to get you someday." Sam chimed.

"Aww, mate. It's been almost two years and you've still yet to. And you know what? It's not your fault. I grew up with an older brother; absolutely nothing can phase me," she said with a chuckle.

Sam pursed his lips and nodded in defeat. *"Yeah, okay, fair. But let it be on record that I'm the show's best."*

"Co-signed," Willa confirmed.

She was back in her chair, swirling around, answering a question about what she missed most in London.

"Oh, God. Everything? My entire family is there, so I miss them a ton. Good fish and chips, which you just can't get here, no offense, Americans. It's not the same. Yes, Target is great, but M&S is better. I miss my mum's cooking a lot, too."

Damn, he wished he could order stuff from M&S for her. Or maybe he could find a place with good fish and chips, but everywhere they'd gone, she'd had at least one complaint about it. One place got the fish right, but the fries—er, chips—weren't.

Still, in her dressing room, she replied to a question asking what the first musical she ever watched was.

"Specifically on Broadway, it was Miss Saigon, but my first musical ever was Beauty and the Beast at the Piccadilly Theatre."

She answered the next question so eagerly that his heart swelled. Someone asked what other Jane Austen production she'd like to see a different version of.

"Oooh, I want to say *Persuasion* because Captain Wentworth in a role like this would be aces. But it would also be so fascinating to actually see *Northanger Abbey* in this light. The spooky and more gothic elements could do so well with the sultriness we have here, so I'd love that. And plus, good boy Henry Tilney growling? I'd lose my shit."

Ethan laughed out loud. God, he loved her.

He loved her so much he didn't know what to do with himself.

24

WILLA

Willa had no idea how she made it through the day. She was more knackered than the singular meme of a child crying and wanting to fall asleep on a beach shore. She wanted nothing more than to go home and tumble onto her bed. But at the same time, she wanted to be with Ethan. It was all so new with them, exciting, easy.

She concluded her account takeover with a few more questions at the night's end, then recorded a video of the fans waiting outside at the stage door for her final frame. It wasn't nearly as anxiety-inducing as she'd imagined, so that made for a pleasant surprise. Without any inappropriate questions or remarks during her takeover, it gave her a bit more hope for the eventual point in time when her relationship with Ethan was publicized.

Willa showered first, then went to his living room to turn on the TV to reruns of one of her comfort shows, *The Great British Bake Off*. She'd had enough of social media and her phone today. Ethan came back out shortly after and flopped beside her.

He pulled her closer and squished her into him, the sea salt and cedar from his body wash filling her nose with the delicious notes of a crisp morning walk underneath a canopy of majestic trees. He whispered something incoherent into her hair that sounded like *fuck,* and *you're amazing* while his lips traveled down to her neck. She brought her legs to the cushion, curled them toward his torso, and leaned further into him.

He drew away from her body and cupped her cheeks with both his hands. He had his glasses on, but she noted his sapphire blues sparkling with an admiration that she could swim in for hours and still not find all the hidden treasures in their vastness. "How do I spend all day with you, then still need you the second you're away from me?" Ethan rasped.

"It's the honeymoon phase. Give it a month, and you'll get over it."

A flash of annoyance evidenced in his gaze. "Is that your way of telling me you'll get sick of me?"

She placed her fingers along his jaw and stroked adoringly, wanting him to catch that she was joking. "No, I'm just prone to believe things will backfire for me."

"Something tells me your therapist wouldn't be happy to hear that."

He had a point. Every time Willa would say something overly pessimistic, Marie always gave her a look that prompted Willa to dispute the negative belief with a pragmatic truth. "You're right. She wouldn't be."

She pressed her lips to his cheek.

"Willa, I've wanted you for a while now. Probably since the very beginning, even when I didn't realize that's what was happening. I only kept it in because I didn't think you'd want me the same way."

The statement made her smile. He'd mentioned their first meeting a few times, but did he really remember the exact details? She didn't. Was it at a table read? Rehearsals?

"Tell me about this first time again—*when* exactly did you start feeling this way?"

His phone vibrated loudly against the coffee table. "Hold that thought," he glanced at the caller ID. "Give me a second, please. My mom and I have been playing phone tag for two days."

"Of course," she gestured for him to pick up.

Ethan's face lit up. "Hi, mom," he answered.

She could hear Mrs. Everett on the other end of the line. "Hi, honey. I'm so sorry I keep missing you. How are you?"

"I'm good. Everything's good here. How's Nick doing?" he asked. Was his brother okay? Had something happened to him?

His mom must've sighed or something on the other end of the line because she grew quiet. "He's good, I guess. Is he not talking to you?" Willa heard. She felt weird listening. But if Ethan wanted to keep the conversation private, he would have sat farther away or exited to another room.

That said, had he and his brother been fighting?

"He still hasn't told me himself. I texted him yesterday to check in, and he kept it dry."

She said something along the lines of "he doesn't want to disappoint you, but he'll be okay. Maybe you can come by soon. We miss you, kid."

He shut his eyes and tensed a bit. "I know I'm sorry, mom. I could make that work. Can I bring someone with me? If they'd be willing to come?"

Was he talking about *her?*

"Of course you can. Who is it? Do I know them?" she asked eagerly, her voice elevating.

He swept his fingers slowly along Willa's forearm.

"You do, yeah, but I'll tell you later if that's okay."

"Alrighty, I can take a hint. I'll let you go now. Are you eating and sleeping normally?" she finished off.

"Yes, to both," he answered.

"Are you sure?" she probed.

He chuckled lightly. "Scout's honor, mom."

"Okay, okay. Goodnight. Love you."

"Love you, too."

She waited for him to hang up and place the phone down before speaking again. He pulled her body closer to him. "Is everything okay with your brother?" she asked.

"He was laid off from work about two weeks ago and hasn't told me himself. He won't respond in the family group chat, either. I'm trying to give him space, but it's odd that he won't talk to me."

Willa's mouth formed into a sad line. "I would understand if he felt like he might burden you."

"I would hate to think I gave him the impression that he could burden me."

Her fingers traced along the side of his face. "It's not something you did or an impression you gave. It's just something people feel sometimes. I could go to Alex about many things, but when I need him, I opt out. I close in on myself and try to handle everything on my own because he's already done so much for me. I don't want him to do more."

"He's your brother. He's supposed to be there as much as he can."

She shook her head slightly. "Tell that to an anxious person's brain."

"It's not like I can do anything anyway, which sucks. I have nothing to do with the academic world."

Willa moved her hand along his shoulder, down to his bicep. She held onto his forearm then. "Don't wait for him to tell you then. You know. Reach out and tell him that you're there for him."

"Nick can be stubborn. He'll get pissed at my parents for telling me. But maybe I can risk it."

"I see."

He nestled his nose in the crook of her neck and breathed her in. It sent tremors down her spine. "Would you want to come with me when I go visit them?" he mumbled.

"So, I was the someone you were referring to?" she asked, holding her breath at the touch of his lips against her pulse point.

He lifted his head so she could see the obvious answer plastered on his face.

"How are you going to explain why you're bringing me?"

Ethan's mouth lowered, trekking to the juncture of her throat again. "You're my best girl. We don't need an explanation."

He kissed her impatiently, greedily sucking and biting down, forcing a low whimper to rise from the pit of her stomach.

"Except it's never happened before. So, why now?" Willa continued.

"Because I want you to. You've met them before; they'd be delighted to have you. Plus, I have plans for you and that first date, remember? And I'm working on a project at the cabin with my dad for my nephew that I want to check in on, too."

"Aww, like a swing set?" she wondered.

"Something like that, yeah," he answered.

"That's adorable."

He took his glasses off and set them aside. His fingers circled around Willa's jaw and ear while he continued to kiss her like he didn't just spend hours tangled with her body in various dance numbers.

"Wait, wait," she called out.

He lifted his head rapidly, eyes blown wide. "What? Did I go too far?"

"No, but you were about to tell me about the first time you saw me before you got the phone call."

The line of his lips curled into an expansive, bright smile. He rested his forehead against hers, "You were wearing that oversized Muppets shirt, black shorts, and choreographing a number to Billie Eilish's 'Bad Guy' with Miles. I walked in just as you came up from the ground, and all I could hear was your stunning laugh. I thought you were the most beautiful woman I'd ever seen, and I would've killed to hear you laugh like that all the time. I still would."

She couldn't believe it. She recalled meeting him and introducing herself, but she didn't recollect anything else about that day. "I—" she started.

The pads of his fingers traced along her arm, interlacing their hands together. He brought hers to his lips and kissed it leisurely. "Since it hit me that I had feelings for you, I've almost blurted it out every time you've worn that shirt."

"I hate my memory for being such shit. I don't remember anything about that day other than we met. I remember you being the only person who understood my jellybeans reference, and that's how we got close, but I don't necessarily remember *when* that was," she replied.

"That was two days later. When we first met, I mentioned liking your shirt, but you didn't seem to think anything of it."

She smiled. "I remember *that*. To be fair, I just thought you were being polite. I'd heard you were one of the kindest people to work with, but how was I to know that you're just as obsessed with the Muppets as I was."

He chuckled. "I would've said it, but I stopped myself. I got weirdly shy. I was too stunned by your pretty face."

She couldn't halt her cheeks from flushing. "I can't deal with you. You should've just said it."

"I have many things I'd like to say to you, but I'm pacing myself," he answered swiftly.

She poked his abs, lean and hard against her fingers. "Like what?"

"Like, when'd you know?" he asked.

He dipped his head back to her throat.

"Know what?" she questioned, drawing out the moment, fingers carding through his hair.

Ethan growled, low and hoarse into her neck. "You know what."

"Why do you think I drank so much that night we went out? When you didn't show up," she confessed through a subdued whimper.

He looked up at her, his eyes blazing with bottomless longing. "That's the night you realized you had feelings for me?"

She shook her head. "That was the night I understood that I was too far gone. I started feeling something when I watched people slow dance at Alex's wedding and wished you were there with me."

"I'm sorry my headache got in the way of us that night," he noted. "I'm also sorry I couldn't come with you to the wedding." She was, too, or maybe she wasn't. Perhaps she wouldn't have realized how much she relied on his presence to feel safe.

"It's okay. Maybe it's exactly what I needed to recognize that *you* are the person I'm searching for in every room."

He groaned, biting down on the slope of her shoulder. "Fuck, Wills, that sounded like poetry."

She tipped his face to look him square in the eyes. "It's the truth."

He seized her mouth hard, surely bolstered by her praise. His phone vibrated on the table again, but he ignored it. It vibrated once more, then a few more times after. He stopped kissing her and looked down. They read the texts together. Sam and his wife, Priya, would be performing at a small venue in Queens next month—the whole cast was invited.

"Are we going?" Willa asked.

He confirmed quickly and then crashed his lips back onto hers.

25

ETHAN

Ethan stood behind the curtains and isolated backstage. His head throbbed, and he didn't have painkillers left on him. He sat against one of the prop chairs that wouldn't be coming out for two more numbers as they ran through a block of rehearsals since Naomi's return.

Willa approached him carefully. She drifted her fingers slowly along his shoulder. "You all right? You seem off."

He nodded. "I'm fine, I just have a headache but ran out of meds."

She drew her fingers lower, brushing them along his biceps now. "Is it really bad?" she asked.

"No. It's annoying as hell, though. It's not going to let me bring my best to the show if I don't get it under control."

"Shit. And I'm pretty sure I only have Aleve and Advil on me, but you're allergic to both. I'll need to start making sure I pack extra Tylenol. Sahar might have some in our dressing room; let me check."

Something as simple but substantial as Willa remembering his allergies despite not having the best memory made his heart squeeze.

As she swerved to walk toward her dressing room, Ethan stood up and stopped her mid-turn, pulling her into his chest. Two seconds. No one was around. It was dark enough in here to hide for a beat. He needed to hold her. Plus, this was normal. This was fine. They weren't strangers to hugging. "It's okay, beautiful. I'll ask around when we're done, or I'll pop into a store real quick and grab it," he hummed against her ear.

Her hands caressed his back in soothing circles. He shut his eyes for a second, giving himself a moment to appreciate her touch. He maybe lingered for a minute too long because he opened his eyes to see Declan smirking from center stage, standing at the right angle to notice them.

Willa pulled away from him, noting the expression in his eyes, then turned to catch Declan, too. She looked back at Ethan, her eyes widened.

"Don't worry. I'll ask him for some meds. It'll throw him off," he whispered.

Willa nodded, parting from him.

In an unsurprising turn of events, despite how close they'd been before they began dating, sneaking around was more challenging than either of them imagined. First, when Naomi returned, she took one look at them and stated that something had changed. They denied it. Then there was the incident with Declan three days ago, and they weren't sure he bought their excuse.

Ethan leaned against the vanity in his dressing room while Willa sat cross-legged on his couch.

"Naomi knows, babe. She one hundred percent knows. She's just not saying anything because she loves us both too much to pry. I'm pretty sure they all do at this point. Dec's not buying the fact that you needed painkillers," Willa commented.

Ethan laughed, shaking his head. "It's your call, beautiful. I'd shout about us being together from the rooftops if I could."

"No rooftops yet, but let's do it. Let's tell the cast. They'd keep quiet if we told them we didn't want it getting out yet. I trust them all fully," she replied.

"I'm good with that," he concurred.

She moved her lips in thought, then picked up her phone and started writing something. "Done," she said, putting the device down. He caught the sight of his lighting up on the coffee table.

He arched a brow at her. "Did you just text it in the group chat, or is that something else on my phone?"

She dipped her chin up and down. "Give it a minute. They're all going to barge in here screaming."

He reached for his phone and quickly read the text:

WILLA

PSA: Ethan and I are dating. Please keep it solely between us. We're very tired of sneaking around all of you.

Sam charged in first. "I *knew* it!" He took Ethan into a headlock.

Ethan pushed him off, stifling a chuckle. "Fuck off. No, you didn't."

"Bro. *Bro!* You know Dec and I made bets. My wife and I made bets. Dec and Carmen have one going. We've known longer than you two have."

Willa gasped with a sardonic huff. "Would've never thought our romantic lives would be so exciting."

Naomi ran into the room with a big, goofy grin spread across her face. "What did I say? Something had changed between you two. It's cute how you tried to hide it and failed." She bounced toward Willa, sat beside her on the couch, and hugged her. "I'm so stinking excited for you two!"

Sahar stood by the doorway. Declan came in and turned to her. "You obviously knew," he remarked.

"I live with her. Of course I knew," she answered.

Ethan's dressing room had become a circus; oddly, he didn't mind it. He turned to Willa, holding her gaze for a beat. He winked at her. She scrunched her nose and smiled.

It was the sweetest sight, a picture to frame deep in his most sacred memories: the love of his life, looking up at him and all their friends thrilled for them.

Miles peeped into the room. "I swear I was going to say something the other day. Did you idiots not realize you'd been holding hands for a solid ten minutes at one point? I straight up counted."

Willa barked out a laugh. "When did we do that? We thought we got caught because Naomi was onto us, and Dec saw us hugging three days ago."

Miles nearly howled and shifted his body toward Sahar to demonstrate by playing with her fingers. "Legit, you were standing in the wings pulling this shit repeatedly. I almost said something, but I let it go."

Oh shit. They thought they were in early on that day, carelessly assuming that no one had come into work yet.

Christian nearly bolted into the room with Innila. "I had to text Dan to tell him it's official. His response was 'finally!'" he affirmed, patting Ethan on the shoulder. He already knew, but it was different now that it was out in the open.

"Who wasn't taking bets on our relationship?" Ethan huffed.

They all laughed, answering his question without any words.

Miles took out his phone and snapped a photo of the entire room. "This is only for our eyes," he clarified before continuing.

"But real talk, I didn't think anything of it at first, and I'm kicking myself a bit because it means my telepathy with Wills is floundering. We gotta get our game back. The thing is, we're all super close, so your vibe felt normal to me. But the night of my birthday, Clyde turns to me when we get to his place and goes, 'You forget to mention the thing between Willa and Ethan.'"

He started cackling. "And I'm thinking I'm drunk as shit 'cause what is he talking about? I'd given him the rundown of who was coming, your partners, etcetera, and he goes, 'Babe, are you serious? Something is going on between those two,' so I started paying attention, and *what do you fucking know!* Even my boyfriend, who'd known us all for a few weeks at that point, could read you two like an open book."

Laughter erupted in the comfortably crowded space again. In truth, Ethan relished knowing that his love for her was on full display, and he didn't have to hide it. Knowing that their friends were all legitimately happy for them, thrilled even, and had been waiting for this moment because of what they'd noticed and decoded.

Sam put Ethan in another headlock and then quickly released him. "Why the secrecy though? Parade this news around. You two are hot as hell together."

Ethan noticed fear engulfing Willa. She shook her head forcefully. "We wanted to tell you lot because we trust everyone here, but I don't want this to be public knowledge right now. There's a lot we need to figure out, and I want to be able to do that without any outside noise."

He felt Sam nod in understanding. "Makes total sense. We got you two, then. It won't leave this theatre," he affirmed.

Willa got up off the couch. "Okay, the party's over now. We love you all. We need to go get ready."

They all left his room, one by one, leaving him and his girl, her cheeks tinted and eyes sparkling. She wrapped her arms around his neck and rocked against his frame.

"That went well. I'm glad we no longer have to hide our relationship from them."

He kissed her nose, the tiny mole under her cheekbone, the curve of her jaw, then pressed his mouth to hers, brushing her lips quickly and reverently with his. "So am I."

She drew her lips to his neck and lingered for a beat before hopping out of his arms. "Okay, bye, getting ready applies to me, too. See you out there."

26

ETHAN

Bittersweet.

That's how the day had been.

Earlier this morning, Tony Award nominations were released, and the entire cast had gathered at the crack of dawn to hear the announcements together. Ethan, Naomi, Sahar, Sam, and Declan were nominated for their respective roles, and if Ethan had any power, he'd give the award to each of them, excluding himself because he was in the running with Broadway legends. Really, he was immensely grateful to be acknowledged, but it was the team beside him he believed in far more.

The best part was that apart from the cast, the show had tremendous chances for accolades, especially Josie's choreography and Marla's costumes. He'd also be shocked if Peter Bradford didn't win for scenic design, as well as Jeffrey for his directing.

Yet, he'd spent moments during the day moving through waves of grief.

Now, the rain was pounding ferociously against his window, and all he wanted to do was spend a few hours with Willa.

Settled in his bed with *his* gray hoodie and a pair of sleep shorts, she had one hand wrapped around a cup of tea while she browsed through some interior decorating catalog with the other.

"You know, I really love this forest green shade in your room. The rest of the place would look so great with more of it. But there's also this stunning navy," Willa added, pointing to an example in the company's book.

God, he loved this woman. She was, and would perpetually be, the best medicine, even while she was talking about things like paint.

"I finally called a plumber for the guest bathroom issue. Their earliest opening is mid-June, literally the Monday after the Tonys."

He'd done a bunch of other things to distract himself today: laundry, grocery shopping, played *Hades 2* right up until the second he had to leave for work.

Taking a sip of her tea, she looked up at him. "Did you schedule an appointment?"

Ethan nodded. "Yeah, I've been putting it off too long already."

"Good. And that'll help with the guest bedroom afterward. Your family should have a place to stay when they visit. There's something else on your mind, though. What is it?"

He shook his head in a wordless *nothing* and then sat on the bed beside her.

Setting her mug aside, Willa leaned closer, resting her fingers along his knee. "I know you, Ethan. What's going on? Something's been bothering you all day."

Another wave of grief drenched him its tide. "It was a really good day, you know? I've never been part of a production where we've all been close enough to even celebrate our nominations together, but I don't know. The group chat with my family has been blowing up. Nick still hasn't said anything to me about his job, but he was enthusiastic with his replies for the first time in a while, and then it sort of hit me again that my grandpa isn't here anymore. And then I started thinking about whether I'm even bringing my best to every show to make him proud—it just..."

He trailed off, swallowing a lump in his throat.

Palming both sides of his face, Willa blocked his mind from the descent it was moving toward.

"Ethan, you're one of the most hardworking men I know. I've watched you grow so much from our very first rehearsal to the show we just had a few hours ago. And my memory might be shit, but my observations are not. How you take care of your voice, listen to your body, and do everything you can to under-stand the character is no small feat, babe. There's no reason for you to have a copy of *Pride and Prejudice* by your bedside table these days, but I know you keep it, as well as the e-book in your phone, so you can look over things, just in case you might catch something new."

She paused, tracing the corners of his eyes. "It's natural that missing him would hit now, especially because this is the first show that he wasn't able to see. Your grief is also pretty new still. I know he was your biggest fan, and I know my words might not be enough, but I'm here to remind you to take a breath. Feel the sadness if that's what you need. Let me be here for you, but don't you dare doubt how fiercely proud he would be of everything you do."

If he hadn't already known that he loved Willa, how she always understood every ache and elation and frustration inside of him would've cemented his adoration in place.

The fact that he never needed to hide any part of him from her.

Her sincerity. Her goodness. Her passion.

"You're the best, you know that?" Ethan said.

Willa placed a kiss on his forehead.

"*You* are," she emphasized, then stood up and stepped out of his room, presumably to take her mug back to the kitchen. Tulip galloped out after her.

"Stay strong, Wills. Don't give her more treats no matter how hard she tries to convince you that she's a starving cat," he called out.

Her laugh came in the distance, but he heard it still.

"Did the vet seriously say Tulip needs to lose weight? I thought you were joking," she asked, walking back in.

He hadn't been joking. Ethan took Tulip for her yearly check-up yesterday morning and learned that his long-haired orange ball of fur was now thirteen pounds.

Ethan bobbed his head up and down. "It's not the biggest deal according to the vet, but I told him I'm incapable of saying no to her, so he said we should opt out of giving her too much after she's had her dinner."

Tulip hadn't returned with Willa. "She knew you were talking shit, and now she's going to stay in the living room."

"See, you're stronger than I am. I would've given in," Ethan noted.

Smiling, Willa plopped herself right next to him on his bed and swung her legs over his.

He settled one arm on her back and placed his other hand on top of her thigh.

"It's her little meows that get you. She's the quietest cat until she wants food, and suddenly, we get all these adorable sounds."

With a low laugh, he ran his fingers up and through Willa's hair, seizing her mouth in a kiss. He didn't want to talk about his cat anymore. *No offense, Tulip.*

Willa kissed him back.

When they paused, Ethan watched her eyes flick to his hand resting on her thighs. She brought hers on top of his, then glided her fingers gently across his knuckles. They stayed like that momentarily, hands brushing intentionally against one another.

Nothing in his life had been as easy as loving Willa. And he wanted to tell her, right here at this moment, even if, to some degree, it felt like it'd be too soon. He wondered if it would scare her away, but since they'd gotten together, Willa had been even more open with him than before. Except he still couldn't believe it—would he ever?

Looking up into her gaze, he realized he'd been staring. Ethan drew his fingertips up to her cheek.

"What?" she asked.

"Just thinking about you."

"Oh?"

"I think that even when we're in our fifties, I'm going to look at you and still question how you're mine."

The brightest, most earnest smile rose along her lips, dimples out and eyes beaming. Tracing her lips along Ethan's cheekbone, she drew lower and kissed his mouth again. Slow and sweet and promising. Parting, she rested her head along the slope of his shoulder.

Words left his lips before he could think them through. "I don't know if you'll remember this, but I called you on your birthday back when we were in Boston."

She raised her head, looking him in the eyes to confirm that she remembered.

"I was so sure that you'd figure out I liked you afterward. I had convinced myself that things would be weird. I kept having to remind myself not to end the call with three words—not to let them accidentally slip." He lingered, tracing his fingers along her cheeks. "But now? I know we're taking things slow, but I'm so deeply and irrevocably in love with you, Willa. I'm sure I loved you from the moment I heard you laugh. And every second we've spent together has only ever multiplied those feelings. Sometimes, I feel like I could explode—like, I don't know how to contain the magnitude of my love for you."

In stunned silence, Willa held his gaze. Her expression was soft and warm, brimming with what he gathered was fear and hope simultaneously.

And then she wrapped her arms around his neck, holding onto him for dear life. A muffled Ethan left her lips but nothing else for a few seconds. He brought her body as close as humanly possible from the position they'd been sitting in.

"I do remember that day. Often, actually, and when I used to think of it before we got together, I had to mentally stop myself from falling for you. But I love you, too, Ethan. I honestly didn't think I'd ever find what we have. You're the closest thing to real-life magic."

"Do you love me more than treehouses?" he asked, eyes widened, a smirk rising along his mouth.

Dramatically, Willa cocked a brow. "Know your place, babe," she deadpanned.

Ethan guffawed, tipping her over, he pressed his lips to her neck. She let out a low giggle and ran her fingers through his hair.

"I've got fifty years to convince you that I'm better."

"What are you going to do, dump me at eighty-four?" she joked.

His hands drew lower to her thigh, and he squeezed. "No, I'll die of sadness instead."

She let out a loud laugh and kissed his lips with searing passion. "I love you more than treehouses," she whispered.

"Thank fuck." Ethan pulled her back over his lap where they stayed for a while, mouths pressed to each other.

27

ETHAN

Willa skipped to his side after the curtain call and nestled herself in the crook of his arm. He'd never get used to this—her nearness, her excitement. It'd been a month since the cast found out about their relationship. He and Willa had been closer than ever, together more often than they weren't. No more hiding. Out in the open, at least here in the theatre.

Most of the cast had plans to go to Sam's show tonight, and Ethan looked forward to it, missing putting on solo concerts more than he thought.

Willa followed him into his dressing room where he was struggling not to gape at her. She was back in the emerald bodysuit, the verdant hues bringing out the gold in her beguiling brown eyes. He wanted desperately to pick her up, set her down on his vanity, and kiss her senselessly until her cheeks reddened into the same color as the crimson on her lips.

She'd said she didn't want him to tiptoe around her, but he knew she wouldn't be ready for some of the things he wanted.

He let his hands trail to her hips, steadying her, holding her gaze. Willa wrapped her arms around his neck. "You look like you're plotting something," she remarked.

"I am," he drawled. "I want to pick you up and set you down on the vanity, then kiss you until you beg me to stop."

A sly smirk landed on her lips. "Let me take off my makeup and change, and then I'm all yours."

"I want you in that costume."

"Do you also want to explain to Marla that you're responsible for a jewel loosening or a tear somewhere?"

She had a point. *Dammit.* He was sure he was openly frowning. "No."

"Then I'll be back," she noted.

Ethan burrowed his face into her neck and sighed. "Okay."

WILLA CAME BACK to his room a few minutes later, makeup off, black fitted cropped top on, and denim jeans hugging her hips. He lifted her onto the counter and drew his hands to cup her ass. Her legs enclosed around him, and he groaned with need, heat pulsing through his bloodstream. Christ, this was a bad idea.

She kissed him hard and fast, her fingers raking through his hair with recurring strokes. He wasn't sure of many things in life, but he knew that the moment he had more of Willa, he'd savor every second with her—preserve every curve of her body and the sounds she made into a sanctified space in his mind.

"Come to my place after you've showered, and we could go together. Your outfit is perfectly fine. You should wear it tonight," she added.

"Sure," he answered, his voice softer, lazier. He was at her disposal. He'd do whatever she wanted him to.

Her gaze was drawn out and searching. She traced the lines

along his face, tipping his chin up to her. "You look like a kid whose parents took away his favorite toy. What's wrong?"

"You changed out of the bodysuit," he answered honestly.

A small laugh chirped out of her. "Wait, are you serious?"

He blinked once, twice, and nodded sincerely. He traced his hand along the rigid denim, angling his hands toward the outer parts of her thighs.

"Oh my God, you're ridiculous," she said, pressing her hands against his chest.

He let out a low grumble. "I miss your thighs. I haven't touched them bare for weeks. You keep wearing jeans or sweats at home," he confessed.

"That's an exaggeration. I wore shorts to bed last week."

"Yes, but you were on your period, and then you almost cried after dropping the Schmackary's cookie on the floor, so I kept my hands to myself."

Grinning, she held his gaze. "Okay, you have a point there. It was cute how you tried to get it delivered for me, then realized it was too late and brought me more the next morning. But also, you realize that you wouldn't be touching me bare, right, but three layers of pantyhose?"

She had a point. But it was the principle—the visibility of her irresistibly toned legs—*her thighs*. "Ssh," he rasped into her neck, kissing her frantically.

Willa sighed in response, dropping her shoulders in a state of relief. "I have a mini skirt in mind I could wear tonight," she proposed.

"Yes," he groaned against her skin, trailing his lips back up to hers to take her in a searing, sweltering kiss.

•　•　•

SAHAR OPENED the door when Ethan knocked. "Hi, hi. She'll be out in a sec. She had a wardrobe malfunction with the top she wanted to wear."

Ethan nodded. He joined Sahar on the couch, where she had reruns of *The Golden Girls* playing.

"Did you start playing *Hades 2* yet?" he asked.

"No! I keep meaning to, but I've been in a shit mood, so I just started *Tears of the Kingdom* from the beginning again."

He gave her a concerned expression. "You okay?"

"Yeah, I'll be fine. You know what won't be fine, though? The fact that I can't share the review key for *Dread Quest,* the game Jay's mate developed, because it's so good, and I don't have anyone to talk about it with. The animation on the zombies is wild."

"When is it supposed to be released?"

"I think at the end of August? Or early September, I'll have to double-check," Sahar answered.

"It's on my list. I tried starting *Elden Ring*, but either I'm getting old, or the lore is too dense for me."

"Oh, I definitely don't have the bandwidth for that one. I mentioned it to Dec the other day, too. Although, to be fair, my brain is mush by the time we get home from a show, so it could also be our exhaustion."

"Yeah, I wondered if that was the case, too," Ethan replied.

"Agreed. But you have to play *Dread Quest* when it's out. You're going to love it. Don't wait."

Ethan bobbed in his head. Knowing it was a frequent talking point for both of them, he was about to ask what she thought of the soundtrack when Willa came out of her bedroom.

She wore a short black skirt with a slit on the side and an oversized heather-grey T-shirt of sorts tied at the front. "Boots or trainers?" she asked Sahar.

Sahar rounded her lips in thought. "Uh...boots. They'd dress up the outfit more."

"Do you have an opinion?" Willa asked Ethan.

Her legs. Her taut calves. *Her thighs.* He couldn't speak his opinion aloud, so he settled for a different version. "You look perfect," he acknowledged.

"Cute, cute, cute. But a friendly reminder that I'm still in the room, and I'm not getting off this couch. You two can go elsewhere if need be," Sahar added.

Shaking her head with a grin, Willa then shimmied her feet into her ankle boots. "You need to go change out of your sweats. Sam said he wanted us there at least half an hour early. We need to leave in ten minutes if we're going to make it."

Sahar bounced off the couch. "Oh shit. You're right."

Willa ambled over to where Ethan sat and snaked her arm around his neck. She lowered herself onto his lap, legs folded together, likely to keep her skirt from rising too much. His arm circled her waist, and his other hand dropped gradually against the top of her knee, moving higher with languid caresses.

He took in the hypnotizing scent of her perfume—reveled in her nearness. "This skirt is going to torture me all night, you know that?"

She raised her unoccupied hand to brush a strand of hair back from his forehead. "And that's why you get a few minutes now to make up for me robbing you earlier."

Ethan drew his fingers closer to her thigh. "So thoughtful. So unaware of how far gone I am that a few minutes will never be enough."

She smiled indolently, lashes darting up and down. "Patience is a virtue." Tipping his chin up, she pressed her mouth onto his, the gloss from her lips catching on.

He repeated the words she'd once spoken back to her. "No, patience is life's most enraging plot device."

Willa guffawed. "What if I tell you I have a surprise for you, and it's one I know you'll appreciate? Can you be patient, then?"

"Anything for you," he croaked, his hand still roaming her legs, touching, kneading, and worshiping the parts that were bare to him. Away from their respective houses and the theatre, he couldn't show physical affection. They had no idea how many fans would show up. He had to get everything—or as much as he could—out of his system until they were back in close quarters again.

"Have you always been a thigh man?" she asked.

He squeezed her flesh demonstratively. "Never knew I was one until I touched yours."

She shook her head, an adorable smile on full display for him. "What's so special about them?"

He shut his eyes, fingers tucked in between her soft skin. "They're yours," he answered candidly.

She kissed his lips again, then wiped the lingering gloss off with the pad of her thumb. He stared at her, still in awe that she was his.

"Ready, lovebirds?" Sahar called out, popping out of her room.

Willa sighed against his arms and passed a look to him. "No," she said in a voice so low he wasn't sure he was meant to hear it. She lifted herself from his lap. Ethan rose afterward, taking her in his arms for a quick hug and a peck along the side of her temple.

Out there, they couldn't be a couple. Out there, he had to master levels of control he wasn't sure he possessed.

28

______

WILLA

There was no doubt in Willa's mind that she wanted more with Ethan—more of his body, his heart, his mind. She couldn't get enough of him, understanding well enough the novelty of their honeymoon stage, but knowing that it was far beyond anything she'd ever experienced. Desires she had never felt before hit her at maximum speed. Her skin prickled with every touch, wanting more of him in the places where she ached for his attention. The things she saw in her dreams and pictured when she was alone in her bedroom.

And she knew where he stood. He was waiting for her. In that regard, the ball was entirely in her court, and she was ready to shoot her shot, land the three-pointer, or whatever it was that they called it.

She forced her attention back to Ethan and Sahar, who were deep in conversation about linen as a fabric. She had been so zoned out that she wasn't even sure how it started.

God, she wanted to reach over and hold Ethan's hand, walk down the street proclaiming that he was hers, and she was his. But secrecy had also been her decision, and it was one she needed to see through until she was ready for their relationship to be publicized. Things were finally looking up for her—everything made sense. Her anxieties had given her a brief and surprising respite, allowing her to bask in the joy of being beside a man she adored. Still, she was terrified of public opinion.

The truth was, maybe people would equate their intimacy with friendship. She could put her arm around his waist, and it'd be fine. Who'd bat an eyelash? But they'd be lying if someone were to call them out on it.

These small, intimate touches were no longer between best friends who shared an easy rapport but two people who cared about each other far more.

"Wills," he called out, nudging her out of her head.

She looked over at them. "Hmm."

"What plant does linen come from?" Sahar asked.

She thought about it for a beat, her extensive knowledge of fabrics coming from her paternal grandmother being a seamstress. "Flax plant," she answered.

They carried on the conversation, and she tried to remain attentive, but Jesus, why were they talking about linen? She opened her phone to text her cousin, Emma.

WILLA

How'd you know Luke was the one?

Emma answered right away.

EMMA

Feelings keep growing for Ethan, yeah?

WILLA

Yeppp.

EMMA

SCREAMING!!

WILLA

It's been magical. I love him with everything in me—I know I do. But I'm scared I'll mess it up.

EMMA

You won't because you're smart, and you two are already good at communicating. The answer to your question, though, I knew right away with Luke because he listened to everything I said and responded honestly. Still, to this day, my favorite thing about him is that he knows how to communicate. Even when I'm stuck and don't know how to put words to what I'm going through, he'll get it out of me with a ton of patience.

WILLA

I love that. And Ethan's really amazing, Em. I've never felt this way before. I want every part of him and keeping it in is getting harder.

EMMA

It makes complete sense. You two are best friends. You're more connected to him than anybody else. Your body is just reacting to all the emotions that have been there for years now. Stop keeping it in if you know you're ready. Life's too short for that. All you need to do is be fully transparent with him. That's what matters.

On another note, I'm so happy to hear this! Between you and Ben, I now have no one else to worry about. I can finally sleep at night.

WILLA

LMAO. Who was asking you to worry so much about our love lives!?

EMMA

The lord. It was my sovereign duty on this earth.

WILLA

You're such an odd human. I miss you a ton.

EMMA

Miss you too, love. As soon as our schedules permit us to get away for a bit, we'll come see you throw down the house.

Ethan leaned over to her. "You good?"

She looked up and put her phone down. "Yeah, sorry. I wanted to catch Emma before she went to sleep."

He pulled her to his chest and released her. Like he hadn't even realized what he'd done, as though he couldn't help himself, and it was his body's instinctual way of reacting to hers.

They trekked down to the 36th Avenue station rather quietly, getting to the newly built venue quicker than they initially timed out.

Sahar and Willa went straight for Sam's wife, Priya. She smirked at Willa, inciting her to roll her eyes. "Spit it out," Willa jested.

"I'm just thrilled. You've no idea. Also, I've missed you beauties. We need a girl's night soon," Priya said.

Willa smiled sincerely. It was adorable how invested their loved ones were in their relationship, so she couldn't fault them in any way.

"We're definitely overdue for one. And ooh, what's on the setlist?" Sahar asked, "Tell me you two will sing 'Exile' and rip my heart out again."

Priya grinned. "We added it solely because of your reaction last time."

Sahar pumped her fist. "Watch me go home and dump Martin."

"I've called him a prick for so long that I legitimately forgot that was his name," Willa noted.

Sahar bit back a laugh. Priya did the same.

Ethan came over to say hi to Priya before walking back to where Declan and Sam stood.

"How's the new pup?" Willa asked.

Priya curved her lips up and pulled out her phone. "She's adjusting so well. And Ravi is obsessed with her," she added, referring to their three-year-old son.

"I want to squish her!" Sahar screeched.

Willa cooed at it. "Please bring her to the theatre for five minutes one day. I need to see her again." Willa and Sahar had been with Sam when he went to the shelter to pick up the pug for Priya as a Christmas gift. They'd deemed themselves her honorary godparents, too, but with their schedules growing increasingly chaotic in the last few months, they hadn't been by in what felt like ages.

She chanced a glance over at Ethan, who was laughing at something Sam had said, and an outbreak of butterflies congregated in her belly. She turned back to Sahar and Priya, taking note of their discussion of the setlist.

"I had to stop him from turning this entire thing into Disney medleys," Priya commented.

Willa grinned. "Somehow, you two would still make us cry with those, too."

Sam and Priya put on shows together at least twice a year, belting their hearts out with their voices gorgeously married as synchronically as they were.

After a few beats, Naomi and her wife, Jeanie, joined the conversation. Lea, Tanya, and Innila did as well. Then, Miles and Clyde came by, and Miles put his arm around Willa. "My calves have been killing me since 'Forbidden Corridors,'" he said.

Willa turned her head quickly. "What'd you do?" she replied.

"I have no idea. I felt something toward the end, but it's such an odd pain. This one's been good to me, though," he replied, pointing to Clyde with the biggest smile on his face.

Clyde smirked shyly. "I hear I was right about you and the other one, but I'm not supposed to say anything."

Willa beamed. "You were. Was it something we did that made you think that? Because really, a lot of us are touchy," she asked, squeezing Miles' ribs to demonstrate. He made a chirping sound. All three of them chortled.

"No, it was the way he kept looking at you. You'd do it, too. Like every time you were separated, you would gaze in the other's direction. And when you'd talk, there was something there. I can't explain it. Sorry, I'm a people watcher. I find it so fascinating," he admitted, placing his hands in his trouser pockets.

Willa wanted to cry. It sounded so wholesome to hear someone else's observations about her and Ethan's relationship.

Miles grabbed Clyde's face and kissed him quickly. "Do you understand how romantic this gem of a human is? God, how'd I get so lucky?"

Clyde wrapped his arms around Miles.

Willa smiled, big and bright. "No need to apologize. I have to thank the universe for your meeting because watching the two of you on that first night made me miss E so hard. I would've probably denied my feelings longer if it weren't for that day."

Clyde smiled wholeheartedly.

THEY TOOK their seats after a few minutes, with Willa and Ethan nestled between Sahar and Christian.

It was nice to be a little guarded and secluded, lights dimmed with the spotlight on Sam and Priya. Some attendees stood in the back near the bar while others sat in designated areas. Upon realizing that the tablecloth draped along the front of the table, Ethan rested his hand against Willa's thigh, his fingers languidly tracing her leg, his watch cool against her exposed skin. The people in the same row as them were their co-workers. This was fine. This was okay. There was no one behind them. The only people they had to be potentially cautious hiding from were the ones in front of them. And there was no way anyone could see their hands or legs like this.

Willa laced their fingers together for a brief period. She caught him stealing glances occasionally. She didn't feel like drinking, but he handed her his whisky sour at one point, and she took a sip, then another. They were together, but they weren't. She was so close that she could feel every tremor and movement in his body.

She leaned her head forward for a beat, wanting a reminder of what Sam and Priya's former band was called. He couldn't hear her through the noise, so he brought his head closer, his hand trailing to inherently hold her face. She asked again, louder this time.

"Discount Shakespeare," he answered, notes of citrus and smokey maple enveloping her. God, she wanted to kiss him. Just like this, right at this very second.

They parted. Ethan's hand continued roving up and down Willa's legs.

The night was a dream of sorts with Sam and Priya and their intoxicating melodies—their gorgeous real-life chemistry bleeding on stage. Is this how it'd been for her and Ethan? Was this what people saw when they were performing together? Fire and warmth, intermingling with love and trust. She wished for it. Wanted it, desperately.

Willa wanted him. She wanted him to try. She wanted his covetous fingers to trail higher and higher without stopping. She was sure of it now. Heat emanated from both the humidity and her desire. Her mind, heart, and body weaved into a completed, picturesque tapestry.

Her best friend. The love of her life. Her everything.

The night ended with another round of drinks, blissful laughter, sing-a-longs, and emotions flying on all cylinders.

She'd consider his headspace when they got home, and maybe—hopefully—she could have all of him then.

29

ETHAN

Ethan could swear something was different about Willa tonight. The way she let his hands linger, how she looked at him, the ease in her frame when they got back to his place. He couldn't have been delusional enough to read into signs that weren't there. There was no way.

She had asked to shower first when they got to his place, grossed out by the fact that her legs had touched the restaurant seats. He had migrated to his living room when the sounds of running water and the knowledge of Willa's nakedness sent his imagination sprinting toward all the ways he wanted to have her.

He sat on his couch, mind rattled. He attempted to mull over his feelings logically without the interference of the throbbing bulge in his pants.

Think with your head, not your dick, idiot. He scolded himself. *You love this woman with everything in you. Don't scare her off.*

And God, how he loved her. His heart had been beating out of his chest for what felt like ages now. It was Willa—it was always Willa. He loved her so intensely that overwhelming emotions took his breath away every time he tried to grasp their magnitude.

Willa stepped out of his room and sauntered to where he was seated.

He was...embarrassingly hard. *Fuck*. She'd see it. She'd run away. It'd scare her off. *Christ*. He seized a pillow from the couch and placed it on top of his jeans, hoping he was suave enough that she wouldn't notice. Except she was smarter than that.

Willa got closer, eyed the pillow, and then cocked an eyebrow at him.

"I—uh..." he tried to say.

She let out a low laugh. "I am well aware of how the human body works, babe. No need to torture yourself with an excuse."

He groaned and leaned his head back against the cushion. "I'm so sorry, Willa."

Ethan felt her stepping closer to him but didn't think anything of it until she straddled him. Carefully. He leaned his head forward, his eyes widened. She smoothed the pads of her fingers along his cheek. "Why are you apologizing?"

"Because I'm trying not to scare you away."

She laughed boisterously, the brilliant one he could perpetually stay drunk on. "It's going to take a lot more than a boner to scare me away. Plus, I—" she started to say, then paused.

"What is it?" he asked. His hand moved to the nape of her neck, behind her hair. He worked his fingers along her scalp.

"I want to try. I want to do more than what we've been doing."

He gaped at her for a long minute, confident that he was fantasizing about the entire conversation. He must've dozed off on the couch. He must've been dreaming about her.

"Ethan?"

No, this was real. Willa looked at him as though the expression on his face was so bizarre she couldn't read it. He blinked a few times, trying to ensure this was real.

"Right now?" he questioned, trying to gain some clarification of what was happening. Maybe she meant days or weeks from now.

She bobbed her head. "Unless you're too tired."

In all the ways he'd pictured this happening, it'd somehow never been like this. Frankly, he wasn't sure what he had pictured. How or when, really, but it wasn't on a random Sunday night after they'd gotten back from a night out with their friends.

Why does that even matter, Ethan? She wants you, he berated himself.

"How much did I drink?" he asked.

Her eyes narrowed, eyebrows arched. "You're asking me?"

"You were next to me the whole night," he added.

She must've sensed what was happening because she unleashed another laugh. Her expression grew wicked, wildly full of want. Willa rolled her hips against him. Ethan groaned, entirely incapable of hiding it.

"Do you think that you're somehow so drunk you're imagining this?"

He confirmed with a nod.

She did it again, slower this time, more calculated. Once, twice, three times.

His breath hitched. She giggled.

"You seem pretty sober to me," she asserted.

He shut his eyes for a beat. "I'm sure I am. I'm just surprised."

Ethan was also so enraptured that if she kept grinding her hips on him, he'd lose it. Come undone way too soon, right here on his couch, and he didn't want that.

He wanted this to be all about *her.*

She lowered her head, taking his ear between her teeth. "If you want me to repeat it, I will," she whispered.

He rose from the couch immediately, carrying her up with him.

No, he wasn't drunk. He wasn't even buzzed. His tolerance was too high.

Willa wanted him tonight.

He'd give her everything he had.

30

WILLA

He lowered Willa onto her feet. "Are you sure? We could wait. I promise. I meant it when I said I'd wait as long as you need me to."

Desires flamed through his eyes. Crimson made its way onto his cheeks. Willa was sure she must've looked the same.

She shook her head with finality, wrapping her arms tight around his neck. "I want you, Ethan. I want to try, not because I think you'll get tired of waiting, but because *I* want you."

He breathed slowly, still processing. His Adam's apple bobbed. "And you'll tell me if you want to stop, right? If there's anything you don't like, or even if you change your mind midway through. You'll tell me to stop?"

She concurred. "I'll tell you to stop."

"Okay," he responded, pausing again like he was looking for the next batch of words he wanted to say. "I, uhm. I bought condoms recently—not because I was expecting anything, but... but I wanted to have them just in case. They weren't for anyone else, obviously. The ones I had were expired. I haven't been with anyone since Michelle."

And this was exactly why she wanted him—the transparency and the genuine, honeyed tenderness in how he looked out for her.

"Well, I'm glad past Ethan was looking out for future Ethan," she acknowledged.

He took her hand, pressed a gentle kiss to the pulse point beating against her wrist, and then guided her to his bedroom.

She imagined the nerves would boil over inside her and spill into a spiral, but nothing out of the ordinary came, only passions parading through the thumping of her heart.

Willa could've never imagined how fiercely her love for Ethan could continue to expand.

Over the past few weeks, day and night, everything grew more substantial. It took all her might to keep the desires suspended inside of her without saying them aloud. She wanted to wait—hold on for a little while longer—to see if their currently secure bubble would burst and leave them confronted with the proof of their incompatibility.

She knew better, yet she was still catering to a small part of her that continued to worry about all the ways they could jeopardize their friendship.

But despite what she tried to control, she fell deeper and harder, like a cosmic explosion spreading and scattering.

She presumed she was ready shortly after they officially got together, particularly during the nights she spent away from his apartment, underneath her own covers, craving his touch in ways she'd never wanted from others.

He turned back to her in the center of his room. "Willa..." he started to say, then stopped and shut his eyes. His fingers glided unhurriedly along her arms. She waited for him to gather his thoughts—to say whatever it was he wanted to.

She lifted her hand to his hair, carding the soft strands.

Ethan inhaled and exhaled, opening his eyes back to her. He looked at her with an expression she couldn't read—something mirroring awe and novelty, like how she must've appeared every time she marveled at nature's latest spectacle: a flurrying snowfall, a multicolored sunrise, autumnal foliage dancing with the wind.

She drew her fingers to the side of his face and held him there, sliding her thumb back and forth.

He dragged his lips through his teeth and swallowed, pushing down what she presumed were nerves of some sort coiling inside. "I love you so much. I can't mess this up; I need everything to be perfect for you."

She traced along his cheekbones, up to his forehead. "You're not going to mess this up. We're good at being friends first. I love you with my whole heart, Ethan. I've never loved anyone or anything like I love you—that's how I know it'll be perfect. Because whatever happens, it's you and me."

She watched him swallow again, longing coursing through her own veins in response. She inched forward and kissed him, taking the reins to show him that she was ready for this—for every part of him. And she was afraid, undoubtedly, but she'd never felt safe enough to believe that her concerns and desires could co-exist in a place that felt oddly right.

His lips moved against hers hungrily, and she pressed her hand against his chest. The beat of his drumming heart caused everything in her to ease. The thoughts that once clouded her with torturous hesitations and, at times, utter disgust were now overflowing with reverential wishes.

Plus, she didn't purposely match her bra and knickers so they would go unnoticed; she opted to bring a brand-new emerald lace set, knowing it marginally matched his preferred costume on her.

Ethan's mouth trailed to her neck, stopping at the center of her throat with a ravenous groan that punctured deliciously straight through her. He kissed and licked, biting down attentively, eliciting a whimper from her mouth.

His lips were molten heat wherever they roamed. He kissed the three little moles along her collarbone, once, twice.

Music almost always played at the back of Willa's head, and Ethan's kisses steadily felt like the start of a perfect bridge, where everything sped up, and emotions were propelled to staggering heights, striking hard and fast.

She slid her fingers underneath his shirt, exploring the taut muscles of his frame and savoring the way they tensed to her touch. He lifted his mouth back up to hers and took her bottom lip with a forceful, searing tug. His fingers trailed across her shoulders, along her arms, then back down to her torso, wordlessly asking for permission to remove her top.

"No tiptoeing," she reminded him. "I'm yours."

He hummed. "Say that one more time."

She kissed the tip of his nose, his cheekbones, his lips. "I'm yours. And you're *mine*," she emphasized.

The dynamic groan that rumbled from him said a thousand words at once, emotions pronounced and profound. His hands dropped to the hem of her shirt, and he lifted it readily, touching her skin with the rising fabric. He tossed it to the floor and stared at her, his eyes flaming in wonder.

"You look like this is the first time you're seeing this much skin on me. Did you forget the cut-out leather ensemble I come out in during 'Forbidden Corridors'?"

"Respectfully, Wills, I stay very far away from 'Forbidden Corridors' because I'd be way too hard to come back out on stage for 'The Letter.' Plus, this is you. It's different." He dipped his head and kissed along the line of the lace.

Eagerly, he confessed. "I love this color on you."

She couldn't help the grin quirking against her lips. "Good. I chose it with you in mind. This was the surprise for your patience."

A low, elongated curse ascended from somewhere deep in his throat.

Willa reached down against his impatient hands and lips to the bottom of his T-shirt and removed it.

Ethan cupped her face, looking at her with entrenched worship glowing in his expression. She could feel his desire against her thigh, the want and fervor present in the restraint he'd consistently shown her.

Something about the moment emboldened her, the intimacy of their friendship, perhaps—the realization of both their longing on full display, so she pushed him against his bed and straddled him.

She'd let him take control again, chase their needs together, but she wanted to see him like this, flushed with yearning underneath her. "What part of 'Forbidden Corridors' pulls you over the edge?" she asked.

He strained against her, and she relished in the feel of it.

"Willa—" he choked out.

She placed a kiss along the jut of his throat, biting down gently and licking the spot in rapid succession. "Tell me," she whispered. Trailing kisses lower against the broad expanse of his chest, she watched him shut his eyes in response.

Ethan's hands slid to her ass, directing her hips up against the hard length of him.

The friction sent an arresting tremor through her. But, no, not yet. She wanted to know the answer to her question first—to see what undid his self-control.

"Is it the way I thrust up the ladder?" she watched his breath catch again. "Or is it when I'm lying on the floor, drawing my hands lower and lower between my thighs? Maybe it's how I lunge my hips three times before the other dancers join?"

He laid his head back farther and groaned. Willa giggled in a comeback. *Oh, this was going to be fun.* "Tell me," she whispered in his ear.

"It's all of it. The entire damn thing kills me," he avowed.

Her hands skated across his abs, moving lower to the top of his sweatpants, where she stopped and stared at his heated expression. "Lucky for you, you'll get to experience everything the dance is meant to showcase."

Some sort of a growl, low and delicious, escaped him, and then he was flipping them over, her body now beneath his.

Hastily, he undid the bow on top of her jogger shorts, pulled them off her legs, threw them across the room, and then gawked at her matching emerald green knickers.

Embers caught fire in his eyes, blazing with urges she was confident matched her own.

"Fuck, Wills. Did you wake up this morning and contemplate how you were going to wreck me to a point of no return?"

"My exact thoughts, yes," she proclaimed.

He slithered his hand to the back of her bra and unclasped it effortlessly, detaching it with care and folding it atop his bedside table.

"Did my shirt and shorts not deserve the same attention?" she examined with a laugh.

A massive grin formed along his lips. "This is special," he said, then lowered his mouth to her breast, prompting a whimper from the pit of her stomach.

He noted the sounds she'd make, repeating whatever he did to her other breast to elicit the same audible reaction.

"What did I do right in the world to be trusted with you?" he declared, his head burrowed in her chest.

Lowering himself then, his lips grazed her abs with purposeful concentration until he reached her legs. He circled his fingers along the inside of her thighs, and he held her in place, kissing every inch of her exposed skin with agonizing slowness. Willa knew her body was conventionally attractive. It's what years of dance and physical training shaped, but as much as people had wanted her before, she knew with utmost certainty that they wouldn't appreciate her the way Ethan could. Obsessed with her thighs to a hilarious degree, sure, but it was beyond that. It was the bruises and scars, too—the dips and curves he found meaning in.

His mouth climbed back up to her lips. They kissed heartily for a few beats, and then Ethan's lips roamed lower again. He kissed her greedily, fervently, and thoroughly, showing every bit of attention to her thighs again.

And then, he touched her atop her knickers, moving his fingers delicately across where she wanted him most. She shuddered slightly at the contact. She needed more of him, his hands —his lips, whatever he'd give.

Ethan drew his mouth back along the height of her thigh, biting faintly and taking a bit of lace in his teeth. His fingers moved reverentially to the top of the fabric.

She lifted her hips with the same motion as during "Forbidden Corridors," forcing his eyes to dart toward her face in understanding.

She smiled cheekily as she caught his gaze.

Delicately dragging the fabric off her skin, he reached back toward his dresser and placed it with its pair.

He sealed his eyes briefly once more, taking a fevered breath.

Ethan drew himself lower, this time with even more methodic and vulnerably transcendent movements. She wasn't even sure he realized he was doing it. He might've believed he wasn't as skilled of a dancer (hint: he was), but Ethan Everett moved with intention and artistry.

And finally, with one swift move, he brushed his lips into her wet heat.

Willa choked out a whimper. His eyes darted intently on her face to read what the sound meant.

"Go on," she rasped, unable to utter more. Willa dropped her hand to wordlessly ask for his—he took it promptly, held on firmly, and squeezed. With permission fully granted, Ethan's lips and tongue collided against her. Delightfully paced and urgent kisses brilliantly fusing together.

He took his time with her, paying attention to all her cues. The vibrations hummed all around her like an impeccably synchronized symphony, and her climax rushed through her entire body.

Ethan took it all in, his eyes flitting up with an unfamiliar expression, something in between wholly satisfied and transfixed. He said nothing, taking notice of her panting moans with a roguishly enamored smirk curving against his lips. He breathed deeply, eyes locked in devotion.

"If this doesn't work out between us. I'm certain I could manage celibacy. I'd never want anyone else after tasting you," he asserted.

Willa smiled at him. This was what she was always missing in others—unwavering adoration and trust. This was why it'd been damn near impossible with others. She didn't trust them. She didn't know them.

She *knew* Ethan better than he knew himself.

He knew her the same.

She steadied her breathing, her gaze fixed at the sight of Ethan still between her legs. She felt bold and free, conviction taking over again. "Take your pants off and get inside me then."

He groaned and sprang off the bed, eyes frantic and starved. She watched him shrug off his jeans and briefs, abandoning them on the floor before rejoining her on the bed.

Inching closer, Ethan pressed his lips to hers with a fervency that made her toes curl. "I love you," he rasped with a tender tug. "I love you so damn much," he affirmed again like he couldn't believe the words were out there, theirs to sigh, say, or scream whenever they wanted.

"I'll go as slow or as fast as you need me, Wills. I just need you to talk to me so I'll know exactly what works and what doesn't."

"I will."

Ethan's fingers traced along her skin, lower and lower, parting and moving inside of her. She gathered how desperately he wanted this to be good for her, to ensure history didn't repeat itself with an unwanted invasion. But this was Ethan— thoughtful and safe, born to be hers.

A moan rose at the base of her throat, and she didn't suppress it, hoping to show him that she'd welcome him. She wanted *him*.

His lips hovered over her neck, and he placed a kiss there, moving up against the curve of her chin, back toward her ear. Nuzzling against her skin while his finger moved inside of her, slowly at first, he picked up the pace only when she bucked her hips in response. Reading her willingness, he added a second finger.

He was so cautious of her body, so keenly aware of her reactions, that it made her want him more.

"Ethan," she begged. He hummed deliciously at the sound of his name—the yearning in her plea.

Reaching inside his bedside drawer for a condom, Ethan took one, ripped it open with his teeth, and placed it around his length.

He held her gaze and climbed fully on top of her. Ethan cupped her cheek. "Do you have any idea how beautiful you are? Do you know how many times and different ways I've pictured this? Never once thinking I'd be lucky enough even to kiss you?"

Willa pulled him forward and crashed her lips to his with searing passion, urging him to go on.

Ethan entered her slowly, carefully.

"Still good?" he asked.

"Still good," she reassured him.

He thrust himself deeper. Willa arched her hips to take what was left, prodding a deep, vigorous growl from his throat.

Everything about them entwined together felt right, like their bodies were made to move and melt against one another—hard and fast, slow and gentle.

It was far beyond what she had envisioned in her wildest dreams.

She was close, so was he. He was good at withholding many things, but his desire for her wasn't one of them.

Her fingers scratched along his back, her climax coming in like shock waves she could barely decipher; Ethan's followed through afterward, a perfect, unguarded groan left in its wake.

The marriage of their breathless longing lulled against the city's bustling noises. Sticky heat and unreserved smiles plastered across both their faces.

She wrapped her arm against his chest, nestling herself into him as close as physically possible. He enveloped her entirely in his arms and squeezed her tighter. She kissed the jut of his throat, where her lips could reach with minimal effort, and looked up at him. "I love you," she said into the kiss. "In case it wasn't clear or anything of the sort."

"Good, because I have no plans to stop loving you or let you go," he muttered lazily.

THEY GOT OUT OF BED, cleaned themselves up, brushed their teeth, and leaped back underneath the covers. Willa didn't bother with a T-shirt this time, deciding to let the emerald ensemble be her outfit for the night.

"I fucking love you in emerald green," he announced.

She gasped sardonically. "I had no idea. You aren't saying it enough."

"I fucking love you in emerald green," he repeated.

She slid beside him, draping her arm against the slope of his shoulder. "I fucking love you in glasses," she added.

"I had no idea. You aren't saying it enough," he mimicked. A big, toothy grin on his face.

Lifting her head, Willa trekked her lips to his. He kissed her hard, then clutched her tight against his chest.

"I'll definitely manage to kick you this close."

He released a close-mouthed chuckle. "It's a price I'm willing to pay."

31

ETHAN

He heard Willa call out his name, but everything was muffled. Had he been dreaming of her? Was last night even real?

"Ethan," he caught again. Her voice shuddered. He forced his eyes open, vision blurrier than usual as he tried to wake up fully.

Turning his head to face her side of the bed, he spotted Willa propped up and visibly upset about something as she looked at her phone. He jerked up and moved closer to her.

His hands flew to cup her face. "Wills, what happened? What is it?" His voice laced with drowsy concern.

She handed her phone to him. He could make out the lights from last night and the figures of the two of them. He reached against his bedside table, grabbed his glasses, and put them on.

Shit.

It was them—specifically, him. His body angled toward Willa, his hand on her face, essentially glued to her. Blurry and from a distance, it looked far more intimate than the moment had been. It was on the stupidly frustrating anonymous gossip site he loathed, which consistently used "sources" to dish out exclusives on celebrities.

The caption read: *Watched these two all night at Sam and Priya Butler's show yesterday. Can't even believe I caught this shot. They say they're best friends, but there's clearly something more going on here. I can confirm that's Midnights at Pemberley's Ethan Everett sitting beside Willa Davidian.*

Tears stained her pretty brown eyes, the happiness from last night eclipsed by anxiety and defeat. And it was all his fault. One little slip that he didn't even think was a big deal. One small, thoughtless move.

"Willa—" he tried to say, but she broke down instantly.

He reached for her and wrapped her securely in his arms, trying to soothe her with strokes along her back. "I'm so sorry," he repeated over and over. Christ, what had they been saying about them? Her? Had the cruelty already begun that this was her immediate response, or was she merely *that* scared of all that could transpire?

"I just wanted more time with us," she cried, her voice strangled.

"No one can take any of that away. No matter what they say or who knows. We're still us, Wills."

He felt her head shake against his shoulder. "Everything changes now. All of it."

He wanted to ask her to elaborate, to dig into all the things that were freaking her out, but he gathered now wasn't the time. This moment wasn't it. There'd be time to talk, hopefully later in the day.

She ripped herself from his arms and leaned back against the headboard, trying to catch her breath. He noticed Tulip's little head look toward them from the footboard bench, and then she jumped on the bed and spread out next to Willa. Whoever said cats were affectionless never had one. They might not like attention as much as dogs, but they could sense discomfort and try to fix it in their own way. She tried to make biscuits against her side of the blanket, gaining Willa's attention.

"How'd you even see this? I thought you had your notifications disabled."

She released a quiet sniffle. "My agent left a voicemail. And then Sahar texted me to tell me to just ignore the internet entirely, but I obviously didn't listen and went searching."

"Wills…"

"Please don't finish that sentence. I know it's my own doing, but it's our personal lives. I couldn't stay shielded from it forever."

He didn't say anything.

Ethan's phone rang suddenly, with Sam's name on the caller ID. He debated answering, letting the silence stretch between him and Willa instead, then opted to pick up.

"Hey, man," he said.

"Mate, I'm so sorry. I just saw the picture. Priya and I can't figure out who was sitting at that angle. They must've been fans. We didn't really recognize any regulars."

"You're fine. It's not your fault."

"I know, but I feel like shit. I know you guys wanted to keep it private. It shouldn't have gone out like this."

Ethan swallowed a lump in his throat. "Yeah, it's not ideal."

"Is Willa okay?" he asked.

Ethan's head spun. "No, not really," he replied.

"Shit, man. I'm so sorry. Are you with her at least?"

He took a breath. "I am, yeah."

"Good. I'll let you go then. Let me know if you need anything. Whatever it is. Me or Priya. We have both your backs. Please try not to let it ruin a day off."

"Thanks, Sam. Will do."

He hung up the phone as Willa got up off the bed. "I need water. Do you want any?"

Inaudibly, he declined.

God, he felt horrible. Her eyes were so dejected, gone to a place he couldn't reach. He didn't want to spend their day off like this. He didn't want her agency robbed of her because of one stupid little thing he did.

Willa returned to the room with a glass of water in her hand, set it down, and then walked to the bathroom. He felt sharp stabs of pain every time he looked at her, unsure of what to do or how to handle the situation. He opened Instagram to check if any comments would've bothered her, scrolling through his notifications first.

Ethan had followed ETHANEVERETTDAILY way back when, and they'd posted a story. He really hoped it wasn't the picture. He clicked on it, seeing white writing against a black background. It read: *"Out of respect for Ethan's personal life, which he's always been very private about, we will not be sharing the photo currently circulating unless something comes directly from him. Frankly, it's appalling how quickly some of you jumped to make assumptions about something we know little about. Ethan, along with all the other cast members, are entitled to their privacy. Thanks."*

He'd met the two women who ran the account a few times, and they were both always respectful. He was thankful for fans like them in his corner, so he sent them a short message for the post: "Appreciate this a lot. Thank you both 🤍."

Willa came back into the room, muffled a whimper, and sat beside him.

He took her hand in his and held onto it. "How can I make this better? Please tell me what to do."

She sighed heavily, apprehension thick in the sound. "There's nothing you can do."

"We can deny it."

"Yeah, and then if we make things public at some point, they'll know we lied. It's all just a mess. What's done is done."

His mind held on to the word *if* and marinated there. She said *if*, not *when*. Was she still unsure about what they were doing? Was she not certain of whether she wanted this in the long run?

"You said 'if,'" he blurted, his voice sounding small and despondent.

She squared her eyebrows and stared at him with confusion. "What?"

"You said *if* we make things public, not *when*. Are you...are you still unsure about us?"

She blinked rapidly. "No. I'm sorry. I'm just angry. I wasn't being precise with my words when I have 'she'll fuck him to the top,' playing on a loop in my mind."

His ears burned, and flames shot through him. His voice came out more intense than he wanted it to. "Did someone say that about you?"

She didn't say a thing.

"Willa..." he called out.

She shut her eyes, biting the inside of her cheek. "You're asking me as if you're going to do something about it. You literally can't. Everyone would advise against it. PR advises against it. So, what's the point?"

"I don't give a shit what anyone tells me to do. I'm not letting comments like that slide." He felt feral. His lungs burned. The pit of his stomach churned with acidity. He knew that some people were a bit too much, but were they truly that low and vile?

He grabbed his phone again, remembering that he was meant to browse through the comments on the gossip page's post.

If this is true, they're hot as hell. I ship it.

I knew it! I knew it! I knew it! Their chemistry is too hot for it be platonic.

Once again, I'm asking if Ethan Everett can fight. I'd do anything for Willa.

Ew, one of the background whores? Unexpected from him.

You realize they're actors, right? Also, wtf. Who talks like this? Get over yourself.

And that ladies and gentlemen is how she'll fuck her way to the top.

What does he see in her?

Should've known he'd get with a girl like this. This production has changed him. I can't call myself a fan anymore.

This is what I've been saying for months. I've been a fan for years, and his behavior lately has been so off. He's out partying more, barely does stage door, and now he's with someone who's clearly a horrible influence.

Okay, first some of you need to calm down. It's not like he was gonna be with you anyway. Second, if you zoom in, it looks like he's saying something??

Naw, I was there (I didn't take the photo), but they were v close.

What is wrong with some of y'all?!! They're adorable. Willa is the sweetest. If this is true, then I'm happy for them.

Some of these comments, my goodness. You people need to relax I'm happy for them.

This is weirdly hot???? Would love to have been a fly on a wall. The way his hand is just covering her whole face? I'm here for it.

The only thing she has going for her is a good body. The rest is so bland.

He looked over at Willa, one pearly-painted fingernail in her mouth as she mindlessly petted Tulip with her other hand. Christ, he felt sick.

She seemed so far away from him now, inches away but untouchable—fully armored, nowhere near the unbarricaded woman from last night.

The last thing he ever wanted to do was hurt Willa, and he did so inadvertently. Ethan got out from underneath the covers and went to the bathroom. He splashed his face with cold water twice, then brushed his teeth, gazing at her toothbrush beside his, trying to hold on to the familiarity, hoping it wouldn't end. She'd been right about the fans; he knew she had, but he genuinely didn't think it would've been this cruel. He had stopped reading comments ages ago. People had generally been respectful and cool during Sam's Instagram lives; he'd forgotten that there was a whole other side to the internet that existed to spread hate.

He also didn't think they would've been caught. He was blissfully hopeful it would've happened on their own terms, comments disabled maybe.

"Betty is calling you," she exclaimed from his room. He rinsed his mouth and walked over, picking it up.

"Hey, Betty."

His manager exhaled a compassionate sigh. "Hi, you. I'm checking in."

"You saw, right?" he asked.

"Mhmm, I'm so sorry that happened to you two. How is Willa?"

He answered honestly. "Not good."

"I'm sorry, E. I really am. How do you want to proceed with this?"

He sighed, sitting on the edge of the bed. "I don't know. I'm pissed. I want to say something, but do you think that's smart?"

"In this day and age, it could work if you're up for it. I'm blanking on who it was, but another actor also had to do this recently. Write a statement, shoot it over to me, and I'll look at it, then turn off your comments when you post. You could also not say anything at all. Do you. Your personal life is no one's business. This isn't a scandal and doesn't need to be. Discuss it with Willa and listen to your gut. I trust you'll handle it well, no matter what you decide to do."

He nodded, considering her words. "Yeah, I'll talk it over with Willa."

"That works for me. Call if you need anything." Ethan had been with Betty since he started his career. She looked out for him like a second mother, and knowing she genuinely cared made trials like this easier to endure.

He looked at Willa. She was on her phone again.

"Please stop reading. It's a mess out there. None of it is true."

She shrugged. "I might not be a gold digger, sure, but one person had a point about my voice having an annoying pitch. Oh, and there's a really lovely comment that said I must be asking for attention because, and I quote, 'Does she own anything other than crop tops?' Jokes on them because I do."

He pinched the bridge of his nose and then pushed his glasses up. "Wills, please look at me."

She did. Her eyes were swollen, red, and trickling with heartache. "Your voice doesn't have an annoying pitch. Let's get that out of the way first. You know that people will come up with anything to make themselves feel better, right?" he asked.

"I know that logically, but it doesn't help at this second."

Sighing, he reached for her hand, but Tulip mistook it as a sign to play, so she swatted him. He pulled his hand away, noting that this wouldn't work.

"Willa, all of this is going to go away someday. You said it yourself. Our contracts will end, we'll get different jobs, and we might even have to spend time apart in different places. But the way that I love you will be the one constant. I'd sacrifice everything to be with you. I'd choose you over any role because I'm certain that even with all the praise in the world and standing ovations every night, nothing compares to how I feel when you smile at me. Or when I hear that perfect laugh of yours. You said it yourself, and I'm right there with you. I could lose all of it, and I'd be fine, but I can't bear the thought of losing you. I'd rather be remembered for the way that I love you than my job. None of it matters without you beside me."

She was in tears again. "I'm sorry for ruining this. I'll get through it eventually, Ethan, but it's hard not to actualize their words in my head right now. And you're worth all of it. I don't regret a single second from last night. I'd do it over again even if I knew this would be the outcome. I just need time to come to terms with this new normal."

He reached forward and gently wiped the tears from her eyes. He brushed wisps of hair from her forehead, tugging them behind her ear, catching Tulip's gaze from beneath. "Take all the time you need, beautiful. You didn't ruin anything—none of this was on you. If anything, it's on me. Just please don't push me away. Let me be here for you."

"It's not on either of us. It's on the people who have no sense of boundaries when it comes to photographing others."

Willa rolled out of bed. This time, Tulip followed, assuming she was going to feed her. Willa looked down and shrugged affectionately. "I was going to stretch, but sure, little orange slice, let's get you fed." She turned to Ethan. "Did you order new cans of wet food? You were down to one yesterday."

"Yeah, I haven't unboxed it, though. It should be by the front door," he answered.

She nodded, then reached for his T-shirt sitting atop a chair and threw it over her emerald ensemble. The two of them ambled out, with Tulip running ahead of Willa like breakfast was an Olympic sport she was determined to win.

He thought of the kind of statement he could make and what

it would entail while he stood up and fluffed the pillows to make his bed. Except looking at his bed trailed his mind to the memories of her intoxicating sounds of pleasure. The way her body moved underneath his, the way she came undone, her gorgeous face flushed with shades of pink. How the flecks of gold around her eyes shimmered.

How unhappy did people have to be to pass judgments as they did when she was the most beautiful rarity he'd ever known? He fell for her honesty, her kindness, her unceasing warmth, and he hated that people couldn't see that.

My cat loves her. That's the only approval I need.

Short and simple, maybe he could post that. No, it needed to be perfect. It needed to be poetic. It needed to reflect every ounce of his heart because Willa was everything to him. His love for her had to be palpable. It's what she deserved.

He finished making his bed and met them in the kitchen, finding Willa sitting on the floor with Tulip.

"Do you ever wonder how much simpler life would be if you were a cat? If you're lucky enough to find a good home, you're entirely oblivious to how gross the world can be, and you just get a bunch of people who love you even when all you do is sleep ninety percent of the day."

He chuckled, sliding down to sit beside her.

Willa curled her arm into his elbow and burrowed her head into his shoulder. He placed his other hand on her fingers, gently grazing his thumb along her skin.

"Yeah, but I think I'd want to be some sort of a sea creature in another life. Be able to breathe underwater," Ethan replied.

"I'd say I want to be a crow so I could fly, but hey, they're just as hated as I am right now." She looked up at him, smiling. "Too soon?"

"A bit."

A sad, strange little laugh left her lips. "I think that's why it hurts so much," she said, eyes fixed on the island in front of them.

"It's bringing up all the bad memories from when I was bullied as a kid. I know I told you parts of it, but I wasn't a cute kid. People were vicious. They called me all sorts of names. It wasn't until I started taking dance classes that I found a place to fit in. I was really shy and quiet—I couldn't defend myself. They didn't bother getting to know me. They just mocked. And I know kids are cruel; most grow out of that, but this feels so similar. It took years of therapy to work through my self-doubts and fears of inadequacy. I know better than to let it get to me, but it stings."

He tilted his head and placed a kiss on her temple. "I'd bully all those kids right back, and then I'd only hang out with you."

"I bet you were adorable when you were little," she replied.

He laughed. "Not many people have glasses kinks. I've been four eyes since I was in elementary school."

"Sucks to be them because they're wrong."

Tulip walked by them, sweeping against their sprawled feet before leaving them alone in the kitchen. "How do you feel about me saying something?" Ethan asked.

She sighed heavily. He hated bringing it back up since she was doing fine for a split second.

"I trust you. If you feel it's right, it's your call to make," she answered.

"But what would you be comfortable with? What do *you* want me to do?"

"I want to hide, except that's not an option."

Moving his arm and facing her fully, Ethan rested his hand against the lines on her face. He looked at her for a beat—his best girl, his best friend, the absolute, unmistakable love of his life. "I can't promise this is the last time something will hurt you. But I can promise that whatever comes our way, I'm going to be right here to take it on with you. Your happiness is always going to be my number one priority."

Willa burst into tears. "You've broken a dam in me. I can't keep crying like this," she sniffled.

He brought his lips to her face this time, wiping the tears away with kisses in their place. "I'm sorry. I'm sorry. Please don't cry."

She bobbed her head from side to side. "These aren't sad tears. These are 'I'm *grateful for you*' tears."

Ethan kissed her with everything in him, pleasantly surprised when she reciprocated by climbing on top of him with her legs, hugging him close.

"Would you be mad if I went home today?" she asked.

Ethan shook his head. "Of course not. Why would I be mad?"

"I don't know. I just need to process it all. Sit with my emotions for a bit."

"Promise me that you're okay," he started to say.

She drew both her hands to either side of his face. "I will be. I didn't want this to get in the way of us. And I'm not going to let it. But I don't want to feel small, and right now, I feel small. I need to be the one to pick myself up if that makes sense."

He tipped his face sideways to kiss her palm.

"I know you know how much all the attention makes me uncomfortable. The times I want to crawl into a hole because it's too much, and I start to feel like I'm losing my humanity," he said.

She stroked his jaw with delicate caresses, cementing her understanding.

"But you've made so much of it easier for me. You know my tells. You read me like an open book. You let me be fragile and uncertain. You celebrate my victories with me."

He sighed heavily. "I knew I loved you when I broke down in

your arms after my grandpa died, and you carried me through those days. You never once looked at me differently. When you stayed awake with me all night and then metaphorically held me upright the next day. We were friends then, but you became my anchor, and I want to be that strength for you, Wills— however you need me to. If you need to be alone, or if you need space, all of it, whatever it is, I'll support you."

"You're my anchor, too. Please don't think you aren't. I meant it when I said you're the person I search for in a crowded room. I don't blame you one bit, Ethan. You're worth this, ten times over. Once the shock wears off, I'll be okay."

She drew her lips to his cheek and kissed him there. "At some point, the words aren't going to matter. I know that. It'll be noise, blurring in the background while we live our lives doing what we love most. I get to have all your smiles and your heart. I'm not letting you go, no matter how crushing the unkindness feels right now."

He smiled faintly and kissed her. They stayed like that for a while, lounged on his kitchen floor, mouths pressed together, hands, teeth, and tongues, taking each other in while the rest of the world raged on.

It was quiet here, silence stretching out before them, creating a safe space.

32

WILLA

Willa walked through her door and threw herself onto the sofa next to Sahar. *The Golden Girls* was again playing on the TV while Sahar was playing a game on her Switch.

Sahar looked up. "How are you feeling?"

"Better, but like shit," Willa mumbled.

Sahar drew closer and squeezed her shoulders. "I had to put my phone down because I was ready to curse everyone out. Christian had to call and warn me against it."

Willa grumbled, laying her head back against the cushion. She slid lower on the sofa. "Everything was so perfect last night, and then this happened."

"Are things okay with you and Ethan?"

Willa nodded. "Yeah. He wants to say something and talked to his manager. I told him I trust him with whatever it is."

Sahar smiled. "If you had to go through something as shitty as this, I'm glad it's with someone like Ethan. Those voices will dim at some point. I also do have a bit of news for you that'd make you happy?" she questioned.

Willa narrowed her gaze. "Go on..."

"I dumped the prick," Sahar said matter-of-factly.

Willa nearly jolted and sat upright. "What?"

Sahar clicked her tongue. "Yup. Man, something about watching Sam and Priya perform. I called him over. I didn't want to be an arsehole and do it over the phone, but he refused to come. Said he was lazy. Told me to come. So I just dumped him."

"What'd he say?"

Sahar belted out a laugh. "He called me a selfish whore and hung up."

Willa's eyes grew wide. She'd wring his neck in if she ever ran into him. "Are you kidding me?"

"Nope."

Willa huffed. "We need to toast being called whores on the same night."

Sahar brought her pinky to Willa's. She took it. "Wouldn't want to be a whore with anyone else but you."

"Cheers, sister," Willa started, then paused. "I really want coffee from Amanda's. And a guava cheese strudel. Want to come with me?" she asked.

Sahar sat upright. "I don't even like strudel, but I do weirdly want one. Let's do it."

A giddy excitement shot through Willa.

"Let me change out of my pajamas first," Sahar noted.

Willa turned off the TV and rose to her feet. She dropped the clothes from her tote into the laundry hamper, then trekked to her room to change the outfit she'd been wearing. Rifling through her clothes, she settled on an oversized Bowie T-shirt and cycling shorts.

She didn't want to let the voices haunt her. She wanted a routine as much as possible.

She'd get through it in time. She'd drown out the negative voices that didn't matter and hype up the better chatter.

Her phone vibrated with a text from Ethan as she strode out of her room.

ETHAN

I have a request for you. Would you be willing to take June 28-30 off with me?

WILLA

That's your birthday weekend. Did you have something in mind?

ETHAN

My parents have a cabin up north; I miss them, and there's that spot I want to take you, too. I figured we could get away for a bit.

WILLA

Would we be able to get it off this late?

ETHAN

It's a little over a month. I can't imagine why it'd be a problem. I haven't taken any vacation days since we started.

WILLA

I have. . .

ETHAN

The show hadn't begun yet.

Oh, right, he had a point. She'd forgotten that minor detail.

WILLA

Your memory needs to be studied in a lab.

ETHAN

Is that a yes?

Sahar wiggled on her Birkenstocks and joined Willa at the door. "A smile! Good news, I hope?"

Willa hadn't even realized what expression she'd been wearing. "He wants us to take a few days off for his birthday and head up to his parents' cabin."

Sahar flapped her arms. "Gah. That sounds fun and everything you deserve."

They locked the door, stepped into the lift, and went down to the lobby.

"How do you feel?" Willa asked, taking a big step to avoid a puddle outside their flat.

Sahar sighed with surprising contentment. "I'm happy with my decision. He wasn't good for me. Seeing all these healthy relationships in front of me, you with Ethan, knowing you've always loathed the prick. How he'd always cause some sort of an argument? I'm happy to have him out of my life. Maybe I'll get lucky and find a best friend who will later fall in love with me."

Willa laughed heartily. "I want that more than anything else for you."

"But I'm swearing off men for a while. I need to be on my own. It feels like it's all drained me—the fights, the one-way commitment. I don't know how much more of myself I can give."

"If that's what you want, then I support you fully," Willa said.

Sahar pursed her lips in thought. "I also think it's high time I stop chickening out and dye my hair red."

Willa gasped. Sahar had wanted to dye her hair red since they first met, always backing out at the last minute because she didn't want to bleach her hair in the process. Willa was the same in that regard; she'd only ever gotten lowlights. Still, Sahar had always debated it. Every year or so, it'd come up, with no action following the temptation.

"I'm serious. Fuck it. I'll make an appointment. Come with me and force me to do it. If I loathe it, I'll dye it back." Luckily, their jobs required wigs, so they could do whatever they wanted with their hair.

Willa looked on proudly, then pondered for an instant. Sahar should do it. It'd look smashing on her, and quite frankly, one of them should be brave in that regard. In response, Willa proposed a wager. "If you dye your hair, *I'll* make a public post about Ethan."

Sahar stopped in her tracks. Her mouth fell open. Willa had never publicly shared about any of her boyfriends before. The shock on Sahar's face made her snort.

"Sod off. You'd never," Sahar huffed.

She said it. She meant it. She'd do it for Sahar. And for Ethan, too. "You dye your hair, and I'll post about Ethan on his birthday."

Sahar lifted a finger. "On your feed. Not in stories."

"On my feed," Willa confirmed.

Sahar brought her hand over to shake. Willa extended hers.

"Then it's settled," Sahar declared.

WHEN THEY GOT to Amanda's Coffee, Jay greeted them from behind the counter. "Sahar, Willa—afternoon."

Sahar looked at him with concern. "Mate, do you ever take days off? Is this legal?"

A closed-mouth chuckle escaped him. "I am the manager," he reminded them. Sahar, more specifically.

"Yes, but even managers deserve time off," Sahar replied.

Jay shrugged. "One called out. Another is sick, so here I am. The usual?" he asked.

"Yes, please, but add in another strudel. This one has influenced me," Sahar answered, pointing to Willa.

Willa made a face that could be translated to "What can I say?"

They paid and watched Jay get to work while Dahlia took orders from the people behind them. Willa looked from the man behind the counter to Sahar.

Physically, they'd be stunning together. He was tall, with a strong bone structure, a great scruff, good hair, *glasses,* a booming, melodic voice, and a killer smile that seemed only to peek through when Sahar was around.

Jay wasn't unfriendly per se; he was always respectful, but there was a clear difference in his demeanor when Sahar wasn't around. Willa had noticed it from the moment he and Sahar started talking about a football match, which led to conversations about a video game they'd both been playing. Something told Willa that if Sahar hadn't been taken, he would've figured out a way to spend more time with her.

"We should sit in here. We never have time to do that," Willa pointed out, taking in the faux succulents and cactus plants covering the place along with the wall of vinyl records and old posters. There were rows of adorable floral mugs aligned against another back wall, which made the place feel like the kind of shop they'd find back home in London. The exterior decorations needed a bit more work, but eh, it'd pass. The interior deserved the praise.

Sahar agreed. "I got nowhere else to be."

They sat down after their orders were called. Willa observed both Jay's surprise at seeing them seated and the opportunities he took to steal glances at Sahar when she wasn't looking. *Ha! He had to have a thing for her. She loved being right.*

"Jay's a director, yeah?" Willa asked, her voice low enough so only Sahar could hear.

Sahar took a bite of the pastry, eyeing Willa through her long lashes. "Mhmm," she acknowledged.

"Have you seen any of the films he's made?" Willa asked.

Sahar looked up finally and took a sip of her coffee. "I've been meaning to, but I haven't gotten around to them yet."

Willa tilted her head. "I wonder if Ethan has."

"He has, actually. When we came here to grab drinks together the first day you went on as Elizabeth, he told Jay how he appreciated one of them. I put it on my watchlist after that."

"Hmm," Willa noted. It must've been sad if Ethan hadn't forced her to watch it with him. He was banned from making her sit through anything too tragic for the rest of the summer.

She chanced another glance at Jay, who now had his back turned away from them and seemed to be writing something on a notepad. "He seems like a good person. I can't exactly pinpoint how I know that, but he does," Willa said aloud.

Sahar echoed the sentiment. "I get that vibe, too, but my radar can't exactly be trusted these days."

Willa narrowed her eyes, noticing the brief sadness flashing through Sahar.

"None of that negative talk. You've always known deep down that Martin was a prick, but you try to see the good people, even when they don't deserve it. And one of these days, when you least expect it, someone will surprise you, Sahar. He'll know what a bloody brilliant catch you are the second he spends five minutes with you, and all those wankers who hurt you will continue to be miserable morons for the rest of their sorry lives."

Sahar smiled. It was a little somber. "Seems like it was only yesterday I was giving drunk Willa a very similar talk in our kitchen."

"And look how well that turned out for me," Willa acknowledged.

"You're a big sap now is what you are," Sahar declared.

Willa lifted her coffee cup in a wordless toast. She was, she truly was.

How could she not be when she watched Ethan's sadness torrent all over his incandescent blue eyes because she'd been in pain? How could she not vouch for love when she knew with utmost certainty that Ethan would do anything for her? How could she not see all the wonders of being adored when he promised her that she'd never have to go through anything alone, ever again?

Willa might've needed a moment to clear her mind, but she would overcome all of this.

She'd overcome the negativity and the hurdles.

She'd fight for him.

She'd fight for their love.

AFTER A WHILE, they said bye to Jay and Dahlia and headed home. It also helped that Willa chose to stay off her phone, not wanting to see any more comments about her and Ethan's relationship, even if they were positive. It wasn't until they were getting ready for bed that Sahar called out to her about Ethan making a post.

Willa came back out into the living room. "I'm scared to look at it."

"It's lovely and honest," Sahar confirmed.

Willa wasn't sure what she was in for. She knew he'd have his comments disabled, so obviously, she wouldn't have seen anything adverse from that end, but still.

It made her nervous, a little—wait, no, very—anxious, too.

"Okay, hand it over," she relented, reaching forward.

Sahar brought her phone closer, already opened to a picture of them Willa didn't even remember taking. It must've been their set photographer, Gary Black. It was back in Boston, and they'd been sitting on the floor, her head against his shoulder, a big, goofy smile across her face. The moment came to her suddenly.

They'd been watching Naomi and Declan run through "Stubborn Bastard." Christian was on the other side of Willa, and they'd been watching from the wings. Gary had come over to them and snapped a few shots of the whole cast. It was still in the early days of their friendship, and at the end of that day, they'd had their first movie night together, wherein she introduced him to another version of *Pride and Prejudice* with *Death Comes to Pemberley*.

He posted that picture on his feed with a red heart and disabled comments, then shared it on his stories with a statement.

Hi everyone. I wholeheartedly appreciate the tireless support and compassion in both my career as an artist and as a person. You've been some of the best fans for the longest time, and I'm always deeply grateful. But at the same time, the events from last night have forced my hand in addressing something that I wanted to keep private for a little bit longer. I'm the happiest and best version of myself when I'm with Willa, who's been my best friend and greatest source of comfort and joy since we met. The vile comments are uncalled for, hurtful, and outright unnecessary. The world is already a shitty place, and we could all use a bit of kindness amid all the turmoil we're living through in our day-to-day lives. Please keep this in mind when wondering if that assumption you're going to make on the internet is something you're proud of.

"I hate that he had to do something like this for the first time in his career."

Sahar sighed knowingly. "It sucks, yeah. But, Wills, fuck it all. You have someone beside you who'd do anything for you. You've got to keep reminding yourself that all those comments are just noise."

"What if it gets more dangerous than that? What if some of those comments are from the same people who repeatedly stalked him when he was on *Detective Vice?*"

Sahar took her hand and squeezed. "Then we'll deal with it. They haven't been seen near the theatre since the show began."

Willa knew Sahar had a point—she did—but it'd take some getting used to. She also needed to stop being so anxious about social media because so much of her career relied on it. It was always fine when she and Miles would post a choreographed number. She never cared when she was part of group photos. Still, all of this felt too intimate, and she'd have to learn to live with it.

But Rome wasn't built in a day, and these things would take time.

33

ETHAN

Ethan turned from his back to face the side of his bed where Willa should've been. His heart fractured again. Even though he wanted it, he didn't expect her to stay with him every night, but today's incident made it all the more difficult to be away from her.

He grabbed his phone to text her, but she'd beaten him to it.

WILLA

I'm going to bed. Not to be dramatic, but I miss your freaking arms and your whole face and YOU. I love you. See you tomorrow!

Fuck. He missed her, too. He always missed her.

ETHAN

Missing you is my default emotion, even when you're sitting right next to me. This bed is too damn big without you in it. I love you, too, beautiful. Sleep well!

He hadn't gone back on social media since making the statement. Frankly, he didn't even want to check. He didn't care. It was done. As long as Willa was okay and felt safe, that was all that mattered to him. Still, he opened the app just to see. He spotted her icon, and surprise dawned on him when he saw a post from her. He clicked on it to see what she'd posted.

It was their photo, with a purple heart underneath.

He didn't expect her to share it. He didn't need her to either. Yet, he hoped that it meant she was feeling a little better about the whole situation. Maybe she was less scared, more hopeful. God, how he wished.

THE FOLLOWING DAY, Ethan's phone rang as he looked for his keys to head out. He swore he hung them on the hook where they belonged, but they were nowhere to be found. His brother's name flashed on the screen.

"Yo," Ethan answered. He almost made a sarcastic remark about how Nick wouldn't return his calls but opted for the casual greeting.

"Hey, man. Sorry I've been MIA," Nick started.

Ethan sighed. He hadn't expected an acknowledgment of his absence. "You're good. Don't worry. How are you?"

"I'm sure mom told you."

"She did," Ethan disclosed.

"I figured she would, even though I hoped she wouldn't. She also told me what happened to you. I'll never know how you put up with it, bro. A bunch of strangers on the internet having an opinion on your love life? That fucking blows."

"It has its downsides," Ethan started. "Not sure I'd trade it to look at essays, though," he added, wanting to lighten the mood.

Nick let out a snort. "Ha! Right now, neither would I. Can I be real for a second?"

"I'd prefer that," Ethan insisted.

"Now that I've had time to sit with it, I think getting laid off might've been a blessing. I used to get home and stare at the goddamn wall, E. I was so drained last year, working extra hard to avoid being axed in the budget cuts, and for what? They got rid of me anyway. Has a role ever made you feel like that? Like you love it, but at the same time, it's sucking the life out of you?"

"Not a role, per se, but the industry often does that. Do you not remember how screwed up I was back in 2017? I'm pretty sure I spoke like two words during Thanksgiving dinner that year," he answered.

Nick sighed. "Shit, yeah, I do remember that."

Ethan sat on the arm of his couch before continuing. "I'm pretty sure that's the case with every person at some point in their career, though. The work is mostly rewarding, but it's tiring. Plus, the gigs aren't always constant, which is a whole other issue, so I get it. Time off isn't always actual time off. The whole system is shit in almost every field. But take some time for yourself right now. Do you have money saved up? If you need..."

Nick interrupted, likely knowing how Ethan was going to finish the sentence. "No, no, no. I mean, thank you. But I have some put aside. I saw an opening at Cal State Long Beach, but I don't even want to apply. I'd rather wait and see if something opens up here or at least along the coast."

"Yeah, I get that. I wouldn't want to move to California, either. I hope something opens for you. You're going to bounce back, Nick. And if you need anything, you know you can tell me, right?"

Ethan recalled Willa's comment about not wanting to burden her brother when she needed him most, so he tried to take the chance to remind Nick that he was there.

"I know. And actually, I went fishing with my buddy Matt. Unplugged a bit, and it got me thinking that maybe I should take Jo's advice and finally see a therapist. I don't think I've properly coped with anything in the last four years, E. Between my breakup with Amelia and then grandma and grandpa dying so close to each other, and now all of this with my job…I'm not sure what I'm supposed to do."

Ethan smiled. He'd never been more proud of Nick's honesty. "I think that's a really good idea. That could help you recharge a bit."

"Yeah, that's how I'm trying to look at it," Nick said. "Good thing is, I don't have to work with Lonnie again."

"Ha! That's the department chair, right?" Ethan specified.

Nick huffed on the other end of the line. "Yeah, I swear, man, he drove me up the wall every fucking day. If he wasn't older than Dad, I would've cursed him out ages ago and got myself fired. Anyway, enough about me. Tell me about Willa. Which of you snapped first and realized that your friendship wasn't normal?"

Ethan let out a laugh and then caught his brother up on the last few weeks. Nick mentioned wanting to take another trip to the city soon and promised Ethan that he'd make his famous honey-garlic glazed salmon for when they were all at the cabin next month.

CHRISTIAN ENTERED Ethan's dressing room shortly after he'd gotten to work. "You're a godsend, E."

"What did I do?" Ethan asked.

His friend and co-star burst with excitement. "Dan is coming in on the twenty-third, and his last day is the morning of the twenty-ninth. I'd initially requested the twenty-eighth off, too, but I took that back when Dina gave me your off days. My man gets to watch me go on for a principal role. I feel like a schoolboy. I'm so psyched."

Ethan balled his hand and gestured for a fist pump, then

hugged Christian with a pat on his back. "Shit, man. I wish I could see it. I'm thrilled that it worked out for you."

"So am I. Nervous as hell but excited."

Ethan gave him another shoulder squeeze. "You're going to be perfect."

He spotted Willa from the corner of his eye, wanting to walk in. They hadn't seen each other yet since yesterday. "Come in, beautiful," he called out.

"Wills! Hey," Christian grinned.

"Hi," she smiled, giving him a quick hug before striding to where Ethan stood. She wrapped her arms around the side of his frame and burrowed herself closer.

Christian tilted his head in response. "Little did you know during that drunken night that this is where you'd be in a few months."

Willa looked up at Ethan, beaming. "I know," she blushed.

Ethan squeezed her to his chest and held onto her. "Christian just told me that Dan will be here when he goes on as Darcy."

Willa nearly screeched. "Mate! That's amazing. How long is he here for?"

"He gets in on Saturday, so I'll be off until Thursday the twenty-seventh."

"That sounds like a blast. I'm so excited for you! Do you have an official date for when he's coming back for good?" Willa asked.

Christian smiled heartily. "Yes, end of September. But we should also do something when he's here if you guys aren't too swamped."

Ethan replied without a second thought. "Absolutely. Let us know when and where."

Willa agreed with a definite nod.

"Alrighty, lovebirds. I'll leave you two alone now," Christian said, walking out the door.

Willa and Ethan waved him off, then turned to each other. She had a look on her face that struck him deep, rotating his insides like a Rubik's cube, with everything realigning for the first time since yesterday. He'd never get used to this. Never.

He tucked a few strands of hair behind her ear and gawked at her. She already had all her makeup on, save for her fiery, red lips, which he knew she left out because she wanted him to kiss her before applying it.

Ethan leaned forward, pausing at the juncture of her neck. "How's my girl feeling today?" he asked, planting a kiss at her pulse point.

She let out a small, delectable sigh. "I'm better. It'll take some getting used to, but I feel okay right now. I almost didn't wear this shirt, but I didn't want to let the noise get to me, so I call that progress."

He took note of the cropped baby-blue tank top she had on with her jeans. She looked incredible. "Good, because you're perfect, and so is the shirt," he said.

"You were a little late today. Is everything okay?" Willa asked then.

It was true; he had been—only thirty minutes or so. "Yeah, I told my parents everything last night, and I talked to my sister. Then Nick finally called right as I was about to head out and mentioned his job, so I lost track of time on the phone."

"I'm so glad you spoke to him. Do you feel a little better about that situation?" If Ethan had to list the things he loved most about Willa, her understanding of his comfort levels would be in the top three. Whether it was realizing that this situation was weighing on him or how she always noticed when he was feeling physically or mentally off, it eased him to know that someone he trusted was ceaselessly looking out for him.

"A lot better, yeah. He said he wants to start therapy because he feels himself shutting down, and I've never been prouder. It sucks being away from my family, which I'm sure you get, but it's worse when you know they're struggling and aren't saying anything."

Her smile was so warm, like sitting in front of a crackling fireplace, soothing and pleasant in the grueling winter.

"It must've been even harder on you because you're the eldest, so you instinctually make everyone's pain your responsibility."

Ethan squeezed her to his chest and swung her in place. "Thank you for seeing me. Thank you for choosing to love me," he whispered.

"I'll always see you, and I'll love you through everything," she confirmed, cuddling closer to him.

He kissed her forehead.

Willa held his gaze. "I do have a favor to ask you," she voiced.

"Name it."

"I don't have the mental capacity to do stage door, at least not for the next few nights. But even if you're not up for it, can you try? I keep wrestling with how people will perceive me, and I don't want anyone thinking that I'm pulling you away."

He shut his eyes for a beat, agreeing wordlessly with a nod.

"I realized something last night, and I wanted to tell you today, but I'm not sure how you'll react," he started.

"Try me."

"Well, now that people know about us, I don't want anyone else beside me at the Tonys," he paused, grazing his fingers across her blush. "But only if you're comfortable by then. I don't want it to stress you out. If it will, then we can sit away from each other or something."

She gave him a sidelong glance. "What about your parents?"

He shrugged. "I'm not winning, so I told them not to bother. Plus, it's graduation week. It's always a stressful time for them."

"Ethan, you don't know that. Why would you rob them of that experience?"

"They've been the last two times. It's not the end of the world."

She gaped at him. "But this could be monumental for you. Your performance is perfect. Your chances of winning are higher than ever."

He placed his hands on either side of her shoulder. "If that's the case, I want you to be the one next to me. You've made me a better performer. You've helped me stay sane every step of the way."

She kissed him, slowly for a moment. "I'll pluck up the courage for you."

34

WILLA

Willa was fortunate to be able to reschedule her regular bi-weekly therapy sessions to once a week to work through the fears and hesitations that kept creeping up after their relationship went public.

It was a process, to be sure, but she was getting there. It helped to continue posting dance videos with Miles, which often led to positive reinforcement about their work as artists. It disconnected her from the noise concerning their personal lives.

It was also reassuring to be made aware of the detail that many people were *waiting* for Ethan and Willa to get together— still, one step at a time.

But tonight wasn't about her. It was about all of them—it was a day to commemorate the best of theatre, and it was a time to celebrate the show that'd perpetually leave a mark on each of them.

She got her hair and makeup redone after the matinee show, where their performance of "Midnights at Pemberley" was recorded to air during the awards later in the evening. Ethan's suit, courtesy of Armani, was pressed and ready to go. Willa was set to wear a gorgeous champagne, sequined dress from Donika Loci Peje.

Their ride to the Lincoln Center was scheduled to arrive in two-ish hours. When she strode in, Ethan was sprawled against his couch in his dressing room. He looked up at her, his expression soft and brimming with contentment.

"Did you write your speech?" she asked him.

"Nope. I'm not trying to be humble, Wills, but there's no way I'm taking it when Henry Niven and Andy Hendricks are also nominated. There's no point."

She scoffed at him. "Ethan. Write *something*. You have a huge chance at winning and you're going to stumble on your words and hate yourself if you have nothing to go off."

"Your faith in me is adorable."

Raising an eyebrow, she then looked around his dressing room for the journal she knew he kept for notes. She spotted it on the edge of his vanity, beelined over to grab it, then set it in front of him. "Write," she demanded.

He sighed, trying not to smile. "Can I just write about how much I love you?"

Willa ogled him for a beat; the vision of him sitting leisurely in her graphic tee was among one of the hottest things she'd ever seen. She had stayed over the night before, and when they had been getting ready for the day, she noticed him eyeing her Muppets T-shirt folded on the vanity.

He had promptly stopped her when she was about to pack it into her backpack.

"Mind if I borrow this?" Ethan had mused.

Willa had laughed. "Sure," she'd consented, watching as he pulled the shirt over his exposed chest. The unisex fabric that was purposely oversized on her fit his frame superbly.

"Looks good on you. How long have you been wanting to steal it from me?" she had joked.

He had guffawed. "You know this shirt on you is my kryptonite, but the need just came to me."

"Well, what's mine is yours, babe. Honestly, it's a little surprising we didn't start swapping tees earlier in our friendship."

He had then taken her face in his hands and kissed her so tenderly that she thought she'd evaporate.

She let the memory settle at the forefront of her mind again. He'd be suited in a few hours, but this moment was a mark of their closeness that well and truly established he was her person. If to no one else, then to every agonizing thought that had once plagued her.

She bent down and kissed the top of his head before leaving him alone.

"I'm going to walk away now. There better be words on paper at some point."

The man dared to laugh. Willa was sure he'd win, and she couldn't wait to experience it—to tell him that she was right. She went back into her dressing room and sat down on her chair. Sahar's sister, Amina, was in town from London, and the two had gone to Amanda's Coffee to grab drinks. Taking in the brief moment alone, she reveled in the quiet comfort of how lovely life was turning out to be.

Willa walked over to her dress hung on a rack and snapped a close-up of the sequins and the colors. She posted it to her stories with the sparkling emoji. This was fine. Little things like this seldom made her anxious. Still, she considered it another step in embracing the new normal.

She knew that life wouldn't always be this bright and exciting. There was much about the industry that needed to change. It was a stunning place in more ways than one, but corrupt, too. Many actors weren't as fortunate as they were. Who knew what the next gig would bring? She had the luxury of ignoring those what-ifs for a while—a chance to temporarily be present in its lovelier corner.

THE THRILL in the room was already infectious after the amount of wins *Midnights at Pemberley* was taking home. Willa was especially ecstatic to be right about almost everything. She did want to fight someone because Naomi, Sahar, Sam, and Declan all lost in their categories—though she was still proud of them beyond measure for the nominations.

She took Ethan's hand as the nominations were announced for Best Performance by a Leading Actor in a Musical.

"And the Tony Award goes to," Noah Gemmell proclaimed, opening the envelope. "Ethan Everett!"

Willa was sure that Ethan was in shock because he didn't move. He simply stared. It dawned on him slowly, then all at once, when she squeezed his hand. The people around them had already begun clapping. The auditorium roared with their ovation. He kissed her, rose to his feet, and walked over to the stage.

He thanked Noah and Iris Ariti as he took the plaque presented to him.

She caught him shaking his head lovingly before he reached into his pocket and took out the folded piece of paper. She was aware that fashion critics often looked down on men for wearing all-black suits—it annoyed her, too, at times—but damn, he was too hot in his for her to care.

"Thank you to the Broadway League and American Theatre Wing for this immense honor. My fellow nominees, it was meaningful for me just to be featured alongside each of you."

Pausing, he smiled and spoke freely. "Mom, Dad, Joana, and Nick, I'm so sorry I told you not to come because I didn't think there'd be a point, but I wouldn't be half the person I am today without the love and support you've all shown me. I once promised my late Grandfather Callum that if I ever won one of these, I'd have to tell the world that he was always right about everything."

His voice broke a little. He caught himself with a breath. "He was right."

"Jeffrey and Greta Henderson, you two brought the world so much joy and light with this production—thank you for choosing me and letting me be your Darcy. It was a big risk to adapt something as beloved as Jane Austen's work like this, but allowing it to be unapologetically happy has made for an unforgettable experience. There's nowhere on this earth that's more open, inclusive, and beautiful than our stages, and I'm so privileged to have this job. It's never something I take for granted. Betty Reyes, my manager who's been with me from the start of my career, thank you for constantly rooting for me. Our entire *Midnights* cast and crew—this show has fundamentally changed me. It's made me a better person and a better performer, and it's brought more light into my life than I ever thought possible. You're some of the greatest people, and I'm constantly in awe of each of you."

And then his gaze magnetized with hers, his smile a breathtaking spectacle of its own. "Finally—Willa, my love—thank you for believing in me as fervently as you do. You're the most extraordinary gift in my life."

Her tears fell openly as she caught his eyes glistening while he walked backstage. When the world tested them, when life got too cruel, she'd take moments like this with her everywhere.

She shared everything from the show's official account, taking an additional step in trying by adding "bursting with unparalleled joy and pride. Congrats, my love! 🩶

35

ETHAN

Ethan stood outside Willa's apartment, leaning against the passenger side of his black Lexus like some eighties movie main character, waiting to whisk the heroine away. He couldn't wait to see her—to show her what was waiting for them at his family's cabin, enthusiastically proud of himself for not blurting it out accidentally.

They both had last minute things they needed to get done before taking a few days off work, so Willa hadn't stayed with him the night before. She'd called him, wanting to say happy birthday at midnight, like he'd done when they were friends. Devotedly sweet wishes had left her lips and settled in his heart.

She radiated when she stepped out, and he swore his heart expanded three sizes from eagerness. He gawked at her, still in a state of wild incredulity that she was his. Her hair was down with loose waves, and she wore a stunning semi-fitted emerald floral dress that stopped at the middle of her calves with white sneakers. She had a couple of gold necklaces stacked together and a few rings, too.

She drew closer and leaped into his arms with such delicious force that his heart thrummed against his chest. "Happy Birthday!" She squealed into his embrace.

Holding on firmly, he clutched her close. "Thank you, beautiful."

When he released her, Willa kissed him like tomorrow would never come. It was formidable and deep, as if she were intentionally carving all her emotions into his bones.

"You look so gorgeous," he groaned into her neck, breathing in the intoxicating scent of her perfume, kissing her there, once, twice.

A giggle soared from her throat, and his legs threatened to give out. He took her weekender bag and opened the passenger door for her, delighting in the small curtsy she did, reading him like an open book splayed out in front of her. She must've spotted the drinks in his console because she tipped her head with an eye roll. "You got us coffee? It's *your* birthday, remember?"

"And you're already the best gift, so..." he proclaimed.

She curved her lips inward.

He knew exactly what she was thinking.

"Scale of one to ten, how embarrassingly cheesy was that?" he asked.

She smiled wistfully, scrunching her nose in the process. "If you rehearsed it, it shoots up to a hundred. If it somehow just came to you, I'll be generous and say five."

"Dammit," he uttered, closing the door lovingly. He popped the trunk, dropped her bag alongside his, and hurried to the driver's seat.

"You rehearsed it, didn't you?" she asked as he sat down.

"I didn't *rehearse* it, no, but I *thought* about it."

She let out a sweet laugh. "Fine, you get a pass since it's your birthday."

He exhaled a theatrical sigh of relief. Ethan started up the engine, and as soon as the car's Bluetooth system recognized his phone, it began playing from her all-time favorites playlist, a gloriously wild mix of happy and sad tracks she'd titled "Dreamy Days in a Treehouse."

She turned from the screen to face him when she caught the first notes for Glass Animals' "Heat Waves." It was convenient considering the month they were in.

Laughing, he reached for her hand. "I swear I put it on shuffle."

Willa entwined their fingers together and shook her head. "What on earth are you doing, Everett?"

"Driving to my parents' place," he answered plainly.

He smiled, looked to his left to check for oncoming traffic, and pulled out onto the road.

"You know that's not what I was asking you," Willa replied, squeezing his hand in hers.

Ethan tried again. "Attempting to ensure that an almost three-hour car ride goes smoothly and with music I know you like?"

"It's *your* birthday, Ethan. Choose the music you want. Let me buy *you* coffee," she exclaimed with an exasperated chuckle.

He chanced a glance at her. "And I want to make sure my girl is comfortable. Doesn't that count for something?"

He caught her trying to hold back a smirk. "I can't deal with you," she declared.

"I love you, too, beautiful," he responded.

Her cheeks flushed scarlet; she shook her head. He adored doing this to her, knowing that all these small reactions were reserved just for him. God, he couldn't wait to show her what he had planned. He was a kid on Christmas, realizing only now what it meant to love someone so fervently that their happiness would be all-consuming.

They stopped for gas and snacks: a box of Cheez-Its, Starburst jellybeans, and Dr. Pepper for good measure. They geeked out over the music and lyrics, told stories about old family road trips, allowed comfortable beats of silence to stretch out between them, and affectionately argued about the *Succession* finale. Again. Ethan would never let go of the fact that it should've been Roman. Willa was a thousand percent "Team Darcy—Tom—and his failed marriage." Her words.

"Okay, so, remember that first official date I wanted to take you on?" he specified.

She tipped her face to him, her legs crossed in her seat. "What about it?" she replied heartily.

"That's where we're going first. It's near my parents' place."

Willa's dimpled smile grew tenfold. "Are you going to finally tell me its significance? Or you're waiting until we get there."

"I'll tell you when we get there," he said, making a sharp left.

She pulled out her phone and snapped a quick photo of him.

"What was that?" he asked.

She shrugged and gave him a clipped but adorable reply. "You'll see."

After a few minutes, he pulled into a small plaza and parked in front of Caro Amico, an old Italian restaurant that'd been in the area for eighty-seven years now.

"Ooh, Italian?" Willa asked.

"Yes. I hope you're good with that and weren't craving something else."

She bobbed her head emphatically. "I wanted pasta last night, so this is excellent."

Good. This eased his nerves a bit. "Stay right there," he said, then went over to open her door.

Willa smiled, swung her bag on her shoulder, and took his

hand. "You're really committing to this whole chivalrous thing right now, aren't you?"

"My grandpa would be rolling over in his grave if I didn't," he replied.

They strolled into the restaurant, hand in hand, and an older gentleman approached them at the door. "Welcome to Caro Amico. Table for two?"

"Yes, I should have a reservation under Ethan."

The man looked at the notebook in front of him. "Ah, there you are. I see you." He turned to the waitress standing by and handed her two menus. "Table seventeen on the patio," he confirmed.

They sat down, and Willa peered up at him, brown eyes glinting with a hundred and one questions. She took his hand, skating her thumb across his knuckles. He was about to tell her the story when the waitress appeared to take their drink orders, to which they both asked for water.

Ethan clicked his tongue and laced their fingers together. "It's kind of cheesy. But this is where my paternal grandparents and parents had their first dates." He smiled, remembering his grandpa's shining countenance as he told them the story. "I don't know if he was joking about it, but Nick and I both sort of held on to this belief like it was some unspoken rule in our family."

He wanted to capture the current look in Willa's eyes in a photograph.

Ethan continued. "My grandpa believed this place was special. So, he said that we should only bring someone here when we're certain they're the one."

Willa's eyes welled up instantaneously. "Ethan…" she whispered, her voice low and reverential.

He leaned closer to her in the booth and cupped her cheek. "You were rightfully scared of giving us a chance, Wills; our jobs are full of unpredictability, but I've never been more sure about anything else than my feelings for you. You're *it* for me. You always will be," he paused. "Plus, Caro Amico essentially translates to *dear friend—best* in my brain—and if that's not some perfectly wild cosmic interference, then I don't know what is. So, yeah, that's why I wanted to bring you here."

Tears pooled in the corner of her eyes. "You're a dream. I don't understand how any of this is real. But thank you for bringing me here. I love you with everything in me."

He drew his lips to her forehead, staying there for a beat. He could swear he felt his grandparents watching over him like they were waiting and hoping for this moment.

He'd always felt particularly close to his grandpa but never quite understood how he'd always been happy until Ethan met Willa. Callum Everett was many things, but he was, first and foremost, a man who revered his wife. And now, at this very restaurant, Ethan fully understood the eminence of everlasting love.

ETHAN'S INSIDES were in knots. He was so damn nervous that it was making him nauseous. What if she hated the surprise? What if she didn't want it like this? But she'd love it. He knew she would. He knew *her*. Inside and out. Yet he couldn't help the nerves simmering as they approached his family's cabin.

Their date went perfectly.

But this. This was the moment he'd been waiting for.

He reached into his pocket and pulled out the blindfolds. "Wills, I need a massive favor."

"Name it, birthday boy."

He passed the cloth to her. "Can you please put this on for me? I have a surprise for you."

She rolled her eyes lovingly. "Need I remind you again that it's *your* birthday? You wouldn't even let me pay at the restaurant!"

"Do you want to hear that cheesy line again about you being my greatest gift?"

She huffed dramatically and tied it across her eyes.

"Can you see?" Ethan asked.

Willa shook her head.

"Promise?"

"I swear it."

"It'll only be about a minute or so," he added.

Taking a deep breath, he continued driving. He was positive that if she heard his heart pounding out of his chest, then she didn't say anything. He was also thankful for Hozier blaring through the speakers.

He pulled up to the driveway and parked the car. "Don't try to step out. It's a little steep. I'll get you."

She nodded.

Ethan nearly jumped out of the car and opened the passenger door, guiding her out with his hands steadily around her elbows. When she was fully on the ground, he wrapped his arms around her shoulder and guided them toward the entrance.

"We're approaching two stairs," he said, watching as she lifted her leg alongside his. It resulted in a synchroneity that was as effortless as one of their dances. He let her go briefly as he opened the door and nudged her in.

"We're going to the backyard for a second. Do you want to leave your bag here?" he asked.

Willa handed it to him. He hung it on a hook stand, then continued directing her movements with careful precision. "There's a small stair here, so just make sure you step down," he added. She moved as so, and they walked a few steps before Ethan stopped them.

He wrapped his arms around her from behind and held tightly for a moment. "You can open your eyes now," he whispered in her ear.

36

WILLA

Willa burst into tears. It couldn't have been cute.

She was staring at a charming, shockingly large treehouse adorned in twinkle lights, with Ethan's arms enfolding her from behind and his lips on her cheek.

What on earth was happening? *It was his birthday!* What was he doing? Christ, those tickets to the Stoic Badger concert and the custom *Muppet Christmas Carol* painting paled on all fronts.

She parted her lips to speak but cried instead. Sahar once joked that actually seeing a treehouse up close would make Willa pass out, and for a split second there, she thought she might. She was sure Ethan was holding her upright.

"Ethan, what is this?" she finally asked.

A delicious laugh rumbled from his throat. "It's a treehouse."

She turned to look at him more closely, her hands resting against his shoulders. "You've had a treehouse this whole time, and you're just now telling me?"

He shook his head. "Remember that renovation project I briefly mentioned I'd been working on with my dad?"

Willa gaped at him. "Go on."

"This was it," he revealed, watching as she puckered her lips and teared up again. He trailed his mouth along her face and kissed the tears away. "He mentioned wanting to build one for my nephew, so when I learned how much you loved them, I went in on it with him and pushed to expedite the construction. We ran into a few issues in the beginning but still managed to finish on time."

She was, quite literally and embarrassingly, speechless.

"I would have brought you here whether we got together or not so you could see it. It was finished about two months ago, so this conveniently worked out. The hardest part was keeping it a secret from you."

She shook her head again, astonishment clouding her brain, happy tears blurring her vision.

Willa threw herself into his arms. "I love you. I love you. I love you," she whispered in a frenzy.

"I love you more. Do you want to go up?"

She perked up like a little girl. "Can we?"

"Yeah, beautiful. It's big enough to fit us," he declared.

Her eyes widened suddenly. "Wait, is anyone else here?"

"No, my parents and siblings will get in tomorrow. I wanted us to have today to ourselves before everyone else joined."

She placed a searing, scorching kiss against his lips. "How are you mine?"

How was he hers? How had she gone from genuinely believing and fearing that she'd never find someone who saw all of her to finding someone who'd turn the world upside down to ensure her happiness never faltered?

How was her best friend and the love of her life the same person?

How was she standing in front of a treehouse, the small, ordinary thing she always dreamed of?

"Okay, but hold on, this dress. I don't want to ruin it," she stated.

Ethan's eyes narrowed. "But I really want to take it off you... up there," he pointed out.

She arched her eyebrows, looked down at the dress, then up at the treehouse again, trying to decipher if she could manage without the fabric catching anywhere or ruining her ascent.

Willa folded the dress to her knees, took her hair band from her wrist, and tied it. It'd be a few seconds. She'd undo it when she got there so the spot wouldn't crease. Ethan let her go first, then followed from behind. She thankfully climbed the steps without any complications and entered.

Inside, there were pillows scattered on the ground, blankets in a woven basket, a small treasure chest-looking stand as a coffee table, two chairs, and one large window.

She strolled toward the window, overlooking a quaint stream beyond the canopy of leaves. It was the most transfixing sight she'd ever seen, a close second to the man who'd just gone back down to grab a few things from his car.

Standing there, she closed her eyes momentarily and counted her blessings one by one.

She had daydreamed about this exact moment without ever realizing it.

Ethan returned with a picnic basket in his hand and set it down on the small chest near the entrance. She ambled back over to him, spotting Dr. Peppers and her favorite jam and cream biscuits from Marks & Spencer.

Her jaw dropped; she picked up the biscuits and stared at them. "Now I know you can't order these online somewhere. *How*?"

He beamed at her. "I'd asked Sahar's sister to bring them in when she visited."

She shook her head affectionately. "Ethan, I physically

cannot take any more surprises today. Please tell me there's nothing else, or I might combust."

He laughed at her. Openly, loudly, strikingly.

He put his hands up as if to surrender. "That's all I've got," he admitted.

And instantly, Willa drew closer, colliding her lips with his in open-mouthed, staggering kisses. His hands flew to her waist, and he tugged her body flush against his.

Ethan's tongue voraciously darted forward, seizing hers in a chaotic dance they'd mastered in all forms.

He stopped for a beat, hands splayed along her waist, gazing at her like she was indeed his bloody gift. Like those words he had said were real and not some frivolous declaration. "This dress, Willa. It's my favorite thing you've ever worn," he acknowledged through panting rasps.

"More than the emerald costume?"

He groaned and pulled her close again. "You'd make a trash bag look stunning. Everything about you is my favorite."

"Oof, now that's a compliment. Thanks a million, babe," she returned.

Willa kissed him again and then turned, taking his hand in hers, she guided them back toward the window.

There, Ethan circled his arms around her belly and pressed his lips to her shoulder. A tiny moan escaped her from contact.

She marveled at the sunset. He bestowed all his attention on her.

"You're distracting me," she rebutted.

His laugh vibrated through her. "That's the point."

She tilted her head back, giving him more access. Ethan kissed his way up her neck, her jaw. He tipped her chin to face him, then seized her lips slowly, yet with an eagerness that made her knees buck. "I promise I'll let you watch the sunset tomorrow when I'm forced to behave myself if you let me have my way with you tonight."

She giggled. "So, we're bargaining now?"

"It's my one birthday wish," he claimed, nipping at her ear.

"Finally pulling the birthday card." She took his face in her hand. "How could I say no to that when it's what I've been trying to get you to do all day."

He gleamed, a smile more transcendent than the sun's routine behind them.

"Whatever you do, I need you to take off this dress as carefully as you'd remove a costume. I want to wear it again tomorrow," Willa added.

He concurred, turning her with one swift move. It dawned on her again how absurd it was to once upon a time be so against dating someone in the same profession. Her reasoning made sense to a degree, but she fully understood now why everything clicked so faultlessly into place with Ethan.

He wasn't delicate or even all that graceful in the traditional sense—yet he was deliberate and soft. Magnetic. Electric.

Ethan moved her hair forward and then kissed the nape of her neck. He traced her spine, lowering his fingers with tender caresses until he reached the zipper. He pulled it down carefully, then one strap after another.

His fingers grazed her skin as he slid the fabric down and helped her step out of it. Lowering himself, Ethan pressed a dizzying kiss to the back of her thigh, one after another, then stood back up. She peeled off her adhesive bra and set it aside with her dress before turning to face him. She heard him catch a breath.

"How are you so perfect?" he asked.

She smiled and placed her hands underneath his shirt. "You're overdressed," she mused, skating it over his head and off his body.

She placed it with her dress and kissed him languidly, fingers spread against his chest. "Happy birthday," she drawled.

"The happiest," he rasped, winding his fingers underneath the curve of her ass.

She looked toward the sheets tucked near the pillows. "We're going to wash these sheets tonight and replace everything," she said in between kisses.

Ethan lifted her and pushed up against the thick bark of wood surrounding them. "Yes, ma'am," he affirmed.

She wrapped her legs around him, kissing him back hard. His fingers charged up and down her thighs. A man obsessed, and she knew it. She could feel it.

Willa almost laughed, momentarily thinking back at how upset she was when their relationship had been exposed to the public. People had been so fixed on the way his hand hovered over her face, but no one could see the fingers he had saddled to her thighs.

Sliding her legs down onto the floor, she moved her hands along the button on his jeans. She unzipped rapidly, brought them down, grabbed a pillow for comfort, and kneeled.

"Wills, you don't have to," he protested.

She looked up at him, his face flushed and gorgeous. Willa would take this image over a sunset any day. "Ssh, I'm tired of reminding you what day it is," she countered, then yanked his boxer briefs down.

He tipped her chin up. "I know exactly what day it is. And as much as I want your pretty lips on me, I'd much rather be in between your thighs."

She laughed. She couldn't make this up. Willa put her mouth around him and was rewarded with a delicious groan catapulting from his throat. It was music to her ears, a surrender from his stubbornness.

Good.

She picked up her pace.

"I had different plans," he rasped.

"What plans?" she asked after finishing him off.

Breathlessly, he answered. "As I said before, that's between me and your thighs."

He dropped down to his knees.

She laughed as his feverish lips inched up against her legs, gasping at the bites and licks and kisses that ruptured into something warm and enticing inside of her.

He pushed her toward the pillows and laid her down gently like she was something precious, not fragile or fractured, but worthy of worship. Ethan took his time with her, tasting every inch of her body as though it was the first time, making her scream with every move he made to cherish her.

"Best birthday ever," he announced after bringing her to an earth-shattering orgasm.

They lay for a while afterward, flushed and naked, tangled in each other's arms against wooden floors, a random sheet he'd snuck into the basket and pillows against their heads. "You've made this the best birthday ever," he repeated into her hair.

"Was it taking the dress off that made it so? Or the fact that you basically forced me to steal your thunder?" she asked.

He kissed the side of her head, keeping his mouth there for a steady beat. "The whole damn thing, but the dress fulfilled some sort of an inexplicable fantasy I didn't even know I had."

She laughed, tipping her head to kiss his lips. "Well, good, because honestly, I'm not sure my gifts will do much now."

"I told you, you're my—"

"Finish that sentence, and I'm taking the train back to the city," she said with a snort.

"Okay, I'll play, what'd you get me?"

She propped herself on one elbow. "Part of the gift is at

home. I couldn't bring it with me, but I have a picture. The other is in my bag, inside the house."

"Tell me because I'm not letting you out of my sight right now."

She reached back and grabbed her phone from somewhere on the floor, opening her pictures app to show him the custom painting.

Ethan sat up so rapidly that it was jarring. "Holy shit! This is from *The Muppet Christmas Carol!*"

"Yes, I found a local artist in New York open to commissions, so I told her about how much you adored it and asked for a custom poster."

He bent down, kissing her hard and fast. "Willa, this is fucking amazing! Holy shit. I can't wait to see it in person. This is the best thing anyone could've gotten me."

"And the second is tickets to Stoic Badger's next show; it falls on a Monday, so we could go."

His eyes lit up. "Did you really think I wouldn't love this, or are you being humble?"

"You made me sob!"

"To be fair, the only thing I love the way you love treehouses is you. Plus, you're adorable even when you cry."

She believed him with everything in her, and that was the wildest part of all this. All the fears she had harbored, the agonizing thoughts that'd tormented and kept her up, evanesced when Ethan looked at her. Because he had been the very embodiment of what she hoped treehouses would be in human form. Comfortable. Warm. Perfectly imperfect, jagged edges and all.

He was the dream she never allowed herself to hope for.

It was captivating how Ethan looked at her sometimes. Thinking back to when they were just friends, she'd catch his gazes from time to time, never really thinking anything of it until more recently. She couldn't find the words to describe the serenity in his eyes or the softness in his smile. His eyes then flitted toward her neck. He drew his finger to one of her now tangled necklaces, spotting the small, simple gold letter *E* she wore for the first time today.

A shimmering smile curved along his lips, the corners of his eyes crinkled. "What's this?" he mused.

"One of my favorite jewelry shops had it in stock, so I bought it a couple of weeks ago."

He smirked. "Is it for me?"

"No, it's for my other lover, Edward. I'm so sorry you had to find out this way," she deadpanned.

He pressed a kiss to where the necklace lay, and she giggled. "Fuck, Willa. I love it. I love it so damn much."

His wholesome elation would never be topped.

Willa beamed. "I was hoping you would," she said, holding his face in her hands. She pressed her lips to his in an emphatic kiss.

Later that night, as Ethan showered, Willa compiled a bunch of photographs to post. Sahar had held up her end of the bargain, now a stunning redhead, so Willa's time had come.

She had prepped for it with Marie during three sessions, actively talking herself into focusing on the truth versus the assumptions, and approached the situation with the reminder that this would always come with the job.

Willa didn't need to change all her ways with social media—notifications would permanently remain off—but she didn't want to live in a constant state of anxiety either.

She wanted to take back her agency.

For the first picture, she chose a candid photo Sam had taken of them three days ago, where Ethan's entire body wrapped around her as she giggled over something he'd said. It was a stark showcase of their relationship in a nutshell—a friendship full of laughter, first, unbeatable comfort, and zero concept of personal space. The second was a selfie shot from earlier today at the restaurant. His arm draped across her shoulder, head tilted as he kissed her temple. The third was a photograph she sneakily took of their hands clasped together in his car. The fourth was his profile while the sunlight haloed his face. The fifth was the treehouse.

She captioned it with—*Happy Birthday to the love of my life. My best friend. My favorite everything.* @ETHANEVERETT—kept the comments on and sent it out into the world.

He deserved to be openly, loudly, and perpetually loved by her.

EPILOGUE
ETHAN

One year and three months later

Ethan and Willa had talked about many, *many* things when they were just friends, but engagements weren't one of the discussed topics. He knew so much about her, but he was never quite sure what kind of a proposal she would've wanted. She'd once mentioned a small fall or winter wedding, so he kept that detail tucked in his vault of memories.

For the proposal, however, he had asked Sahar, hoping that the topic was something the women would have talked about. Sahar told him that Willa had never been specific about the *how,* only that she hoped it was thoughtful.

Well, Ethan thought about it a lot, an agonizing amount, actually. This was Willa—his best friend and his favorite person, the love of his life.

It had to be perfect for her.

She adored the treehouse at his family's cabin, but an unexpected summer storm had caused some damage. He'd discussed repairs with his dad, but with everyone's chaotic schedules, it would take longer than he would've wanted it to.

Time wasn't on his side, and he desperately wanted it to be.

Since their runs in *Midnights at Pemberley* ended, Willa and Ethan would be spending six weeks apart. She had to complete performances in a Broadway musical production called *Fever Fever,* and Ethan was scheduled to shoot a limited series in Alberta, Canada for four months, starting next week. While she and Tulip planned to join him after Willa took her last bow, he wanted—no *needed*—to make this promise to her.

And so what if he was also a little selfish and wanted to start referring to her as his fiancée?"

He was standing in their now shared kitchen, staring at the island's black marble tile, waiting for her to text him that she was on her way home from a Sunday matinee. Once she did that, he'd tell her to first open the envelope sitting on the coffee table and then meet him on the balcony, which he had spent the entire day after she left installing wood panels and new furniture with a construction crew. If he couldn't take her to the tree-house, he'd imitate it as best he could.

As a birthday gift for Willa last year, Sahar had printed out and framed one of the Polaroid-filtered photographs she'd taken of Ethan and Willa during their time as Elizabeth and Darcy. It sat on the vanity in their bedroom. Remembering how Willa choked up when she saw it, Ethan thought of how she'd mentioned loving the fact that Sahar consistently did this because even though they weren't "real Polaroid photographs," they still had the effect.

Shortly after, he'd run the idea of proposing through Polaroids with Sahar, allowing her to help out by printing some of their favorite pictures. There were shots of Ethan and Willa together, along with other miscellaneous pictures they'd individually taken, so he could slowly ease Willa into his little plan.

For the past two weeks, he started by giving her one photo a day. Behind each of them, he'd written notes—*I love you in this dress. Your smile makes me weak. Thinking about the things I did to you in this treehouse, I'd do them again.*

Yesterday's read, *will*, but Willa had been so tired she assumed his pen died before he could finish his sentence.

The photograph he'd used was one he'd taken of her during their first Christmas as a couple. It had been on that day when Ethan had asked her to move in with him.

The one this morning simply said *you.* It was a photo of her smiling up at him. She'd apparently thought the word *you* alone was hilarious because she guffawed, sauntered over to him, and said, "Okay, I have a serious question. Are you concerned that I might forget who I am at some point, so all these photos are evidence so I could remember? What on earth is happening here, Ethan?"

He'd said nothing, kissed her cheek, and walked away.

~

WILLA

Willa enjoyed her run in *Fever Fever*, but she was ready for the next month to fly by. She knew that nothing could ever compare to the magic they'd all uncovered in *Midnights at Pemberley,* and even though the majority of her castmates were great, their principal star was a prissy nightmare to work with. A newer actor who thought he was God's gift to humanity and maybe the worst scene partner she'd ever had.

She stepped through the front door of her and Ethan's apartment and walked toward the coffee table, spotting the envelope he'd told her about. Another photograph, she assumed, smiling. Frankly, whatever little game he was playing was adorable.

"Ethan?" she called out.

No answer.

She set her backpack down on the sofa and headed toward the balcony, envelope in hand.

"Oh my, God!" The regular panels had all been replaced with wooden ones, with a matching new table, a new couch, and throw pillows that looked like the ones from his family's treehouse.

Willa felt Ethan's arm curl around her waist. She drew her fingers to hold his, turning to face him. "This is gorgeous, babe."

He bobbed his head toward the envelope in her hands. "Open it."

Someone's impatient, she thought to herself. But she obliged with a kiss on his cheekbone and opened the envelope. Willa pulled out the photograph of them from when he took her to Caro Amico last year. And then, she flipped it over, every detail from the past two days and week dawning on her.

Marry me.

She spun, finding Ethan behind her, down on one knee, a tiny box resting in his hands.

Butterflies fluttered in her chest. Her heart threatened to beat out of her and latch itself onto his. She blinked, mascara and false lashes now more irritating with the tears stinging her eyes. Oh, how she wished she had taken her makeup off, but she just wanted to get back home to him and their little life.

"Ethan," it came out in a whisper.

His eyes sparkled, tears threatening to unleash on him, too.

"Willa..." he shook his head. "Fuck, I practiced this so many times. I've been proposing to you in the shower for months now, and suddenly, none of it feels right or enough." He took a breath, swallowed, and shut his eyes.

Willa's tears fell freely now. She couldn't hold them in if she tried.

This man—this perfect, thoughtful man.

She ran her fingers along the short beard he'd grown for the new role, relishing in both the feel of it and how stunningly rugged he looked.

Ethan tried to speak again. "Wills, I love you more than I did yesterday, and I know I'm going to love you even more tomorrow and the next day and every day after that. You're my best friend and my favorite person, and I'd *really* love to add my wife in there, too. There's no one else I could ever grow old with, beautiful. There's no one else I'd rather look at and know, with every bone in my body, that they're my home. No matter where we go or what we do, I'm yours, Willa—only yours. And there's nothing I want more than to keep building a life together. Will you marry me?"

Willa bounced her head up and down. "Yes, God, yes. Best friend, love of my life, favorite person, and *husband*? I'm all in. Always."

He glided the ring on her finger and placed a kiss where it'd forever reside.

Ethan rose to his feet, and Willa looped her arms around his neck. He collided his lips with hers, lingering for a few beats. Slow and soft and transfixing, as kissing him would always be.

"I love you," she whispered. "So much. I don't know how you pulled this off right under my nose."

He placed a tender kiss on her forehead. "I for sure thought the 'will' and the 'you' notes would blow my cover."

Willa laughed. "If I hadn't been so tired, I might've questioned them. But I've been too occupied thinking about how lucky I am. I thought you were going to make a gallery wall or something with the way you were presenting them."

Ethan smirked. "Huh, that's not a bad idea."

"Only if you hang them with strings because I want to be able to easily read the notes on the back when I miss you."

He pulled her in for a tight hug. "What do I get when I start missing you, and I can't call at the exact moment I need to because you're at work?"

"Hold, please." She sprung out of his arms and ran to their bedroom. Willa walked to the wardrobe closet and crouched down to take out a bag hidden in a far corner. She had planned to wait until next week to give it to him before he left but now felt like the appropriate time instead.

She beelined back over to him and held the bag in front of him.

He tilted his head and took it from her. "What's this?"

She quirked her lips. "Open it and find out."

Ethan proceeded to take out a black box from inside the bag before setting it aside. He sent another questioning look in her direction. She shrugged her shoulders as he opened the box and gaped slightly.

"You always talk about how much you love the E necklace I wear, and selfishly, there's something *hot* about men and thin gold chains, so the subtlety of this one with the small, personalized rectangle-shaped plate near the clasp screamed at me when I saw it. It was meant to be a *congratulations on this next gig* gift, but there you go—something to turn to when you miss me. But don't fret, I'm going to put little notes in your pockets, too."

His smile shot up to his eyes, and his whole face gleamed. "If I only wear this and glasses, is that enough to convince you to stay in bed all day tomorrow?"

"You don't need any of them to convince me of that, but if you want the extra credit, then absolutely, yes—right away," she replied.

Ethan carefully took the chain out of the box and circled it around his neck. He could've clasped it himself, but she reached forward to do it for him before spinning it around in its proper position.

Willa looped her finger through the fine metal and tugged

gently. She kissed the jut of his throat, up toward his scruffy jawline, then back to his lips.

When they parted, she rested her forehead against his. "I know that there was a moment when all of this scared me. You and me and our jobs, all the noise, distance, and the challenges that could've arisen, but we've got this—all of it. We'll chase our dreams together."

He dipped his mouth down on hers in a devotedly heated kiss. "We've got this," he repeated, his cadence warm and right. "I love you," he breathed as his lips scattered across her face, peppering delicate kisses all over.

We've got this.

ACKNOWLEDGMENTS

People weren't kidding when they said the second book is more challenging to write than the first. I went into this one thinking these two would take me on a fun and sexy journey, but instead, they pulled me into one wringer after another, and I wouldn't have it any other way because, in the end, it became a story about partnership and a type of friendship that I'm in awe of. So, in more ways than one, even though a future story will be my ode to the co-workers who become like family, *Midnights at Pemberley* is the true love letter to that idea. It's a beautiful, colorful, inclusive little world that I believe everyone deserves to experience, and I adored bringing each of these characters to life.

Because of how much this book made me doubt myself and my capabilities, I genuinely couldn't have done it without God. Yes, if this were an actual acceptance speech, I'd stand and thank my savior, Jesus Christ, because I don't know how I would've made it to the end without the prayers and tears I found answers in.

For my late father, *always*. I'm the writer I am because of you. It's that simple.

To my family, I could never ever repay all the support you've shown me. I'm truly the luckiest.

Kate, having you part of this journey with me is something I'll perpetually cherish. Thank you for every question mark you left to the most convoluted thoughts, allowing me to bring out a more fleshed-out story in the process. Thank you for listening to me ramble and talking me out of self-deprecating thoughts. I love you.

Sarah, your encouragement will forever be one of my favorite things. So many of these small ideas became better because of you and your feedback. Every little thing you catch is a gift. Thank you from the bottom of my heart for taking this on with me. I love you.

Jenna, I still remember that first Marco Polo I sent you about this little Broadway production, and you immediately became its biggest enabler. What started as a "maybe" became a definitely because of you and your love for these characters. Your tireless encouragement has been a tremendously irreplaceable gift. And, as always, thank you for visually bringing them to life with another perfectly sensational cover!

Dana, I'm so very grateful for you. Whether it's going off about our cats or the vital notes you've given me for this book, it's made everything delightful and better. I love you.

Amy, I adore you and the fact that you are always the first to read the completed product in its wildest state. I'm so grateful for you and your friendship. Sharing my characters with you is one of the best parts of writing.

Arezou, thank you for loving Ben and Violet the way you did because it made writing this story easier. Thank you for being a text away if I need to vent and for your lovely friendship both in fictional writing and journalism.

Erin Langston, your friendship and your words are irreplaceable in this industry. I'm so very fortunate to call you a friend.

Ada and Kels at be.archetype, I'm so thankful for the gorgeous graphics and all the work you've both done. You two are gems in the romance community.

To every person who's read a paragraph, a chapter, shared posts, encouraged me, or shown excitement for this story, I see you. I love you. I hope you know how much it means to me. Truly.

And best of all, to every reader who picked up *To the Skyline* and gave my words a chance. I could apparently write many words, but I could never find the right ones to sum up my *immense, never-ending* gratitude for each of you.

ABOUT THE AUTHOR

Born and raised in California, Gissane Sophia (pronounced Geese-Enny) is a hopeless romantic who ceaselessly champions that vulnerability is a strength. She's a fan of complex characters, found families, her bright, brilliant family and friends, coffee, forests, and all things autumn. When she isn't dabbling in writing romance novels, she's reading them. And when she's doing neither, she's devouring fiction through TV and film, working full-time as an entertainment editor and writer.

ALSO BY GISSANE SOPHIA

Ben and Violet's Second Chance Romance

TO THE SKYLINE

Coming Soon

MIDNIGHTS AT PEMBERLEY BOOK 2: Sahar's Story